A GOOD FIGHT

Did you hear what I said? You can expect a good fight!" Reverend Harry Dushane repeated, as he was apt to do, and screamed into his awaiting microphone. The preacher's purpled veins popped from his reddened neck, shooting out of his body wrapped in a brand new 1971 polyester suit and shaking gold chains. Rev. Harry almost spit as he yelled at the congregation, causing his tinted glasses to slide down the arch of his nose, as if trying to kiss his walrus mustache, which inched upward, accentuating his anger.

Seven-year old Calvin Elkan was only half paying attention, his ass sore and raw from sitting in that hard, wooden pew in the Lighthouse church for three hours. He opened his drawing pad back up and unsteadily balanced it on his kneecaps. With a worn-out box of oil pastels beside him and a reddish-brown one in his left hand, he resumed drawing his version of the Last Supper, creating a large table to place the bread and wine on. Calvin's younger brother Frank sat next to him on the pew, oblivious to Calvin's drawings and raptly focused on Rev. Harry's performance.

As the oldest son of Sunday school teacher Nancy Elkan, Calvin was required to sit through the entire service. Aware that sitting for so long could be demanding for a kid his age, Nancy allowed Calvin's drawing in church, since she struggled enough just bringing him to Sunday night worship. For one so young, Calvin was shrewd in scheming with his great-grandfather, Pop, to get out of attending. Lately, Calvin had been using the excuse of a headache in a vain effort, because watching people speak in tongues and getting the Holy Ghost was kind of boring now.

As the service dragged on, Calvin listened to Rev. Harry squeezing pigments of sin from the pulpit palette. With chunky flakes of pastels ground into his cuticles and sweat trickling down his round face, Calvin sketched out his comic strip preacher, Brother Cobweb, who was inspired by Rev. Harry but weirdly mixed with TV personalities Bishop Fulton Sheen and Ohio horror host Dr. Ghoul. Brother Cobweb's skin was a ghostly hue, which Calvin made by blending olive green with gray. Calvin scribbled Latin text on Brother's forehead and cheeks. Without knowing what they meant, he had copied those strange foreign words from pages of Chick tracts. The anti-Catholic comic books placed throughout the Lighthouse, along with parishioner gossip, left a vivid image of Romanism: mysterious rituals performed by old men in dresses who looked as though they smelled of cigars. These priests were the torchbearers of a cartoon-like inquisition carrying sinister secrets.

It was this malevolent view of Catholics that forbid even a glimpse of one on TV. Nancy had almost jumped out of her skin when she caught sight of Bishop Sheen flashing across their small TV screen one night.

"Is that Doctor Ghoul?" Nancy had asked desperately.

Calvin had ignored her, staring at the screen. She should have known better—Dr. Ghoul came on late at night, and this was prime time. Still, at a glance, it was an easy mistake because both priest and horror host wore dark-red capes. However, a blasphemous bishop was far more frightening and threatening than a green-painted face introducing movie monsters.

"Oh my Lord," Nancy screeched as she recognized the bishop, "that's that Catholic demon!"

As big a woman as she was, Nancy darted toward the television set like she was years younger and pounds thinner and changed the channel so fast that Calvin thought he had gotten a glimpse of Satan himself. Any good Pentecostal mother would have done the same.

Advance Praise for *Brother Cobweb*

"I was blown away by a naked prose, devoid of superfluous ornamentation, that submerges the reader into the darkest of themes. A gifted artist, Eaker knows how to use boldness and tone to weave a claustrophobic, violent reality that will trap you in a cast almost exclusively populated by increasingly sinister characters from a Midwestern Pentecostal church. And here's where the real talent of his artistry shines as Eaker draws a very personal spirituality of individual liberation and redemption through responsibility, which includes accountability of across-the-board religious abuses—from Mormonism to Pentecostalism and Catholicism.

"He shows us how, even in the most horrendous physical and emotional situations, we can all tap into our inner self, and find within ourselves the means to stop spraying our poison onto others or punishing them for the pain we feel. His words contain such a direct and brutal message that it's impossible to remain indifferent; you'll feel the same raw energy and transforming power as a gaze from any of his painted portraits. Art at its best." —**Mada Jurado**, *Novena News*

"Artists have the uncanny ability to recognize the beauty in challenging and difficult life experiences. Calvin is born into a dysfunctional and abusive family. It is Calvin's skill and understanding of the fine arts that gives him the strength to move into a stable and productive adult life. Interwoven into the story are psychological, theological, ethical, and religious dimensions that call organized religion as well as social and moral structures to accountability. These deeper aspects of the story will challenge readers to reflect on their own lives and to develop the empathy we all need to make our lives ever better and better."
—**Justin Belitz**, OFM

"*Brother Cobweb* is a portrait of Pentecostal crazies that could populate a short story by Flannery O'Conner. Calvin survives religious hypocrisy and a mother's physical abuse with the help of a tolerant, benevolent great-grandfather. No easy, happy endings to this well-told, fast-paced story about the role of 'God' in freakish human experience. Eaker's novel draws a complex picture of religion in which the Weird is graphically made flesh."
—**Jonathan Montaldo**, co-editor with Morgan Atkinson,
Soul-Searching: The Thomas Merton Story

"Alfred Eaker's story is a harrowing tale of violence, abuse, lies, and conflict—yet it ends in hope. There is redemption: in art, beauty, friendship, love, and God . . . Eaker's control of the language and emotional power carries the reader through to the place where the peace that surpasses all understanding dwells. Highly recommended." —**Jason Pannone**, librarian, East Hartford Public Library

"*Brother Cobweb* is a great example of a whole-hearted Bildungsroman—a novel that finds humor and a little horror in a coming-of-age story. By the end, you have insight not only into what it means to be free of a religion you don't need, but also what it feels like to find an actual spirituality that can carry you through."
        —**Keith Banner**, winner, O. Henry Prize and author, *The Life I Lead*

"Alfred Eaker's *Brother Cobweb* is a unique coming-of-age story that explores religious fanaticism, childhood powerlessness, the reverberating effects of abuse, and other influences that shape the adults we ultimately become. A tale of resiliency, reconciliation, and redemption, with plenty of ass-kicking and comeuppance along the way, *Brother Cobweb* is a powerful account of self-discovery that will resonate with readers long after the final pages …"
        —**Michelle Moore**, artist and author, *The Deepest Blue* and *Longing for Lightness: Selected Poems of Antonia Pozzi Translated from the Italian*

"Dark humor at its bleakest. The tragic life of a child reared in an overzealously religious house, his mother, a freak of Pentecostal piety and brutality. *Brother Cobweb* is an artist's escape, his split-caricature-personae, starting at victimized age seven to survival adulthood. Haunting visuals, even without the mastery of illustrator Todd M. Coe."
        —**Cheryl A. Townsend**, poet, photographer, and previous editor/publisher of Impetus/Implosion Press and owner of Cat's Impetuous Books

"As with his surreal and mystical paintings, Alfred Eaker's *Brother Cobweb* portrays both the beauty and the horrifying distortion in the search for self-identity and purpose, all while having been deeply entangled in the swampy roots of a kitschy, hamburger-helper, 'slut-for-Jesus' brand of Pentecostalism. And Eaker makes us laugh. A lot. The true gift of *Cobweb*, however—apart from the gratifying interludes of musical abstractions, for the novel has more (and better) music recommendations than a hipster in a vinyl store—is our young protagonist, Calvin Elkan's sense of religious adventure. While the typical post-modern hero would rationally turn one's back on God and religion after suffering abuses and hypocrisies in their name, we get to experience the faith journey through the thoughtful artist spirit, which is a more rewarding story. In order for there to be divine justice, moral atonement, and maybe even hopeful happiness, Eaker invites all sincere wayfarers to consider a revelation of Calvin's: 'The Church needs me more than I need it.'"   —**Amaya Engleking**, poet, *Gospel Isosceles*

"*Brother Cobweb* is a haunting tale of perversion set within a Midwestern Pentecostal community. Young Calvin Elkin navigates an acrimonious sea of motherly loathing. For many, intimacy is a paradoxical experience, where attraction and repulsion share the same psychological territory. He finally moves on, physically and emotionally, but how does he now relate to others? What is the nature of intimacy for him now? *Brother Cobweb* gives us a lot to process. It is a horror story, but it's a self-reflective one, with a darkly humorous, and ultimately triumphant, outcome."   —**Carla Knopp**, artist, www.carlaknopp.com

BROTHER COBWEB

ALFRED EAKER

ILLUSTRATED BY

TODD M. COE

Open Books Press

Saint Louis, Missouri

Published by Open Books Press, USA

www.OpenBooksPress.com
info@OpenBooksPress.com

An imprint of Pen & Publish, LLC
www.PenandPublish.com
Saint Louis, Missouri
(314) 827-6567

Paperback ISBN: 978-1-941799-74-1
e-book ISBN: 978-1-941799-75-8

Library of Congress Control Number: 2019952283

Printed on acid-free paper.

Cover and interior artwork by Todd M. Coe

Of course, there were Lighthouse mothers who wouldn't even allow Dr. Ghoul to be played on their household sets. The subject of banning Ohio's TV horror celebrity had even once been brought up in the Elkan home. Fortunately, Pop interceded and saved the day, offering a defense in his thick German accent.

"Surely, your Jesus isn't such a weakling that he's afraid of black-and-white monster movies that were made before you were born," Pop had argued. "I've watched those with Calvin. He never gets scared. No one does today. *Hölle*, the daily news is more frightening than *Frankenstein*, absolutely! These movies are more like fairy tales."

As usual, Pop had the last word, but even if he wanted to—and he didn't—there would be no way to ease Nancy's anxiety over a televised Catholic bishop. But the briefness of seeing Sheen on the screen only made his image and the idea of him even more intriguing to Calvin. Nancy's panicked censorship all but prompted her son to rebelliously combine a touch of the priest and the monster when resuming his sketch of Brother Cobweb.

Brother Cobweb's demonic skin was accentuated by a Baptist haircut: an abundant, wavy roll on top, met by bushy lamb chop sideburns spouting downward to an awaiting chin. In contrast to his evangelical bob and polyester suit, Brother was adorned in a priest's stole, decorated with icons of rats and eels running down each side. Carefully drawn within these were wide-open mouths bearing piranha-like teeth. With Rev. Harry's melodramatic words spewing like the blue flames of Pentecost, feeding Calvin's pastel, Brother Cobweb rose like Frankenstein's monster.

Satisfied with what he drew, Calvin leaned back in the pew and drifted to sleep. He began to dream: Brother Cobweb entered the Upper Room and surveyed the church with hungry eyes. Slowly, bit by bit, an image of the Last Supper began to appear. A six-hundred-pound Jesus appeared at the table alongside disciples dressed in polyester suits and a cleavage-bearing Magdalene. Their faces beamed assorted colors as the fleshy prophet and apostles babbled in tongues while large servings of Hamburger Helper materialized on paper plates. Dipping their fingers into the meaty brown heaps, the carnivorous saints feasted violently on their nighttime meal. Carrying a pitcher of cherry Kool-Aid, Brother Cobweb approached and placed it on the table. Jesus poured himself a large glass as he peeked down at Magdalene's movie star titties popping out of her blouse. Brother smiled lustfully.

At dawn, the room morphed into the ruins of a church scarred by fire. The skeletons of Jesus and the disciples crumbled into piles of ash, and a breeze blew their powdery remains across the table. With anxious hands, Brother Cobweb scooped up the relics and placed them inside a gold shadow box on the table, locking it with a key. After bending over and kissing the box, Brother approached a microphone in the center of a stage that looked like a tomb, stepping like Count Dracula passing through a magically intact spider web. Each heavy step echoed up in the burnt wooden rafters. A shattered cross, puddles of salt, bloodied shrouds, dried rose petals, a cracked chalice, and crowns of thorns surrounded Brother. He came to an abrupt stop, mesmerized, as a baby mantis entered. Sensing a threatening presence, the mantis froze, as if in prayer. Its prayer proved unanswered as a mass of ants emerged from the cinders. Brother watched as the ants mercilessly tore apart the small mantis, leaving only its praying hands uneaten. Licking his greedy lips, Brother Cobweb leaned into the microphone.

"Second Timothy, chapter two," said Brother gravely. "The apostle Paul said, 'Therefore, my son, be strong in the grace that is in Christ Jesus.' Paul was simply saying, tough it up, guys, 'cause you gotta endure! I have fought the good fight. I have finished my course, and I have kept the faith. We need to expect a good fight! Everybody repeat: we need to expect a good fight!"

"We need to expect a good fight," echoed a congregation of Pentecostal zombies.

"Turn to your neighbor and tell them you can expect a good fight," roared Brother.

"You can expect a good fight," the unified voice of decaying parishioners rang throughout the church.

The scent of their deathliness aroused Brother as he adjusted his robe.

"You can expect some battle in your life, some fight in your life," Brother resumed in a higher pitch. "Put on the whole armor of God! For we wrestle not against flesh and blood, but against spiritual wickedness in high places! Tell ya what, sometimes I wish we were wrestling against flesh and blood because then I could predict the movement—the action—and know what I'm gonna face tomorrow. By the way, what makes a good fight? A good fight isn't where one fella gets in a single punch and knocks out the other fella. If you paid fifty bucks for a ringside seat to a championship fight that didn't last through the first round, you'd go home a little bit disappointed, wouldn't you? I remember coming home one day and saying, 'Daddy, there was good fight in school today!' 'What do you mean, son?' 'I mean those fellas were dukin' it out. Blood got everywhere! The teachers that tried to break it up, they got hit! Blood got on their white shirts and ties!' I tell ya, sometimes I have faced the devil's temptations and I have said to him, 'In the name of Jesus, get behind me, Satan!' And it seems the devil just stuck out his tongue at me and went BLEHHHH!"

After shoving his thumbs in his ears and sticking out his tongue for dramatic effect, Brother began energetically pacing back and forth across the stage. The sweat stained his made-up face as his passion rose.

"Anybody else ever feel that way? All right, then," Brother continued. "Some of you here tonight have prayed for years about something and have yet to see your prayers answered. Well, can I tell you why? It's because you are involved in a good fight, and you may only be in round four or five in a fifteen-round fight! HELLOOO! Boy, I tell ya, I'm about to feel the preacher come by! If you don't wanna be involved in a good fight, then wimps need not apply! Wimps need not apply!"

Brother tore himself from the drunken sermon and leaned erotically into the body of an awaiting woman below. As Brother forcefully clasped her hips, the woman howled. Collapsing to the floor, she thrashed as if in heavenly orgasm. Somehow, she had lost her shoes, which Brother interpreted as an invitation. As he groped her alluring ankle, Brother quivered.

Jesus's skeleton reappeared, hovering above. Flesh clung to his withered frame, stained in rusty reds.

As it floated down to the stage in the form of a kitty cat, the Holy Ghost purred, "This is my beloved son, in whom I am well pleased."

2

JESUS IS THE LIGHTHOUSE

One week later, Nancy, Calvin, and Frank pulled into the Lighthouse parking lot. The Lighthouse wasn't much larger than a bi-level house and looked just as bland and domestic, minus the steeple: the walls were white with brown trim, and a plain gray cross was perched above the front door. It was small and hidden among the mass of dark, towering trees that surrounded it. Calvin often found himself transfixed by those trees, imagining them as a warning of an unsettling sermon or service ahead, which prompted him to repeat under his breath, for protection, the Cowardly Lion's prayer of: "I do believe in spooks. I do, I do, I do, I do, I do." Calvin took a deep breath as he grabbed his coloring materials and got out of the car.

As she emerged from the car and paraded down the sidewalk, Nancy's robustly matriarchal figure embodied the quintessential Pentecostal mother. To Lighthouse parishioners, she was a model of Christian fashion and holiness apparel. A Jesus bump hairdo—the higher the bump, the closer to God—identified her as part of a tongue-speaking, evangelical body politic. Her pallid floral dress cascaded down to thick ankles, meeting the unwritten requirement of covering callous legs. As Nancy promenaded the path to eternity, she declared: I glow, but not too bright.

Frank followed close behind Nancy as she walked to the church, while a moping Calvin trailed behind, carrying his pastels and a sketchpad. As usual, Nancy dressed her two sons identically; today, they wore red suits with white clip-on ties. Her habit of dressing Calvin and Frank alike often invited comments that they looked like twins, which was Nancy's intent, even though they looked nothing like each other. Calvin was older by nearly two years and had a high forehead, topped off by brown, wavy hair. His smooth, round face was distinguished by a flat nose and full lips. In sharp contrast, Frank had a coarse, angular face, set off by inset eyes, and a Roman nose under a brash, black wiry mane.

"Wow! Look at that cool picture of the pirate! Neat-o," said Frank excitedly, pointing to a new sign on the Lighthouse lawn. "What's it say?" asked Frank, who, at five years old, could barely read, which he hated doing anyway.

"Captain Christ's Vacation Bible School," Calvin groaned as he scrutinized the picture on the sign. With a lopsided mouth, a crooked nose, and decidedly off-season Christmas colors of red and green, the Captain Christ of the sign looked more clown than pirate. He didn't look much like the pirates from the movies or cartoons, nor did he look like any traditional depiction of Jesus, so the image failed on both counts, thought Calvin. The worst part of the sign was the way it was colored. Whoever did the sign used a rusty red instead of a bold red; instead of a bright green, they used a forest green. It was almost as if the artist of the sign held back, not wanting it to be too eye-catching. No, this artist did not love color the way Calvin did, and with the sign's dumb-looking pirate, Calvin imagined Vacation Bible School was going to be as dumb as all the dumb sermons he had to hear, week after week. Of course, Frank, who took pride in being dumb, loved the idea of Captain Christ and was still staring at the sign.

"The picture is painted bad," Calvin grumbled, daring to say it out loud, but he already felt Nancy's eyes on him. It was safe for him to say it there, because although Nancy might indeed belt him at home for such a remark, she would never beat him in church. That would make her, a Sunday school teacher, look bad.

"What do you know?" Nancy countered in a screechy voice. "You get that snooty attitude from Pop, and you can just knock it off, mister!"

"When's it start?" Frank asked. "Can we go?"

"Tomorrow, and you're both going," said Nancy in a tone that said there will be no arguing.

"I don't wanna go," Calvin said defiantly.

"I didn't ask what you wanted. You're going, so you can just shut up about it right now," said Nancy.

Calvin raised his hand, as if to say stop, backed up a step, flinching nervously, suddenly realizing that, perhaps, he should not take for granted that his mother would not beat him on church grounds.

"I heard the Captain has a real hook for a hand," Nancy directed at Frank, ignoring Calvin. Her attempt to inspire enthusiasm worked on her youngest son, whose eyes gleamed with interest.

Both the Sunday morning and evening services passed uneventfully. Nobody got the Holy Ghost. However, Calvin spent much of the next day eyeing the tacky-looking grandfather clock in the living room. It was a countdown to Vacation Bible School, which Calvin dreaded like death itself.

Sure enough, Monday evening arrived with Frank leaping out of the car, heading at full speed toward the Lighthouse door. Calvin lagged behind. When the two brothers arrived at the Vacation Bible School room, they found numerous Lighthouse children sitting Indian style on the floor before a cardboard ship. Captain Christ had three teenage boys for helpers, who were dressed alike as traditional pirates, standing before their captive audience—captive that is, with the exception of Calvin. A loud whistle blew from the cardboard ship, and Calvin flinched. In response to the whistle, the three helpers began a pirate dance. Calvin laughed to himself. Although he couldn't dance himself, he'd seen enough musicals on TV to know good dancing from bad dancing. This was terrible, Calvin thought as the boys repeatedly bumped into each other.

"They look like the Penguin's helpers," Calvin whispered to Frank. "From *Batman*."

"They remind me of the Golddiggers dancing," Frank sniggered.

Calvin's eyes widened as he recalled *The Dean Martin Show*'s bevy of long-legged chorus girls, whose dancing he thoroughly enjoyed because they were actually good, unlike these pirate clowns. He wished he was watching them now with Dino, dressed in black tuxes, smoking cigarettes, holding their glasses of whiskey, and laughing themselves silly. With Frank's prompting, Calvin tried to imagine how the Golddiggers would do a much better pirate dance.

As the teens danced, they shuffled their way through the audience, handing each child a God bag. God's bag is just a white paper sack? Calvin asked himself incredulously as a pimply teen handed God bags to him and Frank.

Frank eagerly reached into his bag to find crayons, stickers, a Bible verse written on printer paper, a toy truck, and candy. Frank went for the candy first, popping two peanut butter taffies into his mouth.

"What'd you get?" Frank asked Calvin.

Calvin ignored Frank's question as the room darkened. Calvin fixed his eyes on a single beam of light, which intensified until the silhouette of Captain Christ appeared. Framed by rising mist, Captain's form was so startling an apparition that it took Calvin's breath away. Calvin had imagined an athletic pirate character, something like the swashbuckling movie star Errol Flynn who played Captain Blood, but Captain Christ was more akin to a whale. His bold and imperious voice rang out—Calvin flinched again.

"Ahoy there, mateys! I am Captain Christ, sailing the seven seas, and I'm here to see who dares play tag with the devil!"

He ain't no Captain Blood, Calvin thought. He's a sea beast!

"Even though I lost an arm and leg in service, I still terrorize the enemy," Captain Christ growled at his young audience.

"Mom was right. He does have a real hook for a hand, and that's a real peg leg too!" Frank whispered to Calvin as the light behind Captain Christ brightened, making him more visible.

Seeing Captain Christ more plainly had the opposite effect on Calvin.

"He looks so dumb," Calvin mumbled as Captain Christ rambled on about the most blessed treasure found by wretched man—Jesus, of course, not gold.

The lights dimmed and the kids turned their attention to a projector screen as a crudely animated cartoon started with an image of a motorcyclist cruising down a highway. Captain Christ narrated:

"It was April, and I was making my way through Frankfort. I didn't realize that tragedy was waiting for me. A car pulled out to pass a truck. He didn't see me on my motorcycle, coming from the other direction. And mateys . . . he hit me head on!"

Not even the rustling of a God bag could be heard now.

"I was thrown into a field with half my body almost torn away," Captain Christ continued. "I was unconscious and dying, but worst of all, I was without Jesus. Sirens were screaming and red lights were flashing! They scraped me up and rushed me to the hospital. My left arm and leg had to be amputated to save my life. But something happened to me in that hospital room, mateys—I accepted Jesus as my Lord and personal Savior."

On the screen, an image depicted Captain Christ as a silhouetted cartoon pirate praying on his knees in a hospital room.

"The Holy Ghost tapped on my heart's door, and I turned my life over to Jesus. He's now enlisted me to hook boys and girls and pin them to God because I am the world's only Christian pirate, Captain Christ!"

The room brightened. Captain Christ and his crew shuffled behind the cardboard pirate ship, moving the ship as though sailing through flimsy waves. Opposite them was a smaller cardboard ship manned by a demon, dressed in a black bodysuit and rubber gargoyle mask, which was so loose that his neck and jawline peeked from underneath. Calvin bit his lower lip, trying not to laugh out loud. The demon's trio of henchmen, also dressed in tight-fitting black clothes, had black makeup smeared across their faces and horns strapped around their heads with shoestrings. They must not have been able to afford any more masks, Calvin thought, and, unable to suppress himself any longer, let out a giggle. Quickly, he put his hand over his mouth, but after a moment his mind wandered to the hypothetical children Captain Christ was "hooking": Are the children under the water? Are they trapped by the devil? Will Captain Christ put his hook in them? How is that better than being trapped by the devil?

The demon peered through a telescope.

"Pirates off the starboard bow! Charge your cannon and stand ready to attack," cried Captain Christ.

The demon raised his fist at Captain Christ, mumbling a curse that sounded like Yosemite Sam gibberish.

"Suggest they lower their colors!" ordered Captain Christ.

"Lower your flags," instructed the seaman.

The demon's henchmen scrambled to their cannon and shot out a puff of smoke, missing their target. Captain Christ and his pirates cheered.

"Captain, we can put a draft through their bow," cried Captain Christ's first mate.

"Show them how to lower those colors! Suck the wind outta the devil's sails," roared Captain Christ.

"Fire!" yelled the first mate. Captain Christ's cannon emitted twice as much smoke and struck the demons' ship with a rubber ball.

"The devil is sinking! Grappling hooks away," hollered the first mate. Captain Christ's pirates invaded the devil's ship, and the room erupted in applause as the lights came up.

During a fifteen-minute break, in which most of the children emptied their God bags, Calvin, having handed his bag over to Frank, grabbed a sheet of paper and pencil from a nearby table and attempted to sketch the image of Captain Christ. The idea of Jesus as a pirate made no sense to Calvin, even at his age. After all, in the movies, pirates stole money and jewels and even killed people. They were bad guys. Yet, Christ, who was supposed to be a good guy, was now a pirate who didn't even say anything from the Bible. Instead, he was shooting people. And why would Jesus need a boat when he could walk on water, like the Bible said? Questions spilled onto the paper as Calvin dashed out a rough sketch of a different, better ending: Captain Christ losing the battle with his boat sinking. Just as Calvin was getting ready to draw the devil shaking his fist in defiance, Luke Dushane walked over. Luke was Rev. Harry's son and eight years older than Calvin. Tall and lanky, Luke was dressed in a suit, ever a preacher's son.

"What're you drawing, Calvin? Can I see?" Luke asked, and although his tone seemed polite, Calvin wasn't going to risk getting in trouble.

"Oh, nothing. I messed up. I'll show you my next drawing if I don't mess it up," Calvin answered as he quickly wadded up the paper and shoved it in his pocket.

"OK, cool," said Luke, respecting Calvin's privacy. "How do you like Captain Christ's Vacation Bible School so far?"

Calvin shrugged.

"I kind of figured you wouldn't like it," said Luke.

"Why did you figure that?" Calvin asked, curious because this was the first time the two of them had even talked.

"Oh, I don't know. It just doesn't seem like it'd be something you'd like. I figured you'd rather be drawing."

"Uh huh."

"This is just the first day of it. Maybe it will get better," Luke shrugged. "I better get going. They'll be starting back up any time."

"OK," Calvin answered as he watched Luke walk off. He knew it wouldn't get any better, and he wasn't sure why Luke couldn't see that.

A moment later, Captain Christ and his first mate reappeared, wheeling in something under a green sheet on a gurney. "We are now in the mortuary of eternal judgment, preparing for Truth. We're going to do an autopsy on a sinner," Captain Christ announced.

"What's a mortuary?" Frank asked Calvin.

"A place they take you after you die," answered Calvin.

"What's an autopsy?"

"Just watch," said Calvin, annoyed.

With a theatrical flip of his hand, Captain Christ half-unveiled a mannequin figure of a male. "This sinner was one of the devil's minions," he said. "Have you ever performed an autopsy on a sinner, matey?"

The first mate shook his head.

"Now, please be quiet, everyone. No whispering. That'll disturb us. We don't want to cut off the wrong limb," Captain Christ said loudly.

The first mate handed Captain Christ a saw, and he reached under the sheet and made a cutting motion.

"Oh, look at that hand," the first mate said as he held up the plastic limb. "This hand has not been praising Jesus! The Bible tells us to praise Jesus! Those hands have not been clapping in church!"

Captain Christ passed the hand off to another Christian pirate, who tossed it into a nearby bucket.

"Oh, look at that foot," Captain Christ yelled as he cut off a mannequin foot. "Where do you think those feet have been going? I don't think these feet have been walking to church. I think these feet have been going to bars."

Captain Christ handed his first mate a knife.

"Now cut out that eye," Captain Christ instructed the first mate. "I wanna look at his eye."

The first mate plopped an eyeball into Captain Christ's hand for closer inspection.

"Hmm, this eye's in bad shape!" Captain Christ cried out in a horror movie voice. "The Bible tells us that if our eyes see something offensive, pluck it out. A little more light here, brothers! I want to SEE the evil in that eye, so I can show our friends what it means to be without the light!"

Captain Christ and his first mate tossed the rubber eyeball between them as if it were a hot potato. The slapstick exchange inspired Frank to giggle, but Calvin rolled his eyes.

"Oh, my—what's that on the gurney? Is that a beer can?" Captain Christ asked. "Those ears have not heard how terrible drinking beer is! Beer has no place in the life of a Christian. What's that? Cigarettes! What do those do to you? They turn your teeth yellow! Who would want to kiss a boy or girl who smelled like a camel?"

The first mate unfolded part of the sheet to expose more tools of the devil.

"Let's remove the heart," Captain Christ said as he pulled a blackened and bloody heart from under the sheet.

A collective "grossss" spread through the audience.

"Man looks at the outward appearance, but God looks at the heart! And only Jesus can take care of the heart! Only Jesus can come into your heart and make it pure, white, and clean—not like this heart! Jesus is the best friend you'll ever have. He can clean up your hands, your feet, your eyes, and your ears, too, because the Bible says your body is the temple of the Lord! We need to offer our bodies to Jesus," Captain Christ advised as he made a bow and scuffed his peg along the floor, exiting stage left.

Captain Christ didn't look at the brain, Calvin thought. Maybe God's like Superman. Superman can't see through lead, and God can't see what we think.

The kids at Vacation Bible School sat there stunned in silence until they were ushered into another room where tables were set up. According to Captain Christ's pirates, who were now handing out crayons and colored pencils, the last part of Vacation Bible School was titled "How Great Thou Art Lessons." Calvin was confused because the only artwork hanging in the entire church was a small, framed print of the head of Jesus. It was a boring painting that Calvin had seen in countless department stores. Captain Christ's pirate helpers asked several children what they thought God is like, and Frank quickly offered his opinion:

"I think he's this old man, and he watches us from his cloud—and—and whenever he sees us having fun, he yells Stop!"

Calvin was relieved that he was not asked because he had previously drawn an image of Jehovah God as a hairy beast with red eyes and bad breath who lived in a wooden box out in the middle of the desert. If anyone got too close to the box, God would reach out his claw for the kill.

The children were given the choice to draw a picture for Jesus or color in Bible coloring books. Anxious to draw again, Calvin sat down at one of the tables away from Frank and the other children. Sensibly, Calvin decided not to draw the Jehovah monster and began drawing a picture of George Reeves' Superman flying to a lighthouse. When Calvin finished his drawing, he showed it to the first mate.

"You draw pretty good, but what does this have to do with Jesus?"

"On TV, Superman was at a haunted lighthouse, and our church is called the Lighthouse," Calvin proudly answered.

"Oh," replied the first mate. "It's a good drawing, but I don't think it's got anything to do with Jesus."

"What do pirates have to do with Jesus?" asked Calvin.

Dumbfounded, the first mate could offer no reply, and without a word, he quickly spun around to find a more compliant child.

3

I WAS MARRIED TO A MERMAID

"We saw a half-man play a pirate in church," shouted Frank, pulling off his shirt as he ran into the living room past Pop, who was sitting in his chair. Calvin and Nancy followed Frank into the house.

Instantly smelling Pop's maple tobacco, Calvin laughed. "Pop's incense."

"No, Calvin's incense," countered Pop.

"That's nonsense, Calvin. It's a dirty habit that you best never pick up," Nancy sternly warned.

Although it was summer, Pop was fully dressed in long johns, a T-shirt, a dress shirt, a waistcoat, a coat, and fingerless gloves.

"Aren't you hot?" Frank asked Pop. "I get hot just looking at you! You smell funny, too!"

"If clothes protect me from the cold, they will protect me from the heat," Pop explained. Frank made a face and scampered away to his bedroom.

Never one to bathe much, Pop ignored comments on his mildew-like body odor, feeling his personal hygiene was his *personal* hygiene. Despite his wrinkled skin, white hair, pipe smoking habit, and questionable hygiene, Pop was fit for his age. He walked three miles a day, drank plenty of water, and snacked daily on bananas, cheese, and a single glass of red wine. Pop was an eighty-seven-year old German Jew whose primary health impediment was eccentricity due to the onslaught of senility. To Calvin, Pop wasn't just his great-grandfather—Pop was dad.

Calvin's actual father was the physically and emotionally absent Dale. Having dropped out of sixth grade, Dale was, as Pop said, practically illiterate, and a solid blue-collar union man who liked poker, beer, hunting, and an at-home wife while he worked. When he was present, Dale earned the nickname "the Couch," blending in silently with the Elkan household furniture. Dale had no time for church—he worked three jobs as a machinist for a car manufacturer, a truck driver, and a car salesman—so rectifying her husband's unsaved status was Nancy's biggest life goal.

Despite the questionable odor, Calvin climbed into a chair beside Pop as Nancy went to start dinner. "Looking at movie star ladies again, Pop?" he asked with a grin, looking down at the scrapbook in Pop's lap. It was a wallpaper sample book titled *Movie Star Titty Book*, according to Pop, who had written the title in crayon on the cover. Glued inside the book were numerous photographs of cleavage-brandishing starlets such as Julie London, which Pop haphazardly cut out of Rona Barrett gossip magazines. Once, Nancy had challenged Pop's lack of morality in spending so much hobby time obsessing over golden bosoms. Pop had rebuffed her, saying that despite the problems and struggles he'd had with his wife, Pop had remained chaste since she had died many years before.

Pop flipped to a page. "This is no lady here."

Calvin looked down. "Darwin?"

"Mr. Charles Darwin," said Pop, admiring the photo.

"How come you have picture of Darwin in a book about ladies?" Calvin asked, confused.

"It's not really a scrapbook just about ladies. I just call it that to annoy your mother. I put all kinds of pictures in here. Anything that interests me, like this . . ." Pop said, flipping to a page with a picture from an opera on it.

"But," Calvin started to protest.

"Calvin, not everything has to make sense."

"But you make fun of the Bible because it doesn't make sense sometimes."

"*Gottverdammt*, if you aren't a great-grandson after my own heart," Pop laughed heartily. "I suppose that makes me a bit of a hypocrite like your mother. Although, not that big of a hypocrite. So, I think you can indulge me a little hypocrisy."

Calvin did like the opera images Pop had flipped to, even if they were roughly arranged and the pages stuck together from too much glue. However, the images of operas and Darwin were few and, as the title indicted, the book was mostly filled with celebrity cleavage and pictures of mermaids, including the aquatic movie starlet Esther Williams. There she stretched out, smiling through stills from her movie, *Million Dollar Mermaid.*

Pop's eyes twinkled. His finger traced the length of Esther's legs and then closed the book abruptly, noticing Calvin's discomfort.

"Where's that grandson of mine?" Pop called out to Nancy, who was opening cabinets in the kitchen.

"He's playing poker with his union buddies—a bunch of Democrats," she said with emphasized disgust. "He'll be home soon." Nancy walked into the living room where Pop was sitting with Calvin. "Calvin has something to ask you," she said.

"Well then, let him ask."

Embarrassed, Calvin shrugged. Pop rolled his eyes, suspecting Nancy was up to typical Pentecostal scheming.

"Calvin's too shy to ask."

"Nonsense," Pop said, turning to Calvin. "You're not shy with your great-grand pop!"

Before Calvin could respond, Nancy interrupted. "Captain Christ is having a contest in Vacation Bible School. Whoever brings in the most visitors will win an illustrated children's Bible, and Calvin wants to win it."

"Who the hell is Captain Christ?"

Nancy sighed loudly. "We told you yesterday that he was coming to the Lighthouse."

"I don't remember, but he sounds like a bad vaudeville act. What does he do? Play like some big fool god?"

"Pop, I try to rear my boys to be good Christian men and you just make fun of God."

"Why do you fill these kids' minds with such nonsense?"

"Nonsense? How about that nonsense that we all came from monkeys?" asked Nancy, pointing to a book by Darwin lying on the end table next to Pop.

"As usual, you are oversimplifying it, but let me tell you something about melodramatic Christian nonsense. I read an article awhile back about the civil rights march that was mighty interesting."

"What's that got to do with my religion?"

"Plenty, woman." Pop's *w*'s sounded like *v*'s, especially when he was agitated. "The sight of colored folk marching on the Capitol sent some Baptist and Nazarene churches into a tongue-speaking frenzy. Mind you, these are Christians who normally do not engage in all that babble, but seeing marching coloreds was enough to convince them that the end of the world was right around the corner."

"About time they spoke in tongues," Nancy snarled, "you can't get into heaven until you been anointed in the gift of tongues."

"If it's a gift, then how is it mandatory? I don't know how the lot of you sleep at night!"

"I sleep just fine, but all that reading is mashing that brain of yours into liberal gravy, old man."

"And your religion keeps you a zealot. Why are you so afraid of change? You'd be better off if you got out and walked a spell," Pop countered.

"Get out and walk? What's walking got to do anything? We weren't even talking about walking? You're plumb crazy . . ."

"You're a silly old woman. Sillier and older than me even."

"You're getting senile, Pop. You're so much older than me."

Knowing that arguing with Nancy was pointless, Pop returned his attention to Calvin. "Why do you want to win that baby Bible?"

"I just want to win something. I never won anything before," Calvin whined, "and I like drawing Bible pictures. It might give me some ideas."

Pop smiled knowingly. "Alright, but I'll show you some images later that are well painted. It's important to be able to tell good art from bad, but now what do they do at Bible School?"

"Just teaching and drawing. Well, only I did some drawing. The rest of the kids just colored."

"So, what did they teach you today?" asked Pop.

Calvin thought for a moment. "Well, I guess I learned this: God can see the heart, but he can't see a kid's mind."

"Captain Christ didn't teach you that," Nancy barked.

"He did so. He cut up a sinner. He cut off his hand, cut out his eye, and even cut out his heart that was black as coal. He cut out everything because he said God could see all those, but he didn't cut out the brain at all. He left that alone. I figure now that must be why everybody at the Lighthouse prays so loudly—God can't hear them if they're just praying to themselves because he can't read their minds."

"That ain't why we pray loud," Nancy shot off defensively.

"Then, why do you? Are you just showing off?" Pop asked, interjecting.

"Like an atheist Jew would understand," Nancy huffed.

"Well," said Pop, ignoring Nancy and turning to Calvin, "no surprise about God not seeing the mind because if there is a God and if he could see my mind, he might just change a few of his tactics knowing how his chosen see him. One question though, what the hell do pirates have to do with Jesus?"

"I asked the same thing!" said Calvin excitedly, which prompted a threatening look from Nancy. "But I didn't say the bad word," Calvin added quickly.

"I suppose I can go to your Bible School for one night, as long as they don't cut out my heart to give to some sky beast."

Nancy and Pop stared each other down while Calvin watched intensely, waiting for an exciting outburst that never came.

"Come on, Calvin," said Pop finally, struggling to get to his feet.

"What are you up to now, old man?" Nancy asked.

"We're going to my room so I can finish up an important story I was telling him. Isn't that right, Calvin?"

"Yup," Calvin answered, excitedly.

Nancy eyed Pop with suspicion. "Don't be filling him up with all that Wag-ner opera stuff. I don't want my son turning into a freak. Kids'll make fun of him."

"It's pronounced 'Vagner' with a 'V,' even though it's spelled 'Wagner' with a 'W,' and Calvin likes my operas, woman, so let him be."

Pop's narrow bedroom was littered with cut-up magazines, classical music LPs, two sets of encyclopedias, and numerous stacks of books—seemingly hundreds of them—haphazardly placed on the floor throughout the cramped living space. Among the books was one of Pop's favorites, *I, Claudius*, which he had recently been reading to Calvin. In the center of the room was Pop's bed, so small that his legs dangled over the end when he slept. However, the old man didn't seem to mind because he never complained about it. At the end of the room was a television set with a ten-inch screen and two big round knobs, framed in ugly sci-fi gold. Atop the set was a pair of rabbit ears wrapped in aluminum foil. Pop and Calvin often sat on the edge of his bed before the idiot box. Although they talked, read, and listened to music a lot, it was selective watching that Calvin and Pop did most together.

Lying on his bedside table was Pop's own unfinished manuscript: *I Was Married to a Mermaid*. Pop's book was opened—he had recently been working on it. Pop's incessant laboring on his mermaid manifesto had initially inspired Calvin to begin *The Brother Cobweb Chronicles*. In contrast to Pop's book, which was over a thousand pages of text, Calvin's *Cobweb* was a mere forty pages of drawings.

Pop had a complete LP set of Wagner's mammoth *Ring* opera. He thumbed through the records and picked the first opera of the four-part cycle, *Rheingold*, placing it on the turntable.

"How come *Rheingold* is the only one we ever listen to?" Calvin asked his great-grandfather as he sat down on the floor across from Pop.

"I've listened to all of them, but *Rheingold* is my favorite because it has mermaids. You'll have plenty of time to listen to the rest. Besides, *Rheingold* sets the mood for my tale."

Pop turned the sound down low so it would not interfere with his unfolding narrative.

"I told all my friends those Nazis were insane," he began. "Did they listen? No. Now they're all dead, and I'm still alive. And just like Superman's father put his baby in a spaceship and sent him to Kansas, I put your great-grandmother on the boat and shipped her to America, even though we were already divorced. Well, not really divorced. We were just separated. I didn't manage money well enough for her, so she got mad and moved across the street," Pop snickered, pointing as if her adjacent house were in front him, "but I still had conjugal visits."

"And you sent my grandpa here, too," added Calvin.

"And his wife," Pop added. "Of course, your poor grandpa died before you were born . . . drank himself to death, as did your great-grandmother. Anyway, I sent her and the whole family here first so I could sail the seven seas. And you know what happened?"

Calvin shook his head.

"I was fishing on the island of Galapagos, and I caught me a mermaid," Pop announced with childlike glee.

Calvin's eyes lit up. "A mermaid?"

"Yes, a mermaid! See, that's what Alberich should have done," said Pop, pointing to the villain on the *Rheingold* LP. "Instead, he wanted gold more than love. Only a fool would choose gold over love, but I am no fool. So, I married my mermaid, and I named her Ariel! Together, Ariel and I outsmarted those Stormtroopers! When they landed on our island—never saw anything like it in my life! She'd twirl up in the air, bring down her tail, and Slap! Slap! Slap! right in the old Nazi kisser, and she drove those Stormtroopers back into the sea! They never knew what hit 'em! And now, I'm writing my great book. It's going to be as big as Wagner's *Ring*! As big as the *Rheingold*! And it's all about Ariel and me. When it's finished, *Reader's Digest* will publish it. You mark my words, Calvin."

"Ahem," coughed Nancy, peeking in through Pop's doorway.

"You might have knocked," said Pop.

"You were not married to a mermaid. There's no such thing as mermaids. You're making up stories again."

"Don't you tell me I wasn't married to a mermaid," snapped Pop.

"What happened to her then? Huh?"

"I made love to her so passionately, she transformed into whoopee butter."

"Pop! I don't want Calvin hearing such porno-grafee!"

"You didn't have qualms letting him watch Clint Eastwood shoot everyone in sight. Would you rather your son grow up to kill people or to make people?" asked Pop, defiantly.

Calvin looked down at the carpet, hiding his smile and avoiding Nancy's stare.

"We're not talking about this in my house. Now, come and eat, both of you."

"I hope it's not Hamburger Helper again," Pop grumbled under his breath.

The old man and his great-grandson left the bedroom, slowly following Nancy.

"You see, after Ariel transformed into whoopee butter, I keep her right here," Pop whispered, patting his heart. "That way she's protected from all the bigots in the world."

Calvin smiled, perplexed, and changed the subject. "Captain Christ talked about the seven seas, too, but his stories aren't as fun as yours."

Pop turned to Calvin, surprised. "He sailed the seven seas, too?"

"Yeah, but all he did was go after the devil."

"He's an even bigger fool than Alberich, then."

Nancy and Frank were waiting impatiently at the table when Calvin and Pop entered the dining room. Nancy was preparing to bless the meal but changed her mind upon seeing Calvin. "Calvin, let's see what you learned in Bible School. Why don't you say grace for the family?"

Caught off guard, Calvin quickly blurted out something he had heard from a kid at school: "Father, Son, Holy Ghost, whoever eats the fastest gets the most. Amen."

"You learn that in Vacation Bible School, did you?" asked Nancy, fuming. Calvin shook his head. "Well, you're lucky you're at the other end of the table, otherwise I'd take a belt to that face of yours!"

"Woman," yelled Pop, "there'll be no belting!"

Pop's command was issued with such sternness that Nancy drew a breath and conceded.

The threat and violence of Nancy's tone startled Calvin. Although Nancy had, on a few occasions, belted Calvin, she had never done so or threatened to do so in Pop's presence. Even when she had belted him, it had been a quick swat to the rump, usually over something that he had indeed done wrong, like the time he conked Frank on the head with a wooden toy for stepping on six of Calvin's favorite pastels. However, the threat of taking a belt to Calvin's face, over something so silly, breached a new level of violent intent that felt like hate. Although he had never felt much in the way of affection from his mother, or even sensed that she liked him much, this was the first time Calvin fully realized her real hatred for him.

Calvin picked at his food, suddenly not hungry. He wondered why she hated him. Was it because he didn't like her church, which her whole life revolved around? Or was it because, as she often pointed out, Calvin was more like Pop's son than hers? Maybe it was both. Despite Nancy's penchant for aggressively making godly points, she respected familial tradition to concede to Pop's pacifism. That she had now been brave and disrespectful enough to threaten Calvin in front of Pop was both shocking and frightening.

The family ate in uncomfortable silence for a short while until Nancy got up and pushed a button on the tape player near her. The sound of Rev. Harry's voice rang out from the small machine.

"We have to prepare ourselves—galvanize our souls! Oh, Lord give me the backbone of a saw log; give me ribs like the sleepers underneath the church floor; give me the hide of a rhinoceros; give me steel-stitched britches and hang a wagonload of determination on the cable into my soul. Help me to sign a contract to fight the devil as long as I have a fist and bite him as long as I have a tooth, and then gum him till I die! Hey, it's a good fight. I might as well brace myself for it! I know it's real! I know I can't get out of it! So, we might as well quit whimpering around, go ahead, and get in the ring!"

"Jesus," cried Pop.

"Pop, you're praying," beamed Nancy.

"The hell I am! I am shocked how much time all of you spend worrying about some devil. What's the point of that? Doesn't seem like much fun to me."

"Mama prayed to the Holy Ghost, Pop! The Holy Ghost said you and Dad won't get saved unless you hear the sermons. The Holy Ghost told Mom to tape the sermons for you so you won't go to hell with the devil," explained Frank earnestly.

Pop spit out a mouthful of his baked potato. "Margarine? I told you butter, woman, butter!"

"Whoopee butter," giggled Calvin, delighting in a humor that Nancy, and perhaps even Pop, failed to see. Although Pop had voiced playful defiance in response to Nancy's assertion that he had uttered a prayer, in a way, Pop's patting his heart to keep Ariel safe was like a prayer. It was an honest prayer: eccentric and personal without unnecessary words. In that brief gesture, proclaiming his mermaid protected, Pop was in a state of perfect grace—perfect because it couldn't be named grace. In a wave of inspiration, Calvin prayed that Pop's grace could remain hidden. He prayed it quick and under his breath, with eyes open, for fear that both Nancy and Pop, each for their own reason, might disapprove. Nancy, sensing his defiance, looked directly at Calvin, her scathing eyes darkening. Just then, Dale walked in smelling of heavy cigars, bargain beer, and deep-fried frog legs. Nancy's tone shifted immediately and sharply.

Anger gave way to exaggerated tears. "Oh, Jesus help me, please," cried Nancy as she sprang up from the table, ran from the dining area into her bedroom and melodramatically collapsed onto her bed. Calvin could hear her large body in the throes of a toddler-like tantrum, flopping against the mattress.

Calvin rolled his eyes upon hearing his mother caught up in a cartoonish wailing of the spirit while Frank gnawed at his knuckle. Dale, stunned by his wife's outburst, descended the hallway, following Nancy's trail. Frank followed his dad, but Dale motioned the boy to go to his room. After hearing both Frank's and Nancy's bedroom doors shutting, Pop was torn somewhere between a fit of uncontrollable laughter and disdain at this common household occurrence. He settled on a heavy, fatigued sigh and motioned to Calvin.

"Calvin, let's go listen to Glenn," said Pop with disgust. "If we're going to have to put up with craziness, it might as well be beautiful craziness."

Calvin nodded in enthusiastic agreement since he had developed a passion of sorts for that eccentric Canadian pianist, Glenn Gould.

Nancy's profuse experience in Pentecostal performance art had rendered her quite the manipulator considering her husband's blue-collar naïveté. Although he knew Dale—who, like Pop, was pacifistic—would not physically discipline him, Calvin expected he and Pop would later have to endure Dale's late-night impassioned plea to keep peace.

"My god. She sounds like a wounded Moby Dick wailing from the shore of yonder lighthouse. Where's Captain Ahab when you need him?" grumbled Pop as they passed by Nancy's room. "Well, Glenn's *Bach* should drown her out."

Although Pop forgot about Vacation Bible School the next day and Nancy saw no reason to remind him, at the end of the week, Calvin won his children's Bible through no work of his own. Nancy, discouraged by Calvin's lame proselytizing efforts, took it upon herself to go door to door and invite all the neighborhood kids in Calvin's name. If she had hoped his winning the children's Bible would prod him to a new enthusiasm for the Lighthouse, her hopes were soon dashed when Calvin immediately gave it away after seeing that Pop's instincts were right. It was filled with awful drawings.

ECUMENICAL ALCHEMY

Three weeks after surviving being lost at sea with Captain Christ, an odd, new scene played out on Sunday night at the Lighthouse: Rev. Harry, rising from his grand red velvet chair, disappeared offstage momentarily. The chair was one of two recently installed thrones, as Calvin called them. The second one was black and reserved for visiting evangelists, but the spotlight was on Rev. Harry alone. For Calvin, there was something menacingly fascistic about the thrones, but tonight he wasn't disturbed by them, as he often was. Instead, his curiosity was piqued as Rev. Harry returned, dragging a television set onto the church stage. It would likely be a perfect thing to draw, but frustrated by the worsening headaches he'd been having over the last two weeks, Calvin felt temporarily defeated and placed the oil pastel back in its box. The pounding and the sweat and the heat would not permit him to capture the scene playing out in front of him, which he guessed probably disappointed Luke, who had chosen to sit in the pew with Calvin.

It was an unofficial tradition at the Lighthouse that when kids turned fifteen, they no longer had to sit in the pew with their parents and could sit anywhere they wanted. Getting to move to another pew was a sign that kids were preparing to become members of the adult Lighthouse community. Everyone had been waiting to see when and if Rev. Harry and his wife, Vernell, were going to honor that tradition with their son. After all, Luke had turned fifteen in late spring, but tonight was the first night that Luke didn't sit next to his mother. Of all people, Luke chose to sit next to Calvin, who made less of this than everyone else. Calvin guessed it was just because Luke wanted to see him draw. Nancy, for her part, was quite pleased in Luke's choice.

"I'll tell you straight up, my wife and Luke are mighty upset with me right now," Rev. Harry announced, "but sometimes we have to make hard decisions as Christian leaders for our families. I tell you this—leadership comes with a price. As a boy is apt to do, Luke went to his mama when daddy took what seemed like a harsh stand. He tried to play Vernell and me against each other, which makes my godly decision a cross to bear."

Even through his headache and young age, Calvin gleaned the cruelty of Rev. Harry knocking Luke down a few pegs publicly on the night of his pew of choice initiation.

"So, Reverend, you might ask, what does a TV set have to do with hard decisions? It's just innocent entertainment. It may seem so, but what comes across that idiot box is not so idiotic, really. We cannot have blinders on to Hollywood's smart agenda. By smart, I don't mean good. I tell you, the devil's no dummy, and we need to be aware of how he uses liberal Hollywood to condition our households."

Rev. Harry took a sip of water. "Oh, Superman seems innocent enough, flyin' through the air, but we all know there's only one real superman, and that's Jesus! Y'all know the Superman story? His father sends his only son, from a planet far away, to save us on earth. Now, what's that sound like? Sounds like Jesus, don't it? It's no accident that the people who made up Superman are Jews. Look it up! I ain't foolin' ya. Jews mocking our Lord and Savior ain't nothing new. They're still doing it. Why do you think that actor who played Superman killed himself?"

"Why?" Calvin whispered to Luke.

Luke shrugged.

"I like Superman, too," Calvin continued. "What's wrong with Superman? He's more fun than Jesus."

"That is why Dad's doing this," Luke answered with hushed disgust. "Superman is competition, I guess."

Rev. Harry continued from up on stage. "But that's nothing compared to what I saw the other day—prime-time witching hour, straight from Hollywood into our living room. I'm talking about *Bewitched*, folks. Yeah, that show with Elizabeth Montgomery twitching her nose, gettin' holy men all worked up."

"Worked up about what?" Calvin whispered, which prompted a laugh out of Luke. Nancy glared at Calvin from further down the pew, and he quickly looked away from Luke.

"She's promoting witchcraft!" Rev. Harry said conspiratorially. "I'm sure it's the devil's favorite program. I'm sure Satanists gather weekly to watch that show."

"Now I'm not going to get to see Uncle Arthur anymore," said Calvin.

"Sorry. Paul Lynde's a great Uncle Arthur. He's my favorite part," Luke said, trying to distract him from the damaging sermon.

"But, she's a good witch, you might say," continued Rev. Harry. "I'm here to tell you—no such thing. Hollywood's been trying to sell us thinly disguised Satanism since that Glenda witch in *The Wizard of Oz*. It's their recruiting poster for their lord and master, the devil. We let 'em beam it right into our holy space! We've sacrificed our prayer hour for their witching hour, and we think it's innocent? No such thing. Over time we've called evil good and good evil. It's time to take a stand. I'm gonna start by putting my money where my mouth is. Nancy . . . ?"

Rev. Harry motioned Nancy to come to the stage, which surprised Calvin. Nancy walked proudly up the aisle, her head held high, before disappearing behind the stage. A moment later, she reemerged holding a baseball bat and handed it, like a sacred instrument, to Rev. Harry.

"Thank you, sister," purred Rev. Harry as he took the bat from Nancy. "Now, the Bible says put no evil thing before our eyes," he said, getting louder and louder, almost yelling now, "so I'm gonna cleanse my house of this abomination." He screamed as he lifted the baseball bat and brought it crashing through the screen. The congregation sat stunned in silence while two men cleaned the stage. Nancy looked on proudly, happy to be part of such a cleansing, while Rev. Harry did a stylish shuffle back to his throne.

"Why'd your dad walk like that?" Calvin asked Luke.

"Oh, he got that from Minnie the Moocher on the *Betty Boop* cartoon."

"On TV? I thought he didn't like TV," Calvin said in a horse protest.

"Oh, don't let that fool you. The picture tube on that TV set went out last week, so it was broke anyway. We got another one. Dad watches TV more than me or Mom—mostly wrestling though."

Calvin tried to laugh, but coughed violently.

"How long you been sick like this?" Luke asked.

"Couple weeks maybe, but bad the last few days," Calvin answered. As the sweat on his face dripped onto his shirt, he shook his head to keep his heavy eyelids from slamming shut.

Moments later, Rev. Harry took the mic again. "As I told some of you on the prayer band, tonight we have a guest gospel trio."

Three black gospel singers mounted the stage and began belting out a spirited rendition of "The Sweet By-and-By." The sound of xenophobic grumbling began to intensify, which took Calvin's mind off his fever, until it dawned on him that he had never seen black folks at the Lighthouse. Unlike the normal Lighthouse singers, who sang in bland hues of brown, white, and gray that echoed the church colors, the visiting black gospel trio produced every color of the spectrum with their voices, and Calvin imagined it was as much their voices as it was their skin tones that was offending.

Returning to the pew, Nancy sat beside Calvin.

"You'll have to tell Pop about this," Nancy said as she whispered to Calvin and pointed to the singers, "because he thinks we're all racists."

On the following day, Calvin was informed that, come Tuesday, he would be joining Nancy, Rev. Harry, and Luke to go see a famous reverend named Ernest Angley.

"Reverend Angley is a prophet. He can cure people just by touching them," Nancy professed. "Maybe he can cure you of those headaches you been having, but you won't be cured, if you don't believe," Nancy said as if compliance produced the tooth fairy. Having only heard half of what she said, Calvin put up no protest and managed a nod. He slept fitfully that night, unsure if the voices of Pop and Dale pleading with Nancy for a legitimate doctor were imagined or real.

On Tuesday afternoon, Rev. Harry unexpectedly opened his station wagon door for Calvin. As Calvin started to climb weakly into the back seat with Luke, Rev. Harry touched the boy's clammy hand and exclaimed, "Nancy, he's burning up!"

"That's why we're taking him to see Reverend Angley," Nancy said as if Calvin's state of health was a way for her to proudly proclaim her faith.

Nancy talked incessantly to Rev. Harry in the front seat on the drive downtown. Calvin said nothing and, drifting in and out of sleep, he could not ascertain what she was talking about. Everything sounded like people speaking in tongues.

Calvin couldn't remember getting out of the car or almost falling over until Luke caught him. He thought he heard Luke's voice saying something about Calvin being drenched. Calvin didn't remember finding a seat in the big stadium. His head flopped over toward Nancy's shoulder, but she pushed him away with a sigh. That he remembered. He didn't remember what Rev. Angley spoke about, and he didn't know how he got to the stage to have hands laid on him by the healer guy. Someone evidently escorted him and had hold of his forearms. Whether it was Rev. Harry or Luke or someone else, Calvin couldn't make out, but he suddenly felt like some guy in a zombie movie, trapped and surrounded by arms—arms, smelling of Sunday-go-to-meeting suits, pulling. Arms prodding. A hand found its way to Calvin's forehead. As he was already inflamed, Calvin didn't even feel the warmth of the seemingly disembodied hand touching him. Then the hand was joined by other hands, and most of them were hairy; hairy, brown hands touching as voices prayed prayers. Yet all Calvin could concentrate on was those swirling browns filling up his eyes. Why is it that brown is the only color you see when you're sick, Calvin asked himself. Even the warped sound of towering voices praying for him sounded brown.

Finally, the hands quit touching him and Calvin was escorted back to the car, but he never felt his feet touch the ground. He imagined himself floating back to the station wagon. It was brown, too. Or perhaps he didn't even go in the car. Perhaps he flew, sidewise, in the sky, all the way back to the Lighthouse while his mother, Rev. Harry, and Luke drove below in their brown wagon, following Calvin's lead. No, that couldn't be true, Calvin thought. I'd get lost. Whatever the truth was, the four of them were back at the Lighthouse. Calvin felt like he might have to throw up, but he couldn't. All he could do was rest his head on a table in the church kitchen.

Cutting through layers of brown fever, Calvin managed to hear his mother concede to Rev. Harry.

"Nancy," Rev. Harry said, "when Jesus told his apostles to teach and instruct in order to heal and convert, do you believe people at the time listened to them?"

"The people of faith did," she answered.

"That's right, because the apostles were the shepherds leading the flock. As your pastor, I am your shepherd. I know you want Jesus to heal Calvin, but you have to remember that Luke was a doctor. That's one of the reasons I named my son after him. God gave us doctors, and he gave them the knowledge to heal. So, as your shepherd, I am instructing you, in faith, to take Calvin to the doctor first thing in the morning."

The next morning, after Calvin's temperature reached an alarming 107, Nancy took him to see Dr. Avery, as Rev. Harry had instructed her to do.

"I hope it's not . . ." Dr. Avery said, stopping himself as he gently pushed Calvin's knee up to his chest. Calvin screamed in pain. "God! We need to get him in right away for a spinal tap."

Calvin's screams, heard throughout the hall, only subsided once he was packed in ice.

For three long hours, Pop, Dale, and Nancy waited in a room with not enough magazines, until a grim-looking doctor walked in.

"Spinal meningitis," the physician informed them.

It was a foreign word to both Nancy and Dale, but Pop's shoulders sagged in recognition.

"If you have religious beliefs, you might want to call a minister."

"Are you . . . ?"

"We lost him, briefly, twice already, ma'am. I'm sorry, but I don't see how he can survive. If, and I must say . . . if, he does live, I wouldn't expect much of him."

"What do you mean?" Nancy asked.

"He died twice, ma'am. He was without oxygen. Most likely he'll be mentally handicapped for life."

"I want him whole or not at all," Nancy protested.

"Nancy," exclaimed Dale, outraged.

"I want him whole, or I don't want him at all!"

"Goddammit, Nancy, shut up," Dale screamed. "I'll take him any way we can get him."

"He'd be better off dead and in heaven than alive here in a retarded hell."

Nancy's fingers desperately dialed Rev. Harry, but he didn't answer.

"We are in a Catholic hospital," offered Pop. "Surely, they have a priest here."

Nancy wasn't able to hide her disgust as the thought of a Roman collar praying over her son flashed across her mind.

"This is not the time for religious pride," said Pop sternly.

A short while later, a priest leaned over Calvin's limp, unconscious form. Dale, Nancy, and Pop sat around the bed, wringing their hands impatiently as they observed this strange Catholic performing alien rituals in a cramped room.

"I want you to pray for my son," Nancy told the priest, "but I don't want you to just pray for my son to live. I need you to pray that God will give him knowledge. That fool doctor says Calvin might end up retarded. I need God to prove that doctor wrong."

The priest nodded uncomfortably and went about his prayers.

"I'll give up drinking if God'll just let Calvin live," said Dale.

"Better be careful—God'll expect you to keep that promise," said Nancy.

A few hours after the priest had prayed over Calvin, Rev. Harry arrived at the hospital, having finally gotten the news about Calvin. Upon hearing that a Catholic cleric prayed over Calvin, Rev. Harry, alarmed, prayed over him as well—just to play it safe. Although he tended to over a hundred families on a regular basis, Rev. Harry spent the night and stayed by the side of the Elkan family. The next day, Rev. Harry left for a few hours, but returned to be with the Elkans. And so the pattern went for three days, until, finally, the doctor announced that Calvin's fever had broken. Relieved, Rev. Harry left and promised to check in nightly.

After Rev. Harry's departure, Dale said to Nancy, "You know, that preacher of yours is a good man. Don't get me wrong, it's not like I'm going to become a churchgoer or anything, but he's a good man."

Pop, privy to the conversation, looked up and smiled at his grandson.

"It's not every day that a preacher will take that much time out of his busy schedule for somebody else's kid," Dale continued. "I'm glad you have him as a preacher."

Nancy, sitting in a chair across from Dale and Pop, looked up from the magazine she'd buried herself in and belatedly responded as if it took her a moment to think about what to say. "Uh huh, but goes to figure, you ain't going to be going to church with us. I knew you wouldn't keep your promise."

Pop looked at Nancy suspiciously.

"I never promised to start going to church. I said I'd cut down on my beer," Dale said defensively.

"You said, you'd stop drinking, you didn't say—" Nancy tried to shoot back.

"Hallo!" Pop shouted, genuinely upset. "Can we knock it off? We're here for Calvin."

With disgust, Pop got up to walk to the bathroom.

A few days later, after Calvin's fever had subsided, the Catholic priest returned.

Nancy sat next to Calvin, who was soundly sleeping. Pop sat sleeping in a chair next to the bed, his body half dangling to the cold floor, and Dale was at work.

"The doctor informed me that your son is going to be all right," the priest told Nancy.

"He's a good doctor," said Nancy, "I tried to thank him, but he told me to thank the old man upstairs. Thank you for praying over Calvin. God's given Calvin a second chance. I pray that Calvin will realize that and start behaving better."

A curious look crossed the priest's face.

"The important thing is that your son has survived this ordeal," the priest offered.

"It ain't gonna be much of a blessing if he survives and never gets saved."

After a few weeks, Calvin had almost fully recovered. Nancy was anxious to ask the question and felt it time.

"The doctor said you died twice, Calvin. Did you see Jesus?"

Calvin shook his head.

"Do you see any light? Do you remember anything about it at all?"

"It hurt."

Later that night, looking up from his *Movie Star Titty Book* as he sat on the floor, Pop realized Calvin was standing at his half-open bedroom door, dressed in Superman pajamas.

"*Guten Abend*," Pop greeted Calvin. "I thought you put on your new Batman pajamas?"

Calvin swallowed.

"Did you have an accident?" Pop asked gently. Calvin had been wetting himself frequently since his return from the hospital. "Bring them here. I'll wash them. Your mom will never know."

After Calvin handed over the soiled PJs, Pop asked, "So, you are spending the night with me?"

"Mom says I'm not supposed to call it spending the night, because my bedroom is just next to yours," Calvin answered dejectedly.

"What is that supposed to mean? You call it what you want to call it, and I will go along with you."

"I want to call it spending the night."

"Then you're spending the night. Have a seat."

Calvin sat opposite Pop. Sorting through a pile of cut-up pictures from the gossip rags, Calvin got to pick which image Pop would glue in next, and for quite some time, the two worked in the silence with a seriousness of purpose, until Calvin relayed his conversation with Nancy earlier.

"So, what was your mother's reaction when you said it hurt?" Pop asked, aware that his grandson was talking about it for a reason.

"I don't think she was happy," Calvin answered.

"I don't imagine that she was."

"I don't want to be in Mom's imagination," Calvin countered passionately.

"Oh my! There's something to what you're saying," said Pop as he glued an image into his scrapbook. "You're not real in her imagination because even though you survived death, she still wasn't happy. Why? Because she expected you to give her the answer that she wanted to hear."

Calvin nodded, but wasn't sure he understood.

"You couldn't give her a satisfying answer of any kind, and I suspect you never will be able to," Pop said, patting Calvin's arm tenderly. "I'm not saying this to hurt you, but you need to be aware of that because survival might depend on knowing it."

A YOUNG PEOPLE'S CONCERT

With his *Brother Cobweb Chronicles* on the floor at his feet, Calvin leaned into Pop's arms. The two had retreated into the old man's bedroom sanctuary, and Pop was giddy with excitement in sharing Leonard Bernstein's televised *Young People's Concerts* with his great-grandson. The handsome conductor, glowing in black and white, bounced onto the stage and waded into Rossini's overture to *William Tell*.

"OK, what do you think that music's about?" asked Lenny.

"*The Lone Ranger*," answered Calvin in unison with the young TV audience.

Pop shook his head.

"That's what I thought you'd say," Lenny continued from the screen. "My daughter agrees. When she heard me play this piece, she thought it was *The Lone Ranger* song. Well, it isn't about *The Lone Ranger*. It's about E flats and F sharps. Music is never about anything. Music is beautiful notes put together in a way that we get pleasure listening to them."

"But *Rheingold's* about mermaids," countered Calvin.

"Sort of," explained Pop. "Wait and see."

"If there is a story connected to music, it's good in a way that gives extra meaning, but it's extra."

Lenny explained with several examples, but Calvin perked when the conductor said, "We're going to play you a piece that has a story, but I'm going to tell you the wrong story. I'm going to make one up that doesn't belong to this music."

The story Lenny gave, which accompanied the music, was about a prisoner meeting Superman on a motorcycle. Lenny followed that with the *Don Quixote* narrative, set to music by Richard Strauss.

"Which story should we use, then? The real one?" Calvin asked.

"If you want," answered Pop, "or the Superman one, or both."

"Both?"

"Sure, or make up one of your own. Like Lenny said, the story is extra, but feel free to imagine whatever you want. It's like your drawings in *The Brother Cobweb Chronicles*."

Calvin opened his book.

"Now," said Pop, pointing to the six-hundred-pound messiah, "I've seen a few Last Supper paintings, but I've never seen one with a fat-assed Jesus eating Hamburger Helper, peeping down at a pair of movie star titties."

For a moment, Calvin feared the worst, detecting the tone of sarcasm in Pop's voice. Maybe Pop got saved when I was sick, Calvin dreaded.

"No, I like your drawing," said Pop reassuringly, sensing that Calvin was afraid of getting in trouble, "but I will give you another example. Mozart wrote his version of a last supper, too, in the opera *Don Giovanni*. The Commander rises from the dead and meets Don at a long table. Now, the Commander issues a warning that this will be the Don's last supper. I imagine you think that the Don was afraid? He wasn't at all, but you see Mozart reimagined that story, just like the New Testament writers reimagined the Passover story to write their version."

"What happened to Don Giovanni?"

"You'll have to listen to it to find out what happens, but my point is that you choose stories from the Bible or stories you hear in your mom's church and reimagine them. Being an artist, I think it's making your own icons that's actually the appeal."

"They don't seem to like art much at the Lighthouse, though."

"Of course not—they're Protestants, and a lot of Protestants are iconoclastic. That means they have a fear of art, and that probably drives you even more to make art. I think you have more than an ounce of my rebel blood in you. Of course, I'm just guessing, but the point is that you don't pick all of the images, just the ones that you find interesting, and when you draw them, you are adding something extra—you draw them the way you choose to see them. You can do that with everything: music, art, and the Bible, too. Pick and choose what you want and throw out the rest."

BAGATELLES FROM A SOUTHERN GOTHIC BIBLE

The U-Haul truck finally pulled out of the drive from the last house on the left of Calvin's street. The appearance of the truck, along with the three people moving in—a man, woman, and son—piqued Calvin's curiosity. This new kid on the block looked about Calvin's age, wore Clark Kent–like glasses, and was dressed in a white sailor's outfit. After his parents disappeared into their new house to unpack, the boy stood at the end of the drive, surveying the neighborhood. After asking Nancy for permission to meet the new residents, Calvin headed over to the new kid's driveway.

"Hi," Calvin said, greeting his new neighbor.

"Hi, back."

"How come you're wearing a sailor suit?"

"That's what my mom gave me to wear today."

"My name's Calvin Elkan."

"My name's Ray Stevens. Wanna see my new bedroom?"

Calvin nodded, and as he followed Ray into the small, brown house, he noticed a framed photograph of a man in a naval uniform perched atop the new family's television set.

"This is Calvin, my new friend," Ray yelled out.

Ray's parents emerged from the kitchen, where they had been unpacking. "Calvin, this is my mom," Ray said.

"Hi, Calvin," Ray's mom said. "My name's Kennedy."

Calvin was somewhat startled to see that Ray's mother wore pants and a tank top and struggled to contain himself. Unlike Nancy, Kennedy was thin, tan, and wore her curly hair down and loose around her shoulders. Calvin eyed her as he might an alien and nearly lost his balance upon seeing a lit cigarette lodged between Kennedy's fingers. Standing directly behind Kennedy was her husband.

"This is my dad, Gary," said Ray.

A quick look back toward the television set confirmed that Ray's dad was the naval officer in the framed portrait.

"Hello, sir," Calvin said nervously.

Gary, with his crew-cut hair, piercing light blue eyes, and broad shoulders, merely nodded in Calvin's direction.

Introductions out of the way, Ray took Calvin on an exploration of the new bedroom, digging through mountains of unpacked boxes until he reached the holy grail of toys.

"Look, the Sea Adventurer GI Joe. He's my favorite," Ray said as he held up the red-bearded military man with his accompanying rubber shark.

"I've got him, too. Frank likes the Air Adventurer GI Joe because he has a parachute and a flashlight, but a shark's cooler," Calvin exclaimed.

"Who's Frank?"

"That's my little brother."

"Oh, my mom and dad only had me. Well, my mom and real dad. They're divorced. Now Gary's my dad."

"Your mom was divorced?" Calvin asked with a mix of sympathy and shock, having never met anyone whose parents were divorced.

"Yup," shrugged Ray, changing the subject. "What makes Sea Adventurer even cooler is his torpedo tank."

A few hours later, when it was time for Calvin to leave, Ray asked, "Do you want to come to the comic book shop with me tomorrow?"

"Yeah! But . . . I'd have to ask my mom first."

"Mom already walked down to your mom's house and asked if it's OK. Your mom said you could go."

This surprised Calvin—would Nancy really acquiesce to a woman wearing pants?—but he chose to be grateful rather than question it.

Calvin went home excited about the next day and the fact that he had a new friend in the neighborhood. Although the Dushanes lived next door to the Elkans, Rev. Harry and Vernell never socialized with Calvin's parents, which seemed to only bother Nancy. Calvin guessed she was embarrassed about having an unsaved husband and living with his argumentative, atheistic Jew grandfather. Luke was always at church, and what few friends he had were mostly Lighthouse kids his age. There were no other kids on the block, and Frank wasn't Calvin's idea of a playmate, so it was luck or blessing that brought Ray.

On Saturday, Kennedy drove Ray and Calvin on a field trip to comic book heaven, so naturally, Calvin was confused when Kennedy stopped the car in front of a Methodist church on the corner of a nearby street.

"How come we're stopping here? I've seen this church before. We're not going to church, are we?" Calvin asked nervously.

"Yeah, we know the church, because we just moved from two streets down," Ray explained. "But we're not going to a church service or anything."

"Then what are we doing?" Calvin asked.

"Just wait and see. I promise you, Mom would never take us to a church service," Ray said emphatically.

Nervously, Calvin walked behind Ray and his mom and hoped that she wouldn't even mention to Nancy about going to a Methodist church, whatever the reason. Nancy would not be pleased, having repeatedly said that only Pentecostals were real Christians. Curiously, Ray stopped at the auto parts store adjacent to the church.

"You two go inside. I'll wait out here," said Kennedy.

"Why're we going in here?" Calvin whispered as he and Ray walked through the door.

"Mom's gonna have a smoky treat," Ray laughed before walking to the counter.

Calvin looked back through the store front window, and sure enough, Kennedy had already lit one up. The coolest people smoke, Calvin thought, thinking of Kennedy and Pop. Calvin quickly turned his attention back to the counter in hopes of discovering what Ray was getting at an auto parts store.

"Here, Ray, got your weekly supply ready for you," said the old man behind the counter. Ray handed the gentleman a penny in exchange for a plastic bag of stickers.

"Thank you, Mr. Owens," Ray said as they headed for the front door.

As the two boys hit the pavement, Kennedy winked at Ray.

"Go ahead," she said, pointing to the church as she exhaled her Virginia Slim.

Curious about encountering Methodist sinners, Calvin followed Ray. His trepidation turned to elation upon discovering it wasn't a church at all—the building had been turned into a used bookstore.

As Ray thumbed through a table of new arrival books, Calvin lost himself in the pages of a book on paintings by Paul Gauguin, whom he had recently been introduced to by Pop.

After a few moments, Ray tapped Calvin on the shoulder.

"Ready?" Ray asked.

Calvin noticed a book in Ray's hand: *The Man with the Golden Gun* by Ian Fleming.

"You getting that?" Ray asked, pointing to the Gauguin book.

"Nah," answered Calvin. "Pop's got a book kind of like it."

"Let's go then," said Ray, anxious to climb into the car that would escort them to comic book heaven.

With his two-dollar allowance along with an extra dollar that Pop gave him, Calvin didn't know where to begin inside Denny Gibbon's Comic Book Shop, but upon seeing a Green Lantern/Green Arrow comic book, he grabbed that first.

"You like Green Lantern?" Ray asked upon glancing Calvin's first selection.

"Yeah, I like that he gets his power from green, but yellow makes him weak."

"You're kind of weird." Ray laughed, then added, "Cool."

"But I like Green Arrow better."

"Me too! Green Lantern's kind of stuffy. Not Green Arrow though. Dennis O'Neil writes the stories, and Neal Adams draws them. That's what we'll do when we grow up. I'll write the stories, and you can draw the comics."

"I already started a comic book called *Brother Cobweb*," Calvin boasted.

"Who's that?"

"He's a Pentecostal preacher monster."

"You *are* weird," Ray laughed.

"My mom's church has comic books too, but they're Christian comics. They got good drawings in them sometimes, but they're as crazy as my mom's preachers."

"My mom doesn't like preachers," Ray said. "She says they're a bunch of hypocrites."

"Pop says that too."

Calvin located the latest issues of *Superman's Pal Jimmy Olsen* and *The Tomb of Dracula*.

"Make sure you get a plastic bag to put your comics in," Ray advised Calvin.

"How come?"

"Because they're art. You need to protect them."

Back in Ray's bedroom, the two boys compared their bounty.

"Gene Colan draws the best Dracula," Ray said. "Marv Wolfman writes all of 'em."

Ray opened his comic book bags and spread a portion of his collection across the wooden floor. Calvin took out *Werewolf by Night* and examined Mike Ploog's illustrations.

"You seem to like monster comics," Ray observed.

"Yeah."

"How come?"

"Me and Pop watch monster movies. We saw *The Wolfman*. He's different than *Werewolf by Night*."

"Yeah, but they're both cool. Here, look at this," Ray said, handing Calvin a comic of a scantily clad vampire girl named Vampirella. "You can have this one. I got two of this issue."

"Thank you," said Calvin, "Pop would love her, but can I keep it here? I'll get in trouble if my mom finds that."

"Sure," answered Ray. "Hey, let's put on our own monster play! We can do it in my backyard. My mom can help us!"

"Really?"

"Sure. We can invite your mom, Frank, and Pop to come see it."

"OK, but what kind of monster?"

"Did you see *Dr. Phibes*?"

"No, but I saw pictures of it in the newspaper."

"That's Vincent Price. He's kinda like the Phantom of the Opera, but he plays jazz. My mom likes jazz. She's got all of Dave Brubeck's records. Come here, I know what we can do," Ray said as he led Calvin to the garage.

"Look," said Ray, pointing to a discarded oven sitting beneath shelves of random tools.

"An oven?"

"Yeah, it doesn't work anymore, so we got a new one and Dad was going take this to the junkyard . . . but we can use it instead!"

"How?"

"We can turn it backwards and paint it like it's an organ. You can paint bright colors on it, and we can hide a tape recorder inside of it to play the music, because I have a jazz tape. Let me go ask Mom if we can use her paints. She'll let us, but I still have to ask," Ray said, getting more excited as he told Calvin his plan.

After getting approval from Kennedy and grabbing her paints, Calvin and Ray got to work. Calvin began painting the oven while Ray started writing down the story. The two boys worked into the evening, each happy to have found a creative equal.

While Calvin and Ray were basking in gothic colors and hatching their plans for a theatrical triumph, Rev. Harry, in his official capacity as Calvin's Sunday school teacher, Vernell tailing behind him, had gone to visit Nancy next door with a concern. The Lighthouse Sunday school teachers were a tight group who met often and frequently discussed problematic students. Naturally, expectations for the group's offspring were higher, and Rev. Harry had a task before him: how to get Calvin more involved in church. Nancy's firstborn was inconveniently introverted and rarely participated in class, only responding when called upon, which reduced Rev. Harry to a state of Pentecostal angst.

"As the good book says, girls are meant to be quiet in church, but boys are expected to be tomorrow's leaders. Sister Nancy, God has revealed to me that he has a purpose for Kilvin," said Rev. Harry, filled to the rim with mispronounced agenda. Vernell, who was as big as Nancy, but wore her weight better, stood silently behind her husband, occasionally nodding.

"He's a smart boy," Rev. Harry continued, "and I know that he reads his Bible and listens in class, because usually when I call on him, he knows the answers, but I have to force it out of him. He never volunteers nothing, and he simply won't participate on his own."

"What do you want me to do?" Nancy asked.

"We got to approach this right. He's just shy, that's all, but I can't help notice how much he draws in church."

"He ain't doing that in the classroom, is he?"

"Oh, no, and I understand it's to keep him busy, but I think now it's in our interest, and his, to put that talent to use for the Lord. Ain't making no promises, but this might just prove to be the acorn that grows into a great oak. I hope you can help us out here, sister."

When Calvin got home from Ray's, Nancy approached Calvin with breathless excitement. "Calvin," she said with intense determination, "Reverend Harry has asked me to ask you something."

"What?" Calvin asked suspiciously.

"We want you to make a poster for the Lighthouse," beamed Nancy.

Calvin's eyes lit up. Having just transformed a broken oven into Dr. Phibes's organ of colors, Calvin was on an artistic roll.

"Really?" he asked.

"Honest. Reverend Harry has noticed your talent and wants to put it to use. You're not going let us down, are you?"

"No, but what kind of poster? I can't draw cars very good. It's not a picture of a car, is it?"

"Not at all. We want you to draw a picture of Fat Albert."

"The cartoon?"

"Yup, the Bill Cosby cartoon. Y'know, Mr. Cosby's about the only famous colored folk that we can look up to. That Martin Luther King Jr. was nothing but a wife-cheating communist, but Mr. Cosby's the only colored fella who teaches Christian family values. That's why we want you to draw Fat Albert—just him with his thumbs down."

"But he always has his thumbs up."

"That's the point! He'll have his thumbs down because we want you to have him saying 'Hey! Hey! Hey! Down with the gay!'"

Calvin was confused.

"We're going to use this at an anti-gay rally downtown on the circle. It's this Saturday, so you need to get to work on it," said Nancy, pulling out a grocery bag with art supplies. "I bought you three sheets of poster board 'case you mess up, and some markers and some colored pencils. Let me know when you're done."

Calvin had no idea what an anti-gay rally was, but when he looked up "gay" in the dictionary, it said happy and merry, and it said "rally" was a drawing together of persons. The Lighthouse was always preaching that everyone needed to show happiness in praising God through song and worship, even if that was rarely the case. Most, if not all the time, the source of inspiration for speaking in tongues and slaying in the spirit seemed to come from Apocalyptic fears, as Pop described it in disdain. Still, either Rev. Harry had finally admitted that the Lighthouse didn't believe in happiness or the rally was against being anti-gay. Unable to figure it out, Calvin wanted to ask Pop, but the flu had sideswiped the old man, and there were only a few days to finish this important first commission.

By the time Saturday morning arrived, Calvin had finished his Fat Albert poster and had even drawn a cartoon balloon for the text. But Calvin did not get to employ any imaginative touches to the finished work and felt it bland compared to his *Brother Cobweb Chronicles* and Dr. Phibes's organ.

Both Rev. Harry and Nancy seemed thrilled with the blandness. Apparently, this finished work was more than good enough for the rally. Calvin found out belatedly that he was also expected to attend the rally and hold the sign—a detail that Nancy had conveniently left out. Still, she promised Calvin ice cream as payment for his endeavors, and the shop on the circle had his favorite peanut butter cones. Once Calvin boarded the bus, he saw why his mother and the rest were happy with his sign. Calvin's was the only sign with any drawing or coloring on it. The rest of the signs were merely words that made no sense, such as "Adam and Eve, not Adam and Steve."

As Calvin stepped off the bus, he held his sign tightly, while Nancy gripped his other hand. The circle was filled with throngs of people emerging from a variety of church buses. The presence of a Southern Baptist congregation surprised Calvin. More than once he had heard that Baptists, who believed "Once saved, always saved" and baptized in the name of the Trinity instead of Jesus's name, were bound for hell. However, Calvin had Baptist friends in school and found that they, just like his mom's church, seemed to love that big God in the sky but hated a lot of people. Of course, they would usually try to justify that mindset with a canned "Hate the sin, not the sinner" response, but even Calvin knew that was bullshit, which for once made the collaborative rally of Pentecostals, Baptists, and Nazarenes even more natural. The murmuring Christian crowd was pissed off and unintelligible, buzzing like those giant ants from the movie *Them!*; although it was not hot, Calvin felt like he was in the desert from the movie. When Rev. Harry held the bullhorn up to his face, he did not sound at all like James Arness.

"Maggots for the faggots burnin' in hell," screamed the red-faced preacher. "Sodomy is a graver sin than murder, and fag-enablers are just as bad as fags. And they're both worthy of death. Politicians who don't rule by biblical authority, don't belong in office!"

Nancy and other members of the Lighthouse joined Rev. Harry in spewing insect sounds. Collectively, the lot looked like fattened, deformed cockroaches, angry and hissing. Calvin shifted his focus sharply toward the crowd's target: a small group of gay people.

This is so dumb, Calvin thought. So dumb it was scary.

"Mom, can I go get my ice cream now?"

"Oh, all right, but hurry back. I can't hold this sign all day," said Nancy, barking in full pit bull mode, before shouting, "Truth, not tolerance!"

Nancy handed Calvin a dollar, and off he darted for the ice cream shop. When Calvin went in, he saw an old man behind the counter.

"Can I have a peanut butter ice cream cone, please?"

"Sure," said the old man. "You with that group?"

"My mom and her church made me come," Calvin said, exasperated and frightened.

"If you want, you can stay in here with me till the rally's over. How's that?"

"OK."

"I tell you what—you can have as many ice cream cones as you want, all for that dollar you got there. Why don't you have a seat? I'll bring it out to you."

Calvin sat in the shop enjoying one peanut butter cone after another until Nancy barged through the door with Rev. Harry. Nancy's eyes sharpened upon seeing her son. Calvin immediately started crying.

"What do you think you're doing?"

Nancy's nasty tone sucked the breath right out of Calvin.

"Well?" she asked.

"I don't know."

"You little coward!" Nancy screamed. Like a predatory cat, she lunged and slapped Calvin hard against the face. He cried out in pain; she'd never hit him that hard before. The shop owner took a step toward Nancy and Calvin.

"Hey! I told him he could stay here with me till the rally was over!"

"I didn't ask you," Nancy bellowed at the ice cream man. "You're probably an America-hating liberal pervert yourself. My son ain't keeping company with the likes of y'all."

"Ma'am, I've been married thirty years," the old man tried to counter, but Nancy had already grabbed Calvin by the wrist, yanking him up. His face burning red and ears ringing, Calvin stumbled and started to fall. Again, Nancy pulled him up, toward her. The level of anger in Nancy even surprised Rev. Harry, but he remained silent as she dragged Calvin out of the shop.

Not a word passed between mother and son on the ride home. However, upon entering the house, Nancy pounced on Calvin, violently slapping him in the face until Pop stormed out from his bedroom.

"What the hell is going on?" screamed Pop.

"You stay out of this," screamed Nancy, red in the face from the workout. Yanking Calvin to his feet, Nancy put her body between the boy and Pop.

"This about that gay thing you dragged him to?"

"Anti-gay rally, old man."

"Hypocritical, isn't it? You don't hesitate to watch Liberace."

"What about Liberace? He ain't gay!"

Pop almost choked in disbelief.

"Besides, Calvin's my son, and it ain't none of your business."

"He is my great-grandson, so it *is* my goddamned business. Now keep your fucking hands off him, else I'll make some calls, and the whole family will be hearing about it!"

An unstoppable wave of indignation flooded Nancy as she realized the magnitude of the afternoon's failure.

"Take him, he's more your son than mine," howled Nancy, shoving Calvin toward Pop as she burst into tears and retreated into her room. Calvin was so shocked by Pop saying the f-word that he was rendered completely numb to his mother's histrionics.

"One, two, three, four, five, six, seven, eight, nine—" whispered Pop as he held Calvin tightly in his arms.

Nancy let out a wail from her bedroom.

"Like clockwork," scowled Pop.

Pop shifted his focus to Calvin. Calvin's pale face was wet with tears and full of pain. Pop leaned in protectively, locking eyes with his great-grandson.

"When I am gone from this earth, you are going to be quite alone battling these Neanderthals, but you are going to persevere. Do you understand?"

Calvin nodded his head and spent the rest of the night in Pop's bedroom. It was an evening that could only have been composed by Pop. They started by listening to *Rheingold*, then Pop added a spicy dash of quotes from the poet Oscar Wilde, then colorfully teleported himself and Calvin to join the painter Paul Gauguin in the artist's myth-crafting journey toward a new, personal iconography and self-styled paradise.

Calvin adored Pop's obsessions. Among them was the TV show *The Adventures of Superman*. As they did religiously every week, the old man and the kid attended their own private religious service zooming into the sterling black-and-white world of the Man of Steel. More powerful than a locomotive and able to leap tall buildings in a single bound, this strange visitor from another planet defended poor little mole men from a lynch mob. Standing up for truth, justice, and the American way, Superman—like Wyatt Earp— enforced gun control, depriving bigots of their ability to slaughter aliens that they feared and demonized. Helping Superman right injustices was feminist Lois Lane, who had a kick that could rival Superman's mighty punch. Pop and Calvin ended the evening, as they often did, devouring swiss cheese on rye crackers watching 8 mm movies of silent film clown Charlie Chaplin. Calvin found a kindred spirit in the Little Tramp, and along with Pop and Ray, Charlie was one of Calvin's favorite people in the world.

The next day, Calvin stopped by Ray's house. After walking through Ray's half-open screen door, Calvin shockingly found Kennedy in tank top and pair of cut-off shorts. He had never seen a woman in shorts in real life—only on TV—and although he felt a pang of Pentecostal-influenced guilt, he was stirred by her in a way that he imagined Pop was similarly stirred by Esther Williams. Kennedy was multitasking: listening to Patsy Cline's "Walkin' after Midnight," feeding her Siamese cat, and watering cacti with a cigarette dangling from her mouth. That she preferred cats to dogs was one of many qualities that rendered her the opposite of Nancy, which Calvin found appealing.

"Hi, Calvin," Kennedy said. "Ray's not here now. He's with his dad. You can wait for him if you want. Can I get you a glass of lemonade?"

"Yes, thank you."

"Heard you had a little trouble at that rally. Your mom told me."

Calvin swallowed, fearing a scolding.

"Of course, as usual, I bit my lip with your mom, and I do that for you, not her. Do you even know what an anti-gay rally is?"

"I do now."

"Well, I'll tell you, if I had been there, I would have been protesting against your mom and the rest of them from that church. I would have walked right over and stood with the gay folk protesting those bigot protesters," she said defiantly, raspy from her Virginia Slim.

"Well, how am I supposed to protest?" Calvin whined, feeling even more guilty now for his participation in the rally.

"You're not supposed to. Just like you shouldn't even be knowing what a rally is. You're too young for all that," Kennedy said as she squirted the last layer of water on her cacti. "Since you got exposed to it, I might as well say it . . . if gay folks are sinners, well heck, aren't we're all? Ain't like your mom or preacher or any of us can go around saying we're not. Now, give me a minute and I'll get your lemonade. Ray and Gary will be home soon."

Talking with Kennedy had validated Calvin's reaction to the rally, and he realized that there was good to be gleaned from it: his failure at the rally guaranteed that the Lighthouse would never present him with another artistic commission. When Ray got home, he and Calvin walked the railroad tracks at the dead end of the street. Away from their families, they plotted out their *Dr. Phibes* play, which premiered the following Saturday.

That next Saturday, the two boys premiered their play in Ray's backyard. As Kennedy, Pop, Frank, and Nancy sat in lawn chairs, Ray emerged, dressed in a black cloak as Dr. Phibes. His face was partly hidden, revealing a scarred monstrosity, thanks to Kennedy's makeup assistance. Ray sat down at the organ oven and pounded the painted keys while Calvin, hidden from view on the other side, hit play on the tape recorder, producing jazz to accompany Ray's melodramatic gestures. His first duty now fulfilled, Calvin emerged as an Ygor-like assistant to Dr. Phibes. Together, they turned toward their audience and promised more horror adventures to come.

Kennedy and Pop laughed and clapped with excitement at the warm-up theatrical trailer for future horror attractions, while Nancy managed a polite smile, unsure what to make of the presentation.

Frank had no such reserve. "Can I play Ygor in the next one?

"Maybe," Ray answered. "Calvin said you've got the Air Adventurer GI Joe."

"Yup, I got it for my birthday," Frank boasted. "It comes with a parachute."

"If you bring it over and let us play with it, we'll let you be Ygor in the next play."

"OK, but what about Calvin? Who's he going to play?"

Ray leaned in to whisper, "The Wolfman. We're going to have a monster team-up."

7

THE ANTI-CHRIST AT A KROGER NEAR YOU!

Nearly a year had passed since the summer of the spinal tap, meeting Ray, and the anti-gay rally. With less than two weeks of the school year remaining, Sunday night at the Lighthouse was almost bearable. As usual, Calvin preoccupied himself with sketching while listening to Rev. Harry read from Isaiah. Having turned eight in March, Calvin had already done some reading in the way of biblical prophets. The death and destruction in the Old Testament were enough for Calvin to find a loose relationship to the TV westerns that Dale obsessed over. The western pageantry was not unlike that of the Hebrews, with similar desert terrain and hiding in mysterious caves. Calvin's interest was piqued enough to adventurously plunge into the biblical prophets and judges. Much to his disappointment, the Old Testament figures were hardly as amiable a lot as cowboy hero Johnny Mack Brown with his pretty home-on-the-range sweetheart Beth Marion.

Calvin developed an intense dislike for biblical figures such as Moses, Samuel, and David—harsh men whose pronouncements and moral behavior Calvin found questionable. What few women Calvin found in the Hebrew cannon, he liked. However, Nancy was not like Sarah, Miriam, Hannah, Ruth, or Esther at all. Nor was his mother like Beth Marion. Rather, it often seemed Nancy was cut from the same prophetic cloth as Ezekiel.

Deep into *The Brother Cobweb Chronicles*, Calvin's pencil captured moments of intrigue in an apostolic B western drama evolving on the page of his sketchpad, while Frank snored beside him on the pew. Calvin was so engrossed in sketching a scriptural Saturday Night Roundup that he failed to notice that his mother was no longer sitting in the pew. As he imagined Nancy in an ecclesiastical vision of western movie bad guy Kenne Duncan, Calvin's pencil came to an abrupt stop upon hearing his mother's acidic voice erupt from the stage microphone.

"There's not gonna be a sermon tonight," announced Nancy.

Calvin looked up with surprise.

"The Holy Ghost has taken over the service."

A murmur of voices could be heard within the congregation: "Praise Jesus!" "Amen, sister, amen!"

"I had a vision, and Reverend Harry has asked me to share it with y'all," continued Nancy. Full of conviction, she placed the microphone securely between both hands, and like a child ready to take a bite of her first hot dog, she devoured the moment.

"Jesus is coming! Soon, every Christian in the world will be raptured! Raptured up with Jesus! When that magnificent day happens, the news media won't know what to make of it! Planes will crash without a pilot. Cars will wreck without a driver. All the babies in all the hospitals in all the world will disappear! The liberal news media—they're gonna blame it on UFOs!"

Calvin had seen his mother get the Holy Ghost during services before, and it never failed to scare the hell out of him, but this time the drama had shifted from pew to pulpit. In excited frenzy, Calvin sketched the good book of fury like a gavel pounding the pulpit.

Calvin leaned into Frank's ear.

"Amen, Brother Cobweb, Amen," Calvin whispered.

Frank's eyes immediately opened upon hearing Calvin's warning code. Calvin giggled, pointed to the stage and took sadistic delight in seeing Frank turn as white as Old Man Holy Ghost himself.

Calvin had used the code so many times that it was easy as pecan pie to lull Frank from counting sheep. The code was sounded upon the intensification of Nancy's swaying in worship. If she started speaking in tongues,

Calvin and Frank knew to duck under the pew fast or make for the aisle. Far too many times, they had reacted slowly, and the result was a lethal walloping by their mother's flailing arms. If Calvin and Frank were sitting in the middle of the pew, the chances of making it to the aisle without getting hit were slim. However, if they were sitting toward the end of the pew, they might escape the blows of Holy Force from a large woman in spirit.

Calvin flipped back a few pages to an earlier sketch that he had made of that devilishly mean Holy Ghost, drawn to look like TV puppeteer Bob Smith, seizing and pulling the strings of Nancy as a Pentecostal Howdy Doody. Calvin was careful not to title his drawing because he had been told time and again that laughing at the Holy Ghost was an unforgivable sin! However, if Old Man Holy Ghost was indeed the third thug of a patriarchal Trinity, then Calvin's thoughts could be free. Because, as Captain Christ indicated, God could read the heart, but not the mind.

Still, this night was different. Nancy's spewed vision was taking effect upon Calvin, whose spirited resistance proved to be of little avail. Nervously, he looked around to make sure that nobody was getting raptured up.

"Then, after that—the great tribulation!" Nancy's arms, blotted by wet spots under her polka-dotted dress, thrashed about in the air. "The anti-Christ will rise! He'll make a pact with the Pope. Y'all ever seen old Charlie Pope without that big hat on? No! And you know why? `Cause underneath that hat on his forehead is carved the number six-six-six! That day will come, and woe to those left behind!"

"Six-six-six," whispered Calvin.

"But one thing's for sure," continued Nancy boldly, "if you don't have that mark of the beast, you can't even go to the store or buy food! They'll be arresting people right there at Kroger grocery store and chopping their heads off in the parking lot."

Calvin tried to take his mind off Nancy's rantings about the mark of the beast by moving his pastels around the page, but he couldn't deny that once in a while, her ideas really did scare him, even if he didn't believe it.

"Avoid being left behind and join us in heaven on that great day when every knee shall bow and every tongue shall confess that Jesus Christ is Lord!" Nancy shrilled from the stage. She looked directly at Calvin, her eyes gleaming with barbaric determination. Calvin lowered his eyes to avoid her gaze.

"Don't think, 'I'm too young,'" her voice boomed in a mimicking caricature of Calvin. "There is an age of accountability, and if you're old enough to know the difference between right and wrong, then you'll be held accountable by God! You're not too young to be left behind! So, come on up to the altar and turn yourself over to Jesus."

Determined not to walk up to the altar, Calvin peeked over the edge of his sketchbook to see everyone getting saved. Even Luke had walked up to the altar. There had long been Lighthouse buzz that if Luke got saved, he would be Rev. Harry's successor. Calvin was disappointed that Luke had caved into the glory walk. Even more surprisingly, Frank had darted up to the altar. Calvin alone stubbornly remained glued to the pew. If the choice came to being able to buy groceries or getting your head chopped off, waiting in long Kroger lines to fill one's belly was a better option. Calvin felt that joining the rest of the Lighthouse parishioners in a glorious rapture would mean doom—the way that Nancy often described heaven sounded like hell to Calvin. With Jesus, God, and the Holy Ghost already proven to be a hate-filled Trinity, Calvin would rather be like Don Giovanni and scream "No!" in the face of pressure to repent.

On the page, Brother Cobweb joined forces with Nancy as Calvin's fingers reached for the red. Once again, Calvin had evaded Old Man Holy Ghost.

LEFT BEHIND?

A week and a half later, Calvin exited the school bus, his black Kmart slip-ons hitting the pavement with purpose. Summer vacation stretched before him, and he could not have been more pleased. Opening the door, he yelled, "I'm home!" Silence. Tossing his half-eaten lunch into the trash can, Calvin opened a cupboard to look for a snack. "I'm ho-o-o-me," he yelled again. Oddly, he heard no response. Calvin left the cupboard door open and went to Pop's bedroom. Finding no one there, he went to his parents' room, only to find it empty. Where was everyone? Calvin wondered. Usually when he got home from school, Nancy was preparing dinner early, prior to Dale's night shifts. Nancy's vision from the Holy Ghost loomed large in his mind. Calvin walked back to the kitchen and looked in the oven. A chicken was sitting in a pan in the final roasting stage, juices oozing out; the oven had been turned off recently and was still warm. It was almost like . . .

The rapture? The RAPTURE! Calvin thought as his heart accelerated. Sweat poured from beneath his eight-year old bangs. Oh my god! It's true! The rapture's hit! Calvin had refused to walk up to the altar. He had ignored Nancy's vision, and now he had been left behind to face the Anti-Christ! The devil would catch him at Kroger and chop his head off!

In the blink of an eye, the entire house changed. The familiar smells of Nancy's tawdry Avon perfume and Pop's maple-flavored tobacco all dissipated into the haunting smell of nothingness. Feeling the effects of acid reflux, Calvin crumpled onto the waxed linoleum into a petrified fetal position. Calvin was caught between breaths for half of eternity.

Just outside the Elkan house, planes were crashing and babies were vanishing. The sky above, veiled by flying arms and hair, had transformed into an epic, ebony wave. Upon its foamy crest emerged the predator Jesus who, upon opening his purple lips, cruelly deprived strollers of babies and Tonka trucks of their drivers. Why did Jesus take Pop though? Maybe Pop got saved, thought Calvin, and that was his greatest fear. He was now stranded and alone because he had refused to get saved. The tyrant deity had cruelly attacked.

The dam broke, and Calvin cried and cried, oblivious to the sound of Dale, Nancy, and Frank entering the house. Nancy rushed to her eldest son on the kitchen floor. Feeling cold fingers devoid of maternal warmth, Calvin looked up, straining through his sobs. "I—I—I thought the rapture had hit, and I got left behind!"

"What kind of fool are you?" screeched Nancy.

"Where's Pop?" asked Dale. "He's supposed to be here!"

"Let me handle this!"

"You know why this happened, don't you? I warned you that you needed to get saved! You refused! You sat there in that pew and mocked me and mocked Jesus—in front of the whole church! This is what you get!" Nancy drove her hands in hard on both sides of Calvin's face. Calvin's cries turned to screams of pain.

Almost in as much a state of shock as Calvin, Dale, with a pained look creasing his face, nearly took a step forward, but stopped himself short. Dale turned halfway, as though he couldn't bear to watch, and began to retreat from the kitchen, but was stopped by Pop entering the kitchen.

"*Gottverdammt,*" Pop yelled at Nancy, who rose to face him. "I don't know what this is all about, but you don't hit a kid. What kind of mother are you? Calvin needs a mother, not some bullying bitch!"

"Dale!!!" Nancy shrieked, unable to defend herself.

"And my great-grandson needs a father! *Gottverdammt*, Dale," Pop screamed at his grandson.

Everything stood still for a seemingly endless second as Nancy decided whether to continue her fight.

"You think Calvin's got a father in him?" screamed Nancy, pointing to Dale as she half sobbed and panted in anger. "Dale, you better do something!"

"What do you want me to do?" asked Dale, who had almost inched his way out of the kitchen.

"Be a man and spiritual leader of this family, for once."

"Spiritual?" scoffed Pop. "You don't have the first idea what that means, woman!"

Nancy ignored the old man and shifted her piercing eyes toward Dale.

"Your son mocked Jesus and your wife in front of everyone!"

"Nancy, I . . ."

"Someday, that son of yours is going to knock you on your ass, and when that day happens, I'm going to laugh in your face," Nancy mocked, before replaying her wailing sea beast episode at high-pitched volume, running into her bedroom. For all concerned, it was a long night. Pop took Calvin into his room, where he tried to comfort the distraught boy. Dale slept on the couch and did not even attempt to comfort Nancy, allowing her to cry herself to sleep. The next day, a fatigued Dale remembered to ask Pop where he was the day before when Calvin came home.

"I was out on my daily exercise walk," Pop explained.

"You always do that in the morning."

"I forgot to this morning . . ."

"Seems you're forgetting a lot lately."

"I'm sorry."

"Tell Calvin that, not me."

"Don't you think I already have? Several times!"

OSCAR WILDE'S
DANCE OF THE SEVEN VEILS, STARRING CAROLINE MUNRO

Following the rapture incident on Wednesday, the week wrap-up promised to be an eventful one with an opera on Friday, followed by a Saturday night at the drive-in theater. Aunt Blanche had come to town. She was Dale's older sister and lived two thousand miles away in Albuquerque. Although Calvin had never met Blanche, she had promised to take Pop and him to an opera while she was visiting because she knew that opera was one of Pop's passions and, since he was afraid to drive, he was rarely able to attend them. Nancy and Dale would certainly never take him.

"We're going to see *Salome*," exclaimed Pop to Calvin as they waited for Blanche to arrive Friday afternoon.

"Isn't that a Bible story?" asked Calvin suspiciously.

"Sure, but it's retold by Oscar Wilde, the greatest of sinning poets," Pop said, trying to contain his laughter. "Strauss wrote this opera of Wilde's story. It will be a corker—and a lot more entertaining than some silly preacher. Old man Wilde had no sympathy for that long-winded Baptist. It's the sinner girl he has us rooting for!"

"Like in the Rita Hayworth movie?"

"Now, I love Rita, but forget that god-awful movie. This will be a good first opera for you. Blanche will enjoy it, too! She is a grandchild from my authentic seed line, far more than your dad. Like your great-grandmother, Blanche is Catholic."

Calvin raised his eyebrows. Would his mother let him go somewhere with a Catholic?

"Despite what your mother says, the Catholics are not so bad," Pop assured Calvin. "They do have sacraments, although I do not know why they limit it to seven . . . there should not even be a limit on sacraments."

"But Pop, you don't believe in God."

"Let me tell you a story about this German philosopher named Heidegger. Now, Heidegger was an atheist. Or, at least he was supposed to be, but he went with a friend to a festival of Mother Mary and this friend saw Heidegger genuflect—"

"What's genuflect?" Calvin interrupted.

"It's kneeling and doing a sign of the cross over themselves. Anyway, this friend called Heidegger out as a hypocrite, and Heidegger responded, a pragmatist like you would never understand."

"Pragmatist?"

"Means, his friend was lacking an imagination. You see, you do not have to believe in gods for a sacramental life. A sacramental life is the best life to have. When I'm with atheists, I feel like an old man of faith. But when I'm with Christians or zealots, I feel like an atheist. So take the things I say to your mother with a pinch."

"What does that mean?"

Smiling broadly, Pop reached forward and pinched Calvin's nose. Sticking his thumb between the fore and middle finger, Pop announced, "Got your nose."

When Blanche arrived Friday night, she barely paid any attention to Nancy and instead greeted Pop, Dale, Calvin, and Frank with open arms. Everyone was happy to see her, except Nancy, who felt threatened by a positive female presence in the house. Despite her small frame, Blanche exuded a take-charge aura and soon led Pop and Calvin arm-in-arm to her awaiting Volkswagen. Calvin could not take his eyes off Blanche. Accented with dark hair, exotic features, and an attractive sharpness, she resembled Jackie Kennedy.

As soon as the three had exited, Nancy huffed, "We take care of Pop every day, year in, year out. Your sister comes in acting like his guardian queen."

Ignoring his wife, a fatigued Dale became one with the couch.

Within minutes of climbing into the back of Blanche's car, Calvin fell asleep, missing the chance to see how she was more of Pop's seed than Dale. Pop shook Calvin awake when they arrived.

Calvin, surprised by the number of people in attendance, clung to Blanche's hand. The opera was in German, which prompted Pop to translate for Calvin in whispers.

"Calvin doesn't need to know the exact words to get it, Pop," whispered Blanche.

"You're right," Pop agreed, sitting back in his seat and letting Calvin take it all in.

The Bible, filtered through Oscar Wilde and Richard Strauss, reached a climax in the building drama when, much to Calvin's horror, Salome's frenzied dance of the seven veils ended with the heroine removing all seven veils—with nothing on underneath. Calvin had never seen a naked woman before, and his instinct was to cover his eyes. Pop, on his end, had no such qualms, and let out a delighted hoot. But when it came time for the beheading of the Baptist, Calvin kept his eyes wide open, unflinching during a bloody decapitation.

On the drive back, Calvin was teetering on the verge of sleep in the back seat.

"Did you see Calvin's knee-jerk reaction to Salome's strip tease?" Pop asked Blanche, believing his grandson to be asleep.

"It's a natural reaction, I guess," Blanche offered.

"No," countered Pop, "it's a programmed one."

"Before we get back, it'd be best if you advise Calvin not to mention the dance of the seven veils to his mother."

Pop nodded, and Calvin drifted off to sleep in the back seat.

The intimacy of the Volkswagen opera trip contrasted sharply with the whole family climbing into the family station wagon on Saturday for the drive-in double feature of *Walking Tall* and *The Golden Voyage of Sinbad.*

For Calvin and Frank, the movies mattered little. More important were the frequent trips to the concession stand for kicking nachos, fresh popcorn, pizza, tasty cheeseburgers, crispy hot French fries, buckets of fried chicken, delicious hot dogs, mouthwatering barbecue sandwiches, their favorite candy, and ice-cold soft drinks. About an hour before Sheriff Buford Pusser began swinging his baseball bat for cinema under the stars, Pop accompanied Frank and Calvin to a swing set near the colossal screen while Dale rearranged the blanket, turned his radio to the correct AM station, and adjusted the heavy speaker on the window rim.

As Frank and Calvin played on the teeter-totter, a small fox made its way to a nearby trash can.

"Look," yelped Pop, pointing to the fox. "It's a sign!"

Pop could not quit talking about the fox sighting, even after *Walking Tall* started. From the front seat next to Dale, Nancy looked back toward Pop, seated next to Calvin and Frank in the rear of the wagon. "Shut up, old fool, it's not a sign. How could an atheist believe in a sign, anyway?"

"I didn't say it was a sign from Jesus, woman. Why do you so-called Christians seem to think you have a copyright on matters such as signs? It's a sign of the imagination. I'd think you could at least get that!"

Although Pop often laced his arguments with humor, Calvin was surprised at the genuine and fatigued frustration in the old man's hoarse voice. He could almost hear Pop exhale a waning patience with Nancy. Calvin rubbed Pop's hand and got a smile in return when his great-grandfather looked down to see comforting youthful pink skin against his own withered, purple flesh. Attempting to speak above the deafening sound of excessive celluloid violence, Pop whispered to Calvin, "Remember that mummy movie?"

"Yeah!" whispered Calvin, unable to forget that magical movie night with Ray and Pop and cheese pizza rolls and apple cider.

"Smack my hand hard enough, and you'll see the dust fly . . . just like Boris Karloff," Pop joked, comparing himself to that mummy. "But you know what? There's not a lot of difference here." Pop held his hand demonstratively against Calvin's hand. "My skin is so thin, might as well be a fossil, and even though you're brand spanking new, it doesn't matter that we come from a different time. You and I—we're soul mates, meant to be together, like crocodiles from the same Nile."

The Golden Voyage of Sinbad was more fun than Buford Pusser's baseball bat. Unlike Captain Christ's ship, Sinbad's boat was big and actually looked real. Of course, the monsters were not as fake as Captain Christ's demons, either. While Frank snored, Pop was fixated on the actress Caroline Munro.

"I'll have to see if I can find a picture of her for my scrapbook," whispered Pop.

When Caroline brandished expansive breasts through a low-cut top, Nancy turned around and barked, "Pop, cover Calvin's eyes!"

Pop stretched his Boris Karloff–like hand over his great-grandson's round face but cheated by slightly parting his long, bony fingers enough so Calvin could see the golden cleavage.

"My God! I really do think your mom would rather have you kill people than make people," whispered Pop. "Pay her no mind, but wouldn't it be something to see Caroline as Salome? I would give anything to see her take off all seven veils!"

10

A BIG BOX OF NOTHING

Peering out from under his great-grandfather's armpit, Calvin was once again being entertained by Pop's scrapbook. The supple figure of Esther Williams as a mythical mermaid danced around haphazardly glued pictures of exotic banana trees.

"Ariel and me, we spent our days swimming and making whoopee," exclaimed Pop as he took a small bite from a banana. The room smelled strongly of fruit due to Pop's private supply of bananas near his chair, which partly masked his lack of hygienic practices. "We made whoopee so often that Ariel kept your grand-pop in shape. She had enough energy for both of us—burned off every one of those banana calories." His gaunt, aged face beamed with youthful delight.

"What're you saying to Calvin?" asked Nancy, appearing suddenly. Knowing how Nancy felt about Pop's stories, Calvin hopped off Pop's chair and sat down on the sofa. Pretending not to hear her question, Pop hummed an aria from *Rheingold*.

"Pop," said Nancy, again. "What were you telling Calvin?"

"I was telling him about Ariel and me on the island of Galapagos. That's Charles Darwin's island, in case you didn't know."

"Not that Darwin nonsense again," groaned Nancy.

"No nonsense. Darwin's discoveries are fact. You can play ostrich and bury your head in the sand—doesn't make it less so."

"What was that I heard about bananas?" asked Nancy, trying to steer the topic away from Darwin.

"I was saying that I might as well eat bananas since we come from the monkeys."

"You did NOT tell Calvin that!"

"No, I'm telling you that!"

Nancy sighed indignantly. "Never mind. You make no sense sometimes." Cutting her glare through the Peanuts comic strip that Calvin was using to shield himself from her, Nancy warned, "Calvin, don't listen to a word he says. You hear me? There is no such thing as mermaids; never was, and never will be."

Calvin leapt from the sofa and returned with his sketchbook and pastels, his mind racing. Never was and never will be, thought Calvin. If there never was and never will be mermaids, then *The Brother Cobweb Chronicles* must have a mermaid! A never was and never will be mermaid can be like the Rhinemaiden, swimming away from all those dumb sermons, Calvin thought as he sketched.

"Pop, you still haven't told me what you want for Christmas." Nancy's voice interrupted Calvin's artistic endeavors. He peeked over the rim of his sketchbook, eager for Pop's expression.

"I told you, woman. I want a big box of nothing, because your Jesus is a big nothing," replied Pop, continuing to thumb through his scrapbook in silence until he came upon a picture of Ann-Margret.

"*Gottverdammt*," yelled Pop.

Calvin flinched and jumped up. Looking over Pop's shoulder, he saw that someone had colored over the starlet's semi-exposed cleavage with a marker.

"Language," called Nancy.

"God doesn't give a damn what I have to say because he's a fairy tale. That Bible of yours is a great big Jew comic book, and you silly Christians believe every word of it."

A Jew comic book? thought Calvin. My *Brother Cobweb Chronicles* is like a Jew comic!

"Whoever heard of a Jew who doesn't believe in God?" asked Nancy.

"I don't know many Jews who aren't atheist. If your God is alive, he's a wanted man! Convicted of crimes against humanity, he is!"

"Quit taking the Lord's name in vain."

"I wasn't taking the Lord's name in vain. I have a very good reason to call on him."

"And how's that?"

"Because you've been covering up my movie star titties, woman!"

God as a comic book fairy tale, thought Calvin. If Jesus is God's son . . . then, Jesus is a fairy tale, too, so he doesn't have to be a six-hundred-pound ghost or the son of a hairy, smelly beast. Jesus can be anything.

11

HAPPY BIRTHDAY, JESUS

Pop was used to Nancy's relentless proselytizing, but during the Christmas season, the tension between the two escalated. Normally, Pop ignored the holiday festivities or grumbled about them under his breath. However, this year Calvin noticed a change in Pop's demeanor.

"Whatcha doing, Pop?" Calvin asked, his curiosity piqued with Pop's sudden interest in the wooden nativity set underneath the Christmas tree.

Pop could not take his eyes off the set. At the front of the set was the crowned infant Christ child, Joseph, male shepherds, two male angels, and three wise men. Behind these pious male figurines knelt a pensive Mary in prayer. Pop got up from his chair and walked over to the nativity, and his face brightened as he lifted Mary from the back and placed her in front of Joseph and the other male figures.

"And just what are you doing?" Nancy demanded as she walked into the room.

"She was a mermaid," Pop said pointing to the small figure of Mary kneeling in prayer.

Wow, I already drew Mary as a mermaid, thought Calvin, pleased that he had a thought Pop shared, before Pop even said it out loud.

"Mary was not a mermaid," responded Nancy defiantly.

"She sure was," exclaimed Pop with such passion that, to Calvin's surprise, his mother made no further counterreply.

She must be in the Christmas spirit, Calvin thought. Once Calvin recovered from the shock of his mother turning down an argument with Pop, he was anxious to dive into *The Brother Cobweb Chronicles*. However, he didn't get far into his sketching when the annual Christmas Eve ritual demanded his attention. Nancy entered the living room in a threateningly puffy red and green skirt. I hope she never wears this when she gets the Holy Ghost, Calvin thought.

"You look like a poinsettia," said Pop, half-joking, half-grumbling.

"Why, thank you Pop," Nancy said. "You know poinsettias are poisonous to cats."

"You thinking of killing a cat?" Pop asked.

"Oh, you're so silly. I was just statin' a fact that I wasn't sure you knew. I read too, you know."

Pop grunted.

"And now it's time for a different reading, one for the season," Nancy said, beckoning the family to gather around. She sat in her large red chair, opened the View-Master *Christmas Story* booklet, and began her homily.

"A long time ago, before there was such a holiday as Christmas, there lived in the country of Galilee, in the little town of Nazareth, a little woman named Mary."

The rest of the family sat, scrunched together on the small couch, across from their matriarch. Dale held the View-Master up to his eyes, briefly looked into its lens, and handed it off to Frank.

"They're like puppets or Calvin's drawings," complained Frank as he peered into the red View-Master.

"Yup, except Calvin's drawings aren't inspired by the Holy Ghost! These are," Nancy said, triumphantly dismissive.

I can draw better myself without divine inspiration, thought Calvin.

Pop made a concentrated effort to keep from laughing. Calvin smiled after being handed the View-Master.

"Mary sure is pretty in her blue and white," said Calvin as he placed the toy into Pop's hands.

"I told you she was a mermaid," said Pop.

"A mermaid?" asked Dale and Frank simultaneously.

"Never mind," said Nancy, irritated at not being in control of the family tradition.

"Pop, hand it back to Dale. Dale, click to the next picture," barked Nancy. "Mary was betrothed to Joseph. One night while Joseph lay asleep, an angel of the Lord appeared before him."

Calvin gaped in awe at the image of an angel hovering over a sleeping Joseph.

"And she's the prettiest angel I've ever seen!" exclaimed Calvin.

"That's a he angel," protested Frank.

"Let me see," said Pop.

"All angels are boys," said Nancy, siding with Frank.

"Sure looks like a girl to me," countered Pop.

"You ain't no Christian. How would you know?" snapped Nancy.

"That's for certain, but at least I know a girl when I see one, and Calvin's right. She's one pretty angel."

As usual, Dale was not going to get involved in a family squabble. For once, Nancy followed her husband's lead, ignored Pop's attempts to provoke her, and continued reading the Christmas narrative according to Florence Thomas via the View-Master brand.

"Can we see the one about Rudolph's uncle now?" asked Frank after Nancy finished her opening ritual. "Rudolph's uncle has a blue nose, Pop."

"No. Now we're going to sing 'Happy Birthday' to Jesus," interrupted Nancy as she directed the family into the kitchen. In the center of the table was a cupcake with a single candle.

"Jesus got gypped," said Pop. "The old boy makes it to two thousand years and doesn't even get a whole cake. All he gets is a little cupcake and one measly candle."

"Pop, are you going to sing 'Happy Birthday' to Jesus with us? Or are you going to keep being a grouch?" asked Nancy.

"What are you going to do after this?" asked Pop.

"We're gonna watch a *Hee Haw* Christmas!"

"I'll continue being a grouch. I'm going to my room to read."

Knowing that he could not get out of singing "Happy Birthday" to Jesus, Calvin joined Pop after the song.

"How'd you come to live with my dad and mom, Pop?" Calvin asked, snuggling into Pop's arms.

"I moved in with your folks just a few weeks before you were born. It was your dad's idea. He had some notion that I was unhappy living in my one-room shack. Not so. I had my books, cheese, and bananas. Of course, it was small, and the books were pushing me out of the door. I never could save a penny, and every business I ever had failed. That's the main reason why your great-grandmother left me. Still, your dad was worried about me being alone at my age and made a kindhearted offer, which I felt obligated to accept. You know your dad—he's practically illiterate, but he has one of the biggest hearts I have ever known . . . the greatest of these is charity."

"Isn't that from the Bible, Pop?"

"Sure. I probably know your mother's Bible better than she does."

12

ARIEL'S ARIA

After *Hee Haw*, Nancy had a surprise for Pop, and she was anxious to see him open it. Normally, the Elkan house opened presents on Christmas morning, but since Pop was not a Christian, Nancy broke tradition by giving Pop his present on Christmas Eve. Pop sat in his living room chair, looking fatigued in contrast to Nancy's animated enthusiasm. Slowly, Pop unwrapped Nancy's gift.

"A big box of nothing," chuckled Pop faintly as he opened the empty box.

"That's right," said Nancy proudly.

"Why?" Calvin asked, his shoulders sagging with exasperation.

"That's what he asked for, and that's exactly what he got," laughed Nancy before leaning in to whisper, "and don't worry, Santa's bringing him a mermaid figurine. He can open it in the morning."

That night, Calvin dreamed of an angel with flowing long, white hair, much like the one in the View-Master, but his dream was cut short by the sound of a commotion in the living room. He imagined it was Frank rummaging through a stocking, but to Calvin's surprise, Frank was still asleep in his room. The lights were on at the end of the hall. Nancy stood near the entrance to the living room, blocking Calvin from entering.

"Stay back," she barked.

Calvin peeked around her and saw Pop sprawled out on the couch, his face contorted. Pop motioned toward the end table. Calvin looked and saw an unpeeled banana on the top of the table.

"Is this what you want, Pop?" Nancy asked, picking up the banana. Pop nodded. Nancy opened Pop's fingers, gently placed the banana in his hand, and closed his fingers around the fruit. Pop held onto the banana tightly as if holding on for life.

"Where's that damned ambulance?" Nancy cried.

Dale left the room to make a second 911 call.

"Jesus will welcome you into heaven, beautiful man," said Nancy as she gently stroked Pop's hair.

After half an eternity, the ambulance finally arrived. When two long-faced paramedics began lifting Pop onto the stretcher, the ailing man became upset when one of them tried to take the banana from his hand. "For the love of Jesus, let him hold his banana!" Nancy ordered. The frustrated ambulance driver conceded, allowing Pop to hold onto his fruit.

As they loaded Pop into the back of the ambulance, Calvin followed. Nancy climbed in after, took Pop's hand, and started to close the door.

"I want to go," said Calvin, hoarsely.

"No," said Nancy. "The hospital's no place for kids."

"Pop came to stay with me in the hospital. I want to be with him, too," argued Calvin.

"Not on Christmas day. Now go back to sleep."

Disappointed, Calvin walked back in the house as the ambulance drove off.

"We'll open presents later with Frank," Dale told Calvin.

Calvin went back to his room but couldn't fall asleep. He was gripped in fear—fear that a sick Pop might be vulnerable to his mother. She'll try to save him, Calvin thought. But, even sick, Pop won't cave in because he's smart enough to know that he'd have to start going to the Lighthouse, and he'd have to throw away his titty scrapbook, and he couldn't write his book no more. So, he won't do that. I know he won't.

Calvin, at first, didn't even entertain the idea that Pop might not be coming back, but as he sat on his bed and the hours wore on, Rev. Harry's sermon played in his mind: "I'm not afraid of Death. No Christian should be afraid of Death. And when I see Death coming, I'll walk right up and kiss it on the mouth!" No, Calvin thought, I'm not going to even think that. Then, it dawned on him—perhaps he should pray. But praying for Pop's recovery should be serious. So, how does one pray like an adult? The Lighthouse prayers were even more childish than any he could muster.

Calvin slipped into Pop's room, pulled out the Gauguin book, and flipped through it intently until he found the image he was looking for: *Christ on the Mount of Olives*. There, Christ, with his opaque orange hair, a hue of faint yellow bruising his face, prayed alone at a rock. Behind him, two darkened figures stood in the distance. Were they those coming to arrest him? Or were they fearful apostles on the verge of fleeing and abandoning him? Whoever they were, Christ was still alone, eyes downcast, hands folded, and Calvin remembered the words of Christ: "My God, why have you forsaken me?" God even turned his face from Christ. Christ then knew what it was like to pray and receive no answer.

Surely, then, remembering that, Christ would answer Calvin's prayer to heal Pop because Pop was beautiful and Calvin needed Pop and the world needed Pop and his stories. This was prayer enough—an adult prayer—and it was silent because if God is God, then surely he can hear a silent prayer. This was Calvin's act of faith. Despite what Captain Christ seemed to think, Calvin would prove his faith by praying silently, trusting that God could read his mind. For such trust, God would surely heal Pop. Calvin closed the book, lay his head on Pop's pillow, and fell asleep.

"Calvin, we're opening gifts now," said Dale, shaking his son awake.

"Is Pop back?"

"No," said Dale, hesitantly. "You can open all but one present. Your mom wants to see you and Frank open one."

Frank tore through his presents like a predator ripping through its prey. Calvin could only muster a pinch of enthusiasm for an 8 mm movie of Charlie Chaplin's *The Rink* and a Jon Gnagy drawing kit. When Frank offered to trade Calvin a set of markers for a twelve-inch action figure of Crazy Horse, Calvin handed over the Indian without hesitation.

They played with their new toys in the living room while Dale napped on the couch until the phone's ring pierced the air. Dale answered it. Calvin tried to play but couldn't. Dale came back into the living room, sat down on the couch, took a deep breath, and said, "Boys, your mother wanted me to let you know that Pop went to heaven."

Calvin gasped, as if all the breath just got sucked out of him, and his cheek bones burned wet. Dale quickly looked up at Calvin and just as quickly looked away, which was fine. Calvin didn't want to look at his dad either. Loss—coupled with anger toward a faceless God who had betrayed him—rendered Calvin momentarily numb to the world.

Calvin's eyes slowly shifted toward the discarded wrapping paper beside him, with three Wise Men on camels following the Christmas star under a dark blue sky. The phone rang again, tearing Dale away from his sons. Calvin didn't fully understand, but he felt more comfortable with Dale entirely out of the room. As for Frank, his presence felt inconsequential. Frank managed a frown for half a second upon hearing the news of Pop's death, but his mind was locked on Chief Crazy Horse.

Calvin could hear Nancy's voice coming through the other end of the phone in the kitchen. "I can't believe he was that stubborn up to the end. He put more faith in a banana than he did God. He died holding onto a banana," Nancy told Dale. "Of all the silly things—think how silly that is, Dale. It's silly not to give your heart to Jesus. Do you want to be silly like Pop? And die lost?" Dale said nothing in reply.

Calvin rose from the living room floor, went back into his room, and crashed into his bed. He slept fitfully off and on for the rest of the day, vaguely aware of family members moving around the house but determined to stay asleep. Everyone else was asleep when Calvin finally woke. He walked into the living room and saw his one unwrapped present under the tree. Then he saw the nativity set under the tree: someone had removed Mary from the front and returned her to the back. Calvin walked out of the back door and stepped onto the patio. He looked up at the big, dark sky and remembered a few years ago when Pop took him out onto that same patio. Pop had pointed to the moon and said, "See that moon up there, Calvin? That astronaut Neil Armstrong is walking on the moon right now. There's just me, you, and the man on the moon. That's all there is right now, and nothing else."

Now, Calvin looked at the moon again and wondered where Pop went. If he went anywhere, is Pop on the moon now? And he felt all there was in the world, in the entire universe, was him and Pop. There's not even you, God, Calvin thought resentfully.

As Calvin walked back into the house, which now seemed as empty as that black sky, he recalled the Rhinemaidens' mournful song from *Rheingold*. Calvin imagined Ariel singing, "Rheingold! Rheingold! Purest gold! If but your bright gleam still glistened in the deep. Now only in the depths is there tenderness and truth. False and faint-hearted are those who revel above."

Calvin retrieved the Gauguin book and closed his bedroom door behind him, feeling that he didn't want to be in a world without Pop. Again, he searched through the book and found *The Green Christ*, which portrayed a woman in front of a sculpture of a green, crucified Christ, surrounded by women mourners. It struck Calvin as odd that Christ and the women were earth green. Behind them was a pink-hued landscape that might very well have been Eden or Paradise. Calvin could see that woman in the foreground wanted to distance herself from the green death—she looked longingly at the pink Paradise landscape. Calvin identified with her and remembered that prayer many children pray: "Now, I lay me down to sleep. I pray the Lord my soul to keep. If I should die before I wake, I pray the Lord my soul to take." And Calvin hoped that maybe, if God were good, he would allow death to visit this house again. Then, Calvin could join Pop, and their Paradise would be pink and bright.

Calvin woke up the next morning, feeling as if the blanket were crushing his chest.

13
THE BROTHER COBWEB CHRONICLES

The Pentecostal Jesus not only ignored prayers but chose the occasion of Pop's funeral to reveal the depth of his cruelty. The funeral home, which was just down the road from the Lighthouse, was small, and matched the size of the crowd. The few people in attendance were Kennedy, Ray, Dale, one of Dale's union buddies, Nancy, Calvin, Frank, and the church secretary. Aunt Blanche, whose husband was in the hospital after suffering a heart attack, could not attend. Pop's closed casket stood at the front of the small room.

"How come we can't open the casket?" Calvin had asked Nancy shortly before the service. "I want to see him one more time."

"No," she answered curtly.

"But . . ."

"Do not argue with me at Pop's funeral. I said no!"

"Why?"

"Because somebody might take a picture of him."

Calvin looked around.

"No one brought a camera."

"Calvin, shut up! I said, no!"

Kennedy, sitting directly behind the Elkans, pierced the tension. "Calvin," she said, "Come here, for a second, would you? I have something for you."

Nancy rolled her eyes and motioned her son that it was OK to leave her side.

Calvin walked back and sat down next to Kennedy and Ray. At her feet, Kennedy had a brown paper sack.

"In our family, when someone loses someone they love, we buy them a gift," Kennedy explained, as she reached into the sack and pulled out an LP record of Leonard Bernstein's *Jeremiah* symphony that also had music from *On the Town*. "That's Lenny's first symphony and, no," she whispered, "it's not Bible-beating music. It's set to Jewish poems."

Kennedy also pulled out a comic book wrapped in a protective bag. "This is Superman's Pal, Jimmy Olsen. That was Ray's idea. It's kind of an old comic, but he goes back in time to infiltrate the Nazis, and the comic book salesman said the Nazis didn't let people read Superman because they said he was Jewish, just like Pop. I'll put them back in the bag for you."

Kennedy noticed that Frank was observing them with a pronounced frown. Promptly, she reached into her purse, pulled out a Babe Ruth candy bar, and handed it to Frank, who then turned back around, satisfied.

"Thank you," said Calvin sincerely. Kennedy and Ray had put generous thought into their gifts, and he was grateful.

Rev. Harry stood up in the front of the room near Pop's casket. Rather than disrupt the service to move back and sit with his family, Calvin remained seated next to Ray and Kennedy.

"Now, I didn't know Pop," Rev. Harry began, as he looked from his notes, "and being a Jew, he didn't believe in Jesus, so I can't speak for Pop or say where he is right now, but funerals are not for the dead. They are for those of us still living. Even at his age, Pop didn't expect death. The Bible tells us that death comes like a thief in the night, and Pop had his stroke at night while his family was asleep. Maybe that's why Pop died—as a lesson for us here because none of us are guaranteed a tomorrow."

Beside Calvin, Kennedy shifted uncomfortably in her seat.

"So the question is, are you ready for eternity? This life, no matter how long we live, is just a minute compared to eternity. And where will you spend eternity? I think all of us here want our eternity to be in heaven, but Jesus said no one can enter the gate but through him. Where would you be, if you died this minute?"

Calvin's palms were sweating. Kennedy put her arm around his shoulders and patted his arms reassuringly. Rev. Harry looked down again, scrutinized his notes, and looked directly at Dale.

"In order to provide for our families, some of us have to work a lot. We may even work more than one job, and we may think, we don't have time for church, we don't have time for Jesus right now. I'll give my heart to the Lord later. Now, God looks favorably upon family providers, but we are warned in scripture that on that day of judgment, every knee shall bow and every tongue shall confess Jesus as Lord. The Jews in Jesus's time rejected him as their Messiah and thought they were covered in being God's chosen, but Jesus said, I can turn these rocks into children of Abraham. What he was saying was, you have to accept me. So, folks, the best way to honor Pop today is, if you haven't accepted Jesus as your Lord and personal savior, I want you to come up here right now and do so."

"God," Kennedy mumbled. Calvin slumped in his seat.

Only Nancy and the church secretary went forward.

A half hour later, Calvin watched as the funeral director, Dale, his union pal, and Rev. Harry loaded Pop's casket into the hearse, which would drive him to the graveyard. Calvin's cheeks were moist as he tried not to sniffle and imagine a world without Pop. Kennedy and Ray, standing beside Calvin, likewise fought back tears. Nancy walked up behind Calvin and patted him on the shoulder. Calvin jumped.

"He's a good boy, and he sure loved his Pop," Nancy said to Kennedy with such saccharine sentiment that Calvin wanted to throw up.

After loading Pop's casket, Dale told everyone it was time to drive to the graveyard.

"Calvin," Kennedy said, "can you go grab me that guest book over there so I can sign it? And the pen too?" Calvin nodded and went to retrieve the items.

"Nancy," Kennedy said quickly, "as close as Calvin was to Pop, I think it's going to be hard for him to see them put Pop into the ground. We could leave now and take Calvin with us. He could spend the day with us and play with Ray to get his mind off this."

"I was going to take him and Frank to a Lighthouse softball game after," Nancy said, offended.

"Like Calvin would like softball," Dale scoffed. "That's a good idea, Kennedy. Thank you. Please do take him. Calvin can spend the day with you."

Nancy rolled her eyes and almost objected, but looked over at Rev. Harry, waiting by the hearse, and closed her mouth.

"C'mon Frank, let's get in the car," Nancy said as she took Frank by the hand, leading him to the vehicle.

"I still get to play softball, don't I?" Frank asked his mother.

"Yes," she said, tugging him.

Calvin walked up with guest book and pen in hand.

"Calvin, you're going to go with Mrs. Stevens and Ray and spend the day with them," Dale told Calvin.

"OK," agreed Calvin without questioning it. It would be a reprieve from going to the Lighthouse after Pop's funeral, which didn't seem right.

Kennedy told Calvin and Ray that the only way to make amends for such a funeral was to let their imaginations rip for an entire afternoon. They did just that, beginning with a promenade down the railroad track that opened important questions, such as who was better: Batman or Superman? From there, they sailed the seven seas on the Stevens' back patio, with the captured lass Kennedy bringing thirsty seafaring rogues lemonade and peanut butter sandwiches for their long voyage. The sea gave way to the stars with Ray as Captain Kirk and Calvin as Dr. McCoy on the bridge of the U.S.S. *Enterprise*, boldly entering the final frontier without that boring Mr. Spock. Calvin, per Kennedy's suggestion, even injected a bit of Pop, at his delightfully crankiest, into his portrayal of the good doctor, and he hoped the day would never end.

Less than a week after the farce of a funeral, Calvin stood in the backyard as Nancy placed Pop's *I Was Married to a Mermaid* manuscript in the trash burner. Nancy hesitated, tearing up as she held the unfinished book close to her chest before lowering it into the awaiting container. Feeling her son's protest, Nancy defended her decision. "It's nonsense, Calvin. You don't wanna remember Pop this way."

"You've never even read it," Calvin blurted out, feeling tears forming in his eyes.

"Don't haveta read it, heard him talk about it all the time. It's dirty lies told by an old man outta his mind."

"You're scared of Pop, and now you're trying to shut him up by burning his book."

"I know you loved Pop, and I'm trying to be patient with you, but you better watch your tone of voice with me."

"You can burn it, but you can't shut him up. Pop still won—he didn't get saved!"

"Get your ass back in the house, right now!"

Calvin turned around and headed to the back door but stopped short of entering. If Nancy was going to burn Pop's book, Calvin was not going to let her do it without a witness. Nancy resembled the faceless God in the Chick tract comic books as she cast Ariel and Pop into her lake of fire. Alberich placed a curse on the *Rheingold* when Wotan stole it, Calvin thought as he mumbled his own curse against his mother.

Nancy looked back at her son, her eyes burning into his as if she were born again through rage. Did she hear me? wondered Calvin, or is she just mad 'cause I didn't go into the house?

Calvin retreated to his room, where he resumed work on *The Brother Cobweb Chronicles*. Pop had chosen a banana to whisk him away instead of a flying Jesus. Calvin and Pop shared the same language, but with his lifeline of a great-grandfather gone, Calvin identified strongly with the people from the Tower of Babel. He was in a house filled with alien tongues, which made him want to spend more time with Ray and Kennedy, where they all spoke a mutually understood language. Still, Calvin had to contend with the family he lived with, and the best way to do that was to banish his mother from the *Chronicle* pages. It was part of her curse. Over the course of a month, Pop and Ariel came to life again on a banana-filled Galapagos Island as they fought Nazis and were watched over by Our Lady of the Mermaids.

14

ARKIMNEL

With no Pop to protect him and help him make excuses, Calvin was obligated to attend more and more Lighthouse nonsense, including propaganda films that Calvin found trite. With its vanilla walls, the church basement made an ideal movie screen, but the images coming from the film projector were hardly entertaining: the double feature grindhouse picture show began with Soviet horsemen shoving a bamboo stick into the ear of a Christian boy to prevent him hearing the Word of God. As the poor tyke for Jesus puked and bled from his ears, Baptist preacher Estus Pirkle warned of a communist atheist takeover coming soon to the USA! From a flat screen, Rev. Pirkle made an impassioned effort to quash all doubts, dramatically depicting commie henchmen, complete with Southern accents and ten-pound sideburns, raping, pitchforking, and decapitating good American Christians. After an hour of Baptist corpses piling up, a chorus of schoolgirls opened the second half of the program, singing "hay-ull awaits you," although Calvin felt alone in being more frightened of half-curled smiles and blank expressions from the fairer sex than eternal flames. Rev. Pirkle joined Rev. Robert G. Lee to scare the bejeezus out of a sleepy Baptist congregation who shared double chins, polyester suits, and ghastly floral dresses in common with real-life Lighthouse parishioners.

Rev. Pirkle gritted his teeth and warned that liberalism was the path to *The Burning Hell*, which was the name of the second feature. In an effort to peddle Pirkle's propaganda, two actors impersonating liberal hippies tried to argue that "God is love" nonsense, which resulted in yet another decapitation—this time from God's wrath in the form of a motorcycle accident. Covered in orange syrup, the dead rider woke up in the burning hell with maggots crawling out from every orifice on his face. Demons grabbed at his limbs, and the rider screamed for all eternity to a melodramatic fade out—something akin to a live-action Chick tract.

After the film, Rev. Harry added a word of caution. "That's what you'll find in hell, if you're fool enough to put yourself there: maggots, demons, and burning forever and ever and ever." The words struck Calvin as comically—yet frighteningly—sing-song, made more surreal by Rev. Harry's new gold herringbone chain that was so big, it looked like it would swallow him. Coo ca choo, thought Calvin as he steadfastly remained seated during the altar call.

With increased overtime factory hours, Dale's presence at home was confined to short naps on the living room couch. While he exhausted his energies, Nancy's collection of ceramic rustic geese, lacy plaques with Bible quotes, and salt and pepper shakers began taking over the house. Although he was resigned to his mother's tastelessness, it was the salt and pepper shakers that unsettled Calvin the most: the Amish figurine–shaped shakers peered around every corner, like spying gargoyles.

Emulating Blondie from the comic strip dailies, Nancy regularly packed lunch for her Dagwood of a husband, which consisted of a monster sandwich and thermos filled with tomato juice. With time to spare behind the suburban paradise's picket fence, Nancy, who refused to watch sin-laden soap operas like her unsaved neighbors did, recently subscribed to television's morning exercise with Jack LaLanne. Calvin had never seen his mother wear anything other than a dress, but now she wore black spandex daily.

On one weekday afternoon, Calvin came home from school and was surprised to find his mother still wearing her spandex. Even more surprising was the presence of Rev. Harry, out of his Sunday best and squeezed into a T-shirt and camo pants, talking with Nancy in the kitchen. They grew quiet when Calvin entered the room.

"Calvin, I've got to go to the store and pick Frank up from softball practice. Reverend Harry is going to take me because your dad has the car. If you'd like, Vernell can watch you," offered Nancy.

"I'll be fine by myself here," Calvin answered.

Nancy frowned. "Vernell will watch you."

"Why can't Kennedy watch me?"

"I already asked Vernell, and she said yes."

Nancy's quick retort did not surprise Calvin. Although she had never said so, Calvin was aware that Nancy did not like Kennedy. She probably would have forbidden him from even going over to Ray's house, but as Calvin had no other friends, Nancy overlooked her trepidations. Unlike Frank, Calvin was hermit-like, and his time with the Stevens granted Nancy a reprieve.

"Why don't you walk over to Vernell's now? She's making a batch of homemade buttermilk."

"I have homework to do."

"Take it with you."

Disgruntled, Calvin knew better than to argue with Nancy in front of Rev. Harry. Calvin did not like the preacher and sensed that the feeling was mutual. When out of his Lighthouse attire, Rev. Harry was scruffy-looking. Calvin had once overheard Rev. Harry say to Nancy, "Kilvin is soft, softer than Dale, even," in a disgusted tone.

Calvin found Vernell in her kitchen.

"Mom told me to come over here."

"Yeah, Harry's going over church business with her," Vernell said. "Then, they're going to pick your brother up, so it'll be awhile. You want some buttermilk?"

"Yes, thank you. Can you put some pepper in it? And can I work on my homework?'

"Sure thing. Just go sit at the dining room table and do it there. I'll bring you some biscuits, too."

Between shooing off an invasion of horseflies and trying to ignore the sight of Dick the Bruiser flashing across the dining room television screen, Calvin found it hard to concentrate on schoolwork. The beefy blonde wrestler in tight navy panties had his opponent in a headlock; as he pounded into the poor man's face, blood flowed like molasses. Calvin felt trashy for having viewed it.

"Oh, sorry," said Vernell, bringing in biscuits and buttermilk. "Harry had that on, forgot to turn it off."

Calvin's eyes darted from the horseflies swarming around his biscuits to the preacher man's row of guns, camouflage-painted toolboxes, and assorted weaponry on the walls. How can she be married to him? Calvin asked himself. After finishing his history assignment, Calvin desperately longed to work on *The Brother Cobweb Chronicles* but realized he had left it at home. He asked to return home, and Vernell assented.

Why is Rev. Harry's car still here? Calvin wondered as he walked into the house. He could hear his mother panting in her bedroom the way she did when exercising. Quietly, he walked toward his bedroom at the end of the hall. Nancy's door was slightly ajar. Unable to resist looking inside, Calvin saw her underwear lying on the floor near her bedroom door. He looked up to the horrific sight of Nancy and Rev. Harry naked together on her bed. Fighting nausea, Calvin stood frozen, unsure which way to step, fearing that either direction would give him away. This can't be real. Am I imagining this? The entire hall rippled before him. Somehow, Calvin stepped aside and made it to his room undetected. After grabbing *The Brother Cobweb Chronicles*, Calvin got the hell out of there.

When Nancy came to pick Calvin up from the Dushanes' home, Rev. Harry and Frank were with her. She immediately noticed that Calvin had his sketchbook with him.

"How'd you get that?" Nancy asked suspiciously. "You didn't take it with you."

"I let Calvin go back to your house when you were at the store. Hope you don't mind," offered Vernell.

"What time was that?" asked Nancy as she exchanged a nervous look with Rev. Harry.

"Between three thirty and four o'clock."

Nancy tried to look into Calvin's eyes, but he avoided eye contact, dodging her inquiry, and kept his distance the rest of the night.

The following Tuesday turned out to be a snow day, and Frank had gone to the house of a new kid on the block. Calvin had told Nancy that he was going over to Ray's house, but when Calvin got there, he discovered that Kennedy and Ray were leaving for a doctor's appointment. Calvin went back to his house and retreated to his bedroom without thinking to tell his mother that he had returned. He was alone in his room, drawing, almost oblivious to the world around him, when he heard voices rising from another part of the house.

"Dale's ruining that boy. You need to toughen up on Kilvin," he heard Rev. Harry say, almost as loud as when he was preaching. "If you don't—"

"Don't you be telling me how to raise my son . . . and Dale's going to be home any—"

Nancy's protest was interrupted by a loud slap. She screamed. Rev. Harry had hit her, but Calvin was hardly inclined to assist his hypocrite of a mother.

"Who do you think you're talking to?" Rev. Harry screamed at Nancy.

The sound of the slamming door startled Calvin, but he was placated in realizing that the filthy parson had exited the house. Bursting into melodramatic sobbing, Nancy retreated to her bedroom and thrashed on her bed. Calvin's revulsion for his mother gave way to consummate hatred, and he laughed out loud. Suddenly, Nancy's sobbing stopped, and Calvin realized that she had heard his laugh.

With bated breath, he waited at the edge of his bed for what seemed an eternity, knowing that his mother was surely going to confront him.

"So how long you been home?" Nancy said as she swung open Calvin's door.

"A few minutes," he choked out, fear rising to his brow. "Kennedy and Ray weren't home."

"That was over a half hour ago when you left to go to their house. You've been here longer than a few minutes."

"I don't know. I was d—d—drawing, I didn't pay no attention."

"You were paying attention alright. You could have told me you were home, but you were spying on me. Weren't you?"

"I wasn't spying. I was just drawing."

"You're a liar! You know what the Ten Commandments say about honoring your mom and dad. That's even before killing and stealing."

Without thinking, Calvin blurted out, "And adultery?"

Within seconds, she was atop him.

"You filthy bastard," she screamed as her body came crashing down upon his, her doubled-up fists slamming into his cheeks, jaw, and neck repeatedly. Calvin threw his arms up, trying to block her punches, until she grabbed his wrists, dug her nails into his flesh, and spit in his face. Heaving as her spittle ran down his cheeks, Calvin tried to lift his arm to wipe it off.

"Cry, baby, cry," she said and, with disgust, let go of him, only to spread her hand across his face and shove him backward. Calvin let out a whimper, his face streaked with her spit and his tears.

Nancy rose from the bed, and just as Calvin thought she was done with him, she lunged forward and brutally slapped him across the face. He screamed.

"If it weren't for you," Nancy said and stopped herself. "Go clean yourself up, and if you think you're going to go crying to your daddy, just you remember, he's working third shift now and you don't have no Pop to protect you now either. Ain't nothing going to stop me, if I feel like it, from coming into your room at night while you're asleep. So, you better think before you open your big crying mouth."

Nancy left. Calvin's face and wrists burned. Still crying, he got up from his bed and went to the bathroom to wash his reddened face. As he was washing, he saw where she had torn the skin on his wrists. Calvin blotted the blood with the washrag and winced from the stinging.

Calvin, still panting, lay down on his bed. His head, like the room, seemed to be spinning. He closed his eyes and fell into a dream.

In the dream, Calvin stood alone in a pitch-black shower stall as water poured down on him. After turning the nozzle off, he reached for the curtain but froze in place and gasped. Fear seized him upon seeing the outline of a woman from behind the curtain. Slowly, he made her out as the white-haired angel from the View-Master. "When you suffer, I suffer with you," she seemed to say.

Calvin woke up mid-afternoon. He had missed lunch, and his mother hadn't bothered to bring it to him. His stomach tightened as he considered that she might have looked into his room and found him asleep, which only heightened his fear of her coming into his room at night as she had threatened.

The rest of the day went uneventfully, except for the fact that they didn't say the normal blessing before dinner. Calvin avoided looking at his mother during the meal and, uncomfortable with the tension, asked if he could take his bowl of macaroni and tomatoes into his room.

"Don't spill it" was all she said, indicating that he could eat in his room.

Calvin woke several times that night, as if jolted awake for fear that she was in his room. Finally, he scooted his heavy box of classical music records that Pop had left him and put it up against the door. That way, if she did come in, he would hear her pushing the box out of the way. This relieved him enough to go to sleep.

The next morning, Calvin woke to find that Nancy had fixed chocolate Pop-Tarts for breakfast. She placed the plate on the table in front of him and bragged, "I toasted them, just the way you like them." As she spoke, her hand brushed against the back of his neck, and Calvin nearly jumped out of his skin.

"Scared of your shadow, silly?" she asked.

She knows why I jumped, Calvin thought. Calvin knew his mother was a phony, putting on an act, as if in church, and wondered why she felt the need to. He would prefer her direct hatred of him. Calvin didn't respond to her, wolfed down his breakfast, grabbed his backpack, and headed out the door. As he waited at the bus stop, he speculated, she knows that I know she's acting.

Calvin sat next to Ray on the bus, but hardly spoke.

"You OK?" Ray asked after ten minutes of silence.

Calvin nodded. "I just got a little headache." He kept quiet because he now felt a surge of jealousy in Ray having Kennedy for a mom.

All through the school day, Calvin was lost in thought, unable to concentrate on his work, trying to make sense of Nancy's attack—to no avail. Math class was the worst. Calvin looked at the multiplication table in his book, but he could not focus on dull numbers. Then Rev. Harry's sermon flooded Calvin's mind: "Exodus twenty-one seventeen says, 'Whoever curses his mother or father shall be put to death!' In Deuteronomy twenty-one, Moses tells us that if a man has a stubborn and rebellious son who will not obey his father or mother, then they shall take hold of him and bring him out to the elders of his city at the gate. Then, all the men of the city shall stone him to death. So, you shall purge the evil from your midst."

It's all my fault, Calvin thought as he stared at the multiplication tables. Despite his state of fatigue, Calvin made it through to art class, the only class that could lift him. Calvin rhythmically sketched narrative images:

Calvin stood in a vast wheat field. Lucy's red booth from the Charlie Brown cartoons stood in the middle of the field. The word "HELP" was scrawled on the booth, followed by "THE DOCTOR IS IN." The View-Master angel, with her white hair and sensual blue robe, occupied the booth. Calvin named her Arkimnel. Standing behind Calvin were children from the Lighthouse. The eldest of these was Rev. Harry's teenage son, Luke; other children were as young as Calvin. The group formed a vertical communion line. After blessing the peanut butter and jelly sandwiches and pink lemonade, Arkimnel motioned for Calvin to approach. She placed the small sandwich into his mouth and lifted the lemonade to his lips. Together they handed out sandwiches and lemonade to the gathering.

15

JOHNNY MACK BROWN & ST. MARY

Dale was taking Frank deer hunting for the weekend, and Nancy would be at a ladies' retreat in Louisville with Lighthouse women. Dale's question was what to do with Calvin: the Stevens would be out of town, and taking him along on the hunting trip was not an option. Dale had taken Calvin rabbit hunting once before, which ended disastrously, with Nancy stepping out of character to carefully shield her traumatized son from the sight of the ritualistic skinning of rabbits in the sink. Luckily, Aunt Blanche announced to Dale that she would be in town for the weekend and offered to take Calvin to visit Pop's grave at the cemetery and watch her nephew for the weekend.

Dale watched with disgust as Calvin dipped his bread into his stew, eating the vegetables and avoiding the meat. Dale had long stopped concerning himself with his eldest son's proclivities. So what that Calvin did not like playing ball or tinkering with cars? That Calvin preferred to spend time with art, books, music, and old movies did not bother Dale. At times, he thought of Calvin more like a daughter than son and simply left parenting the boy to Nancy. What little interaction he had with offspring was reserved for Frank. But the night before his hunting trip with Frank, Dale couldn't contain his disgust for his eldest son's diet.

"What the hell are you doing?" Dale screamed. "Put your damned spoon in the bowl and eat that meat!"

"I don't wanna eat the meat," Calvin protested.

"Dale, leave him alone, for crying out loud," Nancy yelled. "If Calvin doesn't wanna eat meat, then he doesn't have to."

Although he hated her religion and pretensions, Calvin was influenced strongly by his mother's vegetarianism. However, Nancy's avoidance of meat was inconsistent in that she inexplicably broke her religious-like vegetarianism for hot dogs alone. Why hot dogs? Calvin had yet to figure that out. Dale didn't pay any heed to Nancy's eating habits, but Calvin's recent conversion to full-time vegetarianism quickly became a fatherly concern.

"I'll buy you a collie if you start eating meat," Dale shot back temptingly, knowing that the TV show *Lassie* was one of Calvin's favorites.

"Dale, I said leave Calvin alone! You ain't gonna bribe him either. If he wants a dog, we'll get him one, but he doesn't have to eat meat to get a dog. Now shut up!"

"I'd rather have a cat," Calvin bravely announced.

"I said a dog! You ain't getting no damned cat," barked Nancy.

"But Dad just bought you a dog, so we already have one. Kennedy has a Siamese cat. It's quiet and I like it better than your noisy dog."

"Well, Kennedy ain't your mom—I am! If Kennedy jumped off a cliff, would you jump, too?"

"What's wrong with a cat?" Dale asked. "The cat I got at the car lot just had kittens, and it wouldn't cost a dime to bring one home. It'd give the kitten a home, and Calvin could have a pet. Besides, they clean themselves, you don't have to potty train 'em, and . . ."

"Like I told you, you better never bring them back here. I'll drown the damned things if I have to. You get that cat nonsense from Blanche," Nancy scoffed. "I told you before, I hate cats—hate the way they look at you and slink up against your leg. I ain't never heard that sister of yours explain why they do that. Of course, it goes to figure her liking cats, being a pagan."

"She ain't no pagan," Dale grumbled, getting up from the table to avoid an extended argument.

Having lost his father five years before Calvin was born, Dale had genuine, albeit long-distance, affection for Blanche. Nancy, on the other hand, held her husband's snooty sister in contempt, but practiced rare civility in a half-assed effort to keep family peace. However, Dale wasn't sure how Nancy might react to Blanche spending an entire day with Calvin. His wife already believed her son to be contaminated with Pop's "thinks he's better than me" attitude. Additionally, Nancy was becoming increasingly certain that Kennedy was one of those subhuman liberals and complained about how much time Calvin spent at Ray's house. Still, none of that mattered—when Nancy left for the ladies' retreat that night, she assumed that whether he liked it or not, Calvin would have to accompany Dale on the hunting trip this time.

Loaded down with a bulky backpack, Calvin climbed into Blanche's car. As she fastened his seatbelt, Calvin's eyes wandered across her New Mexico skin. Blanche's eye caught the residue of blue pastels on Calvin's cuticles. She reached into his backpack and pulled out pencils, pastels, and a drawing pad.

"You might want these," Blanche said. "It's an hour's drive."

"Thank you," said Calvin, taking the art supplies.

"Do you like to paint?"

"Yeah, but I haven't gotten to paint much. I mostly draw. My mother says I'll make a mess, but Mr. Bugbee lets me paint in his class."

"Mr. Bugbee? What a name!"

"He told me not to color in coloring books anymore. He said I should be drawing and painting, not just filling in. He gave me a praying mantis and an avocado to paint pictures of. They're good, but I did better on this one."

Calvin flipped through his sketchbook, keeping it half-closed to Blanche's view. He pulled out a loose acrylic painting on heavy paper, which depicted a woman dressed in 1940s clothing and a hat. The painting was monochromatic, done primarily in blacks, whites, greens, and touch of red for the subject's lips.

"Calvin, this is good. Is that the actress Ingrid Bergman?"

"Yup."

"What made you want to paint her?"

"She's a natural beauty."

"Yes," said Blanche surprised, "people have said that about her. Where did you pick up that phrase?"

"I read it in a book that Pop gave me about movies, and I saw her in *Casablanca*, so I found a picture of her and painted this."

Blanche smiled as she started the car. Securely strapped in, Calvin carefully opened his pad, positioning it on his lap for some privacy as he resumed working on a drawing. Twice, out of instinct, Blanche nearly turned on the radio but stopped herself short, allowing Calvin to work in silence.

"Calvin, we're here," Blanche said some time later.

Calvin looked up, surprised to see that they were in a church parking lot.

"I want to light a candle for Pop," Blanche explained.

Calvin's fingers shielded his sketchpad as he closed it.

Together, Blanche and Calvin walked into St. Mary's Catholic Church, a pre-Vatican II parish. As they entered the church, Blanche genuflected. The exterior of the church had not prepared Calvin for what he would discover behind its doors. This was not a Lighthouse church. Rather, this church was a cool, carved, and mystic world, the likes of which Calvin had never experienced. Through the dimly lit building, an array of beautifully austere colors adorned sculptures, icons, and stained glass windows of people from New Testament drama and church history. The air was heavy with incense and smoke from the hundreds of candles that flickered on the walls. This was church as art.

Calvin watched with fascination as Blanche reverently lit orange and white candles. Pulling a rosary out of her coat pocket, she tightly wrapped it around her fingers and prayed like a whisper. The diaphanous reds of Blanche's prayer beads emitted spectral beacons, like microscopic lanterns for Calvin's eyes to follow. As if it were a crimson Christmas star, one such light pointed the way to the Stations of the Cross. Calvin stepped away from Blanche and followed the path of ivory reliefs. Their primitive elegance caught him unaware. These images were very different than the passion narrative Calvin had seen in Chick tracts that depicted a universal savior as crucified, blood-soaked slab of beef.

The sense of Catholic surrealism overwhelmed Calvin to the point where he felt as if he had been catapulted into a View-Master reel. Suddenly, the reels got mixed up when Calvin spotted an honest-to-goodness real-life cowboy praying at the church altar. Johnny Mack Brown, thought Calvin. Only the previous night, Calvin had watched Johnny Mack Brown in *Cheyenne Roundup* during Dale's long-standing weekly showing of 8 mm B westerns that he called "Rodeo Roundup." As the movie was only a five-minute excerpt from a longer film, *Cheyenne* had a gaping plot hole: in one scene,

Johnny was riding on his palomino, but the cowboy's destination was never revealed in the abridged version.

I wonder where he's riding to? Calvin had thought. Now, he knew. Like in that song from *My Fair Lady*, Johnny was trying to get to the church on time. Wait till Dad hears I got to see Johnny Mack Brown. After one such evening of B westerns, Calvin had declined Dale's offer to go horseback riding. According to Nancy, Dale had felt let down. Dale himself would never say so, but he apparently told his wife, and she in turn laid a guilt trip on Calvin for disappointing her husband. Dale had assumed Calvin's enthusiasm for westerns would lead to a bonding activity, but Calvin merely liked the image of horses flickering through a projector light. He had no interest in riding the animals. Calvin assumed Dale would understand that. Still, Calvin could make it up to Dale because here was Johnny Mack Brown at St. Mary's.

Calvin walked closer to the praying cowboy. Upon closer inspection, it was not Johnny Mack Brown at all, but the man certainly resembled that movie star of yesteryear. The fully-attired cattleman stood up and began to walk down the aisle. Calvin's eyes started to follow the stranger, but a statue of Mother Mary in the corner not far from the altar caught his eye.

Mary looked down at Calvin with doe-like eyes that possessed a touch of sorrow, fused with maternal desire. Her lush hands were stretched out from an emblazoned heart caressing her breast. The Madonna's light porcelain face was distinctively framed by an impressionistic blue and white robe, swooping down to her diminutive bare feet, and she seemed to be reaching out to Calvin. The View-Master-like vestal stood before Calvin. Arkimnel is *my* Our Lady of the Lucy Booth. She must be a daughter of Mary, he thought. The beastly divine thug in a wooden box temporarily died within Calvin. In its place, the Mother Love of God aroused him. He sat down in a pew and looked at the statue until Blanche said it was time to leave.

Later that evening, after they had placed a holy card and rose on Pop's grave, Blanche and Calvin sat in the bedroom of his much-missed great-grandfather.

"May I see your sketchbook now?" Blanche asked Calvin.

A look of nervousness washed over the boy's face. Blanche, realizing her words alone would not reassure Calvin, touched his fingers. After he handed the sketchpad to her, Blanche opened it. Calvin leaned in, his cheek resting on the roundness of her shoulder. The pad was filled with dozens of sketches depicting scenes of Lighthouse parishioners slaying in the spirit—exactly how Blanche always imagined the services went, exuding backwoods, sawdust-on-the-floor styled Pentecostalism. Blanche flipped to the page with

Calvin's contemporary Pentecostal Last Supper with a disturbingly obese Jesus peeking down Magdalena's blouse.

"Is there a little bit of Pop in this Jesus?" Blanche asked with amusement.

Calvin shrugged. He had never considered that an element of Pop had gone into the making of this Jesus.

The Virgin Mary as a mermaid swam across the next page. Blanche laughed out loud. "That reminds me: what happened to Pop's mermaid book? I asked your mom about it, and she said that she didn't know."

Calvin said nothing, but his eyes and shrugging shoulders revealed the truth.

"That bitch," she mumbled under her breath.

Blanche continued flipping until she came across *The Brother Cobweb Chronicles*.

"Who's this?" Blanche asked.

"Brother Cobweb."

"Who, pray tell, is Brother Cobweb?" she asked.

"He's a preacher I made up," said Calvin.

Blanche found the drawings of Brother Cobweb to be misshapen, malevolent, and disturbing, but wanting to encourage Calvin, Blanche kept her response supportive. As she closed the pad and returned it to Calvin, she said, "You have vivid imagination and an exciting way with color."

16
CASCADING SLIDERS

"Bertie and Tubby are moving back to Ohio? When?" Calvin asked. "They already moved here a couple of weeks ago, and we're going over there next Friday, so you better not be calling 'em Bertie and Tubby anymore. You're supposed to call them Grandma and Grandpa," said Nancy.

"More like Laurel and Hardy," quipped Calvin.

Calvin had only met Nancy's parents twice when they had visited Ohio. Bertie and Tubby had lived in Florida next door to Nancy's brother, Billy. Now, the three of them had moved back home. Bertie stood four feet eight inches tall and was encased in a whopping four hundred and fifty pounds of flesh. Her husband stood six feet four and barely weighed one hundred and eighty. Billy was a retired sailor, and his body was camouflaged in nearly every stereotypical naval tattoo one could muster: a great battleship sailed across his bristly chest, while skulls, mermaids, and hula girls danced atop anchors embellished on every limb.

Billy showed up at the Elkan house alone one Friday night, bringing with him five sacks full of White Castle hamburgers—Florida was deprived of the oniony, gut-busting sliders. Billy, a burly man, ate thirty small burgers by himself. Dale joined the feast but stopped at exactly half that amount. Downing those burgers with a case of Pabst Blue Ribbon resulted in the Elkan household smelling of a wooly mammoth fart. Utilizing their bedrooms as bomb shelters proved futile when the nightlong trail of gastric outbursts still managed to seep through the cracks of their doors, sending Calvin and Frank reeling.

One week after Uncle Billy's visit, Calvin and Frank officially received the order to spend the night with Bertie and Tubby. The genesis of Billy's vulgar ways became clear upon visiting their maternal grandparents for the first time in years. Bertie's short frame could barely support her weight, which resulted in her using a walker just to get around.

Calvin sat on the floor of his grandparents' apartment as Bertie leaned back in her reclining chair, eating through an entire box of Twinkies while she watched television. Bertie's nightly attire was a mangy green robe from which two doughy legs protruded. Excessively long, brittle toenails topped off a pair of reddish, withered feet. Perfectly matching her toenails were equally disgusting fingernails that were yellowed from decades of Virginia Slims. Calvin watched in freakish fascination as Bertie lowered her right hand into a deep robe pocket and pulled out a raw hot dog, which was spotted in green lint. Bertie lustfully rolled the pork between her fingernails before inhaling the meat. A moment later, she reached into her robe, pulling out another dog, and repeated the ritual several times.

"Grandma, do you have any Alka-Seltzer?" Calvin asked as he witnessed the nauseating origin of Nancy's hot dog fetish.

"Tummy speakin' to ya? Don't think so, but got some Rolaids," Bertie said.

"OK, thanks."

"Tubby," barked Bertie.

Dutifully, Tubby got up from his recliner and retrieved the antacids. Returning to his chair, Tubby opened a pack of Raleigh cigarettes. After lighting up, he resumed watching *Captain Blood* on television. Inherently laconic, Tubby blended in with the furniture, just like Dale. He's more like Dad's dad than Mom's dad, thought Calvin.

"Errol was such a dream," opinioned Bertie about the *Captain Blood* star. "He could leave his boots under my bed anytime."

"But those are boy's shoes," said Calvin, confused. "You couldn't fit in them."

Bertie and Tubby laughed. Frank, occupying himself with a Tonka truck, didn't seem to hear or care about the conversation.

"He's no Douglas Fairbanks," said Tubby. They were the first actual words that Calvin had heard his grandfather utter the entire night. "I went to the premiere of *The Taming of the Shrew*. That was a movie Doug made with his wife."

"Mary Pickford," said Calvin.

Impressed, Tubby asked Calvin how he knew that.

"I read it."

"Yeah, well Hollywood ain't been the same since Mary and Doug divorced," Bertie piped in.

"I saw *The Thief of Bagdad* on TV," said Calvin.

"That's his best, and he was a better Robin Hood than Errol Flynn," Tubby declared.

"No, he wasn't," countered Bertie. "I like Doug, but Flynn was a better Robin Hood. In like Flynn."

"In like Flynn," laughed Tubby.

"Hey!" exclaimed Bertie as she pointed to the TV. "That clipper ship is like the one I used to sail on."

"You were on a ship, Grandma?" asked Frank, suddenly awoken from playing with the truck.

"In my previous life, I was a sailor. I sailed with Christopher Columbus."

"Like in reincarnation? I thought Mom said you were a Mormon," said Calvin.

"Unlike your excommunicated mother, we are Mormons, and despite what your grandmother here says, reincarnation ain't exactly a Mormon belief," Tubby interrupted.

"All the same, I was a sailor in my previous life. Want to know how I died?" Bertie asked. "I was a homosexual, and they killed me for it," she continued before receiving an answer from her grandsons.

"Served you right," said Tubby.

"Yup," said Bertie in agreement. "I was a terrible sinner, and that's why I got to come back and be given another chance. This is my third trip. Second time, I came back as a Cherokee warrior, but my life got cut short when a white man killed me. So, here I am the third time around. Our side of the family is Indian, you know."

"My mother was excommunicated?" asked Calvin, uninterested in the family tree information. "I thought only Catholics excommunicated people."

"We sure as hell ain't Catholics," said Tubby. "She was voluntarily excommunicated for leaving the Latter-day Saints and becoming a damned fool Pentecostal."

"Not getting into religious differences," warned Bertie.

Tubby returned to his Raleigh cigarette and *Captain Blood*.

"Your mom says you can paint pictures. Why don't you paint me a picture of a clipper ship?" Bertie asked Calvin. "I'll give you something for it."

"OK. I'm better at painting people, but I'll try," said Calvin.

17

THE DOLOROUS PASSION OF ALVIE AND NANCY

A s the Jim Croce song "Photographs and Memories" seeped out from the cracked door of Calvin's room, Nancy rolled her eyes. Although she only heard the lyrics in part, the song seemed to paint a blithe portrait of sepia-tinted pasts. Not mine, she thought. There was no adequate color for her childhood . . .

That morning in Nancy's childhood, Bertie was still in bed at nine o'clock when she picked up the bell and rang it, signaling that Alvie, Nancy's older sister, had approximately sixty minutes to prepare breakfast: six eggs over easy, four pieces of buttered toast, a full pound of bacon, a bowl of honeyed grits, a stack of pancakes (heavy on butter and maple syrup), topped off with a glass of grapefruit juice.

With Nancy's help, Alvie finished the breakfast within forty minutes. Tomorrow they'd have to start earlier—on even-numbered dates, Bertie demanded biscuits and gravy on top of everything else, which took the full hour. Alvie and Nancy served Bertie breakfast in bed. While their mother fed, Alvie sat Nancy down at the table.

"Eat your cereal. I have to do laundry."

Alvie had three hours to finish laundry and dishes before starting Bertie's lunch. Alvie mumbled a prayer that she would not get distracted today, but the ratio of unanswered prayers to those answered left little room for optimism. When Billy walked into the laundry room, the silence of a God who turned his face reverberated. Billy unzipped his pants, as he always did, then grabbed Alvie and forced her down to her knees. Billy pushed on the back of her head for a long time, frustrated when her mouth got tired. Grabbing a handful of her locks, he used too much force and yanked out a chunk of Alvie's hair. In his excitability, he pulled out, rather than making her swallow as usual, and splattered on her pink dress.

"What's wrong?" asked Nancy when Alvie came back into the kitchen.

Her face red, Alvie stammered, "I—I only got two dresses, and tomorrow we have to go to the temple. Billy messed on my dress, and now I gotta—"

"He does that to me, too," said Nancy with a matter-of-fact disgust.

"When?"

"At night, when he comes into my room."

"Daddy too?"

"Sometimes, but not as much as Billy," said Nancy, shaking her head.

"How long they been doing that to you?'

"Long time."

"I gotta get out of here. I'm gonna run away and go live with my real mom's family."

"Your real mom?"

"Yeah. You're twelve now, guess you ought to know. My real mom's dead. She was daddy's first wife, and she died when she had me. Daddy married Bertie when I was three. Billy and Leigh are your real brother and sister, but I'm just your half sister."

"That's why Mom hates you! 'Cause you ain't hers."

Startled and terrified, Alvie and Nancy shrieked in unison when Tubby, razor strap in hand, seized them both by the arms. He had heard the whole conversation. Without a word, he dragged his two daughters to Alvie's bedroom and threw them on the bed. The crying girls simultaneously turned over on their stomachs, pulled their dresses up, and pushed their panties down to their ankles. Tubby lashed repeatedly at their exposed buttocks, drawing blood. Silently, Tubby left Alvie and Nancy on the mattress, grimacing as they pulled their panties up.

One memory gave way to another, unfolding like a greatest hits compilation of Nancy's adolescence.

As she bit into a piece of chicken Alvie had prepared for lunch and tasted blood, Bertie's eyes rolled over white. She sprang from the bed, breaking her habit of never rising until after lunch. Alvie was changing Leigh's diaper when Bertie barged in the nursery like an orca from a violent wave.

"Nancy, get your ass in here!" screamed Bertie.

Alvie looked up, aghast at seeing her stepmother's unsettling and rare presence in the nursery. Even more foreboding was the sight of Bertie's bloodstained teeth.

Nancy appeared within seconds.

"Take Leigh and change her goddamned diaper," Bertie barked to Nancy.

"That's Alvie's job!" cried Nancy.

Bertie stepped back and launched her fist into Nancy's mouth. Nancy's head snapped back from the blow. Tears streaming down her face, Nancy rushed to Alvie and took baby Leigh from her big sister's hip.

Nancy laid Leigh on the floor. Unflinchingly, the newly crowned nanny stayed focused on changing the infant's diaper as Bertie mercilessly pounded Alvie's face. Whimpering filled the nursery as the odor of shit and blood permeated the air. Bertie was back in bed within the hour as Alvie clipped her stepmother's dense toenails. The spotty blood on Alvie's mouth took its time drying as she pruned away.

To hell with Jim Croce, Nancy thought, done with memories as she dropped the needle on *The Songs of Zion*.

Christmas was going to be spent at Bertie and Tubby's apartment. Uncle Billy would be there, and even Aunt Alvie would be out of the asylum for a few days and was coming for a visit, which compelled Nancy to prep Calvin and Frank a few days before the holiday get-together.

"Your Aunt Alvie's gonna be there for a few days. Now, she's kinda funny in the head."

"She's cuckoo?" Frank asked.

"She ain't gonna hurt you none. Just be nice to her."

When the Elkan clan arrived at Bertie and Tubby's, Alvie greeted them at the door. She was small and bony; her arms, chock-full of needle marks, revealed multiple treatments. She wore a loose-fitting faded pink dress and was barefoot despite the cold weather. Half of her teeth were missing. Her dark hair was straight, parted in the middle; like Bertie and Tubby both, she was balding on top. She clutched a purple pillowcase tight in her hands.

Calvin was the first Elkan at the door. Alvie held her pillowcase up to him.

"You got some cigarettes?" Alvie asked.

"No."

"Well, I'll kiss you anyway," she declared.

Alvie clasped Calvin's face in her wrinkled hands and planted kisses on his forehead, eyelids, and lips. Her kisses were slobbery, and Calvin wanted to wipe his face but cautiously refrained from doing so.

"He ain't got no cigarettes," said Nancy, "He's just a kid. You know he don't smoke, and he ain't gonna start neither."

"I was a kid when I started smoking."

"I brought you cigarettes," said Nancy as she dropped a carton of Winstons in Alvie's pillow case.

"Thank you! Thank you! Thank you! And I—oh, look at you," said Alvie upon seeing Frank. "You're cute, too."

Alvie grabbed Frank by the face and planted kisses all over him, too. Frank wiped his face, frowned, and looked to Nancy for intercession.

As Nancy and Dale entered, Calvin heard Bertie tell his mother, "Thanks for bringing Alvie cigarettes. If she ain't got any, she'll trade the other patients sex for smokes."

Hearing this, Billy's concentration on a sack of treasured White Castles broke long enough to nearly send him into a fit of laughter.

After mountains of deviled eggs and foamy punch, the family began singing along to Christmas songs about Santa Claus, a red-nosed reindeer, and a talking snowman before a Tennessee Ernie Ford song began.

"Tennessee could leave his shoes under my bed, anytime," said Bertie. Calvin was once again confused when all the adults laughed and snorted at the joke.

Presents were next. From his grandparents, Calvin received a book about movie star Errol Flynn. Bertie leaned in and told him, "Errol's life was even more exciting than the movies, but don't tell your mom what's in it!"

Opening an oddly shaped package, Dale pulled out Tubby's gift: a belt. Nancy's eyes darted between the belt, her father, Billy, and Alvie. The inky onyx of the belt reflected in her eyes, which both Tubby and Billy self-consciously averted. Although Alvie was oblivious to the exchange, Calvin perceptively observed, curious about the familial tension.

For Nancy, the belt smacked of Mormon betrayal, once having been administered by Billy and Tubby when they had learned from Elder Dean that Alvie was planning to run away. Being a young teen then, Nancy had naïvely trusted the Mormon elder, confessing Alvie's intent to and reason for running away. Elder Dean quickly went to Bertie and Tubby told them everything. Worse, he told them that Nancy had accused both Billy and Tubby of other things—sexual things. After the sisters pulled their panties back up over flogged buttocks, Tubby and Billy forced them to their knees as punishment. This proved to be the final straw for Alvie. By sunrise, she had fled the house. Two weeks passed before word came that Alvie had found refuge with her mother's family.

Overhearing Bertie talking to Tubby from another room, Nancy whimpered as she fixed her mother's biscuits and gravy.

"Two weeks there, and Alvie's already cut her wrists. No surprise given that her mother was a loon, too. That family's welcome to her. It'll be a cold day in hell before she comes back here."

"No such thing as hell," said Tubby.

With Alvie's absence, Billy and Tubby abused Nancy even more frequently. Nancy's breaking point came even earlier than it had for Alvie, and she left home at fifteen to marry Dale. At nineteen, Alvie met and married Johnny Soots, who lived up to every known stereotype about mean-spirited, drunken white trash. The two already had five children when Nancy discovered the extent of the damage inflicted upon her sister over a telephone call.

"Nancy, do you have any food to spare? Johnny's been gone near a week, and I haven't been able to feed the kids last two days. Tomorrow's Easter Sunday, and I wanna at least have food for 'em," Alvie pleaded.

"Why didn't you say so, Alvie? God! Dale won't be home till late, but I'll be there first thing Sunday morning."

By the time Nancy arrived, Johnny had already returned with a hangover.

"Where's Alvie?" Nancy asked.

"She's in there on the bed. I don't know what's wrong with her."

Nancy walked into Alvie's room. Alvie was lying face up with glazed eyes.

"Alvie," said Nancy, shaking her sister.

Alvie looked at Nancy. There seemed to be no recognition in Alvie's face as she swung at Nancy, missing by a few inches.

Nancy walked back into the living room and angrily told Johnny that he needed to get Alvie to a doctor. Johnny said he would.

The next day, Nancy called Alvie's house repeatedly. There was no answer. With Dale gone, Nancy had no other option but to talk to her neighbor Vernell. Having only lived in the neighborhood for a little over a month, Nancy hardly knew her, but Vernell's husband, Harry, was a preacher of a Pentecostal church. Surely, they must have some charity, Nancy told herself as she knocked on Vernell's door.

"Vernell, I hate to bother you, but could you please drive me to my sister Alvie's house? It's about ten minutes from here. Something's wrong with her."

Vernell obliged. When the two women walked into Alvie's house, they found four children running around the house without clothes.

"It's cold in here," said Vernell, alarmed.

Nancy walked over to the thermostat, then to a floor grid, feeling for heat. She shook her head.

"It seems like there's some heat coming from the kitchen," said Vernell.

They walked that way, finding the gas stove on and door opened. It was the only heat in the house.

"Where's Alvie?" Vernell asked.

"I guess she ain't here. Might be at Johnny's sister's house."

"How far is that from here?"

"Five to ten minutes, maybe."

"Just take my car. I'll watch the kids."

"God bless it," yelled Nancy upon finding Alvie with her daughter Shannon at Johnny's sister's house. "What's wrong with you? You left four babies at home by themselves?"

"Nancy? What're you doin' here?" Alvie asked groggily, half-awake.

The phone rang.

"Hello?" asked Alvie's sister-in-law. "Uh, sure. It's for you," she said, handing the phone to Nancy.

"Nancy," said Vernell, "Johnny came back to the house."

"Put him on the phone. . . . Johnny, you get Alvie to a doctor today, or so help me God, I'm callin' the police and welfare."

"All right, goddammit," grumbled Johnny.

"Give the phone back to Vernell. . . . Vernell, I'm gonna have Shannon with me. When I pull up, I'm gonna honk. When I do, just come out. I'm not going inside, and I ain't tellin' Johnny that I'm takin' Shannon home with me."

Nancy lifted the three-year-old Shannon into her arms and took off. Alvie seemed not to notice.

"Alvie's cut her wrists twice now since she's been with Johnny. If he don't get her to a doctor, I'm gonna do exactly what I said," Nancy told Vernell on the way home as Shannon dozed off in the back seat.

"That'd be the right thing to do," Vernell said. "You know, Nancy, I don't wantcha to take this the wrong way and ain't trying to push this, but have you given any thought about going to church? It seems to me you need God in your life, and what better way than a Christian community? Our church doors are always open."

"Ain't had much use for church since I left the LDS, but you're right. I do miss having a church community. I'll be there this Sunday."

Nancy meticulously redressed the spare bedroom for Shannon. Dale accepted the new occupant nonchalantly—the addition of a child had little bearing with his workload.

Surprisingly, Johnny called.

"I took Alvie to the emergency clinic. They said to take her to a doctor and get her some medicine."

"So, take her to the doctor and get her some medicine."

"I gotta work tomorrow. If you want her to go to the doctor, take her yourself."

Nancy signed the papers, admitting Alvie to the local mental hospital. A few months later, Johnny pulled his wife out. And Nancy took her back. The pattern lasted for two years until Alvie was found screaming naked between two houses and the police got involved. This time, Alvie was taken to a normal hospital, and shock therapy left her a shell of her former self. After two weeks and a hearing, Alvie was made a ward of the state and admitted to an asylum at twenty-nine.

The last time Johnny had taken Alvie out of the asylum for a weekend, he did not return her on Monday as promised. A few days later, a janitor found her outside a locked ward, crouched on the floor and wailing like a cat in desperation.

"Johnny, I did what you told me, now let me see my babies," she moaned.

Johnny had promised Alvie he would take her to see the kids. It was a promise he broke. Whatever it was that he did to Alvie prompted the state to permanently refuse visitation with his wife. Even Nancy could not see Alvie for two weeks following that weekend. After that and several newly acquired burn marks, Alvie was lost to a childlike state.

With her new charge, Nancy did not have time to mourn losing Alvie to the present, but she made up for it by practically adopting Shannon. Nancy adored brushing Shannon's hair, dressing her up, shopping with Vernell on the weekdays, and taking her to Rev. Harry's church on Sunday.

"You're so lucky," Vernell told Nancy one afternoon at their favorite lunch spot, a chain steakhouse.

"What do you mean?" Nancy asked as she tied the bib around Shannon's neck.

"Getting to be a mom to Shannon here," Vernell explained. "As much as we've all gone out together over the last couple years, I feel a bit like a mother to her myself."

Nancy flashed Vernell a look of anger, but her neighbor failed to notice.

"I wanted a girl, but the Lord saw fit to bless us with Luke," Vernell continued. "Course, I know you and Dale haven't had much luck in the baby-making department. With him working as much as he does, don't know how you'd find time to try and make babies. At least you got this pretty little girl."

As Vernell spoke, Nancy avoided her neighbor's eyes. What she didn't know couldn't hurt her.

When time came for legal guardianship, Nancy approached Dale.

"I want to adopt Shannon. I'll make a good mother to her and give her the life Alvie should have had."

"Look, you're finally pregnant, we're moving Pop in, and I can't be a father to a kid who ain't even mine. I just ain't got it in me to love her," he bluntly told Nancy.

Shannon had felt Dale's coldness for two years. Although she was sorry to leave Nancy, Shannon was glad to be reunited with her siblings, even if it was at a foster home. On the day of Shannon's departure, Nancy broke down.

"I asked this one thing from you, Dale," she sniveled as she looked out the window, watching Shannon drive off in her new foster parents' station wagon.

"Oh, get over it. It ain't like she's yours. You'd do better to focus on the one growing inside your belly," said Dale.

December 29 came too soon, and it was time for Alvie to leave Bertie and Tubby's to go back to her asylum.

"I'll come and get you for Easter," Nancy assured Alvie.

"Can you bring me some White Castle?" Alvie asked.

You never had a chance, thought Nancy as she hugged Alvie goodbye.

18

PINK STRINGY THINGS

A brief but brutal winter brought a considerable amount of ice to Wilmington, Ohio, and neighborhood kids took it as an opportunity to talk Calvin and Frank into a game of sled chicken on the Elkans' iced-over patio deck. The goal of the game was to lie belly-down on sleds, ram into one another, and try to avoid being rammed into. Calvin opted for the latter. Awkwardly, he climbed onto his sled as the four other boys, including Frank and Ray, did the same. Someone gave Calvin a push, and it was only a matter of seconds before a rival sled met his, sending Calvin flying off the wooden sled and onto a sheet of ice. Calvin tried to scream as his mouth hit the hard surface. Pain flooded his head. Instinctively, Calvin placed his hands over his mouth and ran into the house crying.

"Mrs. Elkan, Calvin got hurt," Ray screamed.

"What in the world's the matter with you?" Nancy asked Calvin with irritation.

"Calvin hit his mouth on the ice," Ray informed Nancy, afraid that Calvin was hardly able to speak for himself.

"Calm down," Nancy warned sternly, "and open your mouth."

Calvin shook his head.

"I said, open your mouth!"

Calvin, his face simultaneously soaked and stinging, did as ordered. Nancy pulled him close to her and clasped his face in her hands.

"Oh my god. You broke your tooth in half," Nancy told Calvin. "Frank, get me a Kleenex!"

Kleenex in hand, Nancy reached her hand into Calvin's mouth.

"What are those pink stringy things hangin' outta your tooth?" she asked.

"No," yelled a horrified Ray, sensing she was going to do something unfathomably stupid.

Nancy, ignoring the son of a liberal, reached in and yanked the pink stringy things out of Calvin's tooth.

Calvin wailed and covered his mouth again, crying out in even more pain than before.

"I know it probably hurts, but you need to shut up. We need to get you to a dentist," she said as she put the pink stringy things into the Kleenex, folded it, and stuck it in her pocket. Calvin muffled sobs all the way to the dentist.

"Look what I pulled out of his mouth," Nancy told the dentist, brandishing her Kleenex. "He had these pink, stringy things hanging out of his broken tooth."

"Ma'am, do you realize what you did?" the shocked dentist exclaimed, taking the Kleenex out of Nancy's hand. "You pulled out his nerves!"

A nurse gently led Calvin to a back room, where he threw up once on the exam chair. Calvin was embarrassed from having thrown up in the chair. The combination of anesthesia and Nancy's impromptu oral surgery sent Calvin's already fragile stomach to a place of no return. The doctor, a clean-cut, good-smelling man, put his warm hand on Calvin's cheek, and said, "I'm sorry this happened, but I want you know that you're one brave ten-year-old kid—a real tiger, in fact."

On the way home, Calvin sat in the back seat, a towel under his swollen chin to catch blood, but his mind was on the dentist's arm, which Calvin had held onto tightly for security. It occurred to Calvin, that while the accident was his own fault, the severed nerves and blood and towel were his mother's gifts. In her ignorance, that was all she could give. It took the arm of a stranger to brace Calvin against her hate. Why does she hate me so much? he asked, trying to catch the blood from his mouth.

19

THE DEVIL'S COBWEB

During one Wednesday night service, Rev. Harry Dushane delivered a sermon that twelve-year-old Calvin would remember long after.

"Tonight I'm going to tell you about the wiles of drugs and rock 'n' roll, folks, and let me tell you straight up—this ain't one of those Sunday picnic testimonies. Rock 'n' roll is the devil's cobweb, one that will ensnare your children! The devil hisself will scuttle to them like that venomous black spider from his cobweb, injecting poisonous drugs into your babies' lives! Now, I know some of you teens here tonight are going start squirming in your seats, but that's all right. I want you to know I ain't pickin' on you. My generation was bad enough, but each generation gets a little bit worse. Because that's how the devil works! He feeds us like helpless babies, a spoonful at a time, introducing new sins into our culture—a little bit at a time, a little bit at a time."

Calvin had heard a previous version of this sermon several years before. It was a shrewdly calculated performance, and much of the sermon was identical, right down to "that venomous black spider from the devil's cobweb." This had been one of Calvin's inspirations for Brother Cobweb, but now that the sermon had escalated into a revival, it was no longer amusing. Calvin felt a growing sense of uneasiness. Even Frank, sitting beside Calvin in the pew, was nervously tapping his foot.

"I'm talking about the devil's poisons," bellowed Rev. Harry. "I know all about them because he was feeding me for years, a little bit at a time—a little bit at a time. I got news for you folks: the devil ain't no dummy!"

Calvin rolled his eyes. No, and neither are you, really, he thought.

"You think so, and you might as well tell them to put a book of matches in your coffin with you, because you're headed straight for hell," continued Rev. Harry. "I first started smoking pot when I was a teen and I thought it ain't going no further than that. I spent all my time smoking pot and listening to music like Little Richard. Years later, I graduated to harder drugs and harder music like The Beatles—what a godless group if ever there was one, a godless group of so-called musicians. You had John Lennon saying he was better than Jesus, Paul singing about the Virgin Mary goddess, and George chanting to the devil at airports. I tell ya though, it didn't just start with The Beatles and oooooohhhh I'm going to step on some toes here! It didn't just start with The Beatles! You can lay the blame right at Elvis Presley's feet! That's right! But, see how he's accepted, now? Elvis gyrating his hips doesn't even lift an eyebrow. That's how the devil does it—a little bit at a time—a little bit at a time Elvis laid down the devil's cobweb of fornication. You can't deny it."

Deny what? Calvin thought as he sketched a rudimentary image of Elvis from the comeback special in his gold jacket, surrounded by '60s girls in beehives and miniskirts as he sang about trouble, took to fighting a big boss man, and belted out a gospel song. Aptly, Calvin fashioned Brother Cobweb as a big boss man, surrounded by Lighthouse thugs in polyester suits. Calvin realized this highly manipulative sermon was an example of how Rev. Harry and the Lighthouse were locked into either-or thinking. Although Calvin didn't count himself an Elvis fan per se, he found a parallel identity of sorts. Like Calvin, Elvis came from a Pentecostal church, albeit a black one in the south. To their status quo communities, both Elvis and Calvin were a threat. There, the similarities ended, but still, apart from Mahalia Jackson, nobody sang gospel like Elvis with his golden baritone. While Elvis was hardly a complex artist, he was more complex than Rev. Harry's caricature of him. Indeed, in his secular music, Elvis had taken what he learned from gospel and filtered it into a new musical language, but Rev. Harry had a kind of conservative laziness in only being comfortable with the music he already knew, despite his claim of having once listened to rock and roll. It was Rev. Harry who was in denial—denial of seeing that he was spewing far more harm than both Elvis and The Beatles combined.

"God minces no words in the Bible about whoring," Rev. Harry continued. "Ezekiel chapter twenty-three paints a picture that ain't pretty, folks: she multiplied her whoredoms, playing the harlot in the land of Egypt. She doted upon those who had members the size of donkeys and who ejaculated like stallions. She recalled the lewdness of her youth—bruising her breasts for the Egyptian youth. The temptations of sex before marriage have never been greater than for this generation, thanks to the likes of rock 'n' roll. It'll weave its spell, turning your daughters into sluts. Don't let your children be sluts for the devil and his music. Be a slut for Jesus, like John the Baptist was a slut for Jesus!"

Oh my god, thought Calvin, wondering if Rev. Harry realized exactly what he was saying. He knows it, Calvin surmised, and he enjoys it, too.

"Convert, sinners!" Rev. Harry continued. "You'll be held accountable on that day of judgment when every knee shall bow and every tongue shall confess that Jesus—that Jesus—that Jesus Christ is Lord! Hallelujah!" Rev. Harry wiped his brow with a soaked rag and took a sip of water before resuming.

"There's some of you here tonight that are going to say, Reverend, my kids listen to rock music, but they wouldn't do that and they don't do drugs. Rock music is harmless. Well, perhaps. What do you mean, Reverend? Perhaps your kids don't do sex and drugs—yet. Perhaps they already do! Don't think, well, my little Tommy or Susie, they're honor roll students. They wouldn't do drugs. Well, I hope you're right, Mom, I really do, but I've seen it happen too many times. I've seen moms and dads come to me because their kid's knocked up or their kid's got VD, wondering how in the world did that happen? These mom and dads are God-fearing parents, but they were blind to the influence of rock 'n' roll music. I've seen moms and dads bawling their eyes out at Tommy or Susie's funeral—dead from an overdose! I'm not pulling any punches, folks. How arrogant are you going to be when one of your kids is laying on the mortuary slab? How you going to feel knowing that your kid's burning in hell? A little bit at a time . . . a little bit at a time. That's how sex, drugs, and rock music suck you in—little bit at a time."

"That nut has the whole church in a frenzy," Calvin told Frank. For once, Frank nodded in agreement.

The next day, the phone rang. It was Ruby Segal from church.

"Almighty Jesus help us," screamed Ruby into Nancy's awaiting ear. "I saw him!"

"Who?" Nancy asked.

"I saw the devil hisself!"

Ruby's vision played out before the eavesdropping Calvin like 35 mm porn.

"I was walking down the hall when I heard that song 'Afternoon Delight' coming out of Faye's bedroom. I opened that door and I swear, I saw the devil coming out of her Holly Hobbie record player in a puff of black smoke! I made like the Holy Ghost at a banquet, ran to the garage, and grabbed my old man's ax! I chopped that Holly Hobbie into a thousand pieces with my daughter crying like a demon deprived of her master! I grabbed that record player and all her forty-five records, took them all to the trash burner, and purged this house. My home is clean now!"

"Did you call Reverend Harry?"

"Sure did! He said to call everyone on the prayer band! You better look through your boys' records, Nancy!"

Calvin ran to his bedroom, but Nancy was hot on his heels, giving him no time to go through his inventory. He need not have bothered. Having inherited Pop's record collection, he owned an extensive opera collection, which Nancy knew nothing about. This left the bulk of Calvin's music collection safe from his mother, who only seized two albums: Jim Croce's *Life and Times* along with Dean Martin's *Greatest Hits*. The Croce record contained the song "Bad, Bad Leroy Brown," which had a cuss word in it.

"Not going have that kind of language in my house because this is God's house, too! If that would be playing when the rapture hits, Jesus would pass this house by! As for Dino, he had half-nekked women singing a Christmas song on TV! That's blasphemy," Nancy growled before making her way to Frank's room.

Damn, she'll find a gold mine there, thought Calvin.

Rummaging through Frank's room, Nancy seized armfuls of REO Speedwagon, Aerosmith, Styx, and Rush. Like a hawk, her eyes missed nothing. In the closet, she dug out a rolled-up poster of Farrah Fawcett in a red bathing suit. Nancy's talons ripped into the nipples on the poster, the helpless prey shredded to pieces. Nancy looked around until she sniffed out the corner of an LP underneath Frank's ottoman.

"Calvin!" yelled Nancy.

Calvin was already standing in the doorway, playing voyeur.

"Help me lift that ottoman," Nancy barked.

Calvin did as she asked. To Nancy's wondering eyes did appear KISS's *Alive!* and *Hotter Than Hell*.

"Oh, Jesus have mercy," Nancy wailed.

She swooped into the kitchen, placing a telephone call to relay every detail to Rev. Harry, who told her to round up the entire scandalous collection and bring it to church on Sunday.

Later that evening, Frank walked into the house after a game of football. Calvin shot his little brother a look and silently warned him, mouthing the words "Brother Cobweb." Seeing his stack of records scattered across the kitchen table, Frank gulped. He was in deep, despite having been careful. Jealous of Ray, whose mom had allowed KISS records, Frank handed his allowance money over to Calvin's best friend to buy them for him. He had even kept the records at Ray's house for a time, but his lust for "Rock and Roll All Nite" had gotten the better of him. Throwing caution to the wind, Frank finally retrieved his vinyl treasures, although he hadn't even been able to listen to them. He was comforted merely by having them in his room, and now Calvin's Brother Cobweb was demanding his bounty.

"Oh my god," Frank whispered to Calvin, "What you said last night—you prophesied this!"

Calvin rolled his eyes. "No. It's just predictable."

Upon seeing Frank, Nancy walked over to Frank and slapped him across the face. Although his head snapped back from the impact, he did not cry out. This angered Nancy even more and prompted her to slap Frank a second time.

"Hit me again," he said defiantly.

Nancy grabbed a handful of Frank's hair, locked his reddened face in place, and slapped him a third time.

"Hit me again," Frank said, somewhere between laughing and crying.

Nancy arched back, transforming her open hand into a fist.

Calvin grabbed his mother by the wrist, stopping her. For a suspended moment, the two stared each other down until Nancy blinked and wrested herself from Calvin's grasp.

Nancy's response, after recovering from the brief shock, was a howling lamentation. She ran for her bedroom, flopped down on her bed, and revisited the role of a beached wailing sea beast. Her dog, which Nancy kept in her bedroom, joined in her tantrum, whining and yelping along with her.

Frank, for his part, was so shocked that Calvin had stood up to their mother that he was numb to everything else.

"Wait till your father gets home," Nancy bellowed from her bedroom.

Calvin tried to keep from laughing. Wait till your Father gets, wait till your Father gets, wait till your Father gets home! Calvin thought, recalling the TV show theme. God, I hate that song.

Nancy met Dale at the door. Calvin only heard part of the discourse, which ended with "Be a man for once" as Nancy handed him a belt.

"All right, Nancy," Dale said angrily.

Dale had never disciplined Calvin or Frank and now it sounded like . . .

"Frank," Dale yelled as he walked down the hall, heading toward Frank's room.

Frank? Why didn't he say my name, too? I'm not getting in trouble? Calvin wondered

Calvin darted into Frank's room. Frank, sitting on the edge of the ottoman, looked fearful.

"Shh," Calvin said as he hid in Frank's closet.

Calvin was afraid that Frank was about to get the beating of his life. Without a word, Dale, belt in hand, entered Frank's room, closed the door, and pulled an onion out of his pocket.

"Sit down on that thing," Dale said to Frank in a whisper, pointing at the ottoman. Dale handed Frank the onion, brandished the belt, and sat across from Frank on the adjoining chair.

"When I hit it with this belt, I want you to cry out like I'm spanking you. Take a few bites of that onion, too. You've got to have some tears in your eyes to make it look real."

Dale and Frank went through the charade as Calvin voyeuristically watched from a safe distance behind a closet door. Nancy, listening from another room, smiled with pride that her husband was finally being the father of righteous parenting that she wanted him to be—at least with Frank.

Sunday evening at the Lighthouse, everyone met in the back of the church parking lot. A mountain of LPs, forty-five records, 8-track tapes, and tape cassettes were thrown to the ground in a great sacrifice to the beast Jehovah. Lighthouse teens fought back tears, and a few held hands. Of the older teens, only Luke stood apart, glassy-eyed. In contrast, Lighthouse parents watched, convinced that the Holy Ghost was in charge as Rev. Harry brought God's torch down on modern pop music. Jehovah rumbled, its red eyes glowing as it opened a great jaw, swallowing sacrificial smoke. The flames darted skyward, like Babylonians climbing that fateful tower.

Calvin could not bring himself to join in the collective mourning. Instead, he envisioned Arkimnel beside him, whispering a biting, "Amen, Brother Cobweb," into his ear.

"Amen, Brother Cobweb, amen!" he whispered in response, which Frank heard.

"Amen, Brother Cobweb," whispered Frank in return.

20
PENTECOSTAL BOOT CAMP

At thirteen, Calvin was old enough to be sent to the monthlong summer church camp, or Pentecostal boot camp, as some called it. On the plus side, it would get him away from home and his mother's abusive behavior. On the larger negative side, however, it would eat up thirty days of summer vacation. Two weeks had already been shot to hell with a week of Vacation Bible School, followed by a week of revival, and the summer would end with yet another week of revival. Apart from those special events, Calvin's normal week consisted of Sunday school, followed by morning service. With luck, he would get out around noon, but an hour or so of overcooked steaks and heavily buttered baked potatoes at the steakhouse afterward hardly made sermons sit well in the stomach. Hourlong 5:30 p.m. youth services were succeeded by agonizingly long Sunday night services, which obliterated a potential day of rest. Monday and Tuesday were the only certain breaks during ordinary time. Wednesday night service was mercifully brief during the school year, but the summer version of that service was akin to do-it-yourself root canals. Thursday through Saturday was a charismatic crapshoot—often the days were filled with activity services to keep teens preoccupied and away from trouble.

When it came time for the camp, Calvin stepped up into the Lighthouse bus that was taking them to Pentecostal boot camp, hearing Nancy's last words to him—"I'll be praying for you to get the Holy Ghost"—reverberating in his mind.

An hour into the drive, Luke, sitting next to Rev. Harry in the front camp counselors' rows, observed that his father frequently looked back at Calvin Elkan, who was sitting at the back of the bus and looking forlornly out the window. Luke discerned a heightened sense of agitation, or perhaps growing anxiety, in his father toward the artistic Elkan boy. He knew that, on occasion, his father had grumbled about Calvin's behavior in Sunday school class. His father was always vague about whatever it was that Calvin said in class that had proven to be such a disruption. Luke imagined Calvin somehow challenged his father's interpretation of some scriptural passage, because he had heard his father question aloud, "Why does Calvin bother to read the Bible, if he doesn't even believe in it?" Of course, Luke was also aware that Calvin challenging his Sunday school teacher didn't necessarily mean he was an unbeliever. Rather, it was more likely that Calvin interpreted the passage differently than his father—which, of course, his father, who thought entirely in an either-or mentality, would only equate with disbelief. Even if Calvin didn't believe entirely, Luke thought that perhaps Calvin read the Bible to find artistic inspiration or to defend himself against the strong-willed Nancy. Luke did sometimes envy the fact that Calvin had the courage to challenge his father, which was something Luke himself couldn't do. However, Luke didn't envy Calvin having Nancy for a mother. From what little he had seen and heard of Nancy over the years, Luke felt blessed in having Vernell for a mother instead.

Two and a half hours later, Calvin stepped off the bus, his large backpack and suitcase weighing him down. He stepped into the Kentucky campground, imagining himself in the skin of a leather-clad 1968 comeback Elvis who desperately sought to find his own vitality in a culture that had long been alien to him. If you're looking for trouble, you've come to the right place, thought Calvin, humming Elvis's song as he was hustled into the Church of God Youth Camp hall.

Rev. Harry and Luke walked up to the stage and stood next to the camp's director, who handed the microphone off to Rev. Harry.

"Welcome to the Church of God Youth Camp. I'm Reverend Harry Dushane, your counselor, and I'm going to open with a declaration of faith. We believe in the Bible as the literal, infallible Word of God. We believe Jesus is the only begotten Son of the Father. That he was crucified, died, raised from the dead, and ascended to heaven, and today he is at the right hand of the Father. We believe salvation comes from accepting Jesus as your Lord and personal Savior. We believe in water baptism by immersion in Jesus's name. We believe that evidence of salvation and baptism comes from speaking in tongues. We believe in the second coming of Jesus and the rapture of all saved souls into heaven. We believe in the resurrection of the body, that heaven is for the saved, and that eternal hell awaits the unsaved. Now, I'll lead you in a prayer."

Calvin groaned internally. Feeling as if he were in survival mode, Calvin already was actively plotting how to get out of the mandatory camp activities.

Church camp was as ill a fit as Calvin had imagined, and he managed to get out of most daytime activities, remaining alone in his cabin to work on *The Brother Cobweb Chronicles*. Luke had surprisingly allowed Calvin to do so, but not even the preacher's son could grant a get-out-of-jail-free pass from nighttime services that were followed by the mandatory nightly Christian campfire.

After a tedious sermon, Calvin sat a few feet back from rest of the kids roasting marshmallows, trying not to absorb their mind-numbing conversation.

"Hey, let's see who can come up with the best words to replace four-letter-words. What do you call those?" Darryl asked.

"Euphemisms?" someone suggested.

"Yeah. You know, those words that don't break the commandment and you can't go to hell for."

"Shouldn't say those either," piped in one lone protester.

"What are you? Some wussy Jehovah's Witness?"

"Yeah, shut up!"

"We ready?"

"Yeah," said faceless voices in unison.

Calvin rolled his eyes and thought about how to convert this scene into a drawing in *Brother Cobweb* with everyone's faces bathed in the red glow of the campfire.

"OK, I'll lead and start off with gosh darn," said Dwight.

"That's lame. Shut the front door," said Timmy, laughing at his own joke.

"Son of a biscuit."

"Bejeezers," a girl sheepishly offered.

"Son of a motherless goat," a boy bravely proposed.

"Fart knocker."

"Shut your piehole."

"Kiss my grits."

"Jeepers creepers."

"You got any, Calvin?" asked a faceless voice.

"No, you guys are too radical for me," said Calvin sarcastically.

"Yeah?" Dwight asked with pride.

"Yeah, you guys are just too goddamned radical," Calvin added, making sure the point was not missed.

Luke dismissed the report of Calvin's language at the campfire and promised to reprimand him the next day. He did not intend to address the matter at all, but talking with Calvin one-on-one was high on the next day's priorities. As he lay down in his bunk, Luke found himself ruminating on the mystery of Calvin Elkan. Inexplicably, thoughts on Calvin intertwined with memories from his own past.

His dad had been out on a hunting trip when Luke, thinking he was home alone, pulled Stacey White's eight-by-ten senior school picture out of its hiding spot in his King James Bible. Carefully, he placed her photograph on his desk, propping it up against a small lamp. Stacey had given Luke the picture, along with her phone number scrawled on the back. She had liked Luke for years, and the feeling was mutual. Despite this, they never dated. Luke sensed that she harbored a dislike for his dad, which perhaps was the reason that she had repeatedly turned down his date requests. Or perhaps going to the same school and church made Stacey feel that Luke was more like kin than someone she could be romantically attached to. Yet recently, as the two were nearing graduation, Stacey seemed to have a change of heart. Looking intensely into Stacey's face, he was moved by her beauty and innocence. Aroused, Luke unzipped his jeans.

"Luke, I need help with this deer," announced Harry as he flung Luke's bedroom door open. Harry stared at his son in raging disbelief as he caught him in the act. Luke struggled to quickly zip up his jeans.

"You disgusting faggot!" Harry screamed as he seized Luke by the arm and yanked him out into the hall.

Luke did not put up a fight, allowing his dad to drag him out the back door into the snow. A trail of blood led from Harry's truck to the back porch where a slain buck lay belly up. Harry pushed Luke down on his knees, grabbing a fistful of his hair.

"Dad!" yelled Luke, crying out for mercy.

Harry shoved Luke's head down into the open gut of deer carcass. "Eat, faggot!"

Luke's face hit flesh, blood, and bone. "Stop, Dad!" Luke choked.

Harry pushed harder. "EAT!"

Strings of bloodied, raw flesh came back up as Luke vomited. Collapsing on his side, Luke curled up in a futile attempt to protect himself as his father kicked him repeatedly. As the phone rang inside the house, Harry left his sobbing son alone in the bloodstained snow.

Luke rolled over in his camp bunk, trying to erase that memory, and suddenly wondered what he and Calvin Elkan might have in common.

After arriving in camp, Calvin had heard the rumor about an incident several years before that involved Rev. Harry, Luke, and a deer carcass. Apparently, Luke had told a few friends about it, and the story had become a camp legend. Lying wide-awake in his bunk, Calvin sketched out a comic strip-like hallucination:

Christ as a young woman, dressed in a revealing black mini dress, looked up from a slaughterhouse basement. Beaten down by pathos, she looked up at the hanging pig cadavers surrounding her in a St. John of the Cross-like darkness. *Christ Casting the Demons into the Swine*, Calvin titled it. Dissatisfied with what he drew, Calvin shoved the drawing into the pocket of his pants lying on the floor, next to his bed.

"I'm glad I found you alone," said Luke upon entering Calvin's cabin the next day.

Calvin looked up at Luke, annoyed at the interruption and a little concerned that Luke was there to chastise him about his language at the campfire. Calvin closed *The Brother Cobweb Chronicles* and shot out a ready-made defense for failing to join his peers in various activities: "My comrades all snuck out to spy on the girls swimming." Calvin had no qualms about ratting out fellow campers whom he didn't like anyway. The defense also gave the impression that he was a better Christian boy than his peers, or better in the sense that he was above spying on ladies in one-piece bathing suits. Actually,

Calvin didn't give a thought or judgment about his peers' voyeurism. He simply wasn't interested.

Luke laughed. "Do you mind showing me something from your sketchbook?" Luke asked. "I've been curious for a long time, and you promised me once . . ."

Calvin thought about it for a moment and, risking that Luke might be a kindred spirit, pulled out a drawing of his fictional evangelist.

"Is that why you actually came here? To see my drawings?"

"Yeah, for the most part."

"Then, I'll show you Brother Cobweb," said Calvin as he handed over the drawing.

"That's hilarious!" Luke exclaimed. "Or disturbing. I'm not sure which."

"Good, because it should be both."

"He's like a mixed-up vision of all the bad evangelists we've had," Luke observed.

"Amen, Brother Cobweb," Calvin joked.

"It's not going to be like that forever. My dad's going to leave me the church when he retires."

"Do you want it?"

"I'm his son."

"Do you want it though?"

"I can change things. I have to take it."

"No, you don't."

"You don't understand."

"Don't become Brother Cobweb," said Calvin, only half-joking. "By the way, you said for the most part . . ."

"For the most part?" Luke asked, having already forgotten.

"About why you came here?"

"Well, I heard about your language at the campfire and just want to let you know I'll do my best to keep it from my dad."

"Thanks."

"And I just felt like I need to get to know you a little better."

"Why?"

"I don't know. We've lived next door to each other for years and go to the same church. Maybe it's time."

"That sounds a little vague," Calvin laughed.

"I don't know why fully. Not everything has to make sense, Calvin."

Calvin laughed. "Pop said the same thing once. Just remember that when and if you take over the Lighthouse."

Luke promised to do so and left, but Calvin was skeptical that Luke would keep the promise. He also wondered the real reason behind Luke's visit. It wasn't to see his drawings. Although Luke had indeed asked once, that was a long time ago, and this was the first time he had asked since then. Besides, Luke didn't exactly strike Calvin as being particularly interested in art. Nor was it about the campfire curse. Finally, Calvin decided to take Luke at his word of not fully knowing the reason for the visit.

Oddly, as soon as Luke seemed to have opened a door of communication, he just as quickly closed it. Calvin heard nothing more directly from Luke for the remainder of the camp. But Luke did make it known to the other camp counselors that Calvin could opt out of most activities in order to work on his drawings. Calvin even got out of the final Boy Meets Girl night. The idea of chaperoned dating was unpleasant enough, but chaperoned dating with a Pentecostal girl would have been unbearable for Calvin. On the bus trip back, Calvin eavesdropped on Lighthouse gossip—word was that Luke had found a serious girlfriend at camp. Now, he knew why Luke hadn't talked to him more. Calvin hoped this would be good for Luke because he did feel a degree of sympathy for one who was often portrayed and dismissed as the typical two-dimensional preacher's kid. While Luke wasn't terribly deep, he seemed to have quite the heart. Of course, that also had a considerable drawback: Luke was unable to stand up to Rev. Harry, and Calvin hoped—and even prayed—that the deer story wasn't true at all.

When Calvin walked back into his house after the long bus trip back, he immediately retreated to his bedroom and began unpacking his bag. When his mother walked in and grabbed him to hug him tight, he recoiled. Nancy had never hugged him before, and Calvin wondered what her motive was.

"Did you get the Holy Ghost at camp?" Nancy asked him. "I've been praying all month that you'd get the Holy Ghost. Did you speak in tongues?"

Like clockwork, Calvin thought. She's so phony.

"No, but I got a lot of drawings finished," Calvin answered, knowing it would provoke her. It did, and she left within minutes to retreat to the living room to put on a record of Elvis's gospel music.

Calvin suddenly realized—and found it amusing—that his mother had failed to sacrifice her Elvis record in Rev. Harry's infamous rock and roll bonfire purge. With that and the manipulative hug, her hypocrisy was complete. While Calvin was still concerned about Luke and that deer story, he also knew that he had his own immediate worries regarding a mother he didn't like and was indeed fearful of, along with a largely AWOL father, and a month of church camp hadn't changed that.

21
WEDNESDAY NIGHT TESTIMONY

"I wanna give a testimony tonight," said Nancy as she rose from her pew. Calvin, sitting next to Luke a few pews in front of his mother, rolled his eyes, but continued drawing.

"My son Calvin just turned fourteen, and it's only by the grace of God he's even here with us tonight."

Not the spinal meningitis story, thought Calvin.

"Tell us, sister," a voice beckoned.

As Nancy droned on about her son's childhood illness, Calvin whispered to Luke, "Mom's getting better at this all the time, even down to the dramatic 'amen, amen' at the end of each sentence."

Unfortunately, there would be no escape under the pew or into the aisle. Nancy's rendition amounted to a histrionic spinal tap rehash, climaxing with a vision of Jesus swooping down like Superman, saving Calvin from a cliffhanger of a death. Rev. Harry leaned into the microphone. "There won't be a sermon tonight, folks. The Holy Ghost has taken over the service!"

"Amen," murmured the congregation.

"Kilvin, would you get up right now please and come to the altar?"

Shit! Shit! Shit! Calvin thought as he looked to Luke for help, but the preacher's son proved powerless against his father.

Calvin walked up the Lighthouse aisle, mantling two millennia of martyrs.

"I want everyone here to get out of those pews, come to the altar, lay hands on Kilvin, and thank Gawd for the bona fide miracle of this boy's life," Rev. Harry said as he turned Calvin around to face the congregation. "I want you to put your blessings on him because the Lord didn't spare Kilvin for no reason. God wants something out of this boy, and our blessing may help Kilvin find what that is and guide him down the path of righteousness."

Rev. Harry motioned the guitarists to play something soft as he narrated.

"God's Word tells us of two roads ahead. The first road is a broad road that's easy to travel, but I tell ya folks, it's a temptation leading to everlasting destruction. The second road is narrow: a hard journey filled with thorns, glass, rock, and every hardship. The devil tells us no one in their right mind would travel that second road, but it's this road that leads to streets of gold!"

I'm going to be sick, thought Calvin.

Luke and his girlfriend were the first in line to lay hands on Calvin. Gently, they placed their hands on his forehead, said a silent blessing, and walked back to their pews holding hands.

Rev. Harry was third in line. He reached his hand up and brought it crashing down on Calvin's head. Calvin's head jerked back from the impact. Inspired, Rev. Harry leapt over the altar and ran out the church, leaving in his wake a Holy Ghost domino tumble. The next person in line was Ruby, who smacked Calvin with equal force in the same spot. Calvin's brow was already reddened and sweaty when Ruby was overcome with slain-in-the-spirit, speaking-in-tongues spasms.

"Osmekarakodilkemojab! Oshromoleepodeepokrakmo," Ruby broke past a still-reeling Calvin, her entire body jerking as if controlled by a puppeteer from above. Flip-flopping around the other side of the altar, Ruby promptly lost her shoes.

The next person in line was Nancy, who followed Ruby's lead. Calvin braced in preparation and flinched in time to avoid a direct blow but caught an elbow to the jaw. Off Nancy went flopping. The next person in line was a pruned geezer of a man who looked to be 150 years old, which did not stop him from delivering a hard thud to Calvin's awaiting forehead. The geezer exited stage left, passing the Holy Ghost torch to the next parishioner.

The line was momentarily interrupted when Rev. Harry reemerged, screaming, "I did seven laps for Jesus!" Drenched in sweat, Rev. Harry looked like he had indeed done seven laps around the church. He bolted for the altar but ran past Calvin's point of view. Just when Calvin began to wonder where his Sunday school teacher had been raptured off to, the preacher grabbed Calvin's arms from behind and flung them up in the air with unusual strength.

"He is your king! He is your king!" Rev. Harry screeched in Calvin's ear.

That goddamned Luke abandoned me, thought Calvin as he looked around, searching for one sane person to put an end to the barrage of assaults.

As the hour passed, Calvin stood hostage at the altar, his head throbbing while parishioners writhed and chanted on the floor around him. Ruby somehow scooted herself over to an uncarpeted area. While on her back, she was caught up in a Holy Ghost temper tantrum and managed to crack her head open mid-spasm. Within minutes, boxes of tissues and damp rags soaked up and cleaned the Holy Ghost blood trail as Ruby's husband whisked her out the side door. It only served to amp up an electrified holy atmosphere.

God, they ARE efficient—even while speaking in tongues, thought Calvin in-between heavenly migraines. Slowly, but none too mercifully, the Lighthouse began to dim, and the congregation dispersed. Calvin looked back in numb disbelief to see Ruby's husband looking under the pews for her missing shoes.

"What in the Sam Hill happened to you?!" Dale asked when Calvin walked through the door after the service. "Your head's all red!"

After Nancy went to bed, Calvin finally felt safe enough to explain the Wednesday night testimonial nightmare to his dad. As expected, Dale offered no consolation and even laughed at the story.

Frustrated, Calvin retreated to his bedroom and put on a LP of Gustav Mahler's Symphony no. 2, dubbed the Resurrection Symphony, as conducted by Leopold Stokowski. He already had one record of the Mahler Second—a rolling thunder-like version by Lenny—but was curious to hear a different interpretation, so he had bought the Stokowski version, whom he knew as the conductor from *Fantasia*. Unlike most conductors who got their start as pianists, Stokowski began as an organist, which gave his style an enhanced sense of vibrant color. Indeed, this Resurrection was saturated with color and less overtly dramatic than Lenny's.

As Calvin read the liner notes, which focused on Mahler himself and his body of work over nine symphonies, it seemed that Mahler was asking the same question that Gauguin asked in his paintings: "Where do we come from? What are we? Where are we going?" Calvin realized that his long-held attraction to Gauguin—over every other painter he had been exposed to—was due, in part, to that question. Gauguin approached the answer through a journey of color. Mahler's approach, as interpreted by Stokowski, seemed similar to Calvin. Why is it that I am far more spiritually fulfilled through Gauguin and Mahler than I ever have been opening the Bible or going to an iconoclastic church? Or living in this house with Mom, Dad, and Frank? Calvin asked himself. As he listened to the Stokowski performance, Calvin sensed that this was what he needed for himself: a cool-tone, detached resurrection from the monochromatic, simpleminded religious melodrama which had now literally pounded itself into his head.

22

A LONG WAY FROM GALAPAGOS

"**Y**ou would have wound up going to school with coloreds, thanks to that judge and his busing," Dale offered as his explanation for selling the Elkans' house and moving the family out of Wilmington to Sabina. As they pulled up to their new house, Calvin stepped out of the family's Oldsmobile Delta 88 and into a pile of cow shit.

"We've just gone back a thousand years in evolution," mumbled Calvin, trying to shake the shit off his shoes.

"It'll wipe off," laughed Dale, "and you won't even notice the smell after a while. Gotta have that for fertilizer if we want grass to come next spring."

Indeed, the yard was an acre of mud and shit without a single blade of grass in sight. Nancy was not happy about the move, either. Worse, she was still mourning the recent loss of her Pekingese dog, which she'd had for four years before Dale decided to sell it to a coworker without consulting his wife.

"First, you make me give up Shannon, then my dog, then my house," grumbled Nancy as she walked into their new home.

Who is Shannon? Calvin wondered, but knew better than to ask aloud; his parents preferred closet skeletons to remain intact. That was a question he would reserve for Blanche, the next time he saw her. Still, for once, Calvin partly sympathized with his mother, although he was glad the annoying, yappy dog was gone. For him, the move meant he had to say goodbye to Ray and Kennedy, and he wasn't sure what he would do without his friends and a place to go when home life proved to be too much. Nancy continued to mutter under her breath as she paced around the new living room. Dale, exasperated, stopped after his fourth trip from the truck.

"You gonna bitch all day or help get this stuff moved in? We need to be fixing dinner in a bit and—"

"Order a damn pizza!" snapped Nancy before proceeding to her new bedroom to christen it with tears and flailing limbs.

"Get into some boots so we can unload the rest of the car," Dale told Calvin and Frank. "Make sure you grab the phone in the Delta. I already got service turned on. Just need to plug it in so we can call in a pizza."

That night, Dale, Frank, and Calvin sat on the carpeted living room floor as they ate pizza. Incessantly daydreaming, Calvin picked chips of white paint from the carpet, which were the result of Dale having been too passionate in stuccoing the ceiling. Simultaneously, Calvin picked the pork toppings off his pizza, much to Dale's annoyance. Calvin reflected on a recent sermon he heard, which was one of the few interesting ones:

"What was Christ thinking about as he wrote in the sand when religious leaders brought him a woman caught in the act of adultery?" the visiting evangelist had asked. Calvin checked in the Bible when he got home. Indeed, the Gospel did not indicate what Christ wrote in the earth. Nor, as the evangelist made sure to point out, did it say anything about the man she committed the act with. "Perhaps Christ didn't actually write anything. Perhaps he was just doodling, bored with their hypocrisy, judgments, and idiocy," the evangelist concluded in a sermon that actually went beyond two-dimensional interpretation.

Perhaps he was just doodling—something like me picking paint out of the carpet or pork off a pizza, Calvin laughed to himself. Hell, being Jewish, Jesus would have picked the pork off, too. Plus, he drove those pigs into the lake and drowned them. He obviously preferred figs over pigs. Why else would he curse a tree for not bearing figs? He must have been damned hungry to throw a divine temper tantrum like that. Those are such weird stories; it's no wonder they hardly ever read them in church.

"Earth to Calvin," Dale said, raising his voice. "You know I promised you if you'd start eating meat, I'd get you a collie."

"Mom said you'd get me one anyway, but that was a long time ago. Still don't have one, but Frank's got Hutch," Calvin said, sulking, still jealous of his brother's new beagle.

"Yeah and she never followed up on it, neither. Start eating meat, and I'll get you one."

"Bring one home, and I'll eat meat then—not until."

"Alrighty, I expect you to keep your word. Now, have you boys ever seen shag carpet this thick?" Dale bragged. "Two inches thick. I'll bet you ain't never seen shag this thick. You like it?"

Calvin rolled his eyes and turned his attention to the deer head hanging on the brick fireplace wall. It was staring at him. A few inches below the decapitated buck, its hooves reached out, forced to hold the rifle that slaughtered it.

"It's dead. It ain't watching you," laughed Dale, following his son's eyes. "I bagged that ten-pointer. That taxidermist was downright jealous."

"Of what?"

"You're all bleeding heart. You don't go hunting, so you ain't gonna get it. Hunting a buck like this puts me at one with nature and God."

"That's so Saint Francis of you."

"Who's that?"

Calvin shook his head and sighed. At least Dale was consistent in religious ignorance being bliss. Dale not knowing about St. Francis was almost as amusing as when he asked Blanche what a mass was.

"I don't kill for sport. I always eat my meat," Dale protested.

"If you don't do it for sport, then why is its head on the wall?"

"You just don't get it." Dale took a swing of Pabst.

"Whatever, but I think bringing the table and chairs in first should have been more of a priority than hanging a dead head on the wall. At least then we wouldn't be eating dinner on the floor."

In the laundry room the next day, Nancy was still mulling over her first day in Sabina and the news that Dale was getting Calvin a collie in exchange for becoming a carnivore. Damn, Dale got rid of *my* dog. Now he's gettin' Calvin one. And that weak-willed Calvin's cavin' into his dad to boot, Nancy fumed. Reaching down into the hamper, she pulled out a pair of Calvin's pants. As Nancy started to throw it into the washer, she noticed a crumpled piece of paper sticking out of the pocket. Nancy unfolded it to discover her son's sketch of a female *Christ Casting the Demons into the Swine*.

Sitting shirtless on the edge of his bed as he sketched, Calvin looked up to see Nancy standing at his bedroom doorway in broad daylight. She was breathing heavily, and her eyes were black with fury as she held up the crumpled drawing mere inches from his eyes. Sensing she expected a defense, Calvin was determined to disappoint.

"You filthy demon!" Nancy hissed as she lurched forward and dug her long fingernails into Calvin's wrists.

As Calvin tried to break free, his skin tore beneath her nails.

Nancy's fist landed on Calvin's jaw as her other hand grabbed a handful of his hair, yanking out a strand. He attempted to kick his mother off his bed, but fell off the mattress, landing on his knees. Nancy grabbed the only weapon she could find, a wooden canvas stretcher frame leaning against the wall. Nancy swung the wood into Calvin's back repeatedly. Trying to rise, Calvin was hit in the ribs and face before he was finally able to secure the weapon from Nancy.

"Get out of my room!" Calvin yelled.

Taken aback by her son's defiant stance, Nancy stormed out. Out of breath, Calvin pushed his bed against the door, locked it, and slumped to the floor. Only when he heard Nancy storm out of the house and slam her car door did Calvin emerge from his room to shower.

As he stepped into the shower, he looked up at the bathroom ceiling with a washrag in hand. Wrapping the cloth around his palm, Calvin, still inflamed with pain, washed himself, almost blindly, refusing to look at his own body, excessively reddened with scratches and purpled bruises. Overwhelmed by a sense of smallness, Calvin made a point to glance away while in front of the mirror. A knock on the bathroom door shook Calvin to awareness.

"Hurry it up with the water. Don't forget we got well water here—it'll run low," yelled Dale.

Jesus God, thought Calvin as he bandaged up one of the deeper scratches on his wrist.

Still seething with anger and shame from the wounds his mother inflicted, Calvin went to school the next day, irritable and wearing long sleeves to cover the marks on his body. His new East Clinton art teacher approached him on the first day of class as the students painted a still life of an apple.

"That's not too bad," said Mr. Grover upon seeing Calvin's painting, "but you can see the brush strokes."

"So?" Calvin asked sarcastically. Although his work was more illustrational than painterly, he was slowly but surely transitioning into an enjoyment of paint, which he felt Mr. Grover was too obtuse to see.

"You're not supposed to see the brush strokes," Mr. Grover explained.

"You can see Van Gogh's brush strokes," Calvin protested.

"Van Gogh sucks. You can't see Warhol's brush strokes on his *Marilyn Monroe* painting."

"That's because the *Marilyn Monroe* image is a silk screen," Calvin shot back. "You're an art teacher—shouldn't you know that?" Calvin's boldness surprised even him, and he immediately knew he'd be in trouble.

"Alright, smartass, march yourself down to the office," Mr. Grover whispered before standing over another student's shoulder.

Embarrassed, Calvin awaited punishment in a sterile waiting room in the school office. He got off light with a single detention and a warning from Miss Vinkemulder, who sat next to the vice principal for Calvin's sentencing.

"Perhaps you should watch what you say if you want to make this school easier for yourself," she said.

Calvin, who normally loved art class, was relieved that it was time for history class after making a wretched first impression with Mr. Grover. However, Mr. Zucco, who was clearly past the point of retirement, rendered history hopelessly dull. The lethargic teacher gave the class a reading assignment and instructions to spend the rest of their first day studying while he sat half-asleep at his desk.

Calvin took the opportunity to sketch, putting his reading off for the evening. Soon, he became aware that a round-faced redheaded boy next to him was intensely observing his artistic endeavor. Sizing up the competition, the boy pulled out his own sketchpad and began penciling. After finishing, he handed his drawing to Calvin, which was a competently skilled likeness of President John F. Kennedy. Under the drawing, Calvin noticed a phone number and the name Jedediah Perry.

Unable to concentrate on flying softballs in gym, Calvin missed the one coming at him and lost the game for his team, which earned him additional communal dislike. He had already erred by voicing his dislike of Frank's favorite band, KISS. That had almost resulted in an ass whuppin' by a small band of Sabina boys who immediately branded Calvin as "that weird pussy."

Just before gym class started, Calvin had learned that boys must shower together after class. The sons of the town's radical right-wing rednecks (who were merely a secular extension of Lighthouse parishioners) would surely see the evidence of Calvin having been beaten once he stripped and showered with them. They would ask questions. While it would be humiliating enough for someone like Luke, for instance, to be outed as daddy's punching bag, Calvin would be an even greater pussy for allowing his *mother* to beat him.

Calvin recalled a sermon from Rev. Harry on Proverbs 23 that justified taking a rod to a child in order to deliver his soul from hell and Psalms 137, which went even further in its advice to dash unruly children against the rocks. Predictably, Rev. Harry took these lines literally, although it unwittingly exposed the hypocrisy of Christian fundamentalism. The preacher would resort to the tried-and-true defense of "that's Old Testament—Jesus changed all that" when it forbade things like eating shellfish or premarital sex. Yet, they just as quickly utilized the Old Testament to validate beating children or oppressing homosexuals.

While Calvin pooh-poohed much of Rev. Harry's nonsense, his sermon resonated psychologically—not because Calvin subscribed to Rev. Harry's sawdust theology, but rather because as he was apt to do, Calvin, fancying himself a biblical Sherlock Holmes, skeptically researched and pieced together how these passages might have both informed and driven Nancy. Even if his mother would never admit it, the meningitis seemed to only verify her son's imperfection. Calvin was weak, like Dale, or like a girl, and she took to the rod of purification in order to save his effeminate soul from hell. Although Calvin—unlike Frank—received good grades, was studious, and was a bit of a hermit, staying at home and out of trouble, he was well-read and a threat to her brand of patristic ignorance. Or so it seemed—ultimately, Calvin was aware that educated guesswork was just that. He would never really know why she abused him.

Calvin didn't shower after gym that day, using the excuse that he hadn't known to bring a towel with him.

On Friday, when it came time to shower after gym class, Calvin pulled a large beach towel out of his gym bag and meticulously wrapped it around his torso before removing his clothes. Cautiously, he tied it into a sturdy knot to make sure it would not loosen. Calvin could feel the stares and hear the gossipy whispers as he walked into the shower with his towel still on.

Calvin sat on the bench in the locker room, his dripping towel still secured and eyes cast down on his soaked feet, as he waited until the other boys left before he got dressed. Alone, he put his pants on and unrolled his socks as the bell rang. Late to the next class, Calvin's bag already began smelling like Pop's mildew with his wet towel stuffed in it. Calvin collected himself and walked to the nurse's office to secure a late pass.

When Calvin came home from school, Dale and a beautiful collie welcomed him. Calvin chose to name the dog Starsky to go with Frank's beagle, Hutch.

"He can stay outside or in the garage, but he ain't to be in the house," Nancy grumbled.

"Gotcha a quarter pounder with cheese to go with that dog," Dale laughed, digging into the fast-food bag.

Calvin took a bite of the burger, swallowed, and waited for the inevitable unpleasant reaction in his gut. Pleased, Dale walked off, which gave Calvin the opportunity to give Starsky the remainder of the sandwich.

Later that evening, after putting Starsky to bed in the garage, Calvin called Jed from history class. The two talked into the morning, sharing interests and thoughts about their place in the world. Still missing Ray, Calvin chose to connect with Jed, but apart from a shared dream of escaping family and Sabina, they had little in common. Despite that, Calvin sensed an inexplicable connection of sorts between them.

23

JIMMY JIM

February rolled into March, and with March came Calvin's sixteenth birthday, so he was finally able to drive. His first solo trip was borrowing Dale's car to pick up Jed. After hearing about Calvin's mother over the last few weeks, Jed insisted upon meeting her, without giving a reason for wanting to do so. Curious, Calvin agreed.

"Where you boys going?" Jed's father, Jakob, asked on their way out the door.

"Boy? You must have caught me in the water when it was cold. I ain't no goddamn boy," Jed bellowed.

"Whatever. And why the hell you dressed like that?" Jakob asked, noticing that Jed was decked out in a three-piece suit.

"Yeah, why *are* you dressed like that?" Calvin added.

147

"Gonna meet your mom today," Jed said, smiling broadly as he stood and grabbed a large paper sack lying next to the living room desk.

"I'm not even going to ask," said Calvin.

"Good. Don't," smirked Jed. "Hold on, gotta grab something out of the kitchen."

While Jed was in the kitchen, Jakob opened a closet door. "Lemme show ya something," he said to Calvin, motioning him to come closer. "You ever seen one of these?" he asked as he pulled a gun from the closet. "Used that in Korea. See those notches? Know what they're for?"

Calvin shrugged, even though he guessed the explanation that Jakob was going to give.

"A notch for every gook I took out. Wasn't like *M*A*S*H* for Chrissake. Jed says your mom's a Sunday school teacher?"

Calvin muttered an unenthusiastic agreement.

"I used to be a Baptist preacher, but I gave it up for truck driving."

"And whiskey," said Jed with an air of jokiness as he returned from the kitchen with another paper sack, which clearly contained two bottles of something.

"What are you up to?" Jakob asked, looking at the sack. "Don't you be worrying about that poison men call 'whiskey.' Look what it did to me—well, you remember. Don't make the same mistakes I did."

"I remember your boot in my face," laughed Jed. Calvin winced.

"Yeah, well we ain't talking about that no more, because I was a terrible backslider, but I got right with the Lord again. You been saved and baptized, Calvin?"

Jed arched an eyebrow and tried to keep from laughing as he awaited a response.

"I don't like water."

"What do you mean you don't like water? What do you got against water?"

"To quote Saint W. C. Fields: fish f—"

Jed gave Calvin the eye.

"—screw in it."

"We have to go now, Dad. Be back in a few hours," Jed said as he grabbed both bags and followed Calvin out to the car.

After a ten-minute drive, as they were pulling into the Elkans' driveway, Calvin asked Jed, "I can't believe you joke with your dad about him beating you. Did he really do that?"

"Yeah, but he ain't done it in years. If he still did, I probably wouldn't be joking about it," Jed said as he opened the car door. "Now, I'm going to leave this second bag in the car for later. Let's go meet your mom."

As Calvin and Jed stepped into the kitchen, they were met by Nancy.

"Mrs. Elkan?" Jed said as he extended his hand.

"Well, who's this young man?" Nancy accepted the handshake.

"Calvin told me that you like Reverend Jimmy Swaggart. Here's a record of his hymns. I accidently bought it twice. Forgot I had it," Jed continued as he handed Nancy the sack.

"Really?" she asked. "You like Reverend Swaggart?"

"Ma'am, I've got so many of his records, I plum forgot I had this one, too. It's my hope and prayer to follow in the good reverend's footsteps."

"So, you want to be a preacher?" Nancy asked giddily.

"Yes, ma'am. My dad was a preacher for a spell. It's my life's goal to work for the Lord."

"Well, I know what we'll be listening to tonight," beamed Nancy as she placed the LP on the living room record player. Jed could feel Calvin bristle beside him.

"We're going back to my room," Calvin said, hoping the charade would not be pressed to the point of breaking.

"I can't believe you," Calvin said in a hushed tone after closing the door to his room.

"Hey, it worked!"

"We'll see."

"Just trying to help you out a little. Anyway, you've got to see the *Apocalypse Now* movie!" exclaimed Jed, quickly shifting thought. "I just saw it. It's all about 'Nam and this weird song. I'll never forget . . ."

"What song?"

"I don't know what it is, but never heard anything like it—something about riding the snake and the blue bus."

"'The End.'"

"What?"

"Jim Morrison and The Doors. 'The End.' It's from their first album. Ha! Mother's never heard of them. You wanna hear it?"

"You got it? Hell, yeah!" Jed said as he enthusiastically looked at Calvin's record collection.

"It's not about Vietnam, though. I read a book about Morrison. This song's about counter culture and Oedipus and it's influenced by Velvet Underground and they're really a better—"

"Just play it!"

"That's it!" Jed exclaimed after hearing a few minutes of the song. "And that's what we're gonna do. We're gonna create our own culture and change the world, man. We have to." Jed's tone shifted suddenly. "Your house, man . . . it's got more stuff than my parents' house, but . . ."

"But?"

"It's wrong. Let's get out of here and go see *Apocalypse Now*."

Calvin agreed, anxious himself to leave.

In the cinema parking lot half an hour before the movie started, Jed reached down to the floor board and retrieved the second bag, pulling out a bottle of vodka, a bottle of tomato juice, and two paper cups.

"Didn't you say Errol Flynn preferred vodka?" Jed laughed.

"Yeah."

"In like Flynn."

"I liked reading about him. I don't want to be him. Besides, we can't drive home after—"

"Dude, it's a two-and-a-half-hour movie. That'll give us plenty of time to sober up. Man, you're the one who told me all about Flynn. He lived life—to the fullest. Do you want to read about life? Or live it? There must be something about him you identify with, otherwise . . ."

"He hated his mother."

"Dude, that's not cool to say."

"Then fix me a Bloody Mary."

Back at home, Nancy stopped Calvin in the kitchen as he grabbed chips and dip before retreating to his room.

"That Jed's a nice young man. He'll be a good influence on you."

Calvin refrained from choking long enough to call Jed.

"I guess it worked," Calvin told Jed, laughing.

24
REMEMBER YOUR HERITAGE

Aunt Blanche had visited twice in the past few years and had taken Calvin on more clandestine pilgrimages to St. Mary's Catholic Church. Although Nancy resented Blanche's outings with Calvin, time between aunt and nephew was tolerated because it pleased Dale.

No one at St. Mary's spoke to Calvin. He liked that. There was a comfort in the fact that parishioners didn't shake his hand off or backslap him in a show of phony brotherhood. Everyone was there to be an anonymous part of mass. The only greeting from strangers came after the "Our Father" in the way of a "peace be with you," and that was fine—a satisfyingly brief salutation. Even better, his visits to St. Mary's were short and sweet.

It was these memories that Calvin found solace in on Sundays such as this, when a young visiting evangelist couple took the Lighthouse center stage. Wearing a Santa cap to top off his garish red polyester Sunday best, the visiting preacher complemented his wife's green hoop skirt.

"I'm Reverend Joe Noel."

"And I'm Mary Noel," his wife added.

"And we're here together for the joyous Christmas season," they said in singsong unison.

After a few moments of seasonal verbiage, Mary stepped aside, and Rev. Joe took the microphone.

"The title of my sermon tonight is 'Remembering Your Heritage.' Remembering your heritage. Say that with me: Remembering your heritage."

"Remembering your heritage," the fervent followers echoed.

"How many of you here tonight believe that we need to remember our heritage?"

Curious, Calvin stopped drawing.

"Good, because tonight we need to remember our heritage," continued Joe after he received a handful of amens from the crowd.

"Tonight, I'm going tell you part of our heritage that some of you here tonight might not even know about. But some of you here tonight just might know. How many of you here tonight are aware that two thousand years ago, the Romans took your Christian forefathers and fed them to the lions in an arena? That's a part of your heritage. It is! Your Protestant forefathers sacrificed their lives for their faith and your faith. That's the price they paid. Their sacrifice is part of your heritage. Yet, to what extent, do you really remember?"

"We remember," echoed an unremarkable female devotee.

"Do you really? The Romans fed your forefathers alive to those lions in the arena, yet how many of you here tonight stroll into their Italian restaurants and let them feed you pasta? You need to remember your heritage."

Calvin grinned wryly.

"I am here to tell you: ol' Charlie Pope ain't nothing more than a modern-day Caesar, waiting for that dark trumpet call from the anti-Christ. Ol' Charlie Pope's going to be sitting at the anti-Christ's right hand. The Beast will align himself with the anti-Christ. It's happening right before your very eyes! How many of you pay attention to the news?"

"I do, preacher!" yelped out a sycophant.

"You better! The only thing worse than being an atheist is to be a Cath-o-lick! And that ain't all! Be prepared, folks! Six hundred million Protestants burned at the stake in their Roman inquisition. That's your heritage, folks! But I tell you, that's nothing compared to what's a-comin'! It's nothing compared to the great Roman arena they're gonna be building right here in our beloved U-S-of-A! Why do you think we always see those Cath-o-lick priests marching for gun control? Because the Vatican is working with the Mexicans for the Cath-o-lick invasion—don't let them take your right to bear arms and don't be fooled by fancy Roman double-talk. Don't think: it doesn't matter, Reverend. I tell you, it does! They got all these fancy theologians with fancy man-given degrees to prove all their demonic beliefs . . . I tell you the road to hell's paved with master's degrees. Don't be fooled by their theologians and remember your heritage!"

It truly was an inspirational sermon for Calvin—more so than any previous ones, and a reaction to it required something bigger than a sketchbook.

Calvin borrowed Dale's car. He had finally finished Bertie's clipper ship painting and needed to take it to her. Calvin walked into Bertie's apartment to find Tubby groaning as his nurse moved him to change his sheets. Tubby was now bedridden with prostate cancer. He had around-the-clock hospice care, which freed Bertie to dillydally in her hobbies.

Bertie was glued to her recliner but motioned for Calvin to hand her the small canvas he was holding.

"Hmm, looks like the one I sailed on in my previous life! This is supernatural!"

"Oh," said Calvin skeptically.

"Anyways, I got some things for you," said Bertie, pointing to a cabinet under the TV. "Open that door."

Calvin opened the cabinet and looked inside. "What are these?" he asked as he grabbed four containers from the cabinet.

"Kmart bug catchers. Look at the one with the orange lid behind them. See that stick in there? See that little thing on the stick that looks like a walnut?"

"What is it?' Calvin said, holding the fifth container at arm's length.

"That's a praying mantis egg. It'll hatch come summer. 'Bout a thousand will come out of that small egg," Bertie told Calvin, who quickly set the container down.

"If you're lucky, maybe a dozen of them will live. That's why I am giving you four of them bug catchers. See, mantises are cannibals, so what you need to do is separate them. I have an aquarium in my bedroom that I want you to take, too. You can put a screen lid on it and keep some of 'em in there."

Calvin nodded, unsure of what to think of such a gift.

"Be best if you feed them crickets," Bertie continued, oblivious to Calvin's discomfort. "You can get those at the bait and tackle store. Put a little cup of water in each of them, too."

What the hell am I going to do with cannibalistic bugs? Calvin thought as he thanked his grandmother and left.

A few days later, Calvin was flipping through a comic book when he found an Airfix ad for toy Roman soldiers. An idea hatched in his mind; he cut out the order form and mailed it in. Within weeks he had a full Roman army.

Over the next few months, Calvin meticulously painted Bertie's aquarium up like an ancient Roman colosseum. Statues of pre-Christian deities decorated the walls, and glued-in pews were populated with his new plastic soldiers. Dirt covered the aquarium floor for a finishing touch. Calvin carved a scepter out of a thick wood branch and placed it next to a handmade cardboard crown and purple towel that would be used for Caesar's cape. He carefully concealed the items in his closet, keeping them hidden in his temporary monstrance.

When he was satisfied with the visuals, Calvin set to work on the soundtrack, and as luck would have it, both *The Robe* and its sequel *Demetrius and the Gladiators* were playing back-to-back on television. Calvin pulled out a portable tape recorder and caught the sounds of a Hollywood-styled gladiatorial game. All he had to do now was wait.

Come spring, Calvin found himself in role of adoptive mother to a brood of hatched mantises. Containment was short-lived for the mantises—they made their way through tiny holes in the bottom of the Kmart catcher and into Calvin's room. Calvin discovered the breach when, opening his closet, he found half a dozen of the insects perched on hanging shirts, which sent him into a near panic. However, a family of ants put an abrupt end to *The Great Escape*. The surviving mantises were divided and separated into the various containers Bertie had given Calvin and soon adjusted to a diet of crickets from Goodson's Bait and Tackle Shop.

The Dushanes joined the Elkans for the family's annual Indy 500 barbecue on Memorial Day weekend. For Calvin, the only thing more boring than watching cars go around in a circle was listening to cars go around in a circle on the radio.

As usual, Nancy broke her vegetarian rule for burnt hot dogs. As Calvin learned, her vegetarianism was not out of love for living things. Rather, she had read somewhere that beef remained undigested in the stomach for a long time after consumption, and the thought of cow flesh swimming in her belly for God knows how long had compelled her to swear off meat—with this one exception, which made sense only to her. After all, only unsaved Jews refused pork, and with God as her witness, she was a Christian, not a Jew. Calvin watched with fascination as Dale brought Nancy a plate of hot dogs fresh off the grill. Taking one look at the pink pork, Nancy ordered, "Blacker, Dale, blacker! I like my dogs burnt black as coal!"

Dale did an about-face, heading back to the grill. A few moments later, he returned with now burnt hot dogs.

Seeing spots of pink, Nancy reiterated, "Blacker, Dale, blacker!"

Angrily, Dale stormed to the grill a second time.

"Vroom! Vroom!" mumbled Calvin sarcastically.

"Those still ain't black enough, Dale—blacker!"

On the third try, Dale doused the pork rolls with lighter fluid, lighting them up like an Abrahamic sacrifice. Upon receiving the third platter, Nancy woofed down the crumbling, charred frankfurters. Her mouth opened wide, revealing specks of black ash sticking to her teeth as she quoted a verse from the book of Joshua.

"'Pass on before the ark of the Lord your God into the midst of the Jordan, and take up each of you a stone upon his shoulder,'" said Nancy, hoping that some of the words would sink into Dale's thick, unsaved skull.

To everyone's horror, the sight of blackened pork ash sticking to Nancy's white teeth like pepper sprinkled on butter distracted the next Bible quote. "'He restoreth my soul. He leadeth me in the path of righteousness . . .'"

"Oh my," exclaimed Vernell upon seeing King James accentuated by a mouthful of piggy ash.

"Gawd damn," laughed Rev. Harry.

"Thought you were a preacher," said Dale.

Rev. Harry ignored Dale's comment and returned his attention to the radio race.

Calvin had been spending less and less time on *The Brother Cobweb Chronicles*. He was feeling restless to try his art in a new medium, and Mother Nature, by selecting the fittest, was gifting Calvin the opportunity to do so.

Jed was gone for the summer, so Calvin invited some neighborhood kids over. Although Calvin wasn't close to any of them, they all were intrigued enough by Calvin's bizarre invitation to attend the performance. Kelsie, Russ, and Sean were sitting on the floor of the Elkan garage when adorned in towel, crown, and scepter, Calvin appeared as the emperor Caligula. In the middle of the floor were four bug catchers, the decked-out aquarium, and the portable tape cassette player. Calvin sat on a lawn chair and banged his scepter on the concrete floor.

"My loyal subjects. Your emperor is pleased that you have accepted my generous invitation to our annual gladiatorial games," Calvin said in a booming voice.

Calvin reached down and hit play on the tape player. The cheers of a Roman crowd filled the garage. Calvin pointed to the first bug catcher.

"Today we will witness a battle between Reverend Joe Noel Mantis and Calvin Mantis," he said, revealing the large Calvin mantis in the aquarium. He reached into the first bug catcher, picked up the small Reverend Joe Noel, and placed it in the aquarium with Calvin Mantis.

Music swelled from the tape player. Calvin Mantis, perched on a pew next to an unsuspecting Roman soldier, did not react to Reverend Joe Mantis. Impatient, Caligula reached into the aquarium and edged Joe Mantis toward his larger rival. Within seconds, Calvin Mantis spotted the aquarium's newest occupant, seized it, and bit its head off. The live and taped crowds roared simultaneously. Caligula reached his hand up and shouted "Amen, amen!" Although he did the obligatory turning his thumbs down, his mantis counterpart had already made an unmerciful decision.

The gladiatorial games continued over the next few days with Calvin Mantis facing and feasting on Rev. Harry Mantis and Sister Ruby Mantis. Only Nancy Mantis remained to face Calvin Mantis. The neighborhood kids hyped up the event, spreading word of mouth about the final showdown that would take place the next day.

"Senators, subjects, guards," began Calvin in his best imitation of actor Jay Robinson's Caligula from *The Robe*. "We are touched by your devotion." He placed Nancy Mantis in the colosseum with Calvin Mantis. After a few minutes of watching insects dance around each other, Caligula turned to his audience and said, "Claudius, your gladiators are too fond of each other." The crowd giggled. Caligula turned his attention toward Nancy Mantis.

"Christian, do you renounce your false god? This king of an invisible kingdom who expects to come back someday and rule the earth? Kneel to your god! No? Treason is everywhere! Let what you see now be a lesson to all among you who fail in loyalty to your emperor. The instrument of my justice will be the greatest gladiator who ever fought in the arena."

To his shock, Caligula suddenly found the two mantises deviating from the script.

Ted, a newcomer to the gladiatorial games, stood up and pointed to the pair of copulating insects. "Calvin, Nancy's fuckin' ya in the ass!"

Unbeknownst to Calvin, his namesake was not a male mantis, but a female who had just engaged in mating with the male Nancy Mantis. Calvin's mouth dropped, his face red. Suddenly, the garage door flew open, and the real Nancy stood heaving in the doorway.

"I heard that, Ted! Get out of my house!" Nancy growled angrily. Ted squeezed past Mrs. Elkan and made for the safety of the street.

"What's going on here?" Nancy demanded.

"Nothing," Calvin said.

Nancy surveyed the garage like a hawk. The tape recorder betrayed Calvin's lie with the audio of Hollywood-styled ancient Rome. This, with the painted Roman arena and Calvin's attire, added up to blasphemy afoot.

"All of you need to leave, now!" Nancy hissed.

Within seconds, everyone had fled, leaving Calvin to face down his mother alone. Without a word, Nancy walked out of the garage into the connecting kitchen.

What? She can't be letting this go, Calvin thought.

He was right. She came back with a sawed-off broomstick handle and smashed it into the side of Calvin's face. Nancy swung hard and fast, landing multiple blows to her son's body. Calvin crashed to the floor. Once the blasphemer was down for the count, Nancy lifted the broomstick handle again and smashed the aquarium to pieces, then stormed out.

Attempting to sit up, Calvin wiped blood from his nose and straightened his crown, but agonizing pain robbed him of any dignity as he slumped over, landing with a thud and a pained laugh.

Looking through swollen black eyes, Calvin squinted to see the lifeless form of Calvin Mantis lying among the Roman ruins. Go now, go into your kingdom. They're going into a better kingdom, they are going into a better kingdom.

25

TAINTED BLISS

The following Friday night, Dale, Nancy, and Frank had gone to dinner. Because Calvin had opted to stay home, Dale ordered his son a meat-heavy pizza. Rain started pouring down shortly after, and Calvin opened the door to let Starsky in the house, despite Nancy's previous warnings to keep the dog outside or in the garage only. With everyone gone, the boy and his dog sat down to watch a Boris Karloff movie and share pizza. Calvin drifted off during the movie and awoke to Nancy swinging the broomstick handle into his face.

"Damn you, I told you not to let that dog in the house!" she screamed as blood spurted from Calvin's nose. Calvin threw his arms up, trying to block the blows.

"Goddammit Nancy, can't we just have peace for one night?" Dale cried out, jolted at the sight of his son's blood-soaked face.

"Dale, you're not man enough to make him mind because you don't want to be the bad guy. So, I'll be the damned bad guy!"

But as Nancy lunged toward Calvin again, Starsky leapt toward her, biting her leg and drawing blood. Nancy yelled as she swung the weapon at the dog. Fortunately, she missed and fell off balance, and Calvin had time to leap up and open the front door, allowing his heroic dog to escape. Nancy dropped the wooden stick and clawed at Calvin's face, again drawing blood. Through the pain, Calvin grabbed his mother's wrists and shoved her to the couch.

"Dale!" Nancy screamed.

"Dale what? You did this, Nancy," Dale said on the verge of tears, watching the scene from behind the couch.

Frank cried as Nancy ran down the hall and flopped onto her bed, screaming. Calvin nursed his wounds and walked outside to call for Starsky, but the dog didn't come back that night.

Two days later, Calvin heard Starsky scratching at the back garage door. When Calvin let the dog into the garage, Starsky stumbled and collapsed on a small shag rug next to Dale's tool counter. As Calvin leaned into his beloved dog, he felt blood on his fur and realized something was wrong. Calvin ran into the house.

"Dad!" Calvin yelled, "Starsky's hurt! We've got to get him to a vet."

"We ain't got money to be takin' him to no vet," Nancy protested.

"Dad!" Calvin yelled over his mother's protestation.

"We'll take him to the vet. C'mon," Dale said, hurrying into the garage with Calvin.

Calvin leaned into Starsky, rubbing the dog's neck. Starsky looked into Calvin's eyes one last time.

"It's too late. He's dead, Calvin," Dale said, tears blotting his face as he bent down to scoop the dog into his arms. "It looks like he was shot."

Calvin wept as he helped his father bury the dog. Dale had taken a pride in Starsky—and not just because the dog had been his bribe to make a meat eater of his son. Dale took pride in his son's love for the gift he had given him, so much so that one day he had risked his own well-being to save the dog. That was during the blizzard the winter before, when Frank yelled out that Starsky had gotten stuck in the snow after Calvin had let him out of the garage to go pee. Without hesitating, Dale grabbed a shovel and ran outside in below-zero wind chill to help Calvin dig his dog out of the drift. Dale had been gentle and patient with Starsky, lifting the dog with frostbitten bare hands.

Now, Dale's fingers were stained with brown earth as he took the same shovel to gently pad down Starsky's final place of rest.

"I bet that farmer down the road shot Starsky," Nancy said after Dale and Calvin walked back into the house. "He threatened to last time after Starsky got into his chicken coop."

The farmer had indeed threatened to do so after Starsky had killed several of his birds on two occasions, but Calvin immediately thought of Caesar's wife Livia from *I, Claudius*. Once she felt wronged or threatened, Livia held no life sacred and would not hesitate to poison a child—or even a dog. Nancy was cut from the same ancient Roman cloth, and Calvin wondered if Nancy had shot Starsky herself or if she had asked someone else to do the dirty work for her.

Later that night, as Calvin was alone in his bedroom, he put on an LP of Mahler's Symphony no. 4. As he listened to Mahler's sunniest, most atypical symphony, Calvin sketched out a drawing of Starsky with his flowing mane. Attempting to get through the loss, he remembered how the dog loved it when Calvin's fingers brushed through his hair. Starsky would close his eyes and his mouth would open, expelling awful breath, which didn't deter Calvin at all because he knew his dog was in bliss, just like he didn't care about Pop's body odor. Calvin would snuggle with Starsky, just as he had with Pop. Starsky was the first sentient being that Calvin had snuggled with since Pop. Apart from Pop and Starsky, touch from others had been confined to fists in his face. The love between Starsky and Calvin had provoked Nancy and—responsible or not—she wanted the dog dead. He had to remember this because the dark reality—which Mahler being Mahler, even at his most uplifting, didn't shy away from in his fourth symphony's ending—was that in order to get to heaven, one must die first. Yet it occurred to Calvin that perhaps both Starsky and Pop died in a state of bliss: Pop with his banana, Starsky with his chicken coop. What would it be like to die in total bliss? Calvin wondered. And if they had indeed died in a state of bliss, then Nancy, damn her, had lost.

26

BEEP BEEP!

After sneaking out to see Stanley Kubrick's R-rated *The Shining*, Calvin was captivated with the film's score by a Hungarian composer named Béla Bartók. After researching numerous classical music guides in the library, Calvin found a name consistently listed as one of the top preferred conductors for Bartók: the French musician Pierre Boulez. Calvin then looked up Boulez himself, who, very much alive, seemed altogether more interesting than the dead Bartók. To his delight, Calvin discovered that Boulez had been dubbed an enfant terrible and the avant-garde boogey man. All art of the past must be destroyed, Boulez had said. Slash the *Mona Lisa* and burn down the opera houses. We must be cultural omnivores and raid all the art forms to enhance our own medium. We must be cultural terrorists and retain the spirit of irreverence in art. Boulez had even picketed an Igor Stravinsky concert, a composer who had previously been a hero of sorts to Boulez. However, when Stravinsky went through a phase leading him backward to neoromanticism, Boulez labeled the elder composer as a traitor to modernism. Although Calvin did not wholly agree with Boulez's overly simplified assessment, he was drawn to the Frenchman as a protesting spitfire and took to heart Boulez' creed: art is not for entertainment or pleasure, but to disturb, to challenge cultural norms and the artistic timidity of the masses.

Shortly after his initial research, Calvin saw an advertisement for a televised Wagner *Ring* cycle, conducted by Boulez and staged by Patrice Chéreau. Of course, this would include the *Rheingold* that Pop had loved so dearly. Reading music critic Harold C. Schonberg's review of it in a library copy of the *New York Times* only made Calvin long to see the production even more. Schonberg had been outraged by the modernist post-industrialist approach taken by Chéreau and Boulez.

Calvin finally could see Wagner's *Ring* cycle after all these years. Understandably, Pop's taste in music was primarily reserved for German composers, such as Wagner and Beethoven. Now, years after his great-grandfather's death, Calvin reflected on Pop's musical taste, which he found ultimately conservative. As Boulez's *Ring* unfolded over the course of a week, Calvin found himself wondering how Pop might have reacted to his beloved Rhine mermaids portrayed as prostitutes, Wotan as a Mafioso, Valhalla as a New York City skyscraper, or Boulez' chamber-like reading. With Aunt Blanche two thousand miles away and Pop long gone, there was no one to share these discoveries with, which further reminded Calvin of that aloneness his great-grandfather had predicted. Both Jed and Frank (who was increasingly becoming a stranger rarely seen) were only available when they were without girlfriends, and even if they were available, Calvin could hardly share something like Mahler or Boulez with them. However, solitude did have transcendent moments, usually in the way of artistic exploring, such as losing oneself to this *Ring* while Nancy listened to gospel tunes in the living room.

Calvin had special ordered Boulez's own music and a recording of him conducting Bartók on LP from Karma Records in Xenia, Ohio. The records had come in, and with an extra fifty bucks from his last paycheck from his new gas station job, Calvin was determined to go on a spending spree. Although Xenia was a small town, it was the equivalent of a trip to the big city for Calvin. On the way to the beckoning Karma Records in the mall,

Calvin turned the radio on. The first thing that blared from the cheap speakers was David Bowie's "Changes," which sang of spit-upon children trying to change their world.

"Do you have any David Bowie albums?" Calvin excitedly asked the clerk after retrieving his special order. With his bright pink hair and multiple piercings, the clerk had been dubbed "The Karma Guy" by both Calvin and Jed on a previous trip. Jed had immediately felt threatened by the clerk's appearance, but Calvin liked The Karma Guy's soft-spoken helpfulness.

"His new album just came out today," said The Karma Guy as he handed *Scary Monsters (and Super Creeps)* to Calvin.

The white, pink, red, and orange colors on the LP cover drew Calvin in. Bowie, in his Picasso-like Pierrot attire and shadowy, purpled cigarette, immediately spoke a paradoxically alien and familiar language. Having heard little of Bowie, Calvin's initial attraction was mostly visual.

Once home, Calvin put the Boulez records aside, having already heard a snippet of Bartók. Sitting on the floor of his room, he dropped the needle on the LP groove. A cool, beautifully detached feeling flooded over Calvin, despite the sounds of angry protest and "Shut up!" issuing forth from the record player. Safe in his Bowie bubble, Calvin giddily absorbed lyrics that spoke of revolution and degrading fascists; people from bad homes of bland tension and fear; the status quo coming down hard on chained faggots, blindfolded and naked, all thrown into a wagon, trying in vain to be a part of society.

After listening to the Bowie record twice, Calvin switched it out for Boulez. As he read the album's liner notes, Calvin looked up in shock midway through *The Miraculous Mandarin*. It was even more violent in its iciness than Bartók's *Concerto for Orchestra*. Boulez's own music, entitled *Fold Upon Fold*, was pared down, spiky, and sensuous, soaked in gorgeous chords. Calvin plunged though Bowie and Boulez repeatedly, issuing his private revolt from the bedroom. Although the artists were very different from one another, they shared a ravishing, enigmatic quality. Literally spit upon and stomped on, Calvin had discovered a personal kindred spirit in Bowie and Boulez, who were the only kind of authentic saints—both living and unauthorized.

Beep beep.

INJUSTICE FOR ALL

As Calvin and fellow students were exiting the classroom, Mr. Pollock told his class about a new movie playing called . . . *And Justice for All* starring Al Pacino and suggested they might find some insight for their papers on the legal system. Calvin nonchalantly told Nancy he was going to see the movie for classroom study. Although the movie was over-cooked, Calvin took a lot of notes.

"I called that cinema," said Nancy angrily as Calvin walked through the front door a few hours later. "That movie's rated R! You know I don't allow you to see R-rated movies!" Nancy's fingers curled into fists.

"I didn't pay attention to the rating. I went to see it for my paper."

"I don't care! You knew that movie was rated R and you know the rules! You think if Jesus came back right now, he'd rapture you up while you're sitting in a sinful movie? 'Put no evil thing before your eyes.'"

"That's silly, and besides, it's the first R-rated movie I've seen," Calvin lied. "Jesus would know that I went to see it for homework."

"Silly, am I?"

With that, Nancy reached for the broomstick handle that she had hidden behind the couch. She swung the stick into Calvin's body. Calvin held up his arms, trying to block the blows. Inflamed with pain, Calvin ran toward his room but fumbled in the hallway.

Nancy towered over his fallen form, bringing the handle crashing down over him. Calvin lifted his leg and kicked at the stick, knocking it out of her hand.

"You filthy demon!" she screamed at full volume. As Nancy turned to retrieve her weapon, Calvin sprang up through the stinging, ran toward his bedroom door, closed it behind him, and locked it. "You open that door RIGHT NOW!" Nancy screamed as she pounded on it. Calvin leaned his aching body against the door.

"Can't we just have peace?" was Dale's repeated cry as he walked into the house in time to witness yet another scene.

"Damn you! You're always siding with these kids. You're no man!" Nancy cried as she stormed off into her room, flopped down on the bed, and wailed.

Dale knocked softly at Calvin's door. "You all right?"

"Leave me alone," Calvin answered, his voice cracking. He kept it at that, although he wanted to add, "you're no help." Dale, whose parents had divorced while he was young, grew up in an era where, to be the child of a broken family was to be labeled trash. So in his determination not to go the route of his parents, Dale went from one extreme end of the pendulum to the opposite. It wasn't even that Calvin wanted his parents divorced, but Dale, in his paranoia of a marriage ending in divorce, chose to ignore his wife's abuses. But it wasn't just his parents. Although Dale made the money, he counted on Nancy—who was organized and could read—to pay the bills, keep up the house, and get the kids off to school. But clearly, Nancy increasingly resented both Dale and Calvin—Dale for his failure to be a disciplinarian and religious patriarch. Her resentment of Calvin was less clear. In her ignorance, Nancy was supremely self-confident. In contrast, the well-read Calvin was weak and riddled with self-doubts, and she hated him for it. Unfortunately, Dale was not a father to turn to, and Calvin resented his dad's belated, subdued empathy—the result of a willingness to sacrifice his son's well-being in order to maintain the family structure.

Having no real family, Calvin's turned an abstract one, which, this night, took the form of Mahler's ninth symphony. But it wasn't just any Mahler ninth. Calvin couldn't handle Lenny's version right now with its exposed nerve ends. Instead, he dropped the needle on the adagio as performed by Herbert von Karajan and the Berlin Philharmonic. With Lenny, that final movement was just cataclysmic enough to potentially push Calvin over the proverbial edge. Karajan's approach, however, was so illuminatingly beautiful, it was akin to ecstatic breathlessness inside of a perfectly formed icicle. Calvin pushed away the world and became submerged in a gorgeous chill.

A FISHERMEN'S MASS

Calvin was sitting at his desk after school one day when he heard a knock on his bedroom door. He flinched, half-expecting Nancy to burst through the door to beat him for some minor transgression, then he remembered that she never knocked—just burst in. Dale poked his head into the room.

"Blanche called. She's going to be in town for the weekend and wanted to know if you'd like to spend Sunday with her," Dale said. "She'll pick you up if you want to go . . . six-thirty at the latest, since we live further away from that church now. So you'll have to get up early."

"Why do you think I wouldn't get up early? I usually do anyway."

"OK, I didn't know!" Dale barked. He realized his sharp tone and continued in a more civil voice, "So do you want to go or not?"

"Why not?" said Calvin. "And what's wrong with you, anyway?"

"Your mom kept me up all night making me listen to some dumb sermon she taped."

"Ha! She's still trying to get you saved. You don't have to listen."

"Guess not, but don't know why you'd want to go to mass with Blanche either. Not that your mom needs to know that."

"It's not the same."

It had been over a year since Calvin had seen Blanche, and he was grateful for the reprieve from regular family life and the Lighthouse, if only for a day.

"How many masses do they have a day?" Calvin asked Blanche on the car ride to St. Mary's. "I didn't realize they had this early of a service."

"At my parish, Father Clem calls it the fishermen's mass," chuckled Blanche. "It's the mass all the fishermen go to before they head to the lake."

"Gone fishing, I ain't working anymore," sang Calvin.

"Louis Armstrong and Bing Crosby. I remember that song. Do you like fishing?"

"No, I think it's boring, but the song is fun."

The building and its richly decorated interior never failed to stun Calvin even though he had now visited St. Mary's multiple times with Blanche. In surveying the church, he noticed several iconic images he had missed before, such as the Infant of Prague. The glazed bug eyes of the figure stood out on its narrow, waxy-looking feminine face that held an enormous crown atop its curly head. It wore an oversized crimson robe. The sight of a toddler Jesus in drag was an appealing surrealism to Calvin. A statue of Our Lady of Sorrows depicted a robed virgin with downcast, tear-filled eyes—no wonder, as she had seven daggers thrust into her bleeding heart.

"That's Saint Teresa of Avila," said Blanche, pointing to the statue when she noticed Calvin studying it.

"I like that your church has such weird imagery and worships women," Calvin said without thinking.

"Calvin, you need to understand: we don't worship Teresa or even Mary. We venerate them. There's a difference."

"Oh. Well, I don't see anything wrong with worshipping Teresa or Mary."

"I said we don't worship them."

"Maybe you should."

29

BE CAREFUL WHAT YOU PRAY FOR

Calvin knew he had committed the proverbial open mouth, insert foot sin by the look on Rev. Harry's face after he answered his question about the day of the Pentecost.

"From Genesis to Revelation, there's a time span of several thousand years," Calvin began after Rev. Harry called on him, "yet Pentecostals base their whole religion off one day in scripture—the day of Pentecost—and then misinterpret it to begin with."

"How's that?" Rev. Harry asked angrily. The other kids turned to look at the usually quiet Calvin, interested to see how this showdown would go.

"In the Book of Acts, the apostles and Mary are waiting in the Upper Room after Jesus has flown up to heaven. God sends down the Holy Ghost, and everyone start speaking in foreign tongues. It's a kind of midrash on the Tower of Babel story."

"Midrash?"

"It's a kind of New Testament commentary on an Old Testament story. In the Babel narrative, people are climbing up the tower to see God. God is sitting on his cloud playing his harp or whatever he's doing, gets nervous because he thinks they're going to see him and then he zaps the people below, confusing their tongues so they can't finish building the tower. In the Pentecost story, God comes down from heaven as blue flames, and suddenly everyone understands each other's language. Saint Peter appears on the balcony. Now, let's say you, Frank, and myself are below. I speak French, you speak Arabic, and Frank speaks Latin. You hear Peter in Arabic, Frank hears him in Latin, and I hear him in French. That isn't what anyone in this church does. When people speak in tongues here, it's just gibberish. And I've never once seen a blue flame."

"Gibberish?" Rev. Harry asked, his face twitching in anger before deciding now wasn't the time and turning his attention to more submissive students.

Great, thought Calvin, awaiting the inevitable.

Rev. Harry walked into Nancy's Sunday school class as it was finishing up. Demonstrating the story of Joshua and the battle of Jericho on a Velcro board, Nancy swept her hand across the board, knocking biblical figures to the floor as Joshua blew his trumpet. The children cheered in unison, ran up to Nancy, and hugged her before leaving class. A blonde preschooler paused at the door.

"Miss Nancy? Jesus must love you the bestest because you're so nice. I wish you was my mommy and Jesus was my daddy."

Nancy gasped in delight and stepped forward to hug her student, but the girl had already galloped away down the hall.

"You know, I don't get it," Rev. Harry said to Nancy after the last kid exited the room.

"Get what?" Nancy asked, collecting the Velcro figurines.

"These kids adore you. Every one of them. You have an amazing way with them, teaching them to love Jesus and love church."

Rev. Harry closed the door, then reached for Nancy's wrist. Pulling her toward him, he smiled. "You inspire me."

"Thank you, Harry," Nancy said, surprised. "You're the first man to ever say that to me." Shaking her head as if something threatened to ruin the moment, Nancy inhaled. "Anyway, it's nice of you to say that."

"Nancy, about that time—I shouldn't have—well, I know it's not Christlike to strike a woman. You have this power, this—way of getting to me. Perhaps it was best, you moving to Sabina and all." Rev. Harry slipped his arms around her waist. "I'm sorry."

"Harry, you know how I collect those *Love Is . . .* comic strips from the morning newspaper?"

"You mean the ones you got taped all over your cabinets?"

"Yup. I cut those out every day, but one morning there was this one that said, 'Love means never having to say you're sorry.' I didn't cut that one out because I don't believe that! Y'know, Dale ain't never once told me he was sorry. Thank you for telling me that. I've had a lot worse."

"Your daddy and brother . . . I remember. Almost expected, coming from Mormons."

"Yeah, I left that religion once I married Dale and then I found my true home here. But it ain't just my dad and brother I'm thinking about. To Dale, I'm just there to fix dinner, clean the house, and babysit. Even my boys don't really appreciate me."

"That's what I came to talk to you about. You know you have such a way with these other kids, and they love you, but Kilvin . . ."

"What's he done now?"

Calvin's fear that Nancy would hear about the Sunday school incident was confirmed when he heard the way the car door slammed.

"Reverend Harry and I had a talk. Get your ass out here right now," Nancy yelled out as she stormed into the house.

"I don't want to go to that church anymore," Calvin said, calmly emerging from his bedroom doorway. With arms crossed, he leaned against the kitchen doorframe to easily retreat if she moved toward a weaponized kitchen item.

"I don't care what you want. As long as you live in this house, you'll be going to church!"

"Yeah well, things just don't add up."

"Who told you that you can add? Anyway, let's hear it."

"I don't think the Bible's supposed to be read literally. It's not history."

Surprisingly, Nancy humored the discussion.

Calvin continued. "For example, Moses parting the Red Sea."

"What about it?"

"According to the Bible, Moses produced a miracle when he parted the Red Sea, closed it back up, and drowned the pharaoh with his army."

"So, how's that not a miracle?" Nancy challenged her son, anticipating his surrender.

"Well, historians and biblical scholars agree that the Red Sea was only about knee-high in the time of Moses."

"You big dummy—that's an even bigger miracle!"

"How?"

"Because Moses managed to drown those Egyptians in only knee-high water. Better try harder than that!"

"All right. There's a contradiction in the very first book. God made Adam and Eve, and they're the only people on earth. Right?"

"Right."

"He kicks them out of the garden. They have Cain and Abel. Cain kills Abel. Cain marries into another tribe."

"So?"

"Where did the other tribe come from?"

Nancy paused for a moment. "That proves you better be careful what you pray for, because you might just get it." She turned away from Calvin, opening a cabinet.

"What?"

"When you had spinal meningitis, that doctor said you might be retarded, so me and the priest at the hospital prayed that God would give you knowledge to prove that doctor wrong. Well, now I'm paying for it," said Nancy, deadly serious as she stormed out of the room.

30
I'LL FLY AWAY

Calvin could count on one hand how many times Dale had accompanied the family to church, and the last time had been ten years ago. However, Nancy was persistent in taping and playing sermons for her husband. Surprisingly, one of the sermons had gotten to Dale and bubbled in his brain because he was driving the entire family to Sunday night service.

As usual, Calvin sat a few rows in front of Nancy. Unfortunately, he was sitting in front of a pew with a bouncing-off-the-wall six-year-old boy whose mother and siblings were ignoring him. As Calvin tried to draw, the kid kept tapping him on the shoulder, which proved quite the distraction to Dale. Instead of listening to the sermon, Dale's focus was on the kid consistently tapping Calvin on the shoulder from behind and ducking under the pew. Seeing the disturbance, Rev. Harry locked eyes with Nancy.

Calvin feigned listening to the sermon, but he was struck by the visual of Luke now sitting in the second throne on the stage as his father preached. Calvin felt another tap on his shoulder and chose to ignore it. Another tap.

Again, he ignored it until he heard a woman's voice behind him whisper his name.

Calvin turned to see the woman directly in the pew behind him. With an agitated look on her face, she pointed to the pew behind her, where Nancy sat, motioning him to come back to her pew. Not wanting to disrupt the sermon, Calvin nodded and held up his finger indicating that it would be a moment.

Like a strutting peacock, Nancy rose from her seat, grabbed her purse, walked up to the pew where Calvin was sitting. She forcefully pulled her son up by his arm. As Nancy dragged him down the aisle to the basement, Calvin locked eyes with Luke on stage.

Nancy pushed Calvin into her Sunday school room and slammed the door shut.

"I told you to come back, now! It's taken me ten years to get your dad to church, and you let the devil enter you, distracting him from hearing the sermon!"

With each word hissed, Nancy's aggression turned darker.

"It wasn't my fault. That kid—"

"Told you to come back!"

"I didn't want to disrupt the sermon."

"So you didn't just disobey me, you disrupted the Holy Ghost!"

"Oh come on, I—"

Nancy turned around and grabbed a man's belt from her Sunday school room desk. What's that doing here? Calvin wondered. Maybe it belonged to Reverend—

Nancy flung the belt, slapping Calvin across the face. The buckle caught his cheek, drawing blood. Calvin reached his arm up to block, but Nancy's belt hit him repeatedly. Finally, Calvin grabbed the weapon from his mother's hand and flung it across the room.

Nancy screamed as she lunged for Calvin, knocking him to the floor. Once down, Nancy was atop Calvin, scratching his cheeks. Blood gushed down the sides of his face.

Nancy laughed as she grabbed Calvin's hands and dug her nails into his wrists.

"Try to get away from me, you demon, and you'll just tear your own skin! Go ahead! Do it!"

Nancy growled. Calvin was oblivious to words and jerked his hands free, ripping the flesh of his wrists.

Ignoring the pain, Calvin pushed his mother off. "Get OFF me!"

Nancy screamed and lunged at Calvin again. Grabbing Calvin by the face, Nancy leaned in and bit his lip. Blood spilling from his mouth, Calvin spat, "You crazy fucking bitch!"

Nancy wailed and slammed her fist into Calvin's eye, knocking him to the ground a second time. Calvin jumped up, refusing to be trapped on the floor again, but started to sob from his blackened eye.

"Start crying, big baby," Nancy sneered.

"Go to hell. I'm leaving."

Calvin opened the door and started to walk back up the stairs. Running up behind him, Nancy kicked him in the back, knocking him down.

"Get up those stairs and go sit down," Nancy ordered.

Calvin made it past the stairs. As he started to walk up the church aisle, the entire congregation, including Dale, turned around to see him bloodied and bruised. Luke started to rise angrily from his throne upon seeing Calvin's pathetic form. Rev. Harry motioned Luke to sit down. As everyone's eyes were upon him, Calvin did an about-face and started walking toward the exit. Nancy attempted to stop him in the aisle.

"Get back in your seat," Nancy barked.

Calvin continued walking out the door. In defiance of his father, Luke rose and whispered to the church musicians. Luke grabbed the microphone as the band broke into a rollicking version of "I'll Fly Away."

Calvin limped through the parking lot to the family car and sat on the hood, crying uncontrollably. To his surprise, Dale soon joined him on the hood but said nothing. In the awkward silence, Calvin thought how similar his father was to the weak-willed Wotan of Wagner's *Ring*. Wotan's wife, Fricka, had demanded the death of her husband's son, Siegmund. Rather than defending or sparing his son, Wotan caved in to his wife, allowing Siegmund to die, which seemed to be Dale's approach as well. Father and son sat wordless for nearly an hour until church let out.

An embarrassed Frank walked ten steps behind Nancy. Calvin and Dale slid off the hood. Standing between Calvin and Nancy, Dale blocked his wife when she tried to lunge for Calvin.

"Get in the car, Nancy," Dale commanded.

"Damn you," she screamed as she swung at her husband, comically missing his face by several inches.

"Get in the car before I knock you on your goddamned ass," Dale screamed, crafting a new plot twist.

Dale opened the door for Nancy. It was the first time that either Calvin or Frank had seen their father open a door for their mother.

Halfway home, Nancy broke the silence by shoving in a tape recording of a Lighthouse service. After a moment, Dale reached up, hit eject, rolled down the window, and threw the cassette out.

"Calvin doesn't have to go to church anymore," Dale said.

A moment of tension passed.

"What about me?" Frank asked.

Dale thought for a moment. Although Nancy could be abusive toward Frank, she was far worse with Calvin, which Dale could never understand. "Shut up, Frank."

Nancy entered the house and headed straight for her bed. The sound of her lament, coupled with ceaseless mattress kicks, filled the house.

A short while later, after Frank had gone to bed, Dale had left for work, and Nancy had cried herself to sleep, Calvin sat numbly on the floor of his bedroom, wrapping the blanket around himself like a desired, unfamiliar skin. The last vestige of the Lighthouse as any kind of sanctuary—as flimsy as it was—had been demolished by Nancy. She had finally—publicly—beaten the hell out of him in church. As a Sunday school teacher, careful to preserve her standing, it was something she had never done, but now she had exposed herself, and feeling justified, she clearly didn't care. He was no longer safe at all, safe anywhere, and Calvin knew it.

31
SLIVERS

The morning after, finding himself transitioning from shock to rage, Calvin set off for school with purpose, skipped his first class, headed straight to the library, and pulled out books on Gauguin, Picasso, Errol Flynn, and Jim Morrison, along with a Bible. He poured through each and found the impetus he sought, the course for his escape. Picasso had said that one must kill one's parents in order to be an artist. He was speaking figuratively, of course, but Picasso did just that to compose his own promenade. Flynn famously stole his father's boat at the age of eighteen and headed to New Guinea. According to the myth, Gauguin left his job, wife, and family to paint. Morrison enrolled in UCLA, then formed his band and, when asked, told people his parents were dead. Christ's ministry did not begin until he left home, and he advised those marrying or embarking on a religious vocation to leave their families behind. Art was the only thing that had been faithful to Calvin—not religion, not family.

Calvin had been preparing his portfolio for four years and only a few weeks before had mailed it to the art college in Cincinnati, along with his application. His flight from the blood and the bruises, the ignorance and the hatred of Nancy was going to be an artistic one.

Later that evening, before going to bed, Calvin finished his letter, stuck it in an envelope, sealed it, and placed it in his mother's Bible crossword puzzle book. She worked on that book every day. She would see it. The reason was one of survival. His plan of total escape was going to take some time and money, and in that period, he could not risk falling through the cracks. This letter was his insurance, and it simply read "Lay one hand on me again, and Dad will know about you and Rev. Harry's affair." This was the way to do it, thought Calvin: cold, detached, and to the point.

Two weeks later, at the baccalaureate ceremony, Mr. Grover announced that Calvin won an award for four years of artistic excellence and service, and with the award, he handed Calvin a letter.

"This is the acceptance letter admitting Calvin into the Cincinnati School of Art," Mr. Grover said. "The art school requires a minimum of twenty-five drawings for a portfolio submission. Well, Calvin, as we all know, has applied himself diligently to his art. So much so that he submitted over a hundred and fifty drawings. I guess they were impressed, Calvin, because here's a partial scholarship for your first year."

Calvin almost teared up. He accepted the awards with a handshake, and as he descended from the stage, it didn't bother him at all that no one from his family was there. It was hardly surprising that Nancy came up with the excuse of a Lighthouse meeting in order to get out of it. She had not said one word about the letter, but he knew she'd read it because it was gone. Dale had offered to attend the graduation but was relieved when Calvin assured him that his presence wasn't needed. It was a nice gesture, but Calvin was astutely aware that his dad, having only gone so far as grade school, would unintentionally be made to feel inferior.

As for Frank, he was always off with his circle of friends or bevy of girls, none of whom Calvin knew. However, the girls had dwindled down to one, or so Calvin had heard, and her name was Donna, which seemed like a typical Ohio name. Calvin hadn't met her because he and Frank almost never saw each other. If they did happen to be home at the same time, Calvin usually retreated into his room to work on art. However, on one recent occasion, while Nancy and Dale were gone, the two brothers actually spoke for a moment in the kitchen while Calvin was making a pot of coffee. The rare conversation was still fresh in Calvin's memory.

"I'm surprised you're home and not out with—what's her name?" Calvin asked Frank.

"Donna. You know you'd get a date, too, if you didn't spend all your time in that room," Frank chastised.

"I don't want to date. I'd rather be—"

"Drawing. Yeah. You know, the reason you get it more from Mom is because you're home all the time. I stay gone. That's what you should do."

"I'm trying to get into art school. I've got to work on my portfolio."

"Yeah, well you wanna get killed in the process? If you ain't around much, Mom ain't as likely to find some stupid reason to beat the shit out of you."

"I'd never get the portfolio finished."

"So you risk getting into it with her, just so you can draw?"

"Exactly."

"Suit yourself."

"So, what about this Donna? Sounds like you're kind of dating her steady?"

"Yup. She's the one I picked."

"Why her?"

"She ain't never had a boyfriend."

"What's that got to do with anything?"

"Calvin, if you're gonna get a quality girl, you want one that ain't been used. It's like a car. Do you want a new one? Or do you want some old jalopy that's got a hundred thousand miles on it?"

"So in other words, she's a virgin."

"She was," Frank laughed. "You'll find out soon enough."

"Huh? Find out what?"

"Never mind."

"Fine. By the way, were you?"

"Was I what?"

"A virgin when you met Donna?"

"Are you crazy? Of course not. What do you think I am?"

"A hypocrite."

"Oh, look at you, all holier than thou. Now I remember why I don't talk to you much. I gotta go."

Calvin rolled his eyes as Frank exited the house.

As Calvin walked back to his seat from the graduation stage, holding tight onto his awards, the memory of talking to Frank faded. It was replaced by an edifying sliver: the remembrance of Pop, which suddenly overwhelmed Calvin, and now—more than ever—Calvin felt the absence of Pop.

"Oh, good for you," Nancy said sarcastically upon hearing that Calvin was accepted into art school. "Just don't expect us to pay your way. Going to be a big waste of money, and not just the government's money, but our money, too. You know we gotta carry you on your dad's health insurance as long as you're in school?"

"Dad told me it doesn't matter because his insurance has two options: a family package or a single package. It's no different than if he was just carrying you and him or you, him, Frank, and me. It's the same price."

"I always knew you were going to be a stupid atheist democrat—always expecting free stuff."

"I didn't ask to be brought into this world. As a matter of fact, you said you tried for years to have me, although I'm not sure why you even wanted me. You made me read the Gospels, and that was your biggest mistake ever because the Jesus that's in the Bible sure as hell isn't like the Republicans. They don't follow at all what he teaches. You don't follow what he teaches either. As a matter of fact, I don't know of anyone in the Lighthouse who actually follows what Jesus teaches. I never read him saying poor people just want handouts—quite the reverse. He even said he will deny those who don't give shelter to the immigrants, medicine to the sick, or food and clothes to the poor. That guy, I'm all about. I'm just not about you because he never said to worship him. He said to follow him. You've obviously never read the Gospels or else you would have known forcing me to read them would out you for the goddamned hypocrite you are. So, do you have anything original to say, or are you just going to go by the religious right-wing kook playbook?" Calvin boldly asked, bracing himself for a flying fist that never came.

Disgusted, Nancy walked away as Calvin realized his threat of revelation still restrained mother dear.

32

BLUEMAHLER

A mere six weeks after Calvin's graduation, on an early Saturday morning, Nancy, Frank, and Donna sat in the living room, deep in planning. Donna, a petite, shy, dark-haired girl sat quietly on the couch next to Frank, rubbing her swollen belly.

"Of course, you and your dad have left most of the work to me," Nancy said to Frank. "You men are like that," she added, before switching her attention to her soon-to-be daughter-in-law. "Ain't that right, Donna?"

"Yup," Donna squeaked.

"Course, you mother hasn't been much help either, Donna. I know her and your dad are still hopping mad over the whole thing. I don't like it none neither, but get over it, I say!"

Back in his bedroom, Calvin was asleep, submerged deep within a frag-mented dream.

The dream figures came slowly into focus. Calvin himself was in the dream, dressed in a groom's coat with his face painted up like a blue clown. He was with a wedding party that included three groomsmen and Calvin's gas station coworkers, Clayton and Lloyd. Beside the Calvin Clown was Arkimnel. The party stood still and reserved, as if posing for a photograph. Almost as quickly as it had appeared, the gathering began to dissipate within a purplish light, which brightened in intensity, enveloping the party until everyone vanished.

As soon as Calvin woke, he grabbed drawing paper and hurriedly sketched out the dream imagery. Finished with his rough penciling, Calvin showered and readied for his shift at the gas station.

Hoping he might pass unnoticed, Calvin made a swift beeline for the kitchen. Nancy, sitting in a chair across from the silently cuddling Frank and Donna, looked up at him. A wedding list was on the table in front of her, and she had a pair of nail clippers in her hand. Feeling her gaze, Calvin acknowledged her by glancing over at the small pile of toenail clippings on the wedding list. After starting the coffee pot, he searched through the cup-boards for breakfast. Hearing the opening and shutting of cabinet doors, Nancy joined him in the kitchen.

"Shh . . . your dad worked late," she said to Calvin. "You're gonna wake him up with all this banging. He'll be impossible all day long, and I need him fully rested to help me with this wedding. I'll get your breakfast. You just sit down."

Nancy's voice was far louder than Calvin's opening or shutting cabinet doors. Sensibly, Calvin chose not to point that out. "Oats," he whispered.

"I'll make them. What flavor you want? We got apricot, peach, banana . . ."

"Just plain oats."

"Plain?" she asked. "Well you're just plain boring!"

Calvin ignored Nancy's wretched pun and sat down at the kitchen table to drink coffee. It wasn't surprising that Frank and Donna hadn't acknowl-edged him because, even though it wasn't spoken aloud, Calvin sensed a latent attitude from Frank that he was now one up on Calvin. Despite Frank having a closer relationship with Dale, Calvin had always felt that Frank was jealous of Calvin being the oldest child. Calvin could never specifically point to anything Frank said or did that indicated jealousy per se, but Frank was always blunt in telling Calvin he had more in common with their father than Calvin did.

Within the last three weeks, Frank had announced Donna was pregnant and that the two were going to marry as soon as possible before the baby was born. Surprisingly, Nancy took a glass half-full approach. "Don't want to have an illegitimate grandchild," she had said, and Dale agreed. That Frank and Donna were still teens didn't matter. After all, Dale and Nancy had married in their teens, and even though that was the 1950s and attitudes had changed, ultimately, they were excited with the idea of a grandchild, possibly because they believed the odds of Calvin giving them one were slim. In addition to receiving the news of the marriage, Calvin was informed that Donna would be moving in. She, Frank, and the grandchild would live there, at least until they both graduated from high school. The revelation came in the middle of Frank and Nancy introducing Calvin to Donna. It was whirlwind of change in such a short period of time.

Shortly afterward, Frank had taken Calvin aside.

"Calvin, I got a question for you," Frank said to Calvin in private. "You know that ruby ring Dad wears?"

"What about it?" Calvin asked.

"Did you know Dad's dad gave him that ring?"

"He might have mentioned it once. I don't remember."

"Well, I was thinking, I know you're the oldest son, but since Donna and I will be having a boy . . ."

"What if you have a girl?"

"Nah, we had an ultrasound done and saw the baby's ding-a-ling." Frank laughed.

"Oh. OK, well, you were saying?"

"Well, I was thinking since I'm gonna have a boy and I'm closer to Dad, would you mind Dad passing that ring on to me instead of you when he dies? That way, I can give it to my boy and keep the tradition . . ."

"What the hell would I want with a ring?"

"Thanks, Bubba," Frank said patronizingly as he slapped Calvin on the back.

Calvin flinched and walked off, shaking his head, feeling as though Frank was increasingly mantling the attitude of being the older brother, whatever that meant. Obviously, it was important to Frank, and if that's what he wanted, it didn't matter one damn bit to Calvin.

Frank getting married meant that he was going to be stuck at home for quite some time. Not me, thought Calvin. It would be something akin to a reversal between him and Frank—Frank would be home more, and Calvin would be gone. Calvin couldn't help but notice that Donna, who only said "hi" when introduced, was scrutinizing him. What is it? he wondered, before realizing that her eyes were disapprovingly fixated on his blue-paint-covered cuticles. I'm glad you disapprove, thought Calvin. It just makes me want to get the hell out of here even faster.

Calvin silently slipped out of the house and climbed into his Nova. He hated his car, hated maintaining it, and hated driving. Long drives were made bearable with music. This morning Calvin was in a mood for Wagner's "Ride of the Valkyries."

Halfway to work, the Valkyries' heroic ride, blaring from the car cassette player, was interrupted by a guttural sound coming from the engine as the car began an upward climb on a busy road. The vehicle seemed to mock him: Wagner? Ha, you're nothing more than poor white trash. Calvin smacked the steering wheel with the palm of his hand.

A large line of early-morning traffic trailed him. Calvin hoped that he could make it to the parking lot of a convenience store just beyond the stop sign at the top of the hill. Murphy's Law spewed its triumphal truth and the car wheezed out its last breath just as Calvin approached the stop sign. He looked through his rear-view mirror as traffic swelled behind him like an unstoppable sea of threatening predators. Calvin quickly got out of his car and motioned traffic around him until a farmer jumped out of a truck to assist.

"You steer, I'll push," the farmer told Calvin.

Within a few moments, Calvin and his Nova were safely in the mini-mart parking lot. Calvin thanked the farmer and headed for a phone booth.

Nancy was still working on the wedding list when she received Calvin's call. As soon as she heard her son's voice, she guessed what happened. Calvin's car breaking down was hardly a new dilemma.

"Where are you?" Nancy asked.

"Cope Road."

"You on the road? At least tell me you got help and got it off the road."

"It's in that mini-mart parking lot."

"OK. Your dad knows that store. He never can get any sleep. Guess I'll have to wake him after all and have him come get you. He should be there in about twenty minutes."

As he started to dial the gas station to tell them he'd be in late, Calvin looked out the phone booth window. As he looked into a wheat field beyond the stop sign, the previous night's dream came back to him in a wide-awake vision.

Calvin woke and found himself lying on the ground in the wheat field. Arkimnel stood above him, smiling. Motioning Calvin to get up, she turned and began walking toward a road. Calvin followed. The air was cool like the beginning of autumn, but a quick glance at the trees around him indicated that it was mid-summer. Calvin directed his eyes toward the open back of Arkimnel's dress, which stirred his senses.

On the road, while walking with Arkimnel, Calvin spotted the outskirts of a nineteenth-century town. The dirt underneath changed to a cobbled path. Around them, carriages and pedestrians emerged, dressed in eighteenth-century European garb. Two men, carrying a pane of glass, passed by Calvin. Within the glass, Calvin saw his own reflection, painted as a blue clown with unusual markings. His face was a deep blue; above his blackened eyebrows were echoing white brows, creating an expressive contrast. Running down the bridge of his nose and onto his upper lip was a thin, white line. A horizontal line of white paint covered his lower lip. On each cheek was a perfect white circle with a smaller blue circle inside. Calvin christened his new avatar BlueMahler after Gustav Mahler.

The scene shifted, and Arkimnel stopped at the entrance of a great cathedral. Once the pair stepped inside, Calvin stood awestruck, caught up in expansive ceilings, diamond-cut crystal lighting, and the drama of color sweeping along walls where saints were scripted into art, reminding Calvin of Aunt Blanche's St. Mary's.

Calvin spotted a bride-in-waiting, dressed in a gown of white and pink with her trio of bridesmaids beside her. When they sensed he was watching, the bridesmaids whisked her away into a side door. Arkimnel took Calvin by the hand and led him into a large room where three regally dressed boys were waiting for him. One of the boys grabbed Calvin's arm. "Come along! You must hurry and get dressed," he said. Calvin emerged from the dressing room, attired as a Viennese nobleman.

Calvin snapped back to reality with the sound of his father's noisy diesel. Dale exited the car, hiked up his work pants, and eyed his son's Nova with suspicion.

"Did you bother to check the gas?" Dale asked.

"The gas gauge doesn't work," said an embarrassed Calvin.

"Well, my guess is we better fill it up. We'll need to put a little gas in the carburetor, too."

Calvin's coworkers at the gas station didn't mind that he was late, although they did find it amusing that a gas station employee would run out of gas on the way to work. Clayton was in his late fifties, and Lloyd nearing seventy. With the morning rush hour over, Lloyd sat behind a high desk, and after finishing paperwork, slipped into a brunch that consisted of nonfilter Camels and black coffee. During the slow spell, Calvin utilized the backs of cigarette carton boxes to scribble notes: Sigmund Freud counseled Mahler through a disastrous marriage and sensual longing for the Virgin May image, both of which were rendered unrequited love in the mortal plane. Wagner's Tristan died longing for Isolde. Charlie Brown engaged in a never-ending quest for the mysterious redhead girl. For two thousand years, the mummy defied mortality to reunite with his princess. The Tramp finally got his gamin after thirty years of searching. Pink and blue; yin and yang. Boys are blue. Girls are pink. BlueMahler must find his PinkFreud.

"You know what I think?" Clayton asked Lloyd. Lloyd's eyes peeked over the rim of his glasses, waiting for Clayton to continue. "I think Calvin's mind was on that wedding instead of his car."

"What wedding?" Lloyd asked.

"Frank's."

"No, it's not," Calvin insisted. "I'm a thousand miles from that wedding."

"Don't buy it," Clayton insisted to Lloyd. "Frank's younger than Calvin, gettin' married, while Calvin's never even had a first date."

Lloyd sighed. With perfect timing, a car pulled up for gas, which prompted Lloyd to motion Clayton.

"Oh, that's Mrs. Kemp. She's got great titties and ain't afraid to show them off in those low-cut tops. I'll be takin' my time washing those windshields," Clayton said, hurrying to the door.

"I'd pour an entire bottle of pepper in your eyes if you ogled my wife or daughter that way," Lloyd said.

Clayton laughed as he walked out the door.

"Calvin, your brother's trash," Lloyd said as soon as Clayton was outside.

"What?" Calvin asked, feigning shock.

"He's white trash in a polo shirt—nothing but a blowhard. He's gone and knocked some girl up and his marriage won't last five years, but it's him your parents favor. I can sort of understand your dad. They have more in common, but your mom takes hypocrisy to a new level. Why? You did well in school, and you're starting college. If—if!—Frank graduates, it'll be by the skin of his teeth."

Calvin said nothing, but he knew Lloyd was right. Although Frank had said that the reason Nancy was more violent with Calvin was because Calvin was home more, it was more complex than that. Calvin's seclusion was only part of it. Nancy favoring Frank to Calvin was comparable in a way to her favoring the overtly patristic, flamboyant Rev. Harry to the more pacifistic Dale. Frank, it seemed, inherited Dale's game hunting and disdain for education and ran with those as his personality traits, which somehow pleased Nancy.

Calvin thought about Nancy's most recent display of unwarranted favoritism for Frank: while Donna had been visiting last week, Frank emerged from the bathroom. "Donna," he had yelled, "come see this turd I pooped. It's got to be a foot long!"

She laughed him off.

"No, come here," Frank had pleaded to no avail. Finally, after seeing she wasn't going to cooperate, Frank joined Donna and Nancy at the dining room table. Calvin, with his bedroom door cracked, eavesdropped.

"When our boy is born, I'm going to teach him to name his poop," Frank announced to Donna. "I used to do that when I was a kid, didn't I, Mom?"

"You sure did," Nancy laughed, "and those silly doobies."

"What are doobies?"

"They're the little people that live in my butt. There's a whole village of them. They got drills on their heads and drill into your poop and put it in wheelbarrows. Then, they dump them into the poop chute. That's when it comes out. I used to ask Calvin to draw them for me, but he never would. So, I drew them—they're just stick figures with drills on their heads and big smiley faces. I used to name my big turds for the doobies."

"Oh, you're so silly," Donna said. "If I was Calvin, I wouldn't have drawn them for you either, naming your poop like that."

"Well," Nancy piped in, "maybe he can't do art very good, but his drawings were more fun than all that weird stuff Calvin draws. At least Frank, silly or not, is going to be a father."

Never mind that Frank is sixteen, thought Calvin. It wasn't even doobies or naming poop, which might have been cute when Frank was seven, but at sixteen—no, it still wasn't that. Nancy's round table discussion was complete bullshit: an act, and she knew it was bullshit, but she was saying it loud and out loud to herself and her captive knights and within earshot of her son in his bedroom who refused to join her order.

"Calvin," said Clayton, "why don't you ask out that girl in the drive-through at Dairy Queen across the street? She seems to like you. She's always asking if you're working."

"You mean Tina?"

"Asking her out sounds like a good idea to me, too," Lloyd chimed in.

"I hardly know her," whined Calvin. "Why would I ask out a girl I hardly know?"

"'Why would I ask out a girl I hardly know,'" said Clayton in exaggerated imitation. Clayton and Lloyd laughed.

"I'm gettin' hungry. Whatcha y'all want for lunch?" Clayton asked.

"The usual," Lloyd said.

"OK, one steak sandwich. How about you, Calvin? The usual?"

Calvin nodded.

"One Greek salad."

Lloyd and Calvin each handed Clayton a five. Shortly after Clayton left for the Greek restaurant, the station had a rush, with Calvin and Lloyd each attending multiple customers. As the busy period died down, Calvin looked across the street to see Clayton's truck at the Dairy Queen drive-through. That's odd, thought Calvin.

"Why'd you stop at Dairy Queen?" Calvin asked Clayton after lunch, realizing that Clayton did not buy an ice cream.

"Glad you reminded me—you owe me three bucks," Clayton answered.

"What for? I paid you for lunch," replied Calvin.

"Not for lunch," said Clayton. "For the Tweety Bird."

"What're you talking about?"

"The stuffed Tweety Bird you bought Tina," explained Clayton. "The one you gave her with a note asking her out on a date tonight. I handed it to her in the drive-through, just like you asked me to."

"I didn't—"

"She said yes," Clayton said, grinning. "As a matter of fact, she's walking over here now."

Calvin looked up to see Tina approaching. Damn, he mumbled.

The Elkan house was abuzz with news of Calvin's first date at nineteen.

"Calvin's got a date," Frank told Dale.

"With a girl?" Dale asked.

"Course—who else?"

Dale shrugged. "He's not wearing that pink shirt, is he?"

"I'll tell him not to."

"Have you told your mom?"

"Why would she care? I'm getting married tomorrow."

"I'll tell her."

"Here, now put this on if you want to get girls," said Frank as he handed Calvin a leather jacket. "And if you want to get laid, you better start learning to dumb it down."

"I thought that you said I should find a virgin," Calvin said, rolling his eyes.

"I said you don't want to marry a girl that ain't a virgin. This is your first date. You don't know if she's marriage material yet. If she's too easy, you know she ain't worth nothing more than a poke."

"Good grief," Calvin moaned.

"Don't be saying that either in front of her—it's too Charlie Brown. Take her to a scary movie."

"Why?"

"So she'll get scared and hold you. Maybe you can get a feel of her booby. Course, you don't want a girl with too big a boobies or butt. That's why I like Donna."

Calvin bit his lower lip. Indeed, Donna, with her skinny frame, was the opposite of Nancy. Calvin wondered if Frank didn't like boobies or hips, why didn't he get a boy? Sensibly, Calvin kept the thought to himself.

"And don't be using lots of syllables. Girls hate that," Frank shouted as Calvin walked off.

"What's this?" Calvin asked, a few minutes later, as Dale handed over a set of keys to Nancy's new Delta 88 with a Jesus fish key chain.

"Use it for your date."

"But Mom has that embarrassing bumper sticker on it."

"What bumper sticker?"

"'In case of rapture, this car will be unmanned.'"

"Look, you can't take that girl out in your car. It's too old, too dirty, and too unpredictable. Besides, it's supposed to rain tonight. Don't want to get stuck in the rain if your car dies again."

Calvin waited patiently downstairs in Tina's house as she finished getting ready. For a moment, he imagined his date dressed in a white gown like the bride in his vision, awash in a dreamy glow. That dissipated as Tina appeared in blue jeans and jersey shirt.

"You two have fun," Tina's mom yelled as the two left. Calvin opened the door for Tina and found himself at a loss for words during the drive to the theater.

"I hope you like Charlie Chaplin," Calvin told Tina as they stood in line at the ticket counter.

"Never heard of him, but I'm willing to try a new movie."

"Good. You know, some people say we've lost Christ, but for me it's sadder that we've lost Chaplin."

"Lost Christ? What do you mean?" Tina asked as thunder clapped outside.

Calvin remembered Frank's advice of playing it dumb and ignored her question. "This movie's almost fifty years old, but I think you'll like it."

"Two tickets for *Modern Times*," Calvin said to the clerk.

"Most guys would have taken a first date to a scary movie," said Tina as she played with her spaghetti during dinner.

"What did you think of it?" Calvin asked, again ignoring her comment.

"It had some funny parts, and I'm glad he got the girl. I've never seen a silent movie before."

"Besides working at Dairy Queen, what do you like to do? Do you like art?"

"I don't know anything about art, but I'm on the freshmen girls' basketball team."

"Freshman? How old are you?"

"Fifteen."

"I thought you were at least eighteen. Your parents let you date at fifteen?"

"What are you? My dad? I've been dating for over a year. Some of my girlfriends are on birth control! What's the big deal?"

"Birth control? Jesus! Did your parents say what time you had to be home?"

"No," said Tina defiantly.

The outside sound of exploding thunder and heavy rain rocked the restaurant. "Looks like we better hit the road," said Calvin, who at nineteen was not ready to even explore the idea of sex.

Calvin wondered why he had even agreed to the date and what it was he was trying to prove. As the two drove back to her house, Tina inched toward Calvin, her knee too close to his for comfort.

"Better get your seat belt on," he said as he tried to see through the thick rain pelting his windshield. Tina strapped in. She looked disappointed. Calvin couldn't wait for this to end and hoped they were going to make it back to Tina's house in one piece, what with the poorly lit country roads being as slick as they were.

Jesus God, I'm never going on a date again, Calvin thought as he pulled out of Tina's driveway. That was stupid.

He had driven for what seemed like an eternity on winding back country roads, lost amid the torrent when he felt the car jerk and veer to the right. Skidding off the road, he plowed Nancy's car straight into mud on the shoulder. Immediately, the engine stalled.

"Goddammit," he screamed.

Drenched in sweat, Calvin waited a few minutes before restarting the car and putting it in reverse. Moving too quickly, he again lost control. Panicking, Calvin pressed down on the gas pedal. The tires spun hopelessly in mud. He was stuck. After turning off the engine, Calvin staggered out, walked to the front of the vehicle and attempted to push it out of the mud. He failed to do so and slipped and fell into the mud. Calvin stood covered head-to-toe in mud and leaned against the car in defeat as rain and wind enveloped him. As his mother's Delta 88 slowly sunk further into the mud, Calvin succumbed to the vision of Don Giovanni sinking into a fiery pit, condemned by the commander after an ominous last supper. In place of the dead commander, Brother Cobweb grasped Calvin's unrepentant wrist, preparing to fling the sinner into torment at the hands of an awaiting faceless deity. This, Calvin thought, was Brother Cobweb's revenge for having confined him to a purgatory for so long. Indeed, it had been some time since Calvin had drawn or even given thought to the image. With all that had unfolded with Nancy, Rev. Harry, and the Lighthouse, Brother Cobweb almost seemed too real to be funny. But now, the vision of him raised its ugly head and proved more unsettling than volumes of Chick tracts. Condemned to a white trash opera, thought Calvin as he climbed back inside his mother's car to wait out the rain. Calvin was unsure how long he had been sitting in the mud when a burning glow of oncoming headlights blinded him. A truck came slowly into focus through the rain.

"You OK?" the truck driver asked tentatively.

"Yeah," Calvin stammered, looking down at the mud.

"Hop in. We'll give you a lift."

Relieved, Calvin walked through mud to the road and awaiting truck. Calvin's heart jumped upon seeing the driver. A long scar, perhaps the work of a knife, extended from the top of the stranger's forehead to his chin. His appearance was accented with disheveled hair and tattoo-covered arms. The driver's dishwater-blonde girlfriend scooted over to make room for him.

"Thanks," mumbled Calvin, "I'm covered in mud."

"It's all right—not like it's a new truck. Where can we take you?"

"Someplace that's got a tow truck."

The man laughed. "There's a truck stop not too far from here."

"Thanks. By the way, where am I?" said Calvin as he climbed in.

"Just tell the tow truck guy that your car's on Rural Route One."

The ride to the truck stop was silent, apart from a Tammy Wynette-George Jones duet crackling through the Ford's speakers. When he walked into the small truck stop, Calvin noticed the time: 11:30. The waitress at the truck stop diner took pity on him, pointing Calvin to the restroom and handing him a towel from the kitchen so he could clean up. When Calvin returned, there was a steaming cup of coffee on the table. Taking off Frank's leather jacket, which was now caked in mud, Calvin folded it and placed it on the seat beside him.

"Whattayaknow? There's actually a person under all that dirt," laughed the waitress. "You want anything else? A cigarette, perhaps?"

"God, yes," answered Calvin, grateful for the compassion of strangers.

She pulled out a pack of cigarettes from her pocket and handed one to Calvin.

"Thank you."

"What happened? Did you get caught in the storm?"

"I went off the road and got stuck in the mud. I'll need a tow truck."

"Sweetie, with all the trucks at this stop, you would think we'd have a tow truck here. Unfortunately, I ain't seen one tonight, but you can feel free to use the pay phone. It's right over there to the left."

The dial of each number on the phone felt heavy as Calvin called home.

"So, where are you, and where did you leave the car?" Dale immediately asked Calvin.

"Calvin!" called Dale, startling his son a short while later. "Let's find your mom's car."

Calvin picked up Frank's jacket and followed Dale. After getting directions from a police station, they found the car and had it towed. Preoccupied with the wedding, Nancy never said a word to Calvin about the incident. Equally uncaring, no one asked Calvin about his first date, which was a relief. Better yet, Dale didn't tell Nancy about catching his son smoking.

Frank's wedding was performed by the newly ordained Luke; it took place at the Lighthouse amid faint murmuring regarding a bride walking up the aisle in her eighth month of pregnancy, much to Calvin's amusement. In banning Brother Cobweb from his art for a spell, Calvin realized that perhaps the previous night's rainy vision of Brother Cobweb was merely a longing to revive him. With that in mind, BlueMahler's wedding would have to wait. As he sat through the wedding ceremony, Calvin mentally doodled Frank and Donna's wedded bliss as told by Brother Cobweb, which would begin each morning with Donna in her polka-dotted 1950s dress hitting the country kitchen. Of course, it would be decorated to the hilt: little ceramic Amish figures on shelves, plaques with Bibles verses, and a barn painted on a sawblade. What would she fix him for breakfast? Why, a bowl of Brother Cobweb's Christ Crispies, of course. Eat the baby Jesus so you can fight the devil in your belly. Frank would descend the stairs in his work-ready overalls for his morning bowl of Christ Crispies! Each bowl comes with a free prize—a Jesus coin holder—so Frank and the kids can put their coins in it for the church collection plate. Amen, Brother Cobweb, amen.

"How you been doing?" Luke asked Calvin at the reception.

"OK . . . and you?"

"I'm married now and going to be the new pastor."

"I heard you were taking over the church," Calvin said, toning down the disdain in his voice.

"I'm sure you did. From your mother?"

"She told Frank. Frank told me."

"I guess she's afraid of changes at the Lighthouse?" asked Luke.

"Of course."

"And you're going through quite a few changes yourself—art school, Donna moving in."

"They're moving in, and I'm moving the hell out . . . as soon as I can."

"That would be good for you. You know, I hope you'll give me a few months to get situated in."

"Give you a few months?"

"I was hoping you might come back . . . to church."

"Uh huh," Calvin said, rolling his eyes.

IDENTIFICATION LINE

Older, bespectacled, and bearded, Professor Leonard Hillcrest surveyed the classroom, scrutinizing the rows of canvases. It was the first day of class, and Hillcrest had given the simple instruction: "Paint." A short while later, Calvin overheard Hillcrest instructing a fellow student named Jude that if he wanted to make a straight line, then he should grab a ruler and make a goddamned straight line.

Damn, thought Calvin as he reached into his art case and grabbed a ruler. Within a few moments, Hillcrest hovered over Calvin.

"What are you doing?" Hillcrest asked.

"W—w—well I heard you say if you want to make a straight line . . ."

"I said that to Jude because he's a linear painter. You're an organic painter. I would rather see an honest crooked line out of you than a dishonest straight one. Give me your ruler."

Calvin meekly handed his professor the instrument. Hillcrest threw it across the room. Hillcrest sighed and looked at Calvin's canvas for several moments. "You paint like an expressionist," he said. "Who are some of the expressionists you have looked at?"

"Uh . . . El Greco, Gauguin."

"El Greco's long before expressionism. Gauguin, a few years." Sensing Calvin's cluelessness, Hillcrest said forcefully, "Name me five expressionist painters."

Without an answer, Calvin stammered.

"Get your stuff and leave my class."

Humiliated, Calvin gathered his supplies and was on the verge of walking out the door when Hillcrest stopped him.

"Where do you think you're going?"

"You told me to leave."

"For a reason, you idiot. Come here."

Calvin joined Hillcrest at a large desk in the center of the room.

"Here," said Hillcrest as he handed Calvin a piece of paper. "If you want to be a good painter, then you have to know good painting. Get down to the library and look up this list of artists. I want you to spend the next three weeks there. Then, you can rejoin the class. Your grade won't be affected."

Although Calvin had explored music and film, his exposure to painting had been admittedly limited. Being a painter, or rather wanting to be a painter, had stymied his immersion in art history. As he plunged into Hillcrest's list, he became aware of his own limited palette.

The first book on Hillcrest's list was about The Blue Riders, a group of German expressionists at the turn of the twentieth century who changed the very ideas of painting as much as the Second Viennese School altered the language of music. The Blue Riders were not merely painters, but a new priestly order, subverting the social norms with a provocative iconography: spiritually electric animals, floating forms violently clashing, and primitive explosions of color. He strongly identified with what Blue Rider artist Franz Marc wrote about art as a spiritual gift that was often looked at with suspicion by communities who only valued materialism. It reminded Calvin of the Lighthouse community that had long whispered about his artistic endeavors and the time he wasted in devotion to drawing. Of course, most at the Lighthouse were inherently superstitious about art. That was something akin to their claim of being anti-ritualistic, even though they had created their own anti-ritual rituals. Indeed, kitsch art was a part of the charismatic demograhic, which made them suspicious of art that was too original, too emotional, or too complex.

Of The Blue Riders, it was Wassily Kandinsky whom Calvin spent the most time with. What excited Calvin was Kandinsky's complexity. His paintings were not works that one could merely glance at for a moment before going to the next image. Kandinsky's paintings demanded extended engagement, refusing to be solved. Narratively and pictorially, they made little sense, and that was honest—true to life. Yet, when flipping through Kandinsky's book, *Concerning the Spiritual in Art*, Calvin came across the author's claim that children were not prone to create religious imagery. It was a statement that didn't hold true for Calvin, but it didn't diminish his excitement for Kandinsky. Calvin's first efforts were indeed religious, and although he had reaped much negativity from his mother's religion, Calvin realized it had unintentionally gifted him a rich and unique iconography.

As teens were apt to do, Calvin was getting anxious to switch jobs. Although he enjoyed listening to Lloyd's stories, Calvin hated working outside. Fortunately, Jed, whom Calvin had seen less of after high school, called with an offer of a dishwashing job at Nellie's Bar and Grill. After giving his notice at the gas station, Calvin tried to get excited about having another shit job.

Although Calvin had learned much from his painting research and belatedly realized that Hillcrest knew exactly what he was doing with the library assignment, it had not yet translated to Calvin's work. For the first half of the semester, Calvin painted one godawful canvas after another. Finally, Calvin returned to his first great love in painting when he revisited a series of Gauguin self-portraits, discovering within much symbolism that, like Kandinsky, made them all the more appealingly complex.

Calvin stayed after class, late into late night, to set up a canvas and begin his own self-portrait. Instinctively, as he painted, Calvin became aware that he was onto something. One night translated into five, an epic mess of an area, multiple cigarette-filled ashtrays, and three self-portraits. On Monday morning, Calvin set up his triptych.

"You got good," Hillcrest told Calvin before turning to the next student. It was all he needed to say.

A few days later, after photographing his recent canvases, Calvin, eager to get the photos developed, found a local camera shop. Much to his surprise, he discovered the clerk was Ray Stevens.

"Good for you being in art school," Ray laughed. "But let me guess—with no support from your mother."

"'Waste of money and time,'" he screeched, mimicking her. They laughed together. "How are your parents? Are you in school?"

"I'm working toward my bachelor's in chemistry. Dad's a chemist, and he can get me on where he works after I graduate. I've been forced to be pragmatic."

"How come?"

"I'm married and have a son."

"Wow!" Calvin said, not sure how to feel about the fact that both his little brother and childhood friend were married men, but offering to grab a drink with Ray anyway.

Nellie's Bar and Grill was as dilapidated and clichéd as Calvin had imagined.

Jed showed Calvin the ropes the first day. He handed Calvin an apron and took him to the sink area.

"It's simple. There's three sinks. This first sink you wash dishes in. The second sink you rinse them in. That third sink is a sanitizing sink. See that heating coil? That's what heats it and it sanitizes the dishes. You just take the tray and dip the dishes in there for about thirty seconds and then pull them out."

Calvin nodded while thinking, God, I hope I'm not here long.

On the following Monday, Calvin was relieved to be back at school after the first weekend at his new job. Hillcrest motioned to a large table. "Before the model gets here, everyone turn in last week's assignment," he said. It was rare for Hillcrest to give an assignment of any kind. However, with his love of music nearly equaling his passion for painting, Hillcrest was curious about his students' musical vocabularies and assigned them to do a painting to music. They began by looking at Jude's painting.

Jude held up his smallish canvas of a man in a telephone booth.

"It's from the Jim Croce song, 'Operator,'" said Jude before breaking into an unasked-for rendition of Jim calling the operator to find an ex-girlfriend in Los Angeles shacking up with an ex-best friend.

"Oh, God," groaned Hillcrest, interrupting Jude. "Would you please shut up? Calvin, what do you have?"

Feeling anxious, Calvin presented his psychedelic abstraction and blurted out, "The Mahler seventh."

Hillcrest waxed reflective for a moment. "OK, I'll give you a B."

"Why can't I have an A?" Calvin whined.

"Because that's Mahler's worst piece!"

"No," Calvin challenged. "It's his most progressive. Even Boulez—"

"Boulez? Not that atonal shit."

"You're an abstract expressionist. It's the same language."

"Is it now?"

"Yeah, it is."

"Challenging me, huh? It's about goddamned time," Hillcrest said, smirking. "Write me an essay, and if you convince me, I'll upgrade you to an A."

"I'll write the essay, but not for the grade."

"Just write the essay, then we'll see about the grade."

During a break at Nellie's that night, Gina, a thirty-something buxom blonde waitress sat down across from Calvin in the booth.

"So, how long you and Jed been friends?" Gina asked as she lit up her Kool.

"Since ninth grade."

"Jed said you're in art college."

"Yeah. I don't think Jed's going the college route though."

"Nah, he says colleges are just liberal propaganda," Gina laughed.

"He's buying more and more into all that low-informed extremist bullshit."

"He's talking about joining the army."

"Imagine that. Still, with all the chaos he grew up with, he probably needs that structure. I need the opposite. The army will probably be good for him, as long as it doesn't turn him into a cartoon."

"A cartoon?" Gina asked.

Calvin shook his head, declining to elaborate.

"So, what kind of job are you going to get with your art degree?"

"I haven't given it any thought."

"Did you go to school today? What'd you do in class?"

"Drew a couple of models to Mozart."

"What the hell you know about Mozart? You been elbow deep in spaghetti sauce. Don't let those professors turn you all artsy fartsy."

"No artsy fartsy."

"Oh, you've always been artsy fartsy. I heard plenty about you."

"What does Jed know?"

"Not from Jed. From Opal!"

"Opal?"

"The midget night cook manager," said Gina pointing to Opal, who was standing at the grill. "She knows you from your mom's church."

Calvin looked up and carefully studied Opal's short, stocky frame, pale skin, and oversized glasses.

"God, there's no escaping it," Calvin groaned as recognition of the woman slowly set in.

"Escaping what? She says you left your mom's church."

"I sure as hell did."

"Ha! You and I are going to get along just fine."

"Gina!" Opal yelled. "Break's over, and you've got a customer."

Gina jumped up, and Calvin headed back to the dish area.

"Calvin," Opal said in a raspy voice, "You watch out for that Gina. She's nothing but a drunk and a whore."

Calvin nodded and returned to a stack of dirty plates. A short while later, he passed by Opal as he delivered an armful of dishes to the waitress station.

"Throgaz la lona clak grissle stubb pap nada quo og twallow . . ." Opal mumbled quietly as she cooked and raised her hand in the air.

"God, she's speaking in tongues and flipping burgers at the same time," Calvin whispered to Gina.

"Oh. That's nothing. I went to the bank with her once, and she started getting the Holy Ghost right there in line. Do you think it's real?"

"Oh, please," Calvin rolled his eyes.

Unable to muster any enthusiasm for painting on his day off, Calvin opened *The Brother Cobweb Chronicles* with the most recent Hillcrest class fresh in mind.

"Give me your books," Hillcrest had said, pointing to a large stack from the library that Calvin had on the floor in his paint area. Calvin handed them to the teacher, unsure of what was happening. Taking them, Hillcrest walked over to his desk, grabbed his phone, called the library downstairs, and asked them to retrieve the books.

A half hour later, after the library employee had carted off Calvin's reading bounty, Hillcrest, with a chair in hand, again entered Calvin's paint area, placed the chair next to Calvin, sat down, reached over, pulled the cigarette from Calvin's mouth, and began smoking it.

"Go ahead," Hillcrest said, pointing to Calvin's Marlboros. "Light another. I was just too lazy to walk back and get my own."

Calvin laughed.

"Smoking is good for an artist," Hillcrest said. "Actually, more young people should smoke. If everyone smoked, the problems of the world might go away. By the way, you earned your precious A."

"My A?"

"Your paper on Mahler. Quoting Kandinsky was a good touch, but it was the whole cultural omnivore quote that gave you the upgrade. I'm still not entirely convinced when I listen to Boulez, but I get why you like him."

"Why is that?"

"Simple: he's a colorist. Now, you want to know why I took away your books?"

"Of course."

"Odilon Redon, Georges Rouault, Paul Klee, Egon Schiele, Gustav Klimt. OK, you can stop now! You're a painter, not a goddamned art historian. Now it's time to realize your identification line."

"My . . . ?"

"Identification line. Establish who you identify with, and I don't want to hear about everyone who inspired you. I want to see who you identify with. Start burning away the memory of art you don't relate to. The same goes for life in general. The best artists have short memories. Dispose of attachments and retain only what you identify with. After this year, I am not going to teach you again. You've got too much potential, and the best thing I can do is refuse to teach you again. The rest of the semester is going to be tension-filled. Expect it to be brutal and brief. "

Calvin had not looked at *The Brother Cobweb Chronicles* for a long time. Waves of nausea overwhelmed him as he poured over images of Brother and a painfully naïve Lighthouse childhood. Calvin scanned through the book and removed only what he felt would be of use—a few dozen of its hundred-plus pages. Setting them aside, Calvin picked up the remainder of the book, grabbed a lighter, and proceeded to the backyard trash burner. It felt good. It felt goddamn good. He remembered Alberich's curse. Even then, he had found an identification line and used it to place the curse on Nancy for her sacrilege—her attempt to divorce Pop from Ariel. Now, years later, the curse took the form of fire, consuming the filthy images of her and her church.

"Goddammit," screamed Calvin as he jerked his burning hands from the first sink at Nellie's.

"What's wrong?" Gina asked, running back to the dish area.

Calvin looked at the steam rolling up from the first sink and shook his reddened hands.

"He did it to me, too, a couple hours ago," said Gina.

"Who?"

"Your buddy, Jed. He switched the water in the first sink with the water in the third, then put soap on top. It's his idea of a practical joke."

Calvin could hear Jed laughing from around the corner. He told Calvin it had been a prank inspired by the Errol Flynn book Calvin had given him. Calvin was not amused. A short while later, during a break, Gina inched into the booth, sitting across from Calvin.

"Give me your hands," she said, as she pulled out a small bottle of skin lotion from her apron.

"I got it," he said as he reached over and took the lotion. "Thank you."

"What? You afraid to let a woman help take care of you?" she asked, her joking tone masking curiosity.

"I can do it myself," Calvin answered as he rubbed his reddened hands.

"OK," she said, holding up her hands to show she would back off.

"Sorry," said Calvin guardedly, realized he may have offended her generosity but maintaining a degree of distrust in her motive.

"It's OK," she laughed. "Jed says you've never had a girl."

"Does he now?" Calvin asked, rolling his eyes.

"He says you got mommy issues, too."

"Sounds like Jed says a lot."

"Well, he didn't say it exactly like that, but I knew what he meant."

"Jed has his own issues, I think."

"Oh, boy, does he ever."

Calvin raised an eyebrow, wondering why she said it like she knew Jed's issues well.

"So, I'm gonna ask: you ain't never been with a girl?"

"I had a date not too long ago, but it turned out she was fifteen and—"

"So, that's it? One date and nothing?"

"No, I never went out with her again, of course."

"That's not what I mean," Gina said as she leaned in, whispering. "So, you're a virgin?"

Taken aback by the way she said it, almost disbelieving, Calvin, oddly feeling shamed, quickly deflected, "I'm in school . . ."

"—to be a painter. That ain't going to give you no kind of living, anyway. Look, you're young and not a bad-looking guy at all, ain't no reason—"

"House of sin," loudly grumbled Opal, who was at the grill a few feet away from Calvin and Gina's booth.

Both Calvin and Gina looked up to see what had riled Opal and quickly saw that Liz had walked into the restaurant. She was the regular trans customer who was a dead ringer for movie star Elizabeth Taylor. Opal started to shake.

"Poogooonoo, awl emneee, figsur, lacowives," Opal practically spit out.

"Did you hear Opal?" Gina asked Calvin, hiding her laughter from her strange coworker in the kitchen. "What'd she say? What'd she say?"

"I am not a goddamned tongues interpreter," Calvin answered angrily.

Gina started to laugh but saw the frustration in Calvin's eyes.

"I know you're in school," Gina said to Calvin, "and God knows I know you don't make much money here, but I think you need to get out of your mom's house as soon as you can. But look, I need to go take care of Liz."

Calvin lit up a cigarette and thought about Gina's advice. He knew she was right about both leaving home and not making much money.

"Ha! Gina's stuck with queenie there," Jed laughed as he sat down in the booth with Calvin, pointing to Liz. "Give me a smoke."

Calvin handed over a Marlboro.

"I caught up on the dishes," Jed continued, clearly was distracted at the sight of Liz. "You ever talked to him?"

"Who?" Calvin asked.

"Liz. He's a fucking piece of work—acts like the whole world's queer. Well, it ain't."

"Never talked to her."

"Her? That ain't no her, goddammit. He's got a dick like you and me. He just takes it up the poop chute is all."

"I really don't care—" Calvin said, trying to stop the conversation before it started.

"Yeah, I think that art school's turning you into a goddamned liberal. It's probably filled with fags there, too—like that teacher of yours."

"I didn't ask him what his sexual orientation is. I'm there to learn how to paint."

"Paint what? That abstract shit. My grannie could do better than that shit and she's ninety-four and half-blind."

"That's original."

"You are turning into a goddamned liberal."

"Well, I've never exactly been conservative, and I really don't get why you are. It's not like you're religious."

"You don't have to be religious to be conservative. Jesus! What are you, some kind of fag lover? That why you never been out with girls? You ought to join the army with me. I'm seeing my recruiter tomorrow to sign papers."

Calvin just laughed.

"It'd get you away from that goddamn mom of yours. I just hope when I get back from basic, you ain't turned into some kind of anarchist commie fag, man."

"No worries. Commie fag isn't one of my goals."

As Calvin spent the next hour washing dishes, he mulled over his friendship with Jed. Although they shared a history of past abuse, the way it shaped them was different. For Jed, it was something to laugh off; because it was his father who had abused him, it was somehow acceptable. Although Calvin had few friends, he felt he could make new ones, and there was always Ray. That Jed was going into the army was a relief. It spared Calvin the necessity of eliminating Jed from his identification line. Not that he was ever a true part of it anyway. That they had both suffered at the hands of parents simply wasn't enough anymore, and as Calvin looked up to see that the Lighthouse—via Opal—had even penetrated his workspace, he was determined to get the hell out of this job.

Another half hour passed and Calvin was back in the booth with Gina again.

"Have you ever seen *Night of the Living Dead?*" Gina asked Calvin after she put down a newspaper she had been flipping through.

"Oh, yeah, that's a classic!"

"You want to go see it with me?" Gina asked. "They're having a midnight showing at the theater down the road. We'll get out of here in time."

"Are you asking me out on a date?"

"We don't have to call it a date unless you want to."

"OK, I want to," he said, smiling. He headed back to the dishwashing station, counting down the hours until the movie.

"Good job," Jed said to Calvin as he walked up behind him and slapped him on the back, which caused Calvin to flinch.

"Good job?" Calvin asked.

"Your date with Gina. I heard all about it. It's about time. Shouldn't be too hard. Man. She's about the easiest piece of ass I ever fucked."

"You and Gina?"

"Oh, yeah, plenty. Don't worry, I warmed that shit up for you. Ain't nothing wrong with sloppy seconds. Better hurry man, we're closing in a few, and I want a full report later."

The midnight showing at the theater was mostly empty. Black and white zombies came to life on screen as Gina's hand slowly moved from the popcorn bucket to Calvin's knee. He tensed up as her hand left his knee and brushed against his thigh. Calvin immediately stood up. Without thinking, he emptied the entirety of his Pepsi on Gina's head and flew to the exit.

Calvin clicked off the cassette player on the drive home. The music only added to his nausea—nausea for what he had done, coupled with nausea over Gina telling Jed about the date, nausea over Jed having tainted his date, nausea over Gina not having confided in Calvin that she had slept with Jed, and nausea over the thought of Jed having broken her in for him. It was, Calvin felt, one step removed from incest.

He had the next day off school, but Calvin went there to paint alone and to put yesterday behind him. When he pulled up to the campus parking lot, he was surprised to see Jed's car there.

"I called Gina," Jed said with anger in his voice as he slammed his car door and stood alongside Calvin's car. "She told me about your date."

"I can imagine," Calvin mumbled, feeling embarrassed and guilty.

"She had to call a cab. You just left her stranded there. Why don't you man up?"

"About?"

"You're either a fag or—"

"I'm not anything!"

"OK then, but what the fuck? I mean, you going to be a virgin all your life? I know you were raised in church and all that . . ."

"Church has nothing to do with it."

"Well then, if you're gay—it ain't my cup, and I don't want you looking at my ass, but I just say that shit about fags. I don't really give a damn, one way or another."

"Jed, I said I'm not gay, and God knows it's not any kind of religious hang-ups."

"Then what's your problem, man?"

Calvin pulled a cigarette out of his front pocket and noticeably shook as he lit it.

"What is it?" Jed repeated

"I wish in a way that I was gay. I'm not attracted to men, it's just—"

"Just what?"

"Women . . ."

"What about them?"

"I think I'm afraid of them," Calvin said with brutal honesty.

"Your mom? I know she was kind of rough . . ."

"You don't know the half of it," Calvin interrupted. "She waited years to have me and then . . . . My whole life she's hated me—my own mother, of all people—and I don't understand it. What did I do? She didn't want me, and the way she even tried to take Pop from me . . . . It was like she was glad he was dead because then, after—well, the things she did, it was like being in hell for real. Sometimes, I really thought she was going to kill me. I know you understand part of that."

"With my dad, yeah . . . and my mom just let him. Like your dad turned a blind eye to your mom."

"That's the only thing we're really alike in, but—"

"But for me, getting the shit beat out of me, that was only for a few years," Jed said, intentionally interrupting to make it easier on Calvin. "Dad stopped drinking, and he's been trying to make up for the shit he did since. I joke about it in front of him because at least he tries to. You haven't even had that, and I never could figure it out when I was at your house, but something always seemed fucked up about it. I mean, the whole atmosphere there. I think I knew then that she hated you, and to be hated by your own mother . . . . I guess there's nothing more fucked up than that. No, the army wouldn't be right for you. I don't know what is, but you've got to get out of there. I guess for you it's going to be art, but man, that's going to be a hard life."

"I don't have a choice."

"I guess you don't. You're a lot smarter than me, but just promise me you're not going to do anything stupid."

"Stupid? Like what?"

"Never mind. At least I get some of it now. As for women, if it was me, I'd just say fuck 'em all. Hurt them before they can hurt you, but I reckon you're not going to do that. I don't know, man. You sure surprised me with Gina," Jed laughed, and now Calvin felt far worse for what he had done as Jed was taking a kind of perverse pride in it.

"Man, I've got to go see my recruiter and then I'll be leaving in a few weeks," Jed added in summary. "I need to go, and I love you, man, but I think you need me to leave, too."

"Love you too, but maybe I do need you to leave," said Calvin, surprised that Jed had such a moment of insight. Although Calvin had internally theorized a break with things past, he became astutely aware—especially after Jed left—that it was easier in theory than in practice because change was also an inherent fear; so much so, that to alleviate it, he called Ray.

34

A NEW REACH

For second semester, Calvin found himself stuck with a young assistant painting professor, John Smith.

"We are going to start with fruit bowls," announced Smith.

He's as generic as his name, thought Calvin.

Ignoring Smith's instructions, Calvin painted what he wanted. The semester passed lethargically. Having quit the restaurant, Calvin was back to pumping gas, and by semester's end, he had lost much of his enthusiasm for both school and work, resulting in his failing to attend most classes.

One Monday morning, Calvin had just returned from the dentist's office. Nancy was at the kitchen table, clipping her toenails.

"So, what'd the dentist say?"

"No cavities, but I had some plaque issues. He suggested I get a Reach toothbrush."

"He's just trying to make money," Nancy scoffed. "Every time they sell one of those, the national dentist association makes money off it."

Calvin failed to see her logic. "So, he'd probably have to sell a thousand to make a dollar. Who cares?"

"I care, and as long as we haveta pay your health insurance while you're at that stupid school, you ain't gettin' no Reach toothbrush—not as long as you're living in my house."

"That's the silliest thing I've ever heard."

"Silly, huh?"

"And ignorant," Calvin added.

"Nine, eight, seven, six . . ."

Calvin knew he had until the end of the countdown to apologize and go to his room.

". . . five, four, three, two—"

"Do your worst, bitch!"

Nancy let out a beastly howl. With toenail clipper in hand, she leapt from the chair and lunged toward Calvin. Driving the clipper into her son's arm, Nancy tore a chunk of his flesh. Calvin screamed as blood squirted.

Ignoring his wound, Calvin doubled up and drove his fist into his mother's face, bloodying her nose and lips. Nancy fell to the floor, hitting her head against the wall in a loud thud. Panicking at the sight of her own blood, Nancy threw a tantrum, kicking and pounding the floor.

Holding his bloodied arm, Calvin laughed nervously when Frank suddenly walked into the kitchen.

"What the . . . ?" Frank asked.

"Stay out of it," Calvin warned, breathing rapidly.

"Frank, he hit me! Kick his damned ass," Nancy screamed from the tiled floor through a reddened, sweat-drenched face.

"Dammit, Calvin, the baby's asleep in the other room," said Frank. "I oughta—"

"Don't interfere."

"Yeah? Well, I been lifting weights. In a year, I'll kick your ass."

"I'm not waiting a year."

Calvin swung hard, punching Frank in the nose.

"You broke my nose!" Frank cried, clutching his face.

Nancy sprang up from the floor. Screaming, she again lunged at Calvin but was stopped short by a punch.

"Get away from me. I'm moving out—now!" Calvin screamed.

Calvin ran to his room, slammed the door, and locked it.

Within minutes, Nancy managed to unlock it with a steak knife, and upon entering her son's room, she swung madly, attempting to stab him. Grabbing the knife blade, Calvin sliced his palm and managed to wrest the knife from his mother's hand.

"You filthy demon," she hissed. Nancy grabbed hold of Calvin's hair, yanking brutally, trying to pull it out by the root. Calvin slammed his swollen knuckles into Nancy's face again. Screaming, Nancy sank her long nails into her son's cheek, scratching deep. Blood oozed down his face.

"Let go of me," he growled.

Nancy held firm, prompting Calvin to punch her repeatedly until she fell again, crashing to the floor.

"Jesus help me," she bawled melodramatically.

Racked with raging pain, Calvin grabbed some clothes and art supplies, flinging them out the open window. By the time he was out of the house, Calvin realized he had forgotten his car keys. Running back to the front door, he found that Nancy had locked it. Calvin flung his body against the door, splintering the hinges. As he walked into the living room, Nancy, brandishing a knife, confronted him.

"I need my car keys. I'm leaving this hell! Get outta my way."

"Just you try to get past me," she screamed.

Calvin grabbed Nancy by the wrists and shoved her to the floor. She landed hard and wailed. Ignoring her, Calvin ran to his room to retrieve his keys. Fortunately, Frank was nowhere in sight. Calvin was loading his belongings into the car when Dale pulled up to the sight of his bloodied son standing in the driveway in front of a busted front door. Dale stepped out of the car.

"Dad, I'm leaving."

"What happened?" Dale asked, tears streaming down his face.

Calvin couldn't understand his dad's tears. They seemed at odds with his long-held refusal or inability to stop Nancy's violence. Without answering, Calvin put the car in reverse and drove off. Dale, feeling helpless and broken, walked into the house to see his wife on the floor, wailing with blood smeared around her nose.

"What in God's name was this over?" he demanded.

Nancy evasively answered, "It doesn't matter what it was over."

"Oh, something stupid. You couldn't just leave him alone! He's trying to get through college."

"Stupid college."

"Well now, what he's going to do, Nancy? Where's he going to go?"

"Look at me! Look at what he's done to his own mother. He can rot for all I care," she screamed from the floor.

"Yeah, I know you don't care. I've known it since you said you'd rather him be dead than retarded. You made it clear then."

"You ain't got no faith so you don't understand."

"I understand that you say you love Jesus, but you hate your own son."

Nancy shot a look toward Dale and almost said something but stopped herself short. Instead, she screamed, "Ain't you going to help me off this floor?"

Dale looked at his wife in disgust and, without answering, walked out the front door and looked up the road, wondering where his son had gone to and whether he would be OK.

Calvin pulled into a convenient mart parking lot and sat in his car for what seemed like hours, crying and afraid, unsure what to do, until he finally thought to call Professor Hillcrest. Calvin calmed himself down enough to speak in a cooled tone. Thankfully, Hillcrest was home and agreed to put Calvin up for a week. Before leaving, Calvin walked into the store's bathroom. In excruciating pain and with immense difficulty, he tried to clean the blood from himself. While looking at himself in the bathroom mirror, Calvin felt more hurt by and more anger toward his father than he did his mother. Both had deserted him.

Hillcrest quickly saw signs of abuse on Calvin when he welcomed him in to his home: fresh scratches, dried blood, and large bruises. Choosing not to address or ask about it, Hillcrest offered to treat Calvin to a showing of the Mozart movie *Amadeus* followed by a round of pool.

"You're not very good at this," Hillcrest cracked at Calvin's lame attempt at pool.

"I've always found sports boring."

"Pool's the only sport an artist should play," Hillcrest proclaimed as he lit up a Camel and knocked out his first set of solids. "Did you like the movie?"

"It was beautifully devastating. I wanted to protect Wolfie from Salieri."

"It caught the spirit of Mozart's childishness, but it's hardly an accurate portrayal of Salieri . . . except that he was a hack. Still, they both knew that being an artist is a vocational calling—like the priesthood. That's how you separate authentic artists from the pretenders. Television is the rot that's turning potential artists into mush wasting formative years glued to an idiot box. It's getting worse with cable. Now, I have students who act as if anything from a mere twenty years ago comes from a different millennium. If it were up to me, I'd require all students have four years of college before entering art school, but no worries. I won't lump you in with those spinning-tires-in-the-parking lot types. Anyway, my biggest objection to the movie is the attitude that Mozart was divinely gifted. Nonsense! He worked his ass off."

"There's one thing about Salieri that I do identify with."

"Oh?"

"When he says, how could his father understand what music meant to him?"

"Your father doesn't like music?"

"I've never heard him listen to music at all—ever. It's odd. Being a fifties teen, you'd expect him to, but he has no interest. He's missing out on a lot. I'm not a musician at all, but music is my great love, from Mozart to the Statler Brothers."

"Statler Brothers? Oh, please! I think I overestimated you. At least rock and roll has sex and drugs going for it. There's no redeeming quality in country music." Hillcrest laughed, although Calvin sensed his professor was serious.

Despite Hillcrest's occasional lapses into elitism, Calvin was grateful for a place to crash. He was more grateful for not having to sing for his supper and the assistance that Hillcrest gave him in finding an apartment. Calvin suspected that the patient Hillcrest was helpful in that because, even though they hardly saw one another during that week, there was mutual awareness that Calvin would quickly overstay his welcome. Hillcrest, having come from an affluent and educated family, didn't understand Calvin's lower-income white trash heritage, nor did he want to.

FORBIDDEN SUBJECT

A year passed. Calvin's life consisted of pumping gas and painting. He had talked to no one from his past until Nancy unexpectedly showed up at his door with Vernell one day. Calvin kept his hand on the door, not letting her in his apartment, prepared to slam the door in her face for self-protection if need be.

"I got a ton of mail for ya," Nancy said with a familiarity as though nothing had changed and as though she hadn't physically attacked him the last time they spoke. "I finally found out where you live from the post office when they mailed your change of address form here."

"Thanks," said Calvin, taking the mail with indifference.

"You look thin. Ain't you been eating?"

"Well, I don't make much money, and sometimes I have to decide between bills and groceries, so I pay the bills."

Nancy tried to peer around Calvin's shoulder and look into his apartment curiously.

"Look, I have to go," Calvin lied. "Thanks for bringing me the mail."

As he shut the door, Calvin could hear his mother telling Vernell, "It breaks my heart to see my son in such a state."

Calvin rolled his eyes as he locked the door.

An hour later, Calvin heard a knock. He opened the door to find three boxes of groceries outside his door with an attached note reading, "Love, Mom."

Calvin called the house to thank Nancy for the food, but Dale picked up.

"How's your car doing?" Dale asked his son, happy to hear his voice again.

"Overheating nonstop."

"Really? Why don't you bring it by Saturday, and I'll take a look at it?"

"Would you? I really can't afford to get it fixed right now."

"Bring it by. We'll get it fixed."

Upon driving to his parents' house Saturday, Calvin found no one there. Dad must have forgotten, thought Calvin as he headed back to his apartment.

Calvin awoke Sunday morning and made breakfast with some of the food that Nancy had left him. It disgusted him that his breakfast was dependent upon her. Everything was disgusting him. He had quit school, had a cheap, worthless car, and worked at a gas station in the middle of nowhere. Over the past year, he had applied at several higher-paying jobs, only to be turned down every time. Eventually, Calvin stopped applying altogether. He had even gone to a few galleries, planning on showing them his work, but at the last moment couldn't bring himself to do it—fear of rejection gripped him.

Apart from a few luncheons with Ray, Calvin had no contact with anyone. Ray, being busy with his wife, kid, and job, couldn't meet up often, and he always paid, knowing that Calvin had a meager income. Naturally, it made Calvin feel worse, even though that was not Ray's intent. Calvin envied Ray in having a family. Even Frank had a family and circle of friends. Calvin, however, had no one and couldn't bring himself to attend social gatherings, feeling he would be out of place and most likely rejected. He was lonely.

Although he had been prolifically painting and his work was increasingly improving, he wondered why he was even doing it in the first place. It wasn't as if the world cared whether he was a good painter or not; if he were to die tomorrow, what would become of the paintings? Most likely, they would be tossed out. Perhaps they should be, Calvin thought as he stood in the drugstore checkout line on Sunday morning, realizing that he had been alone since Pop died. Having Pop as a spiritual playmate, confidant, guide, coconspirator, and fellow rebel explorer had made for a wondrous world—a childhood paradise of sorts, although there was always the presence of a snake in the garden. The paradise, though flawed, was all too brief. Calvin realized he wouldn't have that with anyone else—ever. Indeed, Calvin had not known happiness since losing Pop. Pop, like Calvin, was dysfunctional in the world. Together, they protected each other, but apart . . . the world became a grotesque parody. I'm afraid of everything. Perhaps I should be tossed out, Calvin thought as the cashier placed the bottle in a bag.

Calvin poured himself a glass of water, dropped the needle on a small stack of LPs, and swallowed the entire bottle of sleeping pills. As he lay down on the couch, Calvin was already feeling the effect of the pills when he thought to leave a note.

No funeral, no showing, no service, Calvin scrawled.

As he got up to return to the couch, the room spiraled out of control. Dizzy, Calvin collapsed to the floor, unconscious.

Dale felt guilty for having forgotten about Calvin's car and, coupled with the weight of Sunday boredom, called the Lighthouse and asked the church secretary for Nancy. Several minutes passed before Nancy got to the phone.

"Hello?" Nancy asked nervously. Dale had never called her at church. "Is everything OK?"

"Yeah. Calvin asked me to look at his car. It's been overheating, I guess. He was supposed to come by yesterday, but I forgot all about it. Figured I'd go look at it while I got the day off, but I don't know his address."

"You interrupted me in church for this?" she asked, then sighed. "Hold on, I have it in my purse." Nancy found the address and read it to Dale. "I guess he can't exactly be without a car, and he sure don't know how to fix it hisself. Course, you never bothered to teach him that kinda thing."

Annoyed, Dale hung up. It turned out that Calvin only lived twenty minutes away. Dale saw his son's car in the apartment complex parking lot.

Well, he's home. No wonder with that piece of junk, Dale thought. Better get the keys from him.

Dale walked up and knocked on Calvin's door, apartment C. Nothing. He looked at the slip of paper again. Yeah, apartment C. Dale knocked again as he heard music playing faintly from inside. He's definitely home. It's that weird music he was always listening to.

Dale tried the handle and was surprised to find it unlocked. The door swung open, revealing his son lying on the floor.

"Calvin," he yelled out as he rushed over to the limp, unconscious form. "What'd you do?" he asked as if somehow Calvin might answer.

Dale looked up to see a piece of paper and bottle on the table. After reading the note, he turned the bottle over. Dale realized that Calvin had taken the whole thing. He scanned the room in search for a phone, which he found on an end table.

"Yeah, I just found my son," Dale told the 911 operator, breathless. "He's tried to kill himself with a whole bottle of sleeping pills. Get someone over here NOW!" he screamed into the phone. Dale rattled off the address, hung up, and immediately dialed the Lighthouse again.

"Goddammit! Answer the phone," he screamed.

"Hello?"

"Get Nancy Elkan!"

"Sir, didn't you just call? She's still in service. We normally don't—"

"Get her, now! I think our son's dead!"

The secretary left the receiver hanging and rushed toward the stage. Interrupting the sermon, she grabbed Rev. Harry and whispered into his ear. The entire church grew silent in curiosity. Gripped with fear, Rev. Harry's face turned pale as he leaned into the microphone.

"I'm sorry. We have an emergency. Nancy, would you follow me?" Rev. Harry asked as he grabbed Luke by the arm, motioning him to follow. Rev. Harry, accompanied by Nancy and Luke, darted down the aisle toward the phone as the congregation sat in shock at what to do without a leader.

"It's Calvin," Rev. Harry whispered to Nancy, handing the phone to her.

"Hello?" Nancy asked, trembling.

"Nancy. I got here. I found Calvin on the floor. He killed himself. I think he's dead. He took a whole bottle of sleeping pills. He doesn't seem to be breathing. He's all white. I think he's dead."

"Did you call nine-one-one?"

"They're on the way, but I think he's dead."

Dale was bawling uncontrollably when the ambulance arrived.

"Nancy, they're here," Dale screamed into the phone. No answer. "Nancy? Nancy?"

"She's on the way with Harry and Luke," said the secretary. "Hang on, Mr. Elkan."

The EMTs arrived at Calvin's apartment, and Dale watched in abject horror as they tried four times to resuscitate Calvin. It worked the fourth time.

"Calvin will be all right, but he is going to be out of it for the rest of the day," said the doctor to Dale and Nancy a few hours later at the hospital. Rev. Harry and Luke sat next to the couple in the waiting room. "I'll keep you posted when he comes to."

"Did you see those awful paintings in his apartment?" Nancy asked Dale after the doctor left.

"I wasn't paying any attention."

"That's your problem. You never pay any attention. You never have and you don't keep your word."

"What are you talkin' about?"

"Do you remember when Calvin had meningitis? You promised God that you'd quit drinking if he spared Calvin. Well he did, and you didn't. Things have a way of coming back on you, Dale! Now you're paying for not keeping your promise."

"Let's not haggle with God or play the blame game," offered Luke.

"You're right, Luke," Nancy said, bankrupt of sincerity. "We just need to make sure Calvin gets the help he needs first and see that he gets right with God."

"Amen," said Rev. Harry.

"I think maybe we ought to leave your religion out of this," said Dale.

"Same as always—you going against me," Nancy grumbled.

Calvin woke to an inflamed throat. His mouth tasted like charcoal, and his stomach churned. He was alone in a stark hospital room. *God, I can't even kill myself right,* Calvin thought. Now he would be the center of an attention that he did not want. It felt as if he were the one now on the Lighthouse stage with his family and the congregation in the pews below, awaiting his testimony of how the devil had grabbed hold of him—the same devil that had possessed him to paint those godless paintings, the same devil in the form of his apartment cat. Only Calvin wasn't going to give them the heart-on-sleeve show that they craved. He would hold fast to his detachment, blind to their lighthouse beam, and refuse all offers to come back to the fold. He determinedly would not admit any wrongdoing, even though he had indeed sinned. He remembered Pop's command: *you are going to persevere.* Yet, the question Calvin had for himself was, now what?

After he was released from the hospital, Calvin reassured his parents, Rev. Harry, Luke, and the doctors that he would set an outpatient therapy appointment with a psychologist. But he misplaced the referral paper. If he was going to seek help, it would be help of his own choosing. Still, it was hard to return to that apartment, which seemed bigger and emptier now than it had before his suicide attempt. Barely able to tolerate the four surrounding walls, Calvin scheduled an appointment with the Art Brut Gallery in hopes of getting a show. Shortly after that, per Bertie's request, Calvin stopped by to see Tubby, who was in the final stage of cancer. Calvin dreaded doing so, knowing that Nancy had told his grandparents about his attempt. The sight of Tubby—riddled with bedsores, breathing through machinery, and feeding through a tube— made Calvin immediately forget his trepidation. With difficulty, Tubby lifted himself and motioned for Calvin. The yellowing, rotting flesh of Tubby's hand touched Calvin's arm. Tubby's wet eyes, filled with yearning, transfixed Calvin.

"I . . . sorry . . . Calvin," Tubby barely managed to say.

Before Calvin could attempt a response, Bertie interrupted. "He's out of his mind. Said the same thing to your mom the other day."

No, he's not, Calvin thought, and he wondered why Tubby had apologized. It seemed as if Tubby were apologizing for Calvin's suicide attempt. Why? And why did he say that to Mom, too? Does Tubby feel that my doing that was in some way connected to Mom? Mom would have never suggested that there was a connection. And perhaps there wasn't. Mom didn't make me do it. Yet, why did I see a look of guilt and responsibility in Tubby's eyes? As Calvin was leaving, the thought occurred to him that, in seeing Tubby dying, he was seeing the death of an enigmatic seed.

FIRST FRIDAY ETIQUETTE

The Art Brut had accepted both Calvin and his work. Additionally, it had been suggested in a group meeting that Calvin should try donning the persona of BlueMahler for the next opening. It was a suggestion that proved revelatory. With a layer of blue paint separating his face from the patrons, Calvin found that he was in his element; he discovered that the protective layer freed him from his introverted baggage. Behind BlueMahler, Calvin found himself animated and self-confident, even in front of a crowd.

But there wasn't a crowd the night that a short woman walked in The Art Brut. Her face was adorned in large, round glasses and topped off with dark hair; she looked the archetypal librarian.

"Is this thing on?" BlueMahler asked her. It had been his opening line to several patrons.

"Huh?" she asked. She looked around with a confused look on her face. "Is what on?"

"Are you on?" BlueMahler laughed. "Actually, it's the name of the show."

"Why?"

"Why what?"

"Why is it the name of the show?"

"Why should I tell you why that is the show's name when I don't even know your name?"

"My name is Cheryl Paddock. What's your name?"

"My name is BlueMahler."

"I don't understand."

"That's the whole point—not to understand. Once you realize that, you will."

"I will what?"

"Understand that you don't understand."

"So, that's what the show is about? Not understanding?"

"Perhaps, but I was referring to my name."

"Well then, what is a BlueMahler?"

No one had asked Calvin that, which surprised and excited him.

"For me, and only for me perhaps, BlueMahler is this: *Where do we come from? What are we? Where are we going?* That was the question of Gauguin's blue gospel painting. The composer Gustav Mahler asked the same question throughout his music. So, I give you BlueMahler."

"OK, that makes sense, but what's your real name behind all that paint?"

That was another first, prompting Calvin to play along.

"Something boring."

"OK, something boring . . . are any of these paintings yours?"

Calvin's interest was piqued and he wanted to see where this would go. Asking about his art was the surest way to prompt further engagement, even from someone he'd never met before.

"No, but some of them belong to Calvin."

"Ah, so you're a Calvin."

"I didn't say that."

"What are you saying?"

"You've already asked. You're supposed to move to 'where?'"

"Then *where* are Calvin's paintings?"

"Follow me."

Cheryl raised her eyebrows. Calvin wasn't used to people being interested in him or his art, and she seemed to be interested in both. Before

Calvin could escort Cheryl to his canvases, a gallery member named Pee-Wee handed him a note. Calvin read the note and blinked.

"How the hell does she know I'm working here?" Calvin asked Pee-Wee, breaking character in front of Cheryl.

"She probably read about it," Pee-Wee answered. "The show's listed in the paper."

"Anything wrong?" Cheryl asked Calvin as they started walking.

"It's nothing—just a call from mother dear that my grandfather has died," said Calvin, feeling nothing but a void of nameless relief. She said nothing else about it, and he showed her his paintings. They talked for hours until the gallery closed. Cheryl asked him out to dinner while Calvin locked the door.

"I do have a question, if you don't mind: your grandfather dying doesn't seem to affect you," she said as they began walking toward a nearby deli.

"Oh. I don't usually think of Tubby as my grandfather. I think of my great-grandfather as my grandfather, but he's been gone for a long time."

"You weren't close to Tubby?"

"Not really."

"You aren't close to your family?"

"No."

"That was definite. Not even your mother?" Cheryl asked.

"Ha! Especially not my mother."

"I can relate."

"Can you now?" Calvin asked. Already tiring of and feeling a bit of self-loathing toward his night of mild gallery flirtation, Calvin chucked the shallow banter in hopes of finding a deeper connection. "Perhaps we should start there. Tell me," said Calvin.

"Well, I got pregnant without being married," Cheryl began after the two sat down to eat. "That was five years ago, and there hasn't been a day since when Mom hasn't thrown my son in my face."

"What about your son's father?"

"We broke up while I was pregnant. My son's never even seen his dad. Me and my son have lived with my parents since he was born. I haven't even dated anyone for five years, but that doesn't matter at all to my mom. She'll never forgive me—and you know what the kicker is?"

"Let me guess . . . she had you out of wedlock."

"Not quite, but Mom and Dad married *four* months before she had me. She's a typical Baptist hypocrite."

"She and my mother should get together and go bowling."

Cheryl laughed. "Is your mom Baptist?"

"Pentecostal."

"Aren't they the ones who—"

"Yup."

"Is your dad Pentecostal, too?"

"No, but he has a Baptist haircut."

Cheryl laughed again. "So, do you have a girlfriend?"

"No," said Calvin as he lit up a cigarette.

"Would you be open to going out on a date together?"

"Sure. We can bitch about our mothers."

As they left the deli, Cheryl leaned in to hug Calvin goodnight, which caused him to flinch. Cheryl noticed. Calvin noticed that she noticed.

37

We've Got a Spiritual Problem Here

A month passed. Calvin took Cheryl on a few more dates. Getting to know her was nice, but Calvin felt most alive when he was in the gallery performing as BlueMahler and interacting with guests.

"Are you the painter?" an elderly gentleman asked as he approached Calvin, who was standing next to one of his canvases. Tall, thin, dapperly dressed with well-groomed silver hair and a mustache, the gallery patron exuded an air of affability. Calvin said he was indeed the painter.

"I enjoy your work. Correct me if I'm mistaken, but I sense a pronounced spirituality in these," said the old man, pointing to Calvin's paintings.

"You're mistaken," answered Calvin. "I'm an atheist, and I hate God."

"You may be angry at God," laughed the old man, "but you're no atheist."

"Why do you say that?"

"You can't hate someone who doesn't exist. By the way, my name is Father Oliver. Nice to meet you."

The priest extended his hand for a shake, which Calvin awkwardly took.

"I'm not a leper," Oliver mused after the handshake. Calvin blushed. "I've found that when most people say they're atheists, what they mean isn't that they're not spiritual. It just means they're not buying into a belief system. Besides, all art is spiritual—even art by a self-professed atheist. Actually, I've often found that art by so-called atheists may be the most spiritual art of all. I tell my parishioners that they should approach their Catholic faith like an atheist would, rather than taking the Protestant route, but OK, that's all I'll say about it. I don't want you to think I'm proselytizing. I'd like to think we've gone past that superficial silliness."

"We?" Calvin asked, thinking Father Oliver was referring to the two of them.

"The Church."

Calvin was taken back. This was not the kind of cleric he was familiar with.

"Here's my card," Father Oliver said. "I think it would be quite something to get to know you. If you ever feel like it, give me a call. Maybe we can talk art and music—anything but spirituality."

Calvin thanked Father Oliver and took the card with no intention of calling him, despite the fact that he was intrigued by such an open-minded religious leader. He hadn't known they existed.

38

BROTHER COBWEB
AT THE ART BRUT

"You're too original to be named Smith," Calvin told Ed Smith. "You mind if I call you Smythe?"

"Right on," laughed Ed.

With his braided beard, long hair reaching down his back, purple corduroy pants, burnt orange Indian linen shirt, and a sitar strapped around his shoulder, Ed looked the part of the quintessential Vietnam War protester and '60s hippie, which was precisely what he was. He was also a board member of The Art Brut and a friend of Ray's. Indeed, it was initially Ray's influence that had gotten Calvin accepted into the gallery, and now Ed had spent the better part of an hour thumbing through what Calvin referred to as his attic canvases. Most of these were Calvin's Pentecostal-themed works. Believing they would never sell or be of interest to anyone, Calvin had shoved them in a back room of the gallery to collect dust.

"Man, it's your religious work I really dig. Of course, all your work's religious, but when you use these overt symbols, you're onto something. I love your Pentecostal paintings," Ed said as he pulled out a Lighthouse painting. "You should do one on wood. It would add to that primitive quality."

Ed offered to buy the Lighthouse painting for twenty dollars, but Calvin insisted on giving it to him for free.

"Cool man, thanks." Ed tucked the small canvas under his arm. "Man, I grew up in a Nazarene church. I can identify with these."

"I never understood the difference between Pentecostals and Nazarenes."

"Man, Nazarenes still do all that slaying in the spirit, too, they just don't speak in tongues," Ed laughed out loud in a nonjudgmental way that Calvin found charming, despite his own long-held judgments. "I think you ought to do a public showing of your Brother Cobweb character. I know you prefer the BlueMahler character—he is more complex and subtler—but you shouldn't dismiss Brother Cobweb as simplistic. He's not. You could do the Brother Cobweb performance art with your Pentecostal paintings. Maybe we could get Ray in on the show, too."

"If he's open, he'd do it justice," Calvin said, eager to once again perform with Ray. "Still, if we're going to do a performance piece, I need two additional people to be preachers. How about you?"

"Oh, I'm not doing performance art. What about Pee-Wee?"

"I'll ask him."

"I think you ought to include your *Our Lady of the Mermaid* canvas in the show, too. You have the pulse of that blue-collar Catholic surrealism. I want to go to one of those Virgin Mary gatherings where everyone's snapping Polaroids to identify some speck of lens dust as Our Lady Light. From the film clips I've seen, they get worked up fierce. It's related in a way to Pentecostalism, but with all that masculinity burned off—the best kind of primitive religious performance art."

The Art Brut was packed for its First Friday opening of "Brother Cobweb: A showing of paintings by Calvin Elkan, with performance art featuring Ray Stevens and Pee-Wee Sanders." After patrons browsed through the art displays for an hour, Ray stepped up to a pulpit in the center of the gallery space. Leaning into the microphone, Ray looked as though he was going to swallow it.

"Hello, my name is Reverend Noel, and the name of my sermon tonight is 'Remembering Your Heritage.' Can you say that with me?" Ray asked the crowd.

"Remembering your heritage," the crowd said in unison with Ray.

"We need to remember our heritage, and I'm gonna tell you about a part of our heritage that some of you here tonight may not even know about. How many of you here tonight are aware that two thousand years ago, the Romans took your Christian forefathers and fed them to the lions in the arena?"

Ray cleared his throat and took a sip of imported beer. "You better not be sticking your heads in the sand," he resumed. "How many of you saw our president shaking hands with the pope a few years ago? It was all over the idiot box—the media proclaiming it a great day. Think about it, though, folks. Ronald Wilson Reagan. R-o-n-a-l-d . . . six letters. W-i-l-s-o-n. Six letters. And R-e-a-g-a-n . Six letters again! Six six six, the devil's number! Don't let his being a Republican fool you! Forces are as silent as the grave, readying this great Protestant land for the Catholic invasion! It's all around us!"

The crowd was transfixed before him, and Ray struggled to keep in the Rev. Noel character, biting his lip to resist breaking out in laughter.

"You know, those Catholics claim to be worshipping Jesus, and they'll show you their bloody crucifixes to prove it! That ain't Jesus! That's a Roman god disguised as Jesus!" Ray bellowed, working himself more and more into the character. "That's why you better not be wearing no crucifix around your neck. If you wanna wear something around your neck, then wear a plain white Protestant cross. Don't be wearing no corpse of a false Roman god 'round your neck! Not only do they worship that false Roman god, but they worship a woman, too! A woman they have the nerve to say is Mary! But that ain't Mary at all! That's some pagan druid goddess. Why do you think Jesus called his mother 'woman' from the cross? Because Jesus looked out with his fiery X-ray eyes blasting across the sands of time, two thousand years into the future, and he saw these Cath-o-licks worshipping his mama! So, he said, 'Mary, you're just a woman.' That's all she is, and she ain't no goddess, neither!"

The crowd erupted in laughter. Shortly after Ray's sermon concluded, Pee-Wee took the pulpit.

"My name is Reverend Harry, and I'm gonna tell you about the wiles of drugs and rock 'n' roll, folks, and let me tell you straight up, it's not one of those Sunday picnic testimonies," Pee-Wee yelled out in full Pentecostal mode.

After Pee-Wee's sermon, Ed brought out a television set and VCR. He played a recording of Jan Crouch of the Trinity Broadcast Network with her pink hair, talking to her white-haired husband, Paul; their white dog lay at Jan's feet, fervently licking its genitals. The sound was muted, and in place of television audio was a recording of Alessandro Moreschi, better known as The Last Castrato. His voice squeaked like an aberration, neither male nor female, singing a perverse "Ave Maria." Although the sound was barely above a whisper, it was bizarre enough that the crowd responded with communal queasiness, which was precisely what Calvin had hoped for.

Dressed in a black suit with Chick tracts glued onto it, Calvin, in the guise of Brother Cobweb, stepped forward.

"In a sense, all art is autobiography, regardless of subject matter," Calvin began. "So, I will begin with a childhood memory. I was, I believe, around ten and . . ."

Calvin relayed the narrative of the pink stringy things, as Nancy had referred to them. The crowd squirmed as Calvin recollected Nancy yanking nerves out of his broken tooth; the performance was punctuated visually and aurally by the shrill Castrato and the bizarre scene unfolding on the television. After Calvin turned off the music and TV, a moment of stillness permeated the gallery as he psychologically transformed into Brother Cobweb and ritualistically placed a four-sided Hindu-like mask of the right-wing televangelist Jerry Falwell over his face.

"I'm tellin' ya', suffering is a part of Christian living; hardship is a part. You can expect a gooood fight! Did you hear what I said? You can expect a good fight, but you can expect an end as well, and you can expect a victor's crown. There's a victory parade every day in heaven!"

Brother's speech now accelerated into a high-octane delivery.

"You can expect hardship, you can expect suffering, you can expect pain, some of you can even expect death, but you can also expect victory! Some of us, we went through the fire, some have gone through the flood, some have gone through a lot of things, but we all went through the blood, and because of that, you and I can expect victory in Jesus . . . our . . . Savior forever! He sought me; he bought me with his redeeming blood! He loved me, and I knew him. He plunged me—he pluuuunnngggeeddd me to victoryyyy 'neath the cleansing flood!"

"Amen, Brother Cobweb," yelled Cheryl, who was standing among the patrons in a flowery Pentecostal dress.

"Maybe you should wear paint all the time," Cheryl cracked to Calvin after the show. He laughed uneasily.

"Maybe you should," Ed added seriously. "It completely burns away that last introverted ounce while you're on stage. You know, whether you intended it or not, your show inspired me to reflect on Christ, and I thought about something from the Sufis in relation to Jesus. I don't see him as a sacrifice. I don't think he knew he was going to die. I think he realized he was dead when he messed with the establishment's money, ya dig? And like any of us when we go up against something like the establishment, Jesus was frightened, man. The Sufis have a phrase for it called 'annihilation.' It's that moth-to-flame metaphor perfected. He had to be utterly destroyed in order to become a Christ. But I'm not literally referring to the crucifixion—that's anticlimactic after the garden. We get everything we need to know about what happened at Gethsemane. I don't think we attain the kingdom through anything intentional. I think we attain it through something primal that has no regard for outcome, but that's my personal perspective. I don't want to mess with anyone's belief system."

"Well . . . yeah," laughed Calvin. "It's a system, and I tend to stay the hell far away from people who seem forever compelled to announce themselves as believers. You know, all that justification by faith versus justification by faith plus works is total bullshit. It's justification by imagination. It's the iconography that counts."

"Speaking of iconography, I think the whole show can be summed up with your *Our Lady of the Mermaid* icon. Yeah, you have the performances and Pentecostal canvases, but *Mermaid* is a real personal step for you. That was smart to say it's not for sale. Of course, you realize that on the other hand, there's some who'd burn you at the stake for Brother Cobweb alone if they had the chance," laughed Ed.

"Of course," Calvin sighed. "Blasphemy is my second language. I speak it fluently."

39

A LITTLE NIGHT MUSIC

It had been a little over a year since the Brother Cobweb show at The Art Brut. Calvin had been dating Cheryl exclusively; their dating was sporadic and more akin to two people hanging out together—by going to an occasional movie or dinner, for example—than an intimate relationship. Their physicality was kept to the barest minimum as Cheryl said she wanted to wait until she was married, having been damned by her mother for having her son out of wedlock. That was fine—even relieving—for Calvin. He hadn't even met her son yet. But after they had been dating for a year, it was clear that Cheryl was getting antsy, feeling the relationship wasn't going anywhere, until she finally insisted that Calvin meet her son and her parents. Calvin agreed. He had wondered why he had agreed, but he knew why without admitting it to himself: Cheryl was the only friend he went out with on a semi-regular basis.

Calvin met Cheryl at her parents' house. She came up to his car when he pulled into the driveway.

"You smell like smoke," she said, eyeing his fuchsia shirt. He shrugged. She told him to wait at his car, went back inside, and returned with a can of air freshener. Spraying some on him, she declared, "Now you're presentable."

The hell I am, thought Calvin.

Cheryl's mother Charlene, with her shaved eyebrows and granny dress, sat on the sofa and eyed Calvin up and down. Tony, Cheryl's dad, with his big round belly, was asleep in the recliner. Calvin glanced over at Cheryl's son Shane, who was playing with a monster truck and WWF action figures under her parents' Christmas tree, which was still up in August. The sight made for a hyper-masculine nativity set, and that—with all the Bible verse plaques hanging on the wall and ceramic geese in every corner—created a kitsch hell that sent Calvin's stomach reeling with memories of his own mother's decorating tastes.

Cheryl excused herself to the kitchen to fetch a glass of pink lemonade, leaving Calvin essentially alone with Charlene.

"Cheryl says you work in an art gallery," Charlene finally said.

Calvin meekly replied yes.

"And that you went to art school."

He nodded.

"Well, you know whoever Cheryl winds up with, if she winds up with anyone, they have to be aware that Cheryl is a package deal. They have to make a secure living and have to accept Shane. You know, I asked Cheryl why she let herself get pregnant by that awful man, and she said Shane gives her a purpose in this life. Cheryl broke her daddy's heart, but we took her back in. It was all for the Lord's purpose because Shane is our purpose too. He's the only important thing in this world for me and Tony."

"I understand." Hello to you, too, he thought, immediately sensing that Charlene considered him dating Cheryl as a threat.

Although he was only there for a half hour, Calvin looked repeatedly at the clock and couldn't wait to leave. After making his goodbyes, Cheryl walked him to his car.

"Can I meet your parents now?" she asked Calvin in the driveway.

"No. Hell, I haven't seen or talked to them in a long time," he answered defensively.

Over the next three weeks, Calvin and Cheryl went on two dates, during which they actually held hands. That somehow made it seem official. The one fortunate thing about Cheryl's parents was that they were convenient babysitters; the last thing that Calvin wanted was a date with Cheryl and Shane. Shane seemed lost in his own world, and it was a world Calvin did not relate to. On their second date during those three weeks, Cheryl brought up the m-word. It sounded thunderous even though she was meek in mentioning it. She clearly wanted an escape from her parents for herself and Shane. Calvin could relate to that, and although he was open to the idea of being married someday, he evaded her subtle mention of it.

During the next meeting with Cheryl's parents, Charlene was on the couch again and Tony was still in his recliner, but wide awake, watching wrestling. He reminded Calvin of Dale. For an uncomfortable fifteen minutes, Calvin sat in a chair, silent until Tony asked, "Do you keep up on wrestling, Calvin?"

Calvin said he didn't.

"You ought to start watching it. Shane has all the toy figures. Give you something to talk to him about. Didn't your dad watch wrestling with you?"

"No."

"What did you watch together?"

"My dad likes westerns."

"I like westerns."

Small world, Calvin thought sarcastically.

"Mommy," Shane yelled from the bathroom, "come and wipe my butt."

Cheryl dutifully rose and disappeared down the hall.

"Calvin ain't seen his family in a long time," Charlene said to Tony, prompting him to quit asking questions.

"How come?" Tony asked Calvin, oblivious to his wife's intentions.

"Been busy," Calvin answered dryly.

"Cheryl says your mom's Pentecostal?" Charlene asked.

"Yep," Calvin answered, unsure of where the conversation was going.

"Good, because if you two ever get married . . ."

Married? thought Calvin, suddenly aware that Cheryl had obviously mentioned the idea to Charlene.

". . . she knows that she can't get married in white. That's a sign of purity. She ain't pure. Pentecostals know that, too, so it ain't like if you ever you do get married, she could wear white in your mom's church either. I told her one day, long time ago, that if she ever did get married, and she wanted to get married in white, she'd have to look elsewhere because our pastor sticks to the Word."

That's not in the Bible, Calvin wanted to say but wisely didn't. He was unsure how to respond and was relieved when Shane and Cheryl came out of the bathroom and Shane said he was thirsty.

"Got his bottle in the fridge," Charlene called out to Cheryl.

Bottle? thought Calvin. He's almost six years old. Calvin watched with fascination as Cheryl got the bottle out of the refrigerator, sat down with Shane at the kitchen table, and held the bottle to his mouth as if he were a calf.

"I'm hungry, too," Shane added after taking a gulp. "I want peanut butter."

Calvin watched as Cheryl spoon-fed her son peanut butter from a jar of Jiffy.

Charlene resumed. "I know that ain't no time soon because, you know, we got Shane and we're as much parents to that baby as Charlene is, and things would have to be worked out. And I don't care if she does or not, but whoever Cheryl marries, Shane ain't going to be calling no man dad."

"Mom, we're not talking about this, please," Cheryl pleaded from the kitchen.

Lost in thought, Calvin thought perhaps the best reason for marriage was revolt. Marriage: the symbol of bourgeoisie normalcy transformed into an act of rebellion.

An hour later, as Cheryl was walking Calvin to his car, he blurted out with a tinge of anger in his voice, "Were you serious about wanting to get married?"

"You know I am," she answered with a touch of elation and longing in her voice.

"Then find an excuse to leave. We'll go get you a white dress and go see a justice of the peace. If you want to do this, we have to do it, now."

"Now?"

"Now! And don't tell your parents."

Calvin and Cheryl didn't manage it that day—they didn't anticipate blood tests and paperwork—but twenty-four hours later, they were husband and wife. Cheryl cried after the exchange of vows, in part because she had wanted a church wedding and hated that her parents and Shane were not there. Calvin rejected the church idea, but it was not for the reason Cheryl thought. Being married by a justice of the peace was a secular ceremony; if things didn't work out, so be it. However, being married in a church would sanctify the marriage, sacredly seal it, and then he felt he would be permanently bound. He inherited this attitude from Pop—Pop the agnostic Jew who married a Catholic woman, in her church, and remained married to her, despite their separation. Pop had even stated the reason without outright saying it: "One doesn't have to be a believer, per se, to have a sacramental life." However, Calvin didn't share his reasoning with Cheryl. He simply offered marriage as a chance to get her and her son out from under her parents' roof.

After marrying, Cheryl called Charlene to tell her the news. Surprisingly, Charlene wasn't surprised. Calvin went back to his apartment to make it ready for Cheryl while she went back home to pack her bags. Cheryl did remember to change her clothes before going back home so Charlene wouldn't know that her daughter married in a white dress. Shane would stay at her parents' for a week longer while the newlywed couple would have a few days of an apartment-styled honeymoon.

When Cheryl returned to her parents' house, Charlene presented her daughter with a wedding gift: a set of dresser drawers. Meanwhile, Calvin was a nervous wreck; the thought of consummating their marriage scared him. He lucked out when Cheryl ordered a pizza, then called her mother to ask her how to put the dresser drawers together. They talked on the phone for hours, and Calvin fell asleep on the couch.

There were no such distractions the next night. They kept the lights out, which helped Calvin feel as if he wasn't being judged. Despite pronounced goose bumps, nervous shaking, and a degree of sweat, Calvin managed; he was even adept with Cheryl's guidance, which surprised them both. Yet, it felt inherently vacant. For Calvin, it was partially related—although he didn't fully understand how—to the fact that they were not married in a church.

40

CRIMES, MISDEMEANORS, AND VENIAL SINS

Shortly after their first noneventful anniversary, Cheryl introduced Calvin to her new boss at Chick-fil-A, who had invited Cheryl and Calvin over for dinner. Her boss's name was Mike, or Mark, or something like that. Calvin couldn't remember because the man's wife just called him "Mr. Husband," which struck Calvin as epically phony and weird—and not a good weird. It's an abso-fucking-lutely bad weird, Calvin thought as Mr. Husband announced he was going to the "latrine" and left the room. Who the hell calls it a latrine? Calvin wondered as he thumbed through the magazine rack holding pamphlets in Cheryl's boss's dining room.

As Mr. Husband was away in the latrine zone, Calvin looked through the pamphlets, which, it turned out, were produced by a group called The Promise Keepers. One pamphlet titled "For Promise Keeper Wives" struck him. In it, these "godly men" advised wives to not greet their husband at the door in a dirty apron, but, after a hard day's work, greet him wearing a pretty dress that he likes. Have his dinner ready, and make sure the kids' homework is done and they are kept quiet. After dinner, turn on his favorite TV show. For a moment, Calvin thought it was satire, but as he read further, he realized these pamphlets were serious. Calvin wasn't sure whether to laugh or be afraid at such a poor caricature of the 1950s. He opted for the latter as Mr. Husband returned, sat down across from him at the dining room table, and explained that the reason God had blessed their home and finances was because he and his wife went to church every week and always paid their ten-percent tithing.

"I'm excited to be working with Cheryl," said Mr. Husband. "I hope we can all become friends."

Calvin was already certain he did not want a friend like Mr. Husband.

"A man should be the spiritual leader in his family, Calvin," Mr. Husband pontificated, seeing the pamphlet Calvin was still holding. "Now, I think the Wifey's ready. Her veal is to die for."

Who the hell calls his wife *Wifey* instead of by her name? Calvin asked himself.

Calvin barely made it through dinner with Wifey and Mr. Husband and brooded through the entire drive home. His mood wasn't helped when Cheryl broke the silence in the car ride to ask whether they could start attending church together. After Cheryl fell asleep later that night, Calvin got up to smoke a cigarette, wondering how he had come to this. Cheryl had known what he was when she met him. She had even been to his showings. She knew, in part, what he came from and that he had steadfastly refused to contact his family and introduce them to her and Shane. When they met, Calvin thought that they shared one thing: contentious relationships with their mothers. He now saw the inherent difference between him and his wife: in sharp contrast to Calvin, who sometimes hoped he would never have to see Nancy again, Cheryl believed being married would win Charlene's acceptance. Almost predictably, it had done just the opposite. Charlene became increasingly jealous of Calvin's time with Shane. Why? He could only guess. There was nothing to be jealous of. Shane already belonged to his grandparents and was far removed from Calvin.

Calvin had even taken the leap of physical engagement in his life in the spirit of dutiful lovemaking once every month or so. Yet there was very little physical affection between them and, indeed, he spent more time painting at the gallery than he did with Cheryl. And with her putting in fifty hours a week at her job, he had become more of a babysitting stepfather than a husband.

Why now the pressure to acclimate themselves in a church community, as Mr. Husband had suggested? Despite her Baptist background, Cheryl had never seemed overtly religious. Perhaps for Cheryl, the evidence of the highly affluent Mr. Husband and Wifey pointed to God equaling mounds of money. That was odd because Cheryl seemed to forget that Calvin knew the Bible, and the Christ of the Gospels was consistent in saying that one was better off without money—and, if you did have it, he advised giving it away. Cheryl often complained that they needed to make money so they could have lots of stuff, which would give Shane a better home. Calvin was beginning to despise the concept of money even more than he had previously. And despite Cheryl's suggestion that perhaps Mr. Husband was right in that Calvin needed to be a spiritual leader, Calvin knew that there was a spiritual void in his life. He did need to do something about it, but for himself—not to fulfill the role of a bankrolling spiritual leader for his wife.

The next day, Calvin took Father Oliver's card out of his wallet. He had almost forgotten about it, but there it was, two years later. Why not? He thought as he dialed the number.

"Father Oliver?"

"Yes."

"Hello. This is Calvin Elkan. We met at the Art Brut—"

"Ah, the artist who hates a nonexistent God. It's been awhile, but I remember. How are you?"

Calvin couldn't believe Father Oliver remembered him. Hoping for some company, Calvin invited him to the new Woody Allen movie that night. Father Oliver accepted his invitation.

Calvin barely had time to soak in the surrounding and architecture before he was besieged by a group of inquisitive elderly nuns at the Benedictine abbey.

"So, you're taking Father Oliver to a movie?"

I don't think there's even one nun here under the age of eighty, thought Calvin. "Yes."

"Father will be out momentarily. I'm so happy that you're taking him. It's my all-time favorite movie."

"Really? I haven't seen it," said Calvin, perplexed.

"Oh my! Well, you'll love that scene when Julie Andrews sings on top of the mountain. It's a classic!"

Oliver suddenly appeared and shot Calvin a look. Calvin took the hint and didn't respond to the nun. Grabbing Calvin by the arm, Oliver hastily whisked the young man out of the clutches of swarming octogenarian sisters.

"Sorry about that," Oliver whispered to Calvin. "I need to stop by the rectory. I forgot my medicine."

Two things immediately stood out as Calvin scanned the interior of Oliver's living quarters: A large collection of theology books coupled with Buddhists masks hanging on the wall.

"So, what was that all about with the nuns?" Calvin asked.

"I didn't lie per se. I merely told them I was thinking about going to see *Sound of Music.* The theater's having a revival of it. I simply said that because I doubt any of them would understand me going to a Woody Allen movie."

"Well, yeah, that is a lie, but not that I care."

"Lying isn't necessarily a bad thing if it spares someone."

"What do you mean? You know we're going to see Woody Allen. Who cares what they think?"

"It would hurt them—they look up to me as some kind of stainless model. Regardless how good an argument you might give for saying it's OK to see a Woody Allen movie, you're not going to persuade anyone with preconceived notions. They need to figure that out on their own. Of course, many never do."

As the two men climbed into Calvin's car, Oliver observed the wedding ring on the young man's finger.

"I didn't realize you were married. Did you recently marry?"

"About a year ago," Calvin said.

"Congratulations."

"Thanks, I think."

"Do you go to movies often?" Oliver asked.

"I write film reviews for our gallery's magazine, so yeah, I suppose I do. Although I try to mix it up by writing about older films as well."

"The first movie I remember seeing was *The Mask of Fu Manchu.* It's a hoot today, although I probably didn't think so then. Anyway, I've seen most of Allen's films, and this one has a marvelous cast. By the way, if you're open, I suggest holding off on cinema junk food. I thought we could eat at the abbey after we return . . . if you have time."

Afterward, the young man and elderly priest waited in the cafeteria line with an army of nuns.

"I think the sisters' chicken and dumplings will be welcome after such a bleak serving," Oliver said as he grabbed a tray.

"You didn't like the movie?" Calvin asked.

"Quite the contrary. Martin Landau was a likeable monster. Do you object to my blessing our meal?"

"No."

Taking Calvin's hand, Oliver felt the younger man's tense reflex. Although he had made marginal progress with being touched by Cheryl, even something as simple as the taking of one's hand, to join in a prayer, was still startling.

"I don't bite," said Oliver reassuringly. He cleared his throat to pray. "Bless us, O Lord, and these thy gifts, which we are about to receive from thy bounty. Through Christ, our Lord. Amen."

The priest humorously rattled off the prayer like a microwave dinner. The delivery was so pressured in speech that Calvin found himself wondering whether he was at an auto action as opposed to a rectory meal. He surveyed the small cafeteria, taking notice of nuns praying over dumplings. Visions of Bertie digging into twinkies, Nancy's blackened wieners, and Jesus with Hamburger Helper all danced before Calvin's eyes, and he tried to stop a laugh.

"Did I do something funny?" Oliver asked, noticing Calvin's smirk.

"Oh, no. I just like your rat-a-tat-tat delivery."

"I can't abide all that drawn-out mumbo jumbo. I prefer practical and cool-toned spirituality. Besides, people have things to do. Do you like your dumplings?"

"Yes, thanks."

"So, since we last met, you've married. Do you want to talk about it? If you're open, I'll lend an ear."

"What would a priest know about marriage?"

"I was engaged once . . . I've heard everything."

"But you chose to become a priest instead of getting married?"

"Something like that."

Hesitantly, Calvin narrated a summary of his what-were-you-thinking kitsch marriage, and Father Oliver listened respectfully.

"I think this is the beginning of a beautiful friendship," Oliver told Calvin a short time later. "However, every priest has a niche. Hostility is not my niche. That's Father Vincent's niche. He's a Franciscan. I'll give you his number. I think you should call him."

"OK?" Calvin questioned, almost offended.

"I'm not trying to pawn you off. Believe me, it's not that, but I used to be the director of Saint Joseph's, and I was the director here before I retired."

"Oh, I'm sure your schedule is—"

"Nothing to do with my schedule. I imagine you have a history of combative relationships with authority. Despite being a priest, Vincent is not an authority figure at all. You and I can continue the way we've begun, but I prefer to avoid talking to you about your spiritual perspectives or lack thereof. You can talk to Vincent first. I think you and I can find plenty of other things to cover. As far as your marriage, I'll say this: I absolutely believe in the sanctity of marriage, and I've seen the tragedy of divorce far too often. But you're not Catholic, so I shouldn't . . ." Oliver stopped himself.

"And if I were Catholic?"

"I'd connect you with my lawyer today and start your annulment process myself the second that your divorce was finalized."

41

A FRANCISCAN RETREAT

"Franciscan retreat," answered a treble-sounding voice, which contrasted sharply with Father Oliver's baritone elocution.

"Is Father Vincent in?" Calvin asked tentatively.

"This is Vincent." The priest's voice resonated with confident joy.

"Hi. This is Calvin Elkan. Father Oliver suggested I call you."

"He said you might call."

"I think it was Father Oliver's idea that you and I should meet. He said every priest has a niche, and hostility is not his niche. It's yours."

"It's my niche, alright!" Vincent laughed. "Are you free Wednesday? We're having a celebration here that you could join in."

Calvin agreed to meet Vincent at noon on Wednesday, unsure of what exactly he was getting himself into.

Vincent smiled as he answered the door for Calvin. The priest's chiseled face complemented his silver hair, which was as perfectly groomed as the retreat's bucolic landscape. A flawless tan peeked out from beneath Vincent's brown friar robe as he asked, "You're Calvin?"

Before Calvin could answer, Vincent leaned in for a hug, and Calvin flinched.

"We hug here," Vincent said, noticing Calvin's reaction, but choosing not to question or judge it presently. "Come on in. You can help me set up for Phoebe's birthday party. She's turning one hundred and two today. You like cake, don't you?"

Calvin and the priest meticulously placed all one hundred and two birthday candles on a white cake trimmed with pink icing. Within the hour, Phoebe was wheeled in, and it took everyone present to help blow out every candle. After that, Vincent celebrated mass. Passing the communion to Calvin, the Franciscan priest whispered, "Go ahead, if you want."

"I'm not Catholic," Calvin answered in a hushed tone.

"Everyone's Catholic."

He makes religion seem kind of cool, Calvin thought.

Calvin opted not to take communion at Father Oliver's more traditional mass the following Sunday at the Benedictine abbey.

"Our reading today is about our blessed Lord's temptation. Let us reimagine that for a moment and give Jesus a more substantial hurdle. Instead of merely tempting one starving person by turning rocks into bread, let's up the ante. 'Turn these rocks into bread' says the devil 'and you can feed *all* the starving children of the world.' What would our blessed Lord do? Well, I think I have an answer to that found in the history pages of our own church. Nazi Germany, 1940. The bishop had been preaching against the Hitler Youth, which prompted a visit from Goebbels, Goering, and the Führer himself. So, the bishop was warned, if you continue preaching against us, we will send all of your Catholics to the concentration camps. However, if you sign this concordant, we will let your Catholics live. Now what do you think that bishop did? That's right. He signed the concordant. And what do you think happened? Hitler killed all of his Catholics anyway, which goes to show that if you go to dine with the devil, you need a loooooooong spoon."

Oliver's humor punched the air, and everyone present felt it.

"I heard you met Vincent," Oliver said as he took Calvin aside after mass.

"Yeah. I connected with him."

"I knew you would. Did the two of you get to talk privately?"

"Actually, we didn't. We celebrated Phoebe's birthday. We made an appointment to talk later this week."

Oliver smiled. "I have a book for you by Julian of Norwich. I think you will find in her a spiritual sibling."

Oliver motioned for Calvin to follow him. Once in the rectory, Oliver handed him the book.

"Thank you, but I never accept a present without giving one in a return. Here," said Calvin as he pulled a wrapped gift out of his suit coat pocket.

"You already had that planned," chuckled Oliver, unwrapping the gift to find a copy of *Mask of Fu Manchu*.

"Tell me your story," Vincent began with Calvin the following week. "I've set aside the whole day because I want you to feel free to tell it. I pass no judgment. I want you to know that first. Calvin, this retreat is self-funded. I don't answer to the diocese or even the Franciscans. I made that decision a long time ago and worked my ass off to accomplish that. So, now I do services here with Protestants, fallen-way Catholics, ex-priests, Buddhists, Muslim, atheists, and gay and transgender people, and I've heard everything. Before we begin, I want to assure you that I believe the Spirit River brought you to where you are right now. The Spirit speaks directly to us, and if you choose to ignore that direction and go your own way, you will limit your life. That is not a judgment—just an inevitable outcome."

Calvin exhaled. Vincent's authentically paternal demeanor, combined with the intimacy of the chapel setting, with its St. Francis icon, all put him at ease. He began. Only once did Vincent interrupt, merely to briefly proclaim Pop's story as a God story, and after Calvin finished his three-hour confessional, Vincent drew a breath to comment on Calvin's reluctance to call Nancy.

"If you feel it's unhealthy to call your mother, then I'd suggest going with that initial instinct. Have you talked to your father or brother?"

"They don't have my new number, and I'd like to keep it that way for a while.

"Ah."

"What?"

"You said for a while."

"They'd pressure me to call Mom."

"Talking to your mother is never going to be a possibility?"

"I'm not saying never, but I can't abide that whole white trash world of hers, and sometimes I'm afraid that I'm nothing more than white trash with artistic ambitions. I don't need her to remind me of it."

"That whole trash mentality, as you call it—it's not a financial status. It's grounded in narcissism, selfishness, materialism, and ignorance, along with selfishness about one's ignorance—a resistance to self-work. There is an inherent fear of evolving, and that's why so many locked in that mindset have repeated broken relationships and tend toward right-wing extremism. Despite being a little hesitant at first, from this outpouring, you're clearly self-aware, so continue working to avoid becoming that caricature. I'm not going to comment about your marriage, except to say that I think it is sad that you feel you cannot share being here, or your time with Oliver, with your wife. Whatever shape your spiritual direction takes, it is not something you should feel you need to hide. However, I will say this: the promised land is not over here or over there. It's beneath your feet. Of course, you have to choose to see it."

42

A SATANIC THEOLOGY

"I met your mother yesterday," Cheryl announced to Calvin, who was half asleep on the couch.

"What? How? Where?" Calvin asked, shocked, as he attempted to sit up on the couch-turned-makeshift bed. The couch, about a foot too short in length, rendered his legs numb. Still, he managed to reach for the Marlboro Lights and lighter on the end table.

"Do you have to smoke first thing?"

"Did you happened to make any coffee?" Calvin asked, deflecting her question.

"I started you a pot. Hazelnut creamer's next to your mug."

"Thanks," said Calvin as he headed for the coffee pot. "Now, how do you know you met my mother?"

"She came into the restaurant and introduced herself."

"How did she know—"

"Calvin, it's been over a year. I'm sure she's heard. After all, they do print marriage notices in the paper. I imagine that someone was bound to have seen it and told her at some point."

"So, what did she say?"

"She'd like to meet Shane. Invited us to lunch."

"Us?"

"Me and Shane. She didn't mention you, other than ask to how you were."

"Well, at least she's sensitive enough not to do that. I think, unless . . ."

"I think she is. I felt there was real regret in her voice."

"Wait, I thought you said—"

"Not in what she said, but how she said it."

"Oh." Calvin swished the hazelnut creamer around his cup of coffee. "Did she say how my dad and brother are doing?"

"Your brother and his wife and kid moved out. They got their own house, but then she left him."

Calvin shook his head and laughed.

"What's so funny?" Cheryl asked.

"Nothing. How's Dad?"

"He's fine . . . working all the time, from what she said."

"OK, thanks," said Calvin, feeling that was enough.

"So, do you care?"

"Do I care about what?"

"If me and Shane meet her for lunch."

"It's not my place to stop you."

Within the hour, Calvin headed to the gallery and tried to put the Chick-fil-A mother-and-wife rendezvous behind him. And so his avoidance routine went until three days later.

"Shane and I had a great lunch with your mom the other day. She even bought him a toy after paying for dinner," Cheryl told Calvin as he was painting in his basement studio.

"OK," he said dismissively without looking up, more irritated at being interrupted than he was over the meeting.

"She invited me to her church."

"Oh, hell no!" Calvin lit up and dropped his brush.

"I want go to a church together as a family, and Mike has been encouraging me . . ."

"Mr. Husband should get a job writing hackneyed motivational posters."

"He has his own business," Cheryl countered.

"Corporate homophobes selling chicken lard for Jesus. I couldn't sleep at night with that on my conscience."

"He makes more money than you do."

"Yeah, because Jesus was one of those money-loving corporate types."

"I don't want to fight, but your mom says the church has changed since Luke took over."

Calvin thought about it for a moment. He had been curious as to what the Lighthouse would look like under Luke's management. "I will check it out . . . for a good laugh."

On Sunday night, Calvin, with Cheryl and Shane in front of him, walked through the Lighthouse doors for the first time in over six years. They took a seat in a pew near the back and Calvin remained glued as the entertainment unfolded before him.

The church stage was made up like a B western set with a rubber cactus and dusty floor. To Calvin's surprise, Frank, of all people, took the stage dressed in a bright orange three-piece suit and matching orange dress shoes.

"Frank?" Calvin whispered.

"Your brother?" Cheryl asked.

"And now I bring you a living video," Frank belted into the mic.

"He looks like a charismatic citrus," Calvin grumbled to Cheryl.

"Shh," she chastised.

Two cowboys entered the stage from opposite ends. The first cowboy was dressed in white, the second entirely in black. They approached each other cautiously until the black cowboy pulled out his pistol with a pentagram painted on it. The demonic figure shot his popgun at the sky. The word "adultery" flashed in smoky neon above the two figures. In reaction to the word, the good cowboy grabbed his chest as if in pain. Rebounding, the man in white pulled out his own pistol (adorned in crosses) and shot into the air, producing the word "marriage." The black cowboy screamed as if wounded.

The two figures on stage went tit-for-tat. Atheism and faith, lying and honesty, greed and tithing viciously combatted. Calvin had forgotten how long these services lasted. It seemed to go on for half of forever until the black figure shot the word "unsaved," which literally drove the Christian cowboy to his knees. He rose melodramatically, pulled out his gun, and "the cross" appeared. The word was accompanied by a giant red and black cross that reminded Calvin of a Third Reich flag. God, that must be bigger than the one Jesus hung on, he thought. The evil figure on stage whooped out a B movie bronco yelp before disappearing like the Wicked Witch of the West into a puff of smoke.

"God, I hope Glenda doesn't appear, too. She's worse than the other one. Jesus, this has turned into MTV Pentecostalism," Calvin grumbled.

The church service finally came to an end.

"Wow, I love this church," Cheryl whispered to Calvin as they stood up to leave. "I bet with your gallery experience, you could do stuff like this here. Shane loves it, too!"

"I'm sure he does," said Calvin disdainfully, hoping to sneak out before anyone he knew tried to talk to him.

"Good to see you," said a voice behind Calvin as someone patted him on the back, nearly causing the Lighthouse prodigal to jump out of his skin. He turned around to find Luke behind him.

"So, what did you think?" Luke asked.

"Of the performance? It reminds me of Captain Christ. Did he stage it?"

"Oh no. Captain Christ died several years ago. I staged it. Glad you liked it."

I didn't say I liked it, thought Calvin.

"Do you have any free time next week?" Luke asked. "I'd like to get together and talk."

"Sure," said Calvin. "What day is best for you?"

"Any day after Tuesday. I'm painting up the small house next to the church. Dad's moving in there."

"I don't work Wednesday. If you need help painting, I can lend a hand and we can talk then," Calvin offered.

"All right . . . Wednesday at noon?"

"Do you want to meet at the house?"

"That'd be great."

Calvin was almost out the front door when another hand grabbed his shoulder. He recoiled, recognizing the firm grip. He turned to find his mother behind him.

"You a little jumpy tonight?" Cheryl asked Calvin, having witnessed his similar startled reaction to Luke, which prompted Shane to giggle.

"This is a wonderful church, Nancy," said Cheryl, beaming pride at her benevolent act of reunification before her mother-in-law and husband.

"I've been trying to get Calvin to see that for years," Nancy said, easily slipping back into her role as victim.

Scheming fundies, Calvin thought in disgust as he looked at his mother and wife.

"Cheryl, you oughta take Shane over to the kitchen. They have some lemon cookies and Kool-Aid."

Calvin recognized Nancy's attempt to distract Cheryl away from whatever she was about to tell him.

"He's a cute boy," said Nancy as she watched Cheryl take Shane by the hand over to the cookies. "So, how do you like having a son?"

Calvin looked at the young boy with his jet-black hair and bib overalls. "I'm just a babysitter. The kid'll probably grow up to be some right-winger selling chicken for Jesus."

"You've changed. You're worse. I should remind you, he's only a child."

"No excuse! Regardless, I don't like him much."

"Like father, like son."

"Meaning what?"

"Your dad didn't like your cousin who stayed with us for a while, either."

"Her name was Shannon. You can go ahead and say it because I heard all about her."

"How did you . . ." Nancy stopped herself short, correctly figuring that Calvin had finally heard about Shannon from Blanche, who was a transparent thorn in the side.

"Besides, it's hardly the same," said Calvin, rolling his eyes. "Would it be easier for you if I lied? I'm not going to apologize for not liking someone, even if he is a kid. Anyway, you asked, so I told you."

Nancy changed the subject.

"I saw you ran into Luke. He may have fancied the place up and got more young people in, but he sure can't preach like his dad. A lot of the old timers here don't like the changes Luke's making. I haven't heard 'Amazing Grace' once since he's taken over. Course some of those changes are his wife's doin'."

"I forgot that he was married to . . . what's her name?"

"Lucy," Nancy said, spitting out the name.

"Do they have kids?"

"Not hardly."

"Why not hardly?"

"Oh, you know how rumors are. They're not just rumors, though."

Predictable, thought Calvin. He wanted Cheryl to hurry back so they could leave.

"But your wife's comin' back. So, I'll tell ya later."

"Can't wait," he replied sarcastically. Nancy's eyes flashed violently for a second before remembering that she was in front of Cheryl and trying to win her over. She painted on a simpering smile and patted Shane on the head as he ran back to her and Calvin with a cookie.

"I'm glad you're back," Luke said to Calvin as they painted Rev. Harry's house on Wednesday. "I've been getting a lot of Christian heavy metal into the church. You'll see if you come to the passion play this Sunday. The kids just can't relate to all that hundred-year-old gospel music. People like your mom complain about the new music and the kids, but . . ."

"Yeah, she does. I wouldn't worry about mother dear. She'll accept it or she won't. If not, she can stay home and watch Jimmy Swaggart."

"About your mom . . ."

"What about her?"

"I'm sorry about that night you had with her."

"Which night?"

"'I'll Fly Away.'"

"Ah, that night."

"You know, when you tried to kill yourself . . ."

"We all have parents . . ."

"If you mean my dad—"

"Yeah, I do. The brutal old school."

"Well, he doesn't come to the church anymore."

"Perhaps that's what you should do across the board—kick out everyone over fifty."

"I couldn't do that."

Calvin shrugged. "Suit yourself."

"When Dad left me the Lighthouse, he started going to another church, but he's sick now. That's why I'm getting the house ready for him. The way people used to do things here isn't acceptable anymore. I'm going to change things, and Frank's with me on that."

"Yeah, about Frank . . ."

"He's the associate pastor now."

The Frank I knew didn't even read the Bible, Calvin thought as he tried hard not to roll his eyes. "What does Vernell think of the changes?" Calvin asked Luke.

"Mom died last year."

"Oh. Sorry. I didn't know."

"Well, you've been out of touch. So, what do you think of the changes at the Lighthouse?"

"I think you've catered the style to younger parishioners, but the message isn't any different."

"You gotta speak their language," Luke replied defensively.

"It's just the language they're familiar with. It's not their language. It's still the language of our parents. I think it's more important to change the language than it is to update apparel."

"What would you do if it was your church?"

"I'd burn the church to the ground."

"You can't mean that."

"OK then, I'd clean house and hire only teachers with at least four years of college plus an additional two years in theology. We have enough illiterate Christians without producing more."

"We're doing our own style of theology here."

"I don't see any theology at all."

"Well, what kind of theology are you talking about?"

"Spiritual irreverence. That's the only honest spirituality."

"And you don't think Christian heavy metal is spiritual irreverence?"

"We're not going to get anywhere in this conversation, Luke."

"OK, but wait till you see the passion play. If that doesn't hit you, I don't know what will."

Cheryl kept asking Calvin to come to the Lighthouse's passion play, even though he kept responding that it was just religious torture porn. Eventually he agreed to go, but he doubted it would have a shred of spiritual irreverence, as Luke claimed. To steel himself for the event, he headed out to the Benedictine abbey Sunday morning to hear Father Oliver preach.

As he was pulling out of the apartment complex parking lot, Calvin noticed a dusty-purple Buick pulling up behind him. At first, he paid it little mind until he realized it had been behind him from the time he left his apartment until his arrival at the abbey, after which the purple car drove on. It looked like Charlene's car. He tried to put it out of his mind as he walked into the abbey.

"I want to address a very real and dangerous theology that has been a staple of Christendom. It is nothing less than a satanic theology," Father Oliver began. "A Satanic theology transforms Christ into the quintessential Pharisee, making him so illuminatingly beautiful, so powerful, so elevated that no one can touch him."

Oliver delivered an intuitive homily—one that was thoughtfully explored, lushly presented, and adorned in wistful humor. Not even Father Vincent probed scripture as contextually. Whenever Oliver was complimented on his homilies, in typical self-effacing response, he countered that scripture was vast enough to withstand any single interpretation—his own included. Of course, Oliver never heard Lighthouse sermons, which sucked ever corpuscle of sanctity out of scripture. Still, as Calvin listened to Oliver each Sunday, his collection of stories was becoming an actual literature, albeit one better heard than read, because despite occasional lapses into weirdness, the Bible wasn't exactly the best read, and later writers, like Julian of Norwich, full of jazzy green metaphors, were more fun to get lost in.

"That's one of the reasons I introduced you to Julian," Oliver quipped to Calvin at lunch after mass. "Although I hate using the word 'spiritual,' I think your spiritual waltz springs from your being an artist, not vice versa, and Julian is a counter to all that pedestaled clerical conservatism. That's why they've never canonized her. God forbid. The conservative Catholics would be running to the store, buying out all of the Preparation H."

"Ha! I would almost prefer the word 'religion' today," Calvin replied. "That whole 'I'm spiritual, not religious' fad makes me want to vomit. Still, I'd rather be in a room with them than the traditionalists who see themselves as guardians of . . . well, something. I'm still not sure what."

"They're not sure either, but they will never admit it," Oliver laughed.

"I have noticed one thing," Calvin added, "the Pentecostals damned my art as of the devil. I've come across a few hyper traditionalist Catholics of late…"

"Ah, the ones that make an idol of tradition?"

"They're the ones and they don't say my work is of the devil, they merely…"

"Deem it degenerate?"

"How'd you know?"

"Fundamentalist cultists are not a majority in the Church, although they seem to think they are. However, there are far too many and they would be right there joining the Gestapo in The Degenerate Art Show. The world over, the two taboo subjects are religion and politics. In America, however, it's religion, politics, and art. You hit all three."

"Two and a half. I'm actually not that political since I dismiss both sides as filled to the rim with hypocrisy, although the side that caters more to the low-informed tends to rage in hypocrisy."

Calvin left the abbey, glancing around for the familiar car. It was nowhere to be seen. He returned home with hesitance, dreading the upcoming pilgrimage back to the Lighthouse, which he knew would probably lead to another fight with Cheryl.

"Terminator Jesus on a Fourth Reich cross," Calvin whispered to Cheryl upon seeing the muscular savior hanging from the red and black cross in the Lighthouse passion play.

"Shh!" Cheryl chastised.

Surrounded by a cheesy set and theater lighting, Terminator Jesus hovered above skinny, black-robed Jews along with Roman soldiers of the weight-lifting variety.

"My Gawd, my Gawd! Why have you forsaken meeeee?" yelped Terminator Jesus in the worst example of amateur acting this side of Sunday as he heaved his tanned biceps and gave up the ghost. "Into thy hands, I commend my spirit!"

Calvin Mantis had been a more effective martyr. At least she elicited some sympathy—and she had far more stylish Roman soldiers, Calvin thought.

The lights dimmed as the curtains closed. A band of young musicians with mountains of hair appeared on stage during the play's intermission. They were adorned in shirts that read "The Savior's Army!"

"On weekdays, they probably play heavy metal covers in their garage," Calvin grumbled under his breath as the band set up their instruments.

"It's Christian metal, Calvin. I told you about it," said Cheryl.

"That's an oxymoron. The whole appeal of rock and roll is sex and drugs."

"You just don't get it."

Two distorted electric guitars, an electric bass, synthesizer, and a drum mercilessly began a morbid ode to Jesus.

> *We are the Savior's Army!*
> *We got the power of the book.*
> *You'll get fried*
> *Unless you get that baptized looooooooooooooooooooooooooooook!*

C-major chords interrupted the screaming vocalist, skipping a few notes on the scale in favor of a screeching bass run—a riff that would have made Jimi Hendrix roll over in his grave. Compounding the cacophony of the electric guitars and bass, the drummer broke into a sudden solo, catching the audience off-guard. The song continued.

> *Every knee shall bow!*
> *Unless you want hell now!*
> *Repent!*
> *Repent!*
> *Repent!*

Jesus paid the price
On Satan's tree!
Jesus paid the price
For all eternity!
Don't get caught without the blood!
We are the Savior's Army
Preparing you for the next flood!
Repent!
Repent!
Repent!

Tearing up from inwardly laughing so hard, Calvin felt Cheryl's elbow jabbing him sharply in the ribs. Mercifully the song ended, followed by an eruption of applause by young congregants.

"Shows how much you know," Cheryl said, glowing and clapping along.

The curtain opened to a set that looked like it might have been lifted from low-budget horror westerns. A bodiless voice narrated: "And for three days, Jesus descended into the bowels of hell." The devil and a half dozen of his minions, clad in black, guarded a small group of people chained together in a corral.

"And Jesus and his angels came to release Adam and the Old Testament sinners from the devil's power," continued the narrator.

Jesus, followed by a small army of white-robed bodybuilders, confronted Satan and his scrawny sycophants. The Lord and personal Savior landed a Batman *Kablam!* to the devil's chin, resulting in an angels-versus-demons domino effect with the white robes fighting black robes.

"Jesus in a barroom brawl," laughed Calvin.

In the middle of the chaos, Jesus lifted the sinners' chain and broke it in half, freeing all of mankind, which inspired an encore from the Savior's Army, accompanied by two center-stage bodybuilders, a set of weights, and a stack of bricks.

Got a warrant for the fallen angel,
A warrant signed in precious blood.
A praying church is Jesus's posse,
Will send the devil to Hades's mud.
We are the Savior's Army,
Bench press this!
We are the Savior's Army,
Jesus is our fist!

On the stage, the two muscley dudes in tank tops with "Bench press this" inked in red lifted weights, and one smashed his head through a pile of bricks.

"What the fuck?"

"Shh, we're in church!"

"Luke has flipped his Pentecostal lid."

"I told you: Luke's taking this church straight to hell," Nancy said to Calvin after the service.

"It's an updated version of Captain Christ and Reverend Harry."

"Yeah, well you don't know about all the sleazy things goin' on here."

Calvin rolled his eyes.

"Well, for one, Lucy! She's had affairs with at least three men here in the church that I know of."

"How do you know that?"

"Sister Opal volunteered to clean the church, and one day she came in and found Lucy and the drummer in the baptismal together. They were hardly baptizin' each other!"

Sounds to me like they were, thought Calvin. "Sorry to hear that."

"He broke it off with her, but I got something he said about Luke straight from a good source."

"And what's that?"

"The reason Lucy does what she does is . . . Luke's impotent."

"Please."

"I heard it from one of Lucy's best friends, too."

"Some best friend," said Calvin, caught between defensiveness and morbid curiosity.

"I'm not saying what Lucy does is right, but things have a way of coming back on you when you ain't doing the Lord's work that you been called to do."

"What're you talking about?"

"Luke—he's so worried about getting young people in and all that, but Frank's a better preacher," she said with pride. "Luke's the pastor here, and he can't even speak in tongues. Not only is he impotent with his wife, but he's impotent with God, too."

"What did I ever do to deserve the likes of you for a mother?" Calvin asked, shaking his head and walking away from her. He found Cheryl and Shane at the cookie table and pulled them out to the car.

"I finally find a church I like, and you have to go and ruin it," Cheryl bawled on the way home.

"Oh, shut up! That was even more crass than anything I witnessed here as a child. If you want to go, I'm not stopping you. Just don't ask me to go, and don't bring it home," Calvin snapped, realizing he was increasingly becoming *both* his parents, stepping into Dale's role of not getting involved, while also imagining himself strangling Cheryl.

43
The Tragedy of Listening

With Shane at school and his wife at work, Calvin poured himself a large cup of coffee to counter the fatigue that had set in from the kitsch cackling of Cheryl's ceramic geese. A handful of markers made the atmosphere bearable, and Calvin took to crafting psychedelic portraits of jazz artists framed in red to be hung on the living room wall. Charles Mingus, Miles Davis, and Thelonious Monk, coupled with Billie Holiday, Sarah Vaughan, and Abbey Lincoln, were far more exciting and welcoming than a generic, fresh-off-the-assembly-line "Home Sweet Home" banner.

Calvin's christened jazz wall stood as a revolt against Cheryl's insipid sense of décor. Once home, she could not take her disapproving eyes off her husband's homage to music.

"Mother's coming over Wednesday," she whined.

Buried in the music of Luigi Nono's weird silvery anti-opera opera, *Prometheus, A Tragedy about Listening*, Calvin had already moved on, forgetting about that morning's creative outburst.

After bouncing several checks, Cheryl begged Calvin to accompany her to Kroger, since he had the money to pay for groceries. Being out of cigarettes was Calvin's sole motive for going. After a half hour of family shopping, Cheryl, Shane, and Calvin were in the checkout lane when Faye Segal walked up behind them.

Calvin groaned silently. With her axed Holly Hobbie record player and "Afternoon Delight" having inspired the Lighthouse parking lot bonfire all those years ago, Calvin had anticipated—and hoped for—Faye's rebellion. Instead, upon returning to the Lighthouse, Calvin had seen that she had merely become yet another Pentecostal minion.

Faye looked disapprovingly at the carton of Marlboro Lights lying atop Calvin's filled grocery cart.

"Cheryl told me what you said, and I've got news for you," Faye told Calvin without so much as a hello.

"Refresh my memory," Calvin answered as he began placing groceries on the conveyor belt.

"What you said about my healing."

Cheryl's face flushed from having been caught.

Calvin recalled that Cheryl had come home from a Lighthouse service with news that a healing miracle had been performed that night. Frank had been preaching about a parishioner, Homer, who had ulcers. According to Frank's sermon, Rev. Harry had told Homer to go home and drink an entire jar of pickle juice—and if he believed, he would be healed of those ulcers immediately.

Inspired by Frank's sermon, Faye, who had been having terrible skin outbreaks, heard the voice of yonder Holy Ghost bidding her to immediately go take a bath in the baptismal. If she did that and believed, her outbreaks would be gone forever. Faye ran to the baptismal, took a quick bath, and ran up to the stage, yanking the microphone out of Frank's hand.

"Sorry, Frank, but I got some great news," Faye belted out. "I just got healed!" After Faye's brief rehashing of Holy Ghost's revelation, Ruby ran to the stage, grabbed her daughter, and started speaking in tongues. Elated, mother and daughter did a Paraclete rumba across the entire church, followed by nearly every parishioner, including Cheryl. It was the first time that Cheryl had ever gotten the Holy Ghost.

When Cheryl came home to share her celebration of getting the Ghost, along with the miracle report, Calvin lit up a cigarette. "I told you I didn't want to hear about the Lighthouse. I can't believe you got all worked up over that. Watch, Faye will have another outbreak in a week," he had told her.

Calvin had erred in his estimation. Within a mere two days, Faye had another outbreak.

"I was cured after all," Faye now announced to Calvin, some months later in the Kroger checkout lane.

"Really?" Calvin asked skeptically.

"Yeah, I went to the doctor, and after some tests, I found out I'm allergic to milk."

"Oh. So, are you still allergic to milk?"

"Well, yeah, silly."

"So, then you weren't cured. Your doctor just found out that you're lactose intolerant."

"Gosh! Some people can't even see a miracle even when it's straight in front of 'em."

"Dammit, Calvin," Cheryl screamed as she tried wiping the phthalo blue paint off her foot in Calvin's garage studio. "I told you to put down a drop cloth."

Calvin looked up. "I did," he said, pointing to the cloth on the floor. "Oils travel."

"Or maybe, you're just a pig. You can't even fold towels right."

"What's wrong with the way I fold towels?"

"You would ask that," Cheryl continued. "You can't even change the oil in your car. The only thing you're good at is painting."

"You're the one who said it was my art that you were attracted to."

"I changed my mind. When was the last time you sold a painting?"

"Or maybe mommy changed your mind for you? I haven't kept track of my sales."

"Well, I do."

Calvin rolled his eyes. Of course she did, he thought.

"It's been at least six months. What good is a painting if it doesn't sell? And about those pictures you hung . . . I want it to feel like home here. It doesn't feel homey. What's wrong with country geese?"

"You mean apart from the fact that I've never talked to a goose? So I sure as hell can't identify with one."

"Frank's wife had geese. She liked geese. Most girls I know do. And every guy I've ever known likes some kinda animal that he can identify with. Frank likes tigers."

"Frank's white trash."

"I think you're like a cheetah," Cheryl proclaimed, ignoring Calvin's comment about his brother.

"How the hell am I like a cheetah?"

"Cheetahs are only good at one thing: speed. You paint fast, and it's about the only thing you're good at, so you paint like a cheetah."

"God! I am trying to work here," Calvin said as he lit up another Marlboro.

"You're just selfish! It's always about you."

"For you, it's not about me at all, so that's pretty hypocritical to say that. God forbid I point out your hypocrisy. Like most thumpers, you can tolerate just about anything, except your hypocrisy being called out."

"Are you going to come and eat?" Cheryl conceded, fatigued.

"I'm painting on my worthless canvas," countered Calvin, practically spitting the words.

"I fixed dinner!"

"I didn't ask you to fix me dinner. I'm not hungry. Go eat with your son."

"You know, Shane's in the next room, and he's already heard you say he's not your son—more than once."

Calvin resumed painting, hoping that if he ignored her, she'd leave.

"You like knowing I'm in the next room, but you won't have anything to do with me," Cheryl whined, storming out of the garage.

Calvin awoke to the sound of the phone on Thursday morning. Stumbling out of bed, he answered the hammering ring.

"Hello?"

"Hi, Calvin, it's Ray. I was wondering if you'd like to get together tonight and have dinner."

"Thanks, Ray, but I promised to take Cheryl to dinner since Shane's spending a few days with Charlene."

"You're kidding? You're taking Cheryl to dinner? Tonight?"

"Yeah. Why?"

"Calvin, have you seen the morning paper?"

"No, actually you just woke me up."

"Sorry, but I think you better grab it and read the City/State section. Page three."

"Hold on."

Calvin laid the receiver down and fetched the newspaper. Oddly, the City/State section was missing.

"That section is gone," he told Ray. "Just read it to me."

"Are you aware that Cheryl's filed for divorce against you? It's in the paper."

"You're kidding!"

Ray's silence told Calvin that he was, in fact, not kidding.

"Let me call you back, Ray."

Calvin dialed Chick-fil-A.

"Chick-fil-A, Cheryl speaking."

"Cheryl."

"Hi. What's up?" Cheryl's voice wavered in anxiety.

"Where's the City/State section of today's paper?"

"Why? What do you want to know for?"

Without responding, Calvin hung up the phone. He was still in a daze as he walked into the living room. Looking up, he noticed his jazz portraits had been replaced by sunflower wallpaper.

"Dammit."

Ignoring the ringing telephone, Calvin rummaged through the trash bags, looking for his jazz photos before it dawned on him to check the outside trash burner. There, he found the ashy remains of his red frames. Calvin lit up a cigarette and walked back inside in time to answer the phone, which was ringing nonstop.

"Hello," Calvin answered.

"Look, I know you know," Cheryl started. "That's obvious. Otherwise, you wouldn't have asked about the newspaper. How'd you find out?"

"A friend called me. He read it in the paper."

"Reverend Luke?"

"Sure," Calvin lied, masking his irritation that Luke obviously knew of the divorce filing.

"Well, I just want you to know—and you can tell Pastor Luke this—I put the divorce on hold."

"Did you now? Tell me, you're always bouncing checks, so how'd you pay for it?"

"My mom gave the money. She told me if I went through with it, I wouldn't have to pay her back, but I . . ." Cheryl trailed off into silence.

"Your mommy paid for it? I should have expected such hackneyed honesty out of you."

"You've got some room to talk about honesty . . . sneaking off to that Catholic church on Sundays."

"So, it was her. You had your mother follow me? Did she tell you to burn my jazz drawings, too?"

"Well, ya know, I can't ever relate to you," Cheryl choked, almost violently sobbing. "I mean, I like jazz, but you go and haveta do to all that weird jazz. I mean, why couldn't you have drawn someone I like? Like Kenny G?"

"Kenny G?" Calvin asked in disgust.

"I know what you're going to say. 'He's not jazz, he's instrumental pop.' I don't care, but you didn't even ask me what I like. If I'm white trash, what are you? Calvin, I do love you and I can't make you see that it's not your art really, but you deliberately ignore me, and you cut Shane down all the time. You're—you're like Nancy. You're mean-spirited, and the emotion you show me the most is anger. Apart from that, you're cold."

Cheryl sniffled on the other end. Calvin realized that Cheryl was right. Nancy's behaviors had subconsciously bled into his behavior, rendering him a wretched husband and father, and he knew that he had to leave her as much for the sake of Cheryl and Shane as for himself.

"I don't think that's who you really are, but that's all I get from you," Cheryl continued. "You forget that I bought you some of those albums— even though I hate them. I've even went out and bought your filthy cigarettes. We barely scrape by, live week to week, and you don't seem to care. You're the man of the house and you're not making much at that gallery, but you act like you seem content there."

"Cheryl—"

"Let me finish. When I met you, I was intrigued, and Brother Cobweb turned me on like I've never . . ."

"You're supposed to be repulsed by him."

"Then that's your fault."

"No, it's yours."

"I swear to God, when you got up there and did that character, apart from the makeup, I'da thought you were a real preacher. You're better at it than Luke or Frank, and you know I love the Lighthouse, but I lied to you. Nancy didn't invite me there. I asked her about that church, and mostly that was because of Brother Cobweb. Have you ever thought about it for real?"

"About what?"

"Becoming a preacher. I'm sure Luke would—"

"Don't you think I'd have to believe in all that first?"

"No, I don't, really. Do you think all those televangelists believe it? I mean, you might grow into believing it, but as good as you are at it, Calvin, we could make a lot of money if you did that. We'd be set, and it'd be a good life without money worries."

"Never mind being able to sleep with myself at night?" Calvin shook his head. He knew she was right—it was his fault, and he had too much baggage to be anything other than a burden for her or Shane. He drew a deep breath. "Cheryl, just please call your lawyer and take the divorce off hold. I'll be gone by the time you get home."

Calvin hung up and didn't answer the phone when it rang again. Despite his anger and incompatibility with Cheryl—and even the fact that he didn't marry her for good reasons—divorce wasn't something he desired. It was too easy and too selfish. But at this point, it was unavoidable. As he walked out the door and into his loaded car, Calvin sat for a few moments, alone in the driveway, and cried with a grief befitting a child.

44

A Big Twilight for Tiny Gods

It had been nine months since Calvin's divorce was finalized, and although the nights were at times too quiet, he had settled into the rut of a single man's routine. However, this particular Thursday day and night, uneventful as they were, inexplicably felt off, and Calvin, feeling he wanted to burn away the day, put on a recording of Wagner's *Götterdämmerung—Twilight of the Gods*. He didn't get far into it before falling asleep. Calvin began to dream vividly.

The rhythmic hammering from the mass's Day of Wrath overwhelmed the Lucy Booth of the field in Calvin's dream. Like the fairy-tale wolf, the music pounded, and despite all that apocalyptic huffing and puffing, Arkimnel's Lucy Booth remained unscathed. Even the gates of hell would not prevail against her. Nancy's 1972 View-Master served in place of the Holy Font; despite its age and dust and wear, it awaited to be reunited with

"

eager eyes. Standing at the entrance of the Lucy Booth, Arkimnel breathed the Holy Spirit upon BlueMahler, who was before her, and like his composer namesake, BlueMahler realized that a work of art, like the world, should contain everything. For his confirmation gift, Arkimnel handed him a *Götterdämmerung* set of View-Master reels with twenty-one three-dimensional pictures, along with the viewer, which BlueMahler placed to his eyes and clicked.

Delighted with the nonsensicalness of the dream, Calvin wrote it down upon waking up before heading to the abbey. He took one of his most recent paintings: an obsessive reworking of the bizarre Christ casting the demons into the swine narrative.

Upon seeing it, Oliver quipped, "It's the Aryan in me: I could never give up my sausage biscuits." Being the perennial nonbusiness man, Calvin offered to give the painting to Oliver. Oliver suggested they hang it in the chapel.

"Why the chapel?" Calvin asked.

"Trench theology, dear sir. Christ the Prophet is more apt for this chapel than Christ the King," Oliver explained as if delivering a mini-homily.

"You know, even a lioness protects its young," Oliver added, guessing that Calvin questioned how the priest reconciled Julian of Norwich's Christ Our Mother to this biblically weird example of divine machismo in Jesus.

I guess he can't help himself, Calvin thought, because, for him, it was the weirdness of the story that was appealing. Calvin almost retorted with "Some animals eat their young," but held his tongue.

Oliver was called away to administer the rite of reconciliation to a terminally ill nun. Satisfied with the placement of the painting, Calvin walked the grounds and was waiting for Oliver's return when he heard a voice say his name.

Calvin turned to see a woman with long, caramel-colored hair staring at him. With tattoos of Buddhist imagery peeking from under the sleeves of her stylish black coat, she studied Calvin intensely.

"It's me, Stacey White."

Calvin barely recognized her. No longer a Lighthouse teen, she was now in her mid-thirties.

"What are you doing here?" she asked.

"Hi," he said, getting that out of the way. "I came to show Father Oliver one of my paintings."

"You know Oliver, too?"

Calvin immediately wondered how, being Pentecostal, she had come to know Oliver, and he nearly became jealous, not wanting to share Oliver with a Lighthouse parishioner. However, he then remembered that Stacey had left the church, even before he did, and Calvin wondered if it had anything to do with that camp story he had heard about Rev. Harry forcing Luke's face into raw deer guts.

"Well, Oliver's gone right now. He'll be back soon."

"I didn't come to see him, actually. I was here to see one of the sisters. I just came back from seeing her, and I was getting ready to leave, but if you don't mind . . . would you like to get a coffee with me? I'd like to talk. If you're free."

"I'm free," Calvin answered, curious.

"I didn't know you were Catholic," Calvin said as they sat down together in the coffee shop across from the abbey.

"I didn't know you were," she shot back.

"I'm not yet. I've been taking the RCIA classes. I'll be confirmed in a few months."

"Well, my mom's Catholic. My dad's Pentecostal. That's why I had go to the Lighthouse."

"How are your parents?" Calvin asked, although he did not remember them.

"Divorced." She sighed.

"Sorry to hear that."

"Are your parents still together?"

"They'll never get divorced."

"That's good."

"I suppose it is," Calvin said, not actually sure that it was good.

"Well, my parents divorced after that mess with Reverend Harry. I imagine you might have heard about it."

"I heard the rumor, but Luke seems to have forgiven it enough—he's the new pastor there."

Stacey looked at him curiously. "I have a cousin who still goes there. I heard Luke took over and that his dad's dying."

"Reverend Harry's dying?" Calvin asked, although it didn't affect him one way or another.

"Well, I might have overstated it. He's got prostate cancer. I don't know if he's dying per se. I heard he's in bad shape. But I don't know if we're actually talking about the same thing."

"I was talking about when Reverend Harry beat Luke up over . . . that picture of you."

"No. I mean, it's kind of related, I guess, but that's not what I was talking about."

"Alright then, what are you talking about?" Calvin asked, feeling a bit silly. He should have known it was something else—that would hardly be a reason for Stacey's parents to divorce.

"You seriously never heard?"

Slightly annoyed, Calvin explained, "I never was up on Lighthouse gossip."

"That surprises me because your mom is—"

"The Lighthouse gossip queen. Yeah."

"She was one of my Sunday school teachers." Stacey reminisced before shifting back to her original thought. "Maybe they were more shut-mouthed about it than I thought."

"Shut-mouthed?"

Stacey took a breath. "That's why I came here—to talk to Sister Norma. When I heard Reverend Harry had cancer, I thought I better deal with it finally, and she's my spiritual advisor, so . . ."

"OK, I'm lost."

Stacey grabbed Calvin's hand and folded her fingers through his. Her revelation unfolded with admirably cool restraint, which was quite remarkable given the unshakable image of one Rev. Harry, his Sunday school room, and sodomy. Not just sodomy—but that was where it ended, after a series of prior abuses—and Stacey was merely one of the Lighthouse children that had, over the years, been lined up and drafted as Rev. Harry's unwilling, branded sluts for Jesus. Calvin had known Rev. Harry to be reprehensible and ignorant, but this was something he had never fathomed. As Stacey talked, Calvin tried to shake from his head that image of Our Lady of Sorrows with an array of daggers thrust in her crimson-red heart. It was no longer confined to some image in his mental folder—it resonated now with his acid reflux. Yet, apart from a wetness in her eyes, Stacey was strong, stronger than Calvin, and he wondered why he had been spared as a victim, but then it occurred . . .

"Oh, no," Stacey corrected his naïve thought. "Reverend Harry made no distinction . . . didn't matter whether boy or girl—I, mean, after all, there's Luke, too."

"Luke? Reverend Harry raped Luke, too? His own son?"

"Both of us, and not just us, several kids, and I think that's why Reverend Harry freaked out when he caught Luke . . . with my picture . . . and I honestly think he was jealous. When my dad found out, he didn't even confront Reverend Harry. He just left the church. That's why my mom left him."

Calvin rubbed his hand across his mouth in disbelief. "Luke's wife . . ."

"Lucy. Those stories about her aren't just stories."

"And that Luke's . . ."

"Impotent? Lucy's blabbed it off to practically everyone . . . to justify her . . ."

"Her being a slut for Jesus."

"You remember that sermon, too? It sure as hell has a goddamned different meaning today, doesn't it? I've been a counselor for years, and I think that's why I got into it. Of course, counselors need counselors . . ."

"Sister Norma."

"Sister Norma." She laughed, and Calvin was surprised that Stacey could find room to laugh.

"Reverend Harry never messed with you?" she asked, abruptly.

"No. Never. Which is weird. I always felt he hated me."

Stacey looked at him deeply and almost spoke but stopped herself short.

She began again, "I never picked up that he hated you. Of course, there's all kinds of abuse, and I don't want you to think mine is any worse than what you went through. I heard about the night you left."

"I'm sure."

"Thank God, I have a supportive mother I can depend on. She told me I ought to come and see Sister Norma."

Calvin scrutinized Stacey for a moment.

"Was your mother as bad with Frank?" Stacey asked.

"She probably would have been, given a chance, but he stayed gone a lot."

"Out with the girls. I remember, and obviously, nothing's changed. Still, I wish he hadn't—I mean if Luke finds out about Frank and Lucy, it'll kill him."

"Frank and Lucy?"

Stacey raised her eyebrows. "I assumed . . . your mom knows about it."

"Does she now? Goddamn hypocrite didn't bother to mention Frank and Lucy. She mentioned Lucy and everyone else, but she conveniently left out Frank. I hardly know my brother anymore, if I ever really did."

He stared off into the distance numbly for a moment.

"What the hell do we do now?" he finally asked.

"Sister Norma felt like I should probably talk to Luke, and I agree, but I'd like to sound off to at least one more . . ."

They waited for Oliver to return. When he returned, they told him everything in his rectory.

"Stacey, I don't know you as I do Calvin, but I know enough that, I believe, at least for this, the both of you to need to gnaw off that umbilical cord with parents, with me, with Vincent, with Norma," Father Oliver told them after a half-day of reasoned listening. He stressed vigilance in accountability on all ends and, with a tone of gallows humor, added a suggestion of a broad sweeping of dead cobwebs with their own brooms.

After leaving Oliver's rectory together, Stacey suggested another coffee.

"Again?" Calvin asked. "I do drink a lot of coffee, so . . ."

Stacey noticed the Marlboros in Calvin's pocket. "Perhaps we should get a real drink in a place where we can smoke."

"You smoke?"

"I do, but I've been trying to quit."

"Oh, please don't."

She laughed. "Yeah, and I think you're going to need to have a drink and a couple of smokes while sitting down."

"Sitting down? For what?"

Oh, but Marlboros and vodka didn't make anything go down easier with what Stacey had to tell Calvin an hour later. Like turpentine, it sunk into his pores and stained his cigarette and seeped into his lips when he went to suck it. Despite its rancid taste, he sucked it anyway. Better a bad taste than the tastelessness of naïveté; what slivers of innocence had remained within Calvin now died. Goodbye degenerate naïve fatty tissues, Calvin told himself on the way home. With the revelation, he knew he needed a fully adult coconspirator—one to protest and provoke and kick over tables with—and Stacey, who had visibly refrained from hugging him as he learned of his family's dark secrets, seemed the perfect fit. There would be time for hugs later—and maybe something else. On the way home Calvin thrust the Sixth Symphony of Mahler in and bit down on yet another Marlboro through Mahler's relentless hammer blows, and he couldn't wait to get out of the fucking car and into the house and onto the phone and he didn't give a damn what time it was.

His finger hit the last number. Calvin tried to picture Nancy in that sickening house on the other end. Almost certainly, she was in her bedroom alone, doing a crossword puzzle, while Dale had likely fallen asleep on the living room couch watching 1950s westerns.

"Hello?" Nancy answered, whispering, likely afraid she would wake Dale up.

"Hello, mother dear," Calvin spit out. "So, were you ever going to tell me that Harry Dushane is my fucking father?"

Calvin felt damned satisfied after listening to his mother try to mask her wails, so as not to wake Dale. Nancy didn't offer any additional revelations. She didn't have to. Everything seemed clear and, for once, something linear was actually good for Calvin. She and Dale had tried to get her pregnant with no success, and then, BAM, when she started porking the holy man, she got knocked up. So she blamed Calvin. It was Calvin's fault that her marriage was stained. It was the fault of her bastard son that her husband wouldn't get saved. And proving that he was conceived in sin and that a dark spirit abided in him, the bastard son took neither to her nor her husband nor even his actual father—but to a perverted atheist Jew. Further proof of Calvin's bad seed was in his effeminacy and weakness and progressive thinking. He had gotten sick and almost died—or, worse, could have been a retard. Calvin had shown his true rainbow of colors at the anti-gay rally. He had mocked her in church and mocked her yet again when he tried to kill himself. Calvin was possessed by a taunting demon that had ruined her entire life. Like the raging narcissist she was, Nancy played the part of Pentecostal heart-on-her-sleeve victim and blamed her missteps on Tubby and Billy, sparing no detail. Although Nancy's own abuse history was dressed up as an explanation, it by no means justified a goddamned thing, and before Calvin hung up in disgust, she asked, "Now what?"

He wished he could mantle the proverbial fly on the wall to witness the scene on her end—he heard genuine fear in her voice. He wanted so badly to tell her, there's not going to be any resurrection for you, mother dear.

"Now what, indeed?" was his curt reply before hanging up, refusing to placate or assure her of anything. Calvin immersed himself in a nicotine daze before sleeping, and he slept good. He slept goddamned good.

Although Calvin couldn't remember dreaming when he awoke Saturday morning, it was the dream from Thursday night that lingered, and in that idiosyncratic spirit, he plotted his Sunday best. He would mentally put on a shielding pair of dark glasses needed to cut up everything that he intended to cut up. And with that, he would don the invisible blue grace of a BlueMahler to observe for his art—his instrument of war. If Rev. Harry and Nancy and the Lighthouse had modeled gentleness, empathy, understanding, and encouragement, perhaps Calvin might have produced a canvas to decorate their living room. Although, that would have provoked them even more because he would have painted something so beautiful that they would have erroneously read hate in it because his art, they felt, was out to make them feel stupid. It made them feel stupid because they were stupid; nothing offended them more than beauty, which is why they built their hackneyed pyramids of righteous, pedestaled morality in the slime of ethical bankruptcy. Come Sunday, Calvin was going to undress and redress because nothing was more incisive than grace—grace to assassinate their hypocrisy because Julian and Oliver and Vincent were right after all: Christ is a symbol of love, manifested in lasting relationships. It was so simple, and the Lighthouse had not only mucked that up for its own members, but they mucked it up for everyone they touched, leaving their trail of a grace so stolen and broken that the trail itself had evaporated.

Calvin met up with Stacey at a cemetery near her work where they could avoid the living and be with only spirits. As they walked, they stopped at a large tree and sat down. They read the names on a tombstone near them: William and Rose, who were born in the 1880s and died a few days apart in the 1950s. It was fitting, and Calvin and Stacey both knew it with astounding clarity. They talked for hours about the saints, philosophers, artists, writers, musicians, and movies they shared a love of. Most edifying, they found they both had a yearning for the authentic sacred that did not shun or condemn blackened flaws or even interests. Their spirituality was comparable to that Johannine tale of Christ and the Samaritan woman at the well, who both could symbolically draw water from an endless well, gifting each other drink, and that segued into their talk of the great romances, both of myth—such as Tristan and Isolde—and history, such as F. Scott and Zelda Fitzgerald. While they talked, Stacey scraped her hand on a rock, drawing blood, which prompted Calvin to run to his car and pull a Band-Aid out of the first-aid kit and tend to her wound. As his hand bandaged hers, they both sensed a feeling of being wrapped.

"Are you aware of the Four Sufi Points?" Stacey asked Calvin. "They are the four points necessary for soulmates. Are you compatible spiritually? Intellectually? Are you best friends?"

"That's only three," Calvin noted.

"Are you compatible sexually?"

Calvin leaned in and kissed her. They kissed, wordless, and the rest of the world was completely burned away. Only these two and the sky existed until finally they realized the time—they had been kissing for hours. They had planned a mass together—not at the abbey or the Franciscan retreat, neither her parish nor his—but one they would go to together: the nearest parish was St. Mark's, and they both saw the necessity and completeness of that. It was not only named after the author of the most ancient Gospel, but it was the Gospel that gave the fullest portrayal of Christ as a prophet, who, after facing temptation, set out on an adventure of kicking over the tables of hypocrites. This was not a Christ condemning sins or baggage, but a Christ who only judged the judgmental, hypocritical, greedy, and those who lacked love and charity. They entered St. Mark's hand in hand. It sanctified them and their relationship, and they both knew they would be joined for life.

They parted after mass, each going to their respective homes, and called each other. Calvin began to talk, but Stacey, being tired, only wanted to fall asleep while hearing him sleep on the other end. It was the perfect end to an even more perfect day; the perfectness was damned necessary for the Sunday ahead.

It was 10:30 a.m. and the Lighthouse children were in Sunday school. That's where they needed to be, because the adults, the ones who weren't teaching, would be gathered together in the chapel. Frank was on the church stage preparing to deliver the sermon. Lucy, sitting in the front row, pridefully looked at Frank, and he looked back at her confidently. Frank carefully placed his notes on the pulpit, but as he leaned into the mic, Stacey White suddenly appeared beside him on stage, grabbed the mic, and said, "There's not going to be a sermon today. The Holy Ghost has taken over the service."

Calvin was confronting Luke in his office. "I know about Lucy and Frank," Luke said loudly and defensively, with more animation than he had ever had on stage. Calvin, standing a few feet away, didn't flinch. "I just shut my mouth—kind of like Mom did with Dad and your mom."

"I never understood your mom's attraction to your dad. Or my mom's attraction to your dad. I don't understand Lucy's attraction to Frank. Fascism is such an aphrodisiac for some women . . ."

"But Lucy is well-read," Luke said as if he himself was trying to understand.

"Obviously doesn't matter, she's drawn to the whole white trash thing like that primal moth to flame."

"I tried to talk to her repeatedly and—"

"She muted and muted you. That's a predictable response to justify her . . . passive-aggressive narcissism."

"Big words."

"They're not big words."

The two men were silent for some time and could hear everything happening in the sanctuary. There was an occasional congregational gasp upstairs whenever Stacey said "penis." They even heard Opal shouting at Stacey for saying the word in the house of God. Otherwise, from what Calvin could discern, Stacey was calm and lucid, instructing and explaining and offering solutions, as opposed to chastising. Yet, he also sensed the inherent spirit of the Lighthouse. The church wanted this buried.

"Thoughts and prayers aren't going to cut it," Calvin said angrily.

"What are you and Stacey trying to accomplish with all this, Calvin?" Luke asked, exasperated.

"Luke, your father fucking raped you. He raped Stacey. He raped others in this church. Sodomy in the Sunday school rooms. That's OK, ignore that, but don't say 'penis' in church? Jesus fucking Christ, Luke. And the climate of hate and ignorance and hypocrisy that's been a trademark in the Lighthouse is what bred every abuse imaginable."

"People don't like changes, regardless. You know that, Calvin."

"Stacey's treating them like they're adults who can reason and strive to think critically."

"They're not adults. They won't reason."

"Luke, it's not going to get prayed away."

"No, it's not."

"You have to do something, and if you won't do it for yourself . . . you're a pastor, and according to that Bible, that makes you a shepherd. So, shepherd."

"I will—immediately," Luke vowed.

"It's not about being immediately effective. The best way for this to take hold is . . . I don't know, something like leaving a trace of poison in their bowl."

"We're brothers," Luke said, almost as if not hearing and already having something in mind.

"How long have you known?"

"Since before you had meningitis."

And you didn't have the guts to tell me, Calvin thought, realizing just how weak Luke was.

"I heard Mom fighting with Dad about it one night," Luke said.

"And she put up with it."

"She was upset when she figured it out, but yeah, she put up with it. I think maybe because it kept Dad off her. It's not like your mom was the only woman that my dad messed with—"

"Consenting adults. Raping children is something else. I know this is hard for you, but did your mom know about you and Stacey and—"

"She knew about his affairs, but I don't think she knew about that. I hope not. I guess we'll never know for sure."

"I know your dad is sick, but he needs to be held accountable."

"Our dad—and he will be," Luke assured.

"No. He's not our dad. I didn't grow up with him. He's just a biological coincidence. Your dad is no more my dad than Nancy is my mother. It makes sense now—the context of what Christ meant when he said to leave your parents, cling unto your spouse, and follow me. Maybe the greatest way to honor parents spiritually is to destroy their parenthood."

"Calvin, you've always understood and believed God's Word more than me, more than Dad."

"I'm not talking about belief. I'm talking faith and—"

"Calvin, everyone is going to know about Dad and me, and Stacey, and your mom and you, and I can't face this."

"But you said you were going to change things."

"I will, I promise."

Calvin left, unsure what or how to feel. The meeting with Luke was anticlimactic, and although Luke had made meager brotherly overtures over the years, Calvin was as disconnected from him as he was as from Frank. Frank and Luke were more like brothers—the brothers cobweb, sharing the same wife, father, and Lighthouse with locked door.

"Well?" Calvin asked Stacey when she met him at his car in the parking lot a few minutes later.

"I stressed accountability, communication, and my services—no charge even," she cracked.

"Are they taking you up on that?"

"If they do—and I doubt it—it will only be to get something for free. How'd it go with Luke?"

"I don't know. He said he is going to act. I think we need to give him time to do that."

"Hmm. Let's give him time and let's get the hell out of here and go to that mystery school you told me about."

They drove to the Franciscan retreat, where Vincent gave a homily and asked Calvin to help service communion, which consisted of wine and multicolored wafers. The white wafers were too boring, Vincent said.

"Oh, Father Vincent is so cool," Stacey laughed on the way back to Calvin's apartment. "I want to dance with him and write a haiku for him and call it 'Sashay This Way.'"

Calvin and Stacey were going to have a two-day shut-in slumber party. He would take the couch at night and she could sleep in his bed, and there would be no answering of phones. They sat up in Calvin's bed with the idiot box in front of them. After mapping out the first evening, Calvin served Stacey a plate of peanut butter no-bake cookies, and the first movie in their marathon was *Freaks*, the 1932 Tod Browning opus that had previously been banned for nearly fifty years, starring a cast of real freaks.

"Oh my god," Stacey exclaimed upon seeing the opening title. "We accept her, we accept her. One of us, one of us," she yelled out in glee, quoting the movie. "I love the bearded lady and the hermaphrodite."

"You've seen it? You want me to put something else on?"

"Absolutely not. I love this movie, and I love that you love it."

"I adore the pinheads." Calvin laughed.

"Let's always fly our freak flags high together," she exclaimed.

"And keep the ink of nonconformity wet. Abso-fucking-lutely, and before we go to bed at night, we'll say a prayer to Our Lady of the Motherfuckers."

She laughed. "And we'll ask her to keep us strong so we don't become like our FOOs."

"Foos?"

"Family of origin."

"Amen to Our Lady of the Motherfuckers," they said in unison.

Following *Freaks*, Stacey asked, "Hey, can we do a Woody Allen movie and *Jaws*? But I've got to have cheese pizza rolls for *Jaws*."

Calvin laughed. "I've got some cheese pizza rolls in the freezer. I can get those started while you look through my Woody Allen collection."

Stacey picked *Zelig*, but because she was craving pizza rolls, they went with *Jaws* first, both quoting the movie by heart. Between movies, they talked incessantly and fell asleep next to each other during *Zelig*. So much for sleeping apart.

The next morning, Calvin made her pancakes—with lots of butter— and already he was enjoying this edifyingly weird domesticity with her. Throughout the day, the phone rang, and the first few times, Calvin was tense, but in the spirit of their shut-in, he tuned it out. He easily could have shut off the ringer, but he wanted to hear it because each time that he refused to answer it, he felt he was making a choice that was right and wanted the verification of that rightness. Their time together reminded Calvin so much of his shut-in magical years with Pop that he opened up to Stacey and regaled her with Pop stories—which she referred to as "God stories"—and after hearing of mermaids and Darwin and movie star titties and the fox at the drive-in, she announced that they should go shopping.

Calvin was reluctant to go shopping, but he sensed she had a creative purpose, and so he accompanied her. They first went to a craft store, where she bought some glue, scissors, and a box. Next, they went to a used bookstore.

"Bookstores are my kryptonite," she said. "I could spend all day in a bookstore, so I'll have to keep focused."

"I'm the same way," Calvin laughed as she led him through the aisles. They found books on saints, mythology, mermaids, and Darwin. The next stop was a clothing store. Stacey wouldn't let him come in with her—she said it was a surprise—so Calvin went to get her a caramel macchiato, with double the fixings—extra whipped cream, nuts, and a cherry.

Once home, Calvin and Stacey sat Indian style on the floor and made a God box. The God box was dedicated to Pop and to her grandmother, whom she called Saint Monica.

"Saint Monica and my grandpa immigrated here from Ireland, and they helped build Saint Patrick's. They were married forever," Stacey explained.

The last pictures they put on the God box were their own.

"Now, when we have something we want to turn over to God, we'll write it on a piece of paper and put it in the God box," Stacey said.

"Let's make a small temple for it," Calvin suggested.

Surrounded by candles and placed on a bookshelf underneath Calvin's *Our Lady of the Mermaid* painting, Stacey and Calvin's God box now was the center of his home.

They both wrote down prayer requests and dropped them in the God box without showing each other.

"Let's go to a mass tomorrow morning," Stacey said. "We've done a Franciscan and Benedictine service. Let's find a Jesuit parish. Jesuits give great homilies. Next week, we'll try a Carmelite parish."

Calvin beamed at such a spiritual sense of adventure. "And we should try a Latin mass."

"Abso-fucking-lutely. Why don't you hand me that coffee and go look up to see if there's a nearby Jesuit parish and what time their morning mass is."

After Calvin handed her the coffee, Stacey grabbed her bag from the clothing store and said, "I'm going to your bedroom. I have to put something together. It may take me an hour or so, so you can busy yourself."

The phone was still ringing incessantly, so Calvin finally turned the ringer off and dived into a book. When Stacey reemerged from his room, she was dressed as a sensual mermaid, which made for a giddy few hours, followed by a night of movies.

If Calvin had been in a conscious state, he might have wondered if a mini-festival of Boris Karloff and Bela Lugosi horror flicks had finally given him a nightmare or if it was merely too many pizza rolls affecting his stomach. His dream kicked into overdrive as he was trying to wake up.

Finding a broken View-Master on the Lighthouse grounds, BlueMahler of Calvin's dream leaned down to pick up three of the toy's still frames, which had been knocked out of the reel. Holding the frames up to Arkimnel's torchlight, he looked into the images contained within.

Arkimnel, whose face now strongly resembled Luke's, proceeded up the Lighthouse aisle with torch in hand. Reaching down, she set fire to the floor and pews. Burnt wooden rafters, shattered cross, puddles of salt, bloodied shrouds, rose petals drained of life, a cracked chalice, and crowns of thorns accented her mournful steps toward the tomb-like stage.

A baby mantis entered the fatal atmosphere. Sensing an ominous presence, the mantis froze, as if in prayer. Its prayer proved unanswered upon being engulfed by a mass of ants emerging from the cinders.

Rev. Harry was alone on the stage, screaming as he felt his skin melting from the flames devouring him. Desiring his body and soul to be raptured up with flying Lighthouse ash, Rev. Harry felt himself restrained by a hulking apocalyptic angel. Tilting his head to see out of his melting eyes, Rev. Harry identified the saint enveloping him as Captain Christ. Rev. Harry's facial muscles tried to form a smile but transformed to sheer terror as he realized that the Vacation Bible School leader was not there to escort him to St. Peter's pearly gates. Instead, the Captain had hooked Rev. Harry for the fiery pit. The ground beneath them opened its mouth. Rev. Harry tried to scream, but no sound came out. His soul was rendered Hamburger Helper for hell's banquet.

Calvin was unsettled as he stepped onto the front porch to smoke a cigarette at two in the morning, trying to shake his nightmare before going back to bed.

On Wednesday morning, Calvin was preparing scrambled eggs for Stacey.

"We still doing the Jesuit mass after breakfast?" she asked from the couch where she had slept.

"Sure," he answered, preoccupied with the eggs.

As she sat up, Stacey put aside her schoolwork and turned the TV on. She flipped through the channels until . . .

"Local news. Father and son ministers perish in Lighthouse Pentecostal Church fire," announced the TV anchor. "It has been confirmed that Reverends Harry and Luke Dushane died in the fire at the Lighthouse Church yesterday. Firefighters are still investigating the cause, but arson is suspected. Reverend Harold Dushane began his ministry in . . ."

45

MOSES UND ARON

S tacey offered to drive on the way to the Lighthouse to give Calvin time to process. For having just found out that their childhood church was gone and that his biological father and half-brother had died a fiery death, Calvin was numb. Calvin could tell this worried Stacey even more than if he had shown an emotional reaction, whatever that reaction might be. Stacey's reaction had been stunned grief for her rapist and his son, whom she once had a crush on. Although Calvin had nearly dropped the plate of eggs upon hearing the news, he quickly recovered, and his demeanor was duty-bound on the ride to the Lighthouse.

"Do you want to call your mother or Frank?" she had asked him.

"Not yet," was his curt reply.

As they hit the road, heading toward a heap of Lighthouse ash, Calvin sat in the passenger's seat, revisiting an old man's bedroom from a still vivid childhood memory.

"Help, I'm drowning," Pop had cried in mocking falsetto voice, imitating the TV show parrot. "Jeepers! That poor Jimmy Olsen can't tell a parrot from a mermaid!"

"Or Clark Kent from Superman," exclaimed Calvin as the show's familiar theme music swelled to a close.

"Superman's like Wotan, except he's a nicer god," Pop declared.

"Shut up, old fool," Nancy had said, interrupting as she walked into Pop's bedroom without knocking. "Some God! Blowing his own brains out. Quit saying that. You'll just confuse Calvin."

"Woman," Pop had said in his impassioned German accent, "I wasn't talking about the actor. I was talking about Superman, and your Jesus killed himself, too. Take up your cross and follow me, that is what your Jesus said. It seems he wants you Christians to kill yourselves, too. I never heard Superman say that and I never read of people killing people in Superman's name or using Superman as an excuse to be a bigot. Superman punched those racists in the face, saved the hound from the water well, and flew that little cripple girl across the sky. What does Jesus do? Nothing! He says wait until after you die, then you can see me. What kind of nonsense is that?"

"Jesus is the only real god, Pop. You're just an old fool," Nancy barked before walking away.

"That Lighthouse lady called the parrot an old fool," giggled Calvin.

"That parrot was no fool. The parrot and Superman were the only ones that knew there were shady things going on at the Lighthouse. *Hölle*, it was a lighthouse that didn't even work!"

"This looks like a job for Superman," Calvin beamed. "But how come Superman killed himself?"

"Perhaps he wanted to become a god for real. That book we've been reading about Claudius—do you remember Livia? She was Caesar's wife, but she did terrible things. So, when she was old, she summoned Claudius. Now, if you remember, she had always made fun of Claudius because he was a cripple, but she also knew that he was going to be emperor someday. So she made him promise to make her a goddess because the gods, even if they have done bad things, don't get punished."

"How come?"

"Because once you become a god, you can't get punished anymore."

When Stacey and Calvin pulled into the Lighthouse parking lot, a crowd had already formed. Calvin saw the fire marshal and several parishioners, including Frank and Lucy, who clearly had been crying fiercely, their faces red and wet. Calvin's eyes scanned the parking lot and crowd. Nancy was conspicuously absent.

"Where's Mom?" Calvin asked Frank as he exited the car.

Without answering, Frank leaned into Calvin and hugged him, which took Calvin by surprise and made him feel awkward. Backing up, Calvin repeated the question.

"She's not here," Frank answered in a hoarse voice.

"I can see that."

Stacey walked over to Lucy, put her arm around her, and together, they walked off to the middle of the parking lot to talk privately.

"We been trying to get ahold of you for the last two days—first to ask you why Stacey said all that stuff, and last night to tell you about this. Why didn't you answer your phone or call us back? I left a bunch of messages," Frank whined.

"I had the phone turned off."

"Well, Stacey saying all that . . . this is the result . . . and more. You guys have no idea what you gone and done."

Calvin bit down on his lower lip and listened attentively to Frank's explanation. According to Frank, after Calvin and Stacey had left, all the poisons in the mud had been drawn out. Humiliated in the revelations of Rev. Harry's pedophilia, in being one of the victims, and humiliated in the ousting of the affairs of Rev. Harry and Nancy and Frank and Lucy, Luke—apparently unable to face anyone—literally fled the church. No one knew where he went or even if he was returning. Taking charge, Frank and Lucy repented to the church for their infidelity, asked for forgiveness, and vowed to "clean house," starting with Rev. Harry and Nancy, who were no longer welcome at the Lighthouse—not for their affair, but for their abuses. Frank had revealed Nancy's violence and described his and Calvin's childhoods. To right wrongs, Frank claimed, as the acting pastor, he would show no favoritism.

"So, you essentially excommunicated Mom?" Calvin interrupted.

"Yeah, I did, and Reverend Harry, of course. I mean, I know he's your real father, but—"

"No, he's not. He was just dressed-up Pentecostal sperm."

"Calvin, don't be talking like that. This is a church ground."

"Really? You just said that? Don't be a hypocrite. Anyway," Calvin said, shaking his head. "Does Dad know?"

"Yeah. He tried to call you, too, to tell you he doesn't feel no different about you, none. You're still his son, as far he is concerned."

"I'll call him," Calvin assured Frank. Although Dale was flawed and they were not close, Calvin knew that he genuinely loved his dad, although Calvin questioned if he could say the same about Nancy. "What about Dad and Mom?"

"He friggin' left her, yesterday."

"He actually left her?"

"Well, he's staying at the car lot. Said he needed time apart from Mom. I don't think he's going to divorce her, though."

"Probably not," Calvin agreed.

Frank resumed explaining that Lucy had not heard from Luke since he had driven out of the church parking lot on Sunday.

"I figured Luke was just too scared," Frank surmised. "But somehow, he wound up back here, with his dad, and they got caught in that fire. You think one of the other kids that Reverend Harry messed with did this?"

"No," Lucy answered solemnly, interrupting Calvin's response. "Just got this letter delivered," she added, waving a piece of paper. "It's from Luke. Guess he mailed it before—"

"Before he came back, got his father, set fire to the Lighthouse, and killed them both?" Calvin guessed.

"You knew?" Stacey asked, as she stood behind Lucy.

"I suspected as soon as I heard it on TV," Calvin answered.

"Why?" Frank asked, shocked.

"Talk is cheap. This was Luke's revolt. He showed what he was going to do about it. Luke didn't burn down the Lighthouse and take out Reverend Harry and himself for what was done to him. He did it for Stacey and us," Calvin said, seething.

"Are you defending this?" Frank asked incredulously.

"I thought Luke had gone weak, but, man, it took guts and nobility to burn down this blasphemy. Normally, I wouldn't defend it at all, but Luke didn't have it in him to change anything, so I guess I have to respect him and his action."

"I can't believe you're saying this," Frank argued. "Yeah, we were abused, too, not like Luke was . . ."

"And Stacey," Calvin countered angrily.

"I meant her, too."

"No, you didn't. It's telling that you didn't mention her."

"Calvin, I ain't being . . . look, what Mom did to us was terrible, and I think that's a big part of the reason that I was so bad in marriage and—"

"You can stop now. Mom is no more a reason for your failed marriage than she is for mine. Nothing that Mom did justifies what you and Lucy did to Luke. Just like what Tubby and Billy did to Mom had nothing to do with the way Mom did us. We're not heroes by any means."

"OK, I'm sorry," Frank said. "I'm going to get right with myself and God, but after you call Dad, can you call Mom, too?"

"No, but I'll turn the ringer back on. If she wants to talk to me, she can call me."

Stacey took Calvin aside and suggested they give Frank and Lucy some space and an offer to get together and talk. Calvin did so, which Frank showed appreciation for but didn't fully commit to.

"I think Frank is worried about their future. The Lighthouse was their income," Calvin said to Stacey as he was driving them back to his apartment.

"The tragedy of this aside, that's perfectly normal to be worried," she reasoned.

"That wasn't part of Luke's concern."

"No, and it didn't need to be. I'm like you, I definitely don't agree with what he did, but I guess Luke felt he had to stay focused."

They rode on in silence for some time.

"I know you're avoiding this," Stacey said slowly, "but you did lose a father and brother, of sorts, today, and I think you need to face that."

"I do face it. I don't need a funeral for closure. I need to work my ass off. The other day I was listening to Luigi Nono. I've kind of developed an obsession with his music."

"Imagine you having an obsession! But what's that got to do—"

"Nono was an almost militant atheist, but he came across an inscription on the wall of a Toledo monastery that immediately altered his art and existence."

"What was the inscription?" Stacey asked, intrigued.

"Wanderer, there may be no destination, but you must travel."

"Damn right," Stacey said.

A few hours later, Stacey got through about ten minutes of Nono music flooding Calvin's apartment and announced, "Calvin, I love you, but that sounds like the noise an orchestra makes while warming up. I can't handle that. Sorry."

They both realized she had said "I love you" and shared an unspoken, authentic smile.

"I love you, too, Stacey. And I'll turn it off, of course. That was probably my reaction when I first heard his music, and, hell, I was already weaned on Schoenberg, Berg, and Webern."

"Ha! Schoenberg, Berg, and Webern. Schoenberg, Berg, and Webern. Schoenberg, Berg, and Webern. Say that ten times real fast, I dare you."

Calvin laughed and retreated to the kitchen to make them dinner. After a few moments, Stacey yelled out, "Hey, the paper says they're doing a concert of Schoenberg's opera *Moses und Aron* in Chicago. It's being directed by a conductor named Pierre Boulez."

"When?" Calvin asked, perking up.

"Tonight."

Calvin looked at his watch. "Alright," he said putting the food back in the cabinet. "We'll stop somewhere and get something to go."

"Something to go?" she asked.

"On the way to *Moses und Aron*. If you're game, make sure you pee before you go."

"I'm game," she said as she dashed off to the bathroom.

A few hours later, Calvin and Stacey sat transfixed in the audience. Boulez's hands cut through and shaped the dissonant reds and oranges and slashing purples of the music, amounting to a prismatic powerhouse, but it was the sung dialogue that resonated even deeper. Moses, angered over Aron's making of the golden calf image, heatedly and violently fought with his brother. God is unconceivable and inexpressible. "God is up there, above us," argued Moses, "and he abhors the image. He must be spoken of only—and invisible."

"Not so," countered Aron. "He appeared to you in the form of a burning bush. That is an image. He brought forth a fiery pillar, which is also an image. The tablets, on which the commandments were given, is an image. No, people cannot connect to an invisible God in the sky. God must be seen and present among us," Aron argued from his prison cell. Because Moses stuttered, Aron had been his mouthpiece, but in anger—and ultimately unable to argue with Aron's point—Moses reacted by killing his own voice.

Calvin found numerous personal parallels. Nancy, unable to silence Pop, burned his mermaid. Unable to counter Calvin's conscience and honest questions, Nancy tortured her son. Like Moses and Aron, Frank and Calvin were similarly contrasted. Unable to identify with an invisible God who spoke only the word "No," Calvin visually expressed God as an idea of profound maternal love. Frank envisioned a paradoxically concrete invisible deity and climbed a stage to only speak of that authoritarian phantom who must be worshipped without question. Naïvely, Luke tried to alter the image of the Lighthouse, yet the only real language he knew was that which Rev. Harry had given him, and when he finally found the courage to stand up to his father, his only recourse, he felt, was to kill them both. Calvin then remembered a homily that Father Oliver had given on a Mother's Day: he had suggested that if one desires to see Christ, he need not try to look above for an invisible God. Rather, he need only look into the flawed face of his spouse to see Christ.

46
GOOD FRIDAY SPELL

It took approximately forty-eight hours for Nancy to call Calvin. He was surprised it took that long.

"You were never your dad's son, but you weren't Harry's, neither," Nancy opened during their phone conversation. "You're Pop's son, but Harry was the worst of all. What he did to my poor Stacey. He ruined her."

"Stacey's not ruined," Calvin corrected, as he dragged off a Marlboro, drank his coffee, and pressed the phone to his ear.

"It's men like Harry that—look, I know I wasn't the best mom . . ."

"The best mom?"

"Calvin, I promised your dad that I'm gonna get help. You know, some therapy. I already called and made an appointment. I'm trying, Calvin. I was hoping your dad might understand a little. I know I did your dad wrong and I was too strict on you and Frank—"

"Too strict?"

"Calvin, nothing compares to what they did to me and Alvie."

"You better stop while you're ahead."

"I didn't mean—"

"I'm sure you didn't, but goddamn!"

"Would you please quit taking the Lord's name in vain? It's bad enough your being an atheist."

"If I am an atheist, then I had the perfect model . . ."

"I know, Calvin. I know! And I'll never forgive Pop—"

"I'm referring to you."

"Me? Calvin," Nancy whined melodramatically, "I'm no atheist. I—oh, Calvin! Pulllleaaazzzeee, I'm getting help and I'm asking you to forgive me. I forgave my dad."

"So, you're willing to forgive your dad for everything, but you just said that you would never forgive Pop. You're as big a hypocrite now as you've always been."

"I didn't mean that about Pop, Calvin."

"Yes, you did. *I Was Married to a Mermaid*," he reminded her.

"And I just want you to forgive me—you and Frank both," Nancy continued, not listening. "And even though you're an atheist, pray for me and pray that your dad ain't gonna divorce me. I ain't never worked a job. I wanted to, but your dad wouldn't let me, and now I'm too old. What am I gonna do? Will you talk to your dad for me?"

"I forgive you as much as I can, but I'm not going to talk to Dad for you."

"Calvin, I don't want to talk on the phone. I want to talk face to face. Would you come over please?"

"No," was his stern reply. He expected a complete about-face and waited to hear Nancy curse him and hang up the phone.

"Goodbye," Nancy said as she tried to subdue her sobs.

Calvin wondered how long it would take for her to call him back. His talk with Dale had been briefer, with Dale revealing that he would go back to Nancy, but he was going to let her sweat it out and asked Calvin to keep that to himself. Dale hadn't even mentioned Calvin being Rev. Harry's son. Instead, Dale droned on that he hoped Rev. Harry was burning in hell. Then, suddenly, Dale asked, "So, when you becoming Catholic?"

"A few months."

"I told your Aunt Blanche. It's funny, in a way, Blanche and I both had a hand in you becoming Catholic."

"How did you have hand in that?" Calvin asked, balking that Dale was giving himself undue credit.

"Well, I let you sneak off to that church with her, didn't I? Your mother still doesn't know that, and don't you be telling her, neither. Anyways, Blanche wasn't surprised. She said you told her that you were gonna become a Catholic someday the first time she took you there."

"I might have." Calvin sighed, choosing not to go too deep with Dale.

Four months later, in the back of the Art Brut, Ed Smith, Calvin, and Stacey sat in a semicircle at a round table with a sand box centered so each could reach it. Ed brought out a box of colored sand in bags, Q-tips, stirring rods, and stencils.

"I think you have every color in the spectrum," said Calvin.

"I don't think we need the stencils," said Ed. Stacey agreed.

The three slowly began their Buddhist sand painting, pouring and working the sand into nongeometric shapes. Calvin and Stacey chain-smoked cigarettes while Ed occasionally smoked reefer.

Several hours later, they were immensely pleased with having finished the sand painting.

"I think it's a beautiful work—real intricate. Let's get a picture of it," said Ed.

Ed produced a camera and snapped away.

"Man, we ought to get a picture of the three of us."

Ed walked outside for a moment and reemerged with a shabby-looking homeless man.

"What did you say your name was?" Ed asked the man.

"Randy," he answered in a gravelly voice.

"Randy's going to take our picture," Ed announced to Calvin and Stacey.

They posed next to their sand painting. Randy clicked a button, did his duty, grabbed a five from Ed, and exited.

The three took the sandbox out the back door and turned it upside down. The breeze blew the remnants of their work through blades of grass and mounds of earth. Whatever the process of their collaboration, the work itself, and destruction of it meant to each was kept private.

It was Holy Saturday Easter Vigil at St. Patrick's. Looking out over the expanse of the parish, Calvin saw Ray, Father Vincent, Ed, and Stacey among the small group of supporters who had shown up for his baptism and confirmation. Surprisingly, there was no sign of Father Oliver.

The entire congregation held up golden candles illuminating their shimmering chorus, The Litany of the Saints.

> *Holy Mary, pray for us.*
> *Holy Mother of God, pray for us.*
> *Holy Virgin of virgins, pray for us.*

Following overwhelming water, fire, wind, flowing white robes, bells, Psalms, and the Litany, Calvin's hour arrived as he stepped up to be baptized by Father Kirchner. The parish priest unexpectedly moved aside, conceding to Father Oliver, who suddenly appeared to administer the rite of baptism to Calvin Elkan.

"Have you chosen a confirmation name?" Oliver asked Calvin.

"Thomas Maximilian," Calvin answered. He had chosen Thomas, the doubting saint who he most identified with, and the saint he most admired—Maximilian Kolbe.

On Easter morning, Calvin and Stacey went to visit Oliver, whom they found in the rectory.

"I hope last night was everything you anticipated," said Oliver to Calvin.

"It was a sublime mass," Calvin answered.

"I've always preferred the Easter Vigil, even to Christmas Eve midnight mass."

"I didn't want last night to end. I realized last night that the best parts of my life have been just that. My great-grandfather composed a liturgical world for me that was so personal that it could have lasted forever. His granddaughter took me to a Catholic parish, and again, I found joy in a liturgy that I've kept coming back to. Last night was, paradoxically, a beautifully familiar plane."

"Joy in repetition," Oliver replied. "Calvin, I think you fell in love with our religion. I want to caution you on something: you are on the high of conversion right now, and it's going to be a wonderful time, but do not delude yourself. There is . . . something festering. I'm going to apologize for sharing this so soon, but I think the sooner the better."

"What?" Calvin asked, curious.

"When I was the director of Saint Joseph's, the bishop wrote and instructed me to start doing night guard. I was to be on the lookout for masturbating seminarians and deal with them accordingly. I did too—like iron. I compromised, and all that accomplished was a drinking problem. That's in the past, but physically and spiritually I suffered for that. Remember, the bishops are ancient men in pointy hats, and never underestimate the influence of money, especially with those who claim they have no use for it. Despite what they claim, the hierarchy isn't the Church. You are. The Holy Spirit is moving the Church, whether we like it or not. We will reap what we sow, especially if we choose not to move with it."

47

THE HOUSE OF SHADOWS

It had been a year since Calvin's confirmation, and almost everything chugged along as predicted. Dale had gone back to Nancy. Frank and Lucy got together officially and then split up; Frank started rebuilding a new Lighthouse and got a new wife. Stacey and Calvin had blossomed into a full-blown relationship, and while she was deep in her PhD, Calvin painted and toyed with the idea of either finishing his art degree or getting a degree in theology. Although he loved donning the BlueMahler person in performance art, it was too readily accepted at the Art Brut. He needed to feel a jolt.

On Sunday, the jolt arrived for both Calvin and Stacey. They left mass numb. Father Vincent had been away on a European tour for several months. In his place, others had been running it; depending on who was leading the mass, at times it felt like happy happy, joy joy–styled spirituality for suburban housewives and the ladies auxiliary club. Sometimes, something deeper was needed, and it was one of those days when it woefully fell short: sixteen priests had been arrested for pedophilia in neighboring diocese.

Stacey had dared to bring it up in a prayer request.

"Can we please just do that as an unspoken request?" a fellow parishioner had asked. "I come here so I can get away from negative thoughts."

"Let's just think happy thoughts and do bumper sticker theology," Calvin grumbled as he and Stacey were leaving. "Forget kicking over the tables."

"Yeah, and isn't it odd that was the gospel reading? Gong! Ignored!"

"I didn't leave the Lighthouse because of the abuse, per se. I left it for other reasons, but I am thinking of something Vincent said during a LGBT service: if your conscience compels you to leave the Church, then do so because we can never violate our conscience. That's the spirit speaking directly to you, and the goal of the Church, like a mother, should be to make herself obsolete in the lives of her children, so they can make their own spiritual path. On the other hand, Vincent said he's been tempted, at times, to leave the Church, but couldn't because then he'd be conceding that it belonged to the conservatives. They're like super-patriots. Believe exactly how we believe or get out."

"Do you feel you need to leave the Church?"

"No—there's joy in repetition. I do love the art of the mass, but I'm not going to be humble. I think the Church needs me more than I need it. It needs me, not just me, of course, but me too, to bring them, perhaps violently, into the present, giving them a dose of contemporary spiritual common sense. The medieval monk never heard of the sexual revolution, but this is a different world. We take young seminarians, at the height of their sexual awareness, tell them they must be celibate, and then put them around children. It's a recipe for disaster. They will wax offense at our art, but look the other way at priests diddling altar boys. I need to be a part of a provocative climate. My iconography needs it."

"Why don't you look into that theology degree?" Stacey asked. "It's one thing to bitch about it—and I bitch about it, too—but a degree would at least give you some validity in doing something about it and a career goal. You can't expect to work in galleries for the rest of your life, making minimum wage, and waiting for your art to pay off."

"Ha. A theology degree would certainly do more for my art than finishing an art degree. Of course, pragmatism isn't my strongest point, but you're right . . . but not here. I'm sick of this suburban climate."

"Then why don't we move to . . . Portland?"

"Why Portland?"

"It's not far from where I'll have to finish up the last leg of my doctoral work, and the city's motto is 'Keep Portland Weird.'"

"God, I could use some weird."

"I'm feeling Willie Nelson's 'On the Road Again.'"

Stacey and Calvin finally made it out to the Portland galleries three months after moving there. Although the galleries were filled with patrons who fancied themselves art lovers, there was no real movement in the scene—the galleries were more akin to a stroll through a department store with art solely as product. The Portland art scene had nothing to say.

Calvin's frustrations ran deeper. He had applied and been accepted at a local school to begin his theology degree, but he was less lucky in the job market, and he and Stacey were dependent on her salary. Calvin had applied for openings at a couple of churches, hoping that the references of both Oliver and Vincent would secure him a position. However, in both cases, the parish priest had looked Calvin up online and discovered write-ups for the Brother Cobweb showing at the Art Brut, which cost him the jobs.

They had skipped mass on the Sunday when Calvin skimmed through the employment ads and came upon one that read "House of Shadows Haunted House attraction looking for artistic director."

Although the idea of a haunted house attraction wasn't altogether appealing to Calvin, Stacey was encouraging, since she had a passion for the season.

"What brought you out to Portland?" Boris asked Calvin during the interview.

"I'm doing my degree here," Calvin explained to the House of Shadows owner during the interview. "It's part of my goal to be a student for life."

Boris, a big brunette of a young man, hired Calvin on the spot after glancing over the artist's portfolio. He even offered to give Calvin a ride to and from the haunt daily so Stacey could have the car that they shared to get her back and forth to work.

After Calvin's first week, Boris knew he had made a sound decision and outlined his ideas for the entire haunt. The amount of work was considerable, but Calvin was comfortable in commercial speed painting. It helped, too, that Boris had the seasonal plans so locked down.

"Am I starting the Classic Monsters mural today?" Calvin asked as he climbed into Boris's truck the next day.

"No, I changed my mind," Boris answered. "I looked you up."

"And?" asked Calvin curiously, as he had no arrest record.

"Brother Cobweb."

"Oh!" Calvin laughed. "That's a performance art character I used to do."

"Yeah, I read about it. Man, I grew up in that shit, too—the whole Pentecostal thing. My mom's a fanatic."

"And so you became a haunter?"

"It's in my DNA. I want you to do that here."

"Do what here?"

"Brother Cobweb. I want you to play him in the haunt and paint the sets."

"You said this is a haunted house attraction. That's not—"

"Horror? The hell it is. Growin' up in that is true horror, and you and I know that better than anyone because I was raised in that whole Pentecostal thing too. It's a helluva lot scarier and weirder than some guy in a hockey mask. 'Keep Portland Weird' will eat it up! You game?"

"Baby sister, I was born game."

"That's John Wayne from the *Rooster Cogburn* movie. I remember that."

"It'll be a hoot jumping into the trench work again, calling out all the Pharisees," Calvin laughed.

"Cool. Let's get some coffee and map it out. Give me a cigarette."

"I didn't think you smoked."

"I don't."

"How old are you?"

"Twenty-eight."

"Well, now is as good a time as any to start."

The haunt needed additional help, so Stacey took the part-time position of casting coordinator, scheduling and repeatedly calling actors to remind them to show up for work. Apart from the haunt, Calvin and Stacey settled into a comfortable routine filled to the rim with conversations on shared interests and new discoveries, mini-film festivals, mass at a Jesuit parish on Sundays, and taking Stacey's dog to the park. Calvin's cat opted to stay home, of course. On a few occasions, Calvin and Stacey talked family and a Lighthouse past, and both found that it was satisfying to see a dysfunctional oppressive religious past unintentionally transformed into horror entertainment for Portlandian horror aficionados. For Calvin, those early years of watching monster movies with Pop, paired with speaking-in-tongues Sundays, had produced a Brother Cobweb on paper. Now, here he was with his own church—albeit one within a haunted house attraction—where he painted murals, was free to create his own work, continue schooling, and, best of all, do everything with an authentic soulmate with whom he yearned for a present and future that was profound and orthodox.

Back in Ohio, Frank's new wife, Cindy—who looked alarmingly like Nancy circa 1973—was proud of the hard work and time Frank had put into their church community. Cindy tried to contain her son, Donnie, who was bouncing up and down with excitement when they stepped into the new Xenox Zone of the Lighthouse, which was something akin to entering a video game bathed in laser lights.

"I'm going with Zelda greens," Frank had told Cindy. He hadn't been exaggerating.

Donnie heard his stepdad's voice booming through the microphone from the sound booth above. "You have now entered the Xenox Zone, where the forces of light must do battle with the legion of darkness. This is the realm of angels and demons, but the light of the world will prevail with steadfast warriors."

As Donnie looked up, he gasped at the sight of a tall mannequin costumed as a demon zombie appearing on one corner of the stage and a second mannequin dressed as a Christian crusader opposite him, holding a sword.

"Is Frank's son coming to play the Xenox Zone?" Donnie asked his mother as she handed him a lightsaber-like weapon.

"No, I don't think Cosmo is the type who likes this kind of thing." There was disgust in her tone, recalling Nancy's surprisingly expressed hope that Frank would grow up and accept the fact of having a gay son. *Guess that liberal therapy's ruining her,* thought Cindy.

Indeed, Nancy's therapy—though long overdue—was a case of better late than never, and it was going so well. She no longer needed church and, even more shockingly, quit donating to the Republicans. All that suited a retired Dale just fine. He actually had to be around his wife now, and so, according to Frank, Dale and Nancy's life consisted of getting up, discussing where they would go for breakfast, followed by talking about the breakfast they just had. Then, a few hours of back-to-back westerns since they had gotten cable. Sometime between the second and third western, Dale and Nancy would discuss where to go for lunch, eat lunch, talk about the lunch, and go back to the house in time for Nancy to watch Doris Day movies while Dale napped in the recliner. Figuring out where to go for dinner was the highlight of the day. Usually, it was a steakhouse with good salads—Nancy had finally gone full-blow vegetarian and no longer even ate hot dogs. The steakhouse with unlimited peanuts was her favorite. She liked to crack the nuts. Dale was usually tired after dinner, and so he didn't talk too long about the cow he just consumed, but after Nancy watched her favorite game show, he liked to fall asleep watching *Spider-Man*. The web-slinger was a lot like the gun-slingers of old, Dale tried to explain to Nancy, but she didn't care what he watched. She had a new crossword puzzle book.

Dale would occasionally call Calvin and Stacey. He especially liked to call them on their birthdays and sing "Happy Birthday" to them, followed by "When you coming back for a visit?" and "You want to talk to your mom for a minute?"

Calvin and Stacey humored Dale and would say to him, "Maybe we'll come back for a Christmas visit. Or Easter. We'll let you know."

"OK, you do let me know. When you two getting married?" Dale always asked.

Frank sent Calvin and Stacey photos of the new Lighthouse. They both felt they had made personal leaps because their reaction was merely, "I wonder how we could work that into the haunt?"

"The show starts in eight minutes," announced the vintage drive-in theater ad playing for the House of Shadows crowd, which included Stacey and Ray Stevens, who had come to Portland for a visit. "Yum, yum, it's time for a tasty and refreshing snack," said the disembodied voice as a red and white bucket of hot buttered popcorn shuffled through a mint green, star-filled sky. The wiener dog and its bun danced on air like Fred and Ginger, soon accompanied by a barbershop quartet of popsicles and sparkling soda pops. "We promise to satisfy your hunger, your thirst, your sweet tooth, so visit our refreshment center now. Let's go! Show starts in five minutes. Visit our snack bar and treat yourself to some delicious Castleberry pit-cooked barbecue sandwiches, cooked the Castleberry way—slowly over open pits of glowing charcoaled fire, then seasoned with a sauce that's zesty, yet delightfully mild, to please the entire family. It's showtime."

After Cornfed Killers and Bedlam, Angels and Demons served as the immediate precursor into the Church of Brother Cobweb. Standing before the entrance to Calvin's lair was the buxom scantily clad Whore of Babylon, who bade all to enter. Painted on the door to the church was Brother Cobweb himself. A tight passageway behind the door lead to a church brought to life from a chronicle that Calvin had burned in a trash bin.

Over twenty thousand square feet of floors painted in flaming colors segued into Calvin's center mural of the Last Supper, which featured tel-evangelists gorging on Chick-fil-A with a dead Savior. A side panel paint-ing depicted children lining up to receive communion next to a hanging gutted deer and homophobic texts once spewed by the late pedophile Reverend Harry Dushane at an anti-gay rally. Yet, amidst all that horror was a white-haired angel offering HELP from the temple of St. Lucy's Help Booth.

As patrons entered the church, Brother Cobweb pointed and bellowed from the stage.

"C-H-C-H. What's missing? U-R! Didn't mummy and daddy teach ya to get to the church on time?"

As the Whore of Babylon handed patrons a pack of mints, Brother advised from the stage, "Now, grab a Testamint—a scripture verse comes with every pack. Have fresh, minty breath before you speak in tongues!"

As Stacey and Ray sat in a pew by Boris in the guise of a good old boy patron, cast into the role of unwitting voyeur to the Whore of Babylon's pole dance. As she ground with abandon, Brother yelled at Boris's character, who was clearly aroused. "If thy eye offends, pluck it out. Better to enter into heaven with one eye than hell with two."

Taking her cue, the Whore of Babylon ripped out the bloodied eye of her victim Boris and threw it to the stage with a piercing scream.

"Don't be such a wuss," Brother screamed to the poor one-eyed man. "The demise of our great 'Murican culture is the fault of sissified men, overly influenced by women! It's the same the world over, folks, and it's our duty to invade their countries, kill their leaders, and convert them to Christianity. We don't need to be wastin' our time protectin' the environment 'cause the second coming is at hand. But we do need to purge Jehovah's world of the feminization crisis, and make no mistake about it: feminism was established to allow ugly women access to mainstream society and convert men to sissified ways. Back in the old days, a good butt-whippin' and prayer was the remedy, but with today's crisis, it's not enough."

Brother Cobweb motioned to Boris. Accompanying Boris was an eleven-year-old boy who dutifully lay on the stage's table.

"Now Brother Boris here caught his boy playin' the princess in *Mario Kart*. That's what I'm talkin' about, folks," Brother Cobweb said as he put his arm around the now one-eyed Boris. "In times like this, we need to go to the Bible story of Abraham, willin' to sacrifice his son to God, but if you remember, Father Abraham chickened out!"

As Brother Cobweb spoke, below the stage, the devil, adorned in long red horns and a black robe, ripped pages out of a Bible, stuffed them in his mouth, and spit them onto the floor.

"Brother Boris here is a man of guts. He's willin' to sacrifice his boy Bobby to the devil in order to save Bobby's soul for Jesus!"

Boris, pulling an actual snake out of his pants pocket, approached Bobby, waving the reptile before the face of his young son. Reaching in close enough,

Boris mimicked the snake biting the boy, who screamed out a melodramatic death wail.

"Praise be to God," Brother Cobweb screamed. "You're doin' the Lawd's work, Brother Boris."

Smiling broadly, Boris rolled up his shirt sleeve, showing off his tattoo of Leviticus 20 inscribed on his arm.

"Leviticus twenty: If a man lies with a male as with a woman, both of them have committed an abomination; they shall surely be put to death; their blood is upon their heads," Brother Cobweb read Boris's arm with glee. "But brother, I'm afraid you forgot Leviticus nineteen, which says, Do NOT put tattoos on your skin, for I am the Lord your God!"

Boris's face turned pale.

"Gotta do my sacred duty!" Brother Cobweb growled, ripping off Boris's arm.

Boris screamed and spewed what looked like a half gallon of blood. Leaning down from the stage, Brother Cobweb threw Boris's arm into an awaiting pail.

Deviating from the planned performance, Brother Cobweb broke into a weird song, called "God Said," which Calvin took from Lenny Bernstein's mass. Pentecostal horror and rock opera proved a weird enough mix to arouse the 'Keep Portland Weird' crowd.

"Stand to your feet and give Brother Cobweb a handclap of praise," the one-armed Boris growled, leading the patrons in a chain-like Holy Ghost rumba as Brother Cobweb paced the stage, speaking in tongues.

The patrons applauded and lined up to receive Brother Cobweb's blessing as they left the church. Brother Cobweb leaned down and touched an awaiting forehead. "Be a slut for Jesus," he growled with salty glee. The patron, a young lady, raised her fist enthusiastically and shouted out, "Hell yeah." Caught up in the theatrical spirit of hypocrisy as horror, the Oregonians proved to be an eager lot, receiving Brother's blessings of "be a slut for Jesus" and "don't forget to get your bowl of Christ Crispies, on sale in the lobby."

As the patrons departed, Calvin heard someone in the crowd say, "We love Brother Cobweb."

But you're supposed to hate him, thought Calvin.

After driving Ray to the airport, Calvin and Stacey went home, both glad that the season was over. Calvin retrieved a letter from the mailbox. It was from one of the few art galleries he liked in Portland and had sent his portfolio to. He read the letter aloud: they had accepted him for a one-man showing of paintings, along with doing a BlueMahler performance. Finally, Brother Cobweb is dead, Calvin thought, craving a more complex art.

"Maybe we should start practicing," Calvin suggested to Stacey.

"We? Practicing for what?" she asked.

"BlueMahler needs his PinkFreud."

Stacey nodded. Unexpectedly, she said, "The other night, you were very tender, and it was lovely."

Calvin nodded a thank you, curious as to why she brought that up.

"But tonight . . ." she said as she unbuttoned her blouse, "what was that music you had on a few days ago? Where the music came down so hard with the drums that your cat jumped off the speaker?"

"You mean the Stravinsky?"

"Yeah. Put that on."

COMING SOON . . .

Brother Cobweb will soon be a graphic novel!

Sign up for our newsletter to find out when *The Brother Cobweb Chronicles* will hit store shelves near you.

www.openbookspress.com/BC

Author Bio

Alfred Eaker has been obsessively working on his first novel, *Brother Cobweb*, for the last five years and, off and on, for a quarter of a century. Additionally, his first eighteen years were spent in a ho-de-ho, backwoods, sawdust on the floor, wooden pews Pentecostal Church in the Midwest. In other words, Eaker's been working toward this novel his whole damned life.In his career as an artist, Eaker's work has been paradoxically labeled as degenerate, orthodox, heterodox, modernist, mystical theology, provocative, academic, and blasphemous. Indeed, blasphemy is a language that Eaker seems to speak fluently, even when he doesn't mean to, and he's been doing it through painting, performance art, independent film, and film criticism for three decades.

Eaker attended John Herron School of Art with a focus on fine arts paintings, attained his bachelor of theology from St. Mary-of-the-Woods and a master of theological studies in the arts from Christian Theological Seminary. Additionally, Eaker has done extensive studies with both the Conventual Franciscans and Third Order Franciscans.